Mackenzie E. C. Walcott

Cathedralia

SALZWASSER
VERLAG

Mackenzie E. C. Walcott

Cathedralia

Reprint of the original, first published in 1865.

1st Edition 2022 | ISBN: 978-3-75258-789-0

Verlag (Publisher): Salzwasser Verlag GmbH, Zeilweg 44, 60439 Frankfurt, Deutschland
Vertretungsberechtigt (Authorized to represent): E. Roepke, Zeilweg 44, 60439 Frankfurt, Deutschland
Druck (Print): Books on Demand GmbH, In de Tarpen 42, 22848 Norderstedt, Deutschland

CATHEDRALIA:

A Constitutional History of Cathedrals

OF THE

WESTERN CHURCH.

BEING

AN ACCOUNT OF THE VARIOUS DIGNITIES, OFFICES, AND MINISTRIES OF THEIR MEMBERS,

FOUNDED ON CAPITULAR STATUTES, AND ILLUSTRATED FROM THE CANON LAW AND WRITERS OF REPUTE.

BY

MACKENZIE E. C. WALCOTT, B.D.,

OF EXETER COLLEGE, OXFORD

PRÆCENTOR AND PREBENDARY OF THE CATHEDRAL CHURCH OF CHICHESTER;

F.R.S.L., F.S.A., F.R.S.N.A., MEMB. ARCH. INST. OF GREAT BRITAIN AND IRELAND;

MEMB. CORR. SOC. FRANÇ. D'ARCHEOL., SOC. DES ANTIQ. DE NORMANDIE, ETC.

"Immo mente revolve omnes in choro dextro, omnes in choro sinistro. Amabant quæ amamus, optabant quæ optamus, sperabant quæ speramus. Mors omnes dedit oblivioni. Cogitemus quod et nos similiter eadem manet oblivio. Certemus omni nisu quærere quod duret, quod stabile sit, quod differt a somno, immo quod aliquid sit, quia hæc nihil sunt."—*Hen. Huntingdon. ap. Ang. Sac.* II. 696.

LONDON

MDCCCLXV.

PREFACE.

It is all very well to see the noble mass of a cathedral looming through the misty morning, the view so infinitely fine of tower and spire, transept, nave, choir, and chapels; to note the quiet life of the city, the charm of the close, the venerable precinct, the associations of glorious architecture and sublime music, and yet to know nothing more of the laws and customs, the traditions and memories of the great minster than of the little parish at home or the modern church in some great city. This may be sufficient to the mere visitor of the day, or the hasty traveller; but the archæologist and the intelligent layman, and those of the clergy who have not access to the capitular muniments, require now to know somewhat of the constitutional history of these noble foundations. With the exception of the agreeable outline given of such matters in England and Ireland by my learned friend Dr. Jebb, in his delightful work, "The Choral Service of the Church," and the scattered information to be gleaned from the Appendix to the Report of the Cathedral Commission, the student could not find any account of the duties of the members or the development of the system. Materials, however, existed for the undertaking in the printed histories of some few cathedrals, many invaluable MSS. of the British Museum, and the series of documents contained in the new edition of the Monasticon. It was necessary, however, to consult Continental writers, and it was a subject of wonder to find that no complete work of this nature had even been attempted.

I may therefore claim, in the following pages, to have achieved the first treatise on the constitutional history of cathedrals which exists in any language, in which the origin, development, and modification of the system, the duties of every constituent member of the body, the contents, comparison, analysis, and nature of Statutes, have been related in a manner which it is my hope will supply a gap in literature; being founded on primary authorities, and authenticated by references to the manifold sources from whence it has been drawn. It is not a mere compilation, but a systematic work, requiring thought as well as research, in which the customs of each cathedral have been employed for common illustration, and one which I have found, from a wide experience, was much needed. No difficulty has been evaded, and it is my hope no particular of interest will be found to be omitted. I have used condensation, and have not printed the original Statutes, partly for the purpose of producing a volume of moderate size at the smallest cost to the purchaser, and partly to render it available to those who are not conversant with the barbarisms and difficulties of mediæval Latin.

Although it is not agreeable for an author to appear to parade his labours, which readers and reviewers will estimate by the result, yet even a special allusion to them, as being independent and original, may be pardoned as an act of personal justice. I only trust that the result may prove of use and interest both to the existing members of our cathedrals and those in power who may at any time meditate changes in their administration, and so preclude such serious evils as have already accrued to them from hasty legislation and incomplete information on the part of the reformers in future. I may say with Heylyn that it has been "a business of so intricate and involved a nature that I had no guide to follow nor any path to tread but what I have made unto myself," and add with Bishop Hacket my belief that "these corporations are the strong ribs of the kingdom."*

CATHEDRALIA.

"Most certain truth it is, that churches cathedral and the bishops of them, are glasses, wherein the face and very countenance of apostolical antiquity remaineth even as yet to be seen, notwithstanding the alterations which tract of time and the course of the world hath brought."—HOOKER.

"EVERY cathedral in its first institution," writes Bishop Stillingfleet, "was as the temple to the whole diocese, where the worship was to be performed in the most decent and constant manner; for which end it was necessary to have such a number of ecclesiastical persons there attending, as might still be ready to do all the offices which did belong to the Christian Church, such as constant prayers, and hymns, and preaching, and celebration of Sacraments, which were to be kept up in such a church, as the daily sacrifice was in the Temple." The cathedral was designed for the celebration of the most solemn service which devotion could devise in a fabric as worthy of its holy purpose as the highest art of man could frame; a daily service "cum cantu et jubilatione," with chanting and great joy, as the statutes of Ely say.

The origin of cathedrals has been dated by some to the age of Constantine the Great, by others to a still earlier period, whilst another class of writers refer them to the age of Anacletus, and parish churches to that of Evaristus. (Mayer, i. 37.) The signs of cathedralitas are: 1. The right of ringing bells before other churches; 2. The right of processions beginning and ending in it; 3. The residence of a bishop; 4. The existence of a theological prebend; 5. The election of a capitular vicar by the canons. (Scarfantoni, ii. 268.) Cathedrals take precedence according (1) to the rank of their bishops; some being (i.) patriarchal (Frances, c. xxxiii. n. 64); some (ii.) metropolitan (n. 135), which are subdivided into patriarchal, wherein is a primate having prerogative of authority over other archbishops (ibid., n. 75), and metropolitan simple, in which the prelate is metropolitan and archbishop (ibid., c. 77, 87), and (iii.) simply cathedral, whereof the bishop is suffragan to a metropolitan (ibid., n. 92); or (2) antiquity of foundation (Frances, c. xxxiii. n. 58, 59, 109); or (3) precedence of bishops (ibid., xxxiii. 58, 95.) The archbishop presides over many bishops; the primate presides over metropolitans and archbishops (Frances, c. i. p. 13; Mayer, i. 34.) A metropolitan is the same as an archbishop (Frances, p. 14, num. 120; Mayer, i. 158), but formerly was the president of the lesser province (Mayer, i. 34); primate merely denoted the president of a chief or first-rate city; the metropolitan is the same as an archiepiscopal church (ibid., c. xv. p. 152, comp. 114). A cathedral church (Germ. Höhe Stifter) derives its name from the see or seat of the bishop (Frances, c. v. n. 152; Mayer, i. § iv. p. 35): "according to the same sense," Hooker observes, "wherein S. Ignatius, speaking of Antioch, termeth it his throne." The word itself is confined to the Western Church, and is not older than the 10th century; and for the honour of his chair, the cathedralicum (first mentioned in the 6th century) was paid (Frances, 152) Scarfantoni says, in the time of Honorius III., by all the clergy of the diocese (Scarf., iii. 149, 150, 171). For this reason they are styled simply cathedral church of such a city, not of such a saint, as are other churches (n. 158, c. xv. 184), the bishop taking his title from his diocese or city in which his church stands. According to Celtic custom, the Bishops of Meath, Ossory, Sodor and Man, Galloway, Argyll and the Isles, Moray, Orkneys, and Caithness, did not take their titles from the cathedral city. The cathedral is the mother or parish church of the entire diocese (Mayer, i. p. 35, Frances, num. 173; c. xvi. n. 16; c. xxi. n. 17) all other churches being but chapels; the bride of the bishop (c. vii. p. 108; xvii. n. 177; Scarf., i. 244), who imparts to it prerogative and superiority over all inferior churches; and the rule and pattern of the diocese (Frances, c. ii. n. 139; Council of Noyon, c. iv.); the bishop being the parish priest of the diocese (Mayer, i. 55), and president and rector of the cathedral, and prelate of all other churches in his diocese (Frances, c. ii. n. 138). In some places the cathedrals were called at an early period Cardinal (Mayer, i. p. 42); in Germany, Domkirche, the Lord's house; and by contraction, in Italy, Duomo; as Mayence was formerly known as the Dom; whilst subordinate churches were known as Basilicæ or Oratoria (Mayer, i. p. 39). Basilica is applied to Chichester (Gale, ii. 166), Rochester (ibid., i. 347, 351), and to large churches (ib., ii. 109; Matt. Par., 1029; and Ann. Waverl. Gale, ii. 234; see also my "Church and Conventual Arrangement," p. 56); and to churches before consecration (ibid.) Minster is also a generic name for cathedrals, as they were often monastic, and founded on the monastic system (Mayer, i. 36). The mere will of the sovereign constitutes a city, which does not depend on the existence of a see in it for its title (Frances, c. iv. n. 89, p. 64), even if he addresses it as a city, or endows it with civic privileges; but there cannot be a cathedral without a bishop, for he is its head, and the chapter are its members (c. iii. n. 21, pp. 43, 610). The collegiate church had no bishop's chair, but possessed merely a chapter of canons with their vicars.

A cathedral ought to be built only in the larger cities, according to the Councils of Sardica, c. vi.; Laodicea, c. lvii.; and Canon Law (c. iv. pp. 58, 64), in order to maintain the high dignity of the Episcopate; and a cathedral city has precedence of all others (p. 70). The reasons for the change and alteration of old cathedral churches, and the erection of new, have never been strictly observed, being founded on usefulness or necessity. For instance, the site has been changed on account of an inconvenient or bad situation, as "Old Sarum" (n. 178, c. vi.), owing to the presence of war, plague, unhealthy climate, floods, a barren soil, inroads of enemies, or the society of evil persons (c. vi. n. 178, 146, 150), but not owing to the increase of the city (n. 58). A new cathedral is to be erected when a diocese is divided (n. 116). By the union of a cathedral and collegiate church both become the bishop's church (c. viii. n. 153). Where two sees are united, the bishop in episcopal instruments was to place the name of the cathedral in which he was resident before that of the other (c. viii. n. 361); but if one is acknowledged to be more eminent in age or dignity, then that always is to take precedence (n. 369). If a church is no longer a see, by suppression or translation (c. i. n. 60), then it retains neither its name (c. vii. n. 62) nor honours (c. ix. n. 103), as in the case of Westminster, Hexham, Lindisfarne, &c., unless by special reservation. The minster of Monte Cassino was reputed to be cathedralis habitu, although it had no bishop (Frances, p. 610). In the case of building a cathedral, the bishop and chapter are to consent to the model and design of the fabric (c. xii. n. 44), the bishop having the choice of the site (n. 84), which should be in the centre of a city (c. xiv. n. 28, 29), near the palace (c. xxix. n. 29).

As the parish church of the diocese, all others being chapels (c. xvi. n. 16, p. 258), it possesses the right of sepulture, which all in the diocese can claim (c. xvii. n. 59, 176). In it daily service should be said (c. xviii. n. 195), and it has the right of Baptism (c. x. n. 118; Mayer, i. 49; Martene, de Ant. Eccles. rit. i. 5); and, out of respect, all parishioners were bound to visit it at Easter (ibid., lib. iii. 171. Comp. Thes. Anec., iv. 902, 955.) At Chichester, the payment of S. Richard's pence was paid by way of compensation for omission to visit the church, as S. Chad's pennies were at Lichfield. It is at once a cathedral and a parish church (Frances, c. xxi. n. 17), and possesses the rights of a parish church (c. xxi. n. 144), of daily public prayer (c. xviii. n. 195, p. 290; c. xxxi. n. 96), administration of Sacraments (c. xvii. n. 146; xxi. n. 101, 110, 83), burial of the dead (c. xxxiv. n. 95), matrimony (c. xi. n. 131), tithes (c. xxi. n. 158) and first-fruits, offerings and oblations (c. xxi. n. 23—29). In cathedrals, councils were held; academical honours conferred; and manumission granted, on the petition of the serf's lord, who laid his petition on the altar at Easter, to be signed by the clergy, while a priest opening the doors, exclaimed, "Jam passæ sunt portæ," implying that the freedman might now go whither he pleased (Mayer, i. 49). Coronations and solemn processions likewise took place in the cathedral (ibid., 50, 51). An enclosure at 40 paces (about 60 yards) distance was drawn round the cathedral, to serve as a cemetery (c. xxvi. n. 115; xiii. n. 72), and a close within which the houses of the clergy might be built, but none other. The privileges of the church extended to this precinct—porches, and cloisters, and gardens; and, in consequence, all secular cases and proceedings, markets, fairs, traffic, and business, were forbidden in them (c. xxvi. 452). In consideration of its being the chief or mother church of the diocese, the cathedral was permitted to have seven bells (c. xxiv. n. 154), and control the number and size of the bells of other churches (n. 158). A collegiate church, if raised to the rank of a cathedral, loses its ancient privileges (c. xxx. n. 347). The collegiate church took its origin in the fact that there was not sufficient room in cathedrals for the number of candidates for vacant places, so that parish churches were converted into capitular establishments (Mayer, i. 169). The clergy of the cathedral were called clerus major primi generis, and the collegiate clergy clerus major secundi generis. These furnished four deacons and four subdeacons at a pontifical mass (ibid., 166). Frances (c. xiv. n. 54) inclines to the belief, that when the Church grew in strength, there were three classes of clergy: 1. Clergy seculars, living on their own means and apart; 2. Clergy having their own property, living in a collegiate manner, but without vows; 3. Clergy living in a college, under the three vows. When P. Dionysius I. (n. 86) instituted or revived benefices, and allotted incomes to the individual clergy, he reserved a certain portion for the superior clergy, who were named canons, from their rule of life and order in their churches, which served as a model to the rest. Simplicius in 472, Gelasius, Gregory the Great, and Gregory II. (Ducange, ii. 101) divided the revenues into four parts: 1. For the bishop; 2. For the clergy, according to their rank and merits; 3. For the poor; 4. For the church (comp. 1st Orleans, c. v. 14; Worms, c. vii.; Carpentras, c. xi.; 1st Mayence, c. x.; Thom. iii. 184, 185, 189); and Pope Gregory, in his reply to Augustine, directed him to have his clergy living in common with him, according to primitive practice. One trace of this old custom long survived in the retention of the cellarer as the second dignitary in a cathedral; from that office, those of the almoner, the hospitaller, and infirmarer were afterwards detached. The constitution of a college or capitular body of seculars and regulars alike embraces the possession of a seal, the right of electing a dean, of constituting a syndic, of holding chapters, and enacting statutes (J. Mayer, Nov. Thes., i. § 28, p. 61), and in a cathedral, of electing the bishop (ibid., xxxvi. p. 70).

According to Beyerlinck (Theatrum Magnum, iv. 66), the primary idea of a cathedral was that of a corporation or college of regulars, following the Apostles' rule or κοινωνία (Acts ii. 42), and living under the rule of a provost; but Mayer more correctly defines it as a collective body, of which canons are the members, and the bishop the head (Mayer, i. p. 60). The name of canons is attributed to Pelagius I. (c. 579); or Gregory (c. 615; Frances, c. xiv. n. 61), and is used by the second Council of Tours, c. xx., fourth Council of Arles, third Council of Tours, and the Councils of Mayence and Aix-la-Chapelle, in the reign of Charlemagne: the idea being, that the title of canons implied the observance of the Apostles' rule, and that of regulars (Frances, c. xiv. n. 69) that on it were engrafted the three monastic vows of obedience, poverty, and chastity, when certain canons were not content with the simpler form of life. Azorius (lib. iii. p. 2) says that secular canons were so called from the canonical portion or regular annual pension yearly paid to them (so Frances, c. xiv. n. 43), the remaining members of the establishment receiving only the daily portion of the commune, known as the quotidian: the prebend being the technical name for the yearly payment. He also attributes the foundation of secular canons to a love of independence, they wishing to reside in separate houses arranged within a close or round a cloister, upon a common site; and that at length the cloister disappeared, and the close only was retained. These canons preceded abbots in their cathedrals. Beyerlinck attributes the introduction of vicars to the inability of canons to sing, as their office bound them (Frances, c. xiv. n. 96), and adds that in some places, birds, which were not song birds, were in consequence called canons! (u. s. p. 67). Another reason was no doubt the non-residence of the canons. Canon, according to Steffanucci, in the 6th century, was a generic title for all clergy, borne on the church books, and paid out of its revenues (Mayer, iii. 274). There are three classes: 1. Canons of cathedrals and collegiate churches; 2. Canons secular and regular—the latter observing, the former not observing the three rules of profession; 3. Canons capitular and non-capitular, the latter including domicellares, the canons elect waiting for an actual vacancy (ibid., 275).

Frances states that c. 372 S. Jerome (Frances, c. xiv. n. 46, 53), or c. 400 (n. 68), S. Augustine was the first founder of canons, and that other bishops followed his example (c. xxxi. n. 4). Posidonius, in his life of S. Augustine (see also Serm. 355), mentions that he established in his church of Hippo a monastery, composed of doctors and students of divinity, for the purposes of a theological college; having formerly, whilst only a priest, lived in a stricter foundation, instituted by him in that city. Similar colleges of candidates for holy orders, and priests living under a certain cœnobitical rule (probably in accordance with canons of different Councils), less strict than the monastic, were founded elsewhere. Their rule embraced residence within the precinct, attendance at the choir services, eating in a common hall, sleeping in a dormitory divided into cells, and acknowledging community of property, from which they were provided with food and clothing (Counc. of Tours, 813, c. xxv.), the number of residents being limited by the bishop in proportion to the revenues (Frances, u. s. n. 9). Such colleges, from their imitation of a convent (Frances, xiv. n. 3), were often called monasteries, and their inmates (clerks presided over by the bishop, and afterwards by a provost), from their rule (ibid., n. 4, 45), were called canons (comp. Muratori, Ant. Ital., 5, 158, 185, 164, 540), as affording a perfect example of liturgical observance (Gal. vi. 16), and observing canonical rule (Ivo of Chartres, Ep. cciii., lxix.; Hugo de Cons. Hær., iii. c. 2), and also from being enrolled on the list or canon of the Church (Conc. Antioch, c. ii. vi. xi.; Chalcedon, c. ii.; Trullo, c. vi.; 3rd Toledo, c. v.; Friuli, 791, c. i.; S. Athan. in vit. Antonii.)[1] Pope Urban I., in 230, directed bishops to provide all necessaries out of the funds of their cathedrals, for the maintenance of clerks willing to live in common. According to Onuphrius, Gelasius, in 490 (Frances, c. xiv. n. 72), established canons regular of S. Augustine in the Lateran; and Ivo of Chartres, in 1080, introduced them into France.[2] S. Gregory of Tours, in 580, mentions (lib. x.) canons at Tournay and Tours.

Bishop Chrodegang, of Metz, in 763, who died 766 (Fleury, Hist. Eccl. s. a.; Hardouin, Conc. iv. 1181; Mansi, xiv. 313;

[1] "Canons, from the word canon, because such persons' names were entered into the register or matriculation book of the church; or because they do receive a portion or stated allowance out of the treasury of the church, which was by the ancient lawyers called a canon, and not a prebend."—Ayliffe's Parergon, p. 139. In all probability the confusion between κανωνία and κοινωνία (Ducange, ii. 102) was made by an age not adept in Greek and fond of artificial analogies, and so gave cause to this singular meaning attached to the former word; and the term communa, designating the entire revenue, lends additional likelihood to the supposition. Carpentarius shows that canonicare and vivere regulariter was applied to conventuals and seculars. (Ducange, ii. 101, Ed. 1842). Mayer derives the term from the fact that Chrodegang bound them not by vows, but by canons derived from the writings of the Fathers and the monastic rule, and so called them canons, in distinction to the clergy of the lesser churches, who did not live in common. (Mayer, i. § 26, 60.) Hitherto all constituti ad titulum bore the name (ibid.) Matricula signified the revenues as well as the roll of a church. Canon was also a military term for the muster roll and payment of those whose names were in it (ibid. 162.)

[2] "Volaterranus informs us that the Abbot Arnulphus founded the order of regular canons c. 1066; but Munster says that the canons of Spires, Worms, and Mayence, laying aside the profession of a monastic life, became secular, and began to live asunder c. 966."—Ayliffe's Parergon. p. 140.

Harzheim, i. 96), established with endowments a community of clerks, under a rule drawn up by himself; and the word canon, formerly applied to all clerks inscribed in the church-roll, and bound by canons ecclesiastical, was restricted to these clerks living in common. He founded his rule on a modification of that of the Benedictines. (Mayer, i. 256; vi. 340.) Each member, though free from a vow of poverty, was (c. xxxi.) to give his property to the cathedral, but enjoyed its use and disposed of his moveables during his life. (c. xxxii.) Priests disposed of all offerings made at private masses, confession, and visitation of the sick (the first notice on record of offerings at mass, or for any ecclesiastical office). Canons (c. iv.) might leave their cloister by day, until the time of compline, after which neither food nor conversation was permitted till after the morrow's prime. They were to rise at 2 A.M. for nocturns (c. v.), and learn the psalms in the interval before matins or lauds. The infirm only were to use staves in church (c. ii.); their rank was that which they held among the clergy. (c. viii.) Chapter was to follow prime daily, with reading of the rule or good books, discipline and direction; and then manual labour succeeded. Meat was ordinarily permitted; and two daily repasts were served. There were seven tables in the hall—the first, for the bishop, archdeacon, guests, and strangers; the second, for priests; the third, for deacons; fourth, for subdeacons; fifth, for clerks; sixth, for abbots and guests of the superior; seventh, for city clergy on festivals. Soup and a portion of meat were served at dinner, with beverages, wine or beer; at supper one portion was allowed. (c. xx.—xxiii.) All canons were to serve in the kitchen by turns. (c. xxiv.) They could be punished (c. xv., xvii.) by penance, corporal discipline and imprisonment, or even excommunication. The city clergy who did not live within the cloister assisted on great festivals in the cathedral and in chapter, and had a table in hall. (c. viii., xxxiii.) The elder received a new habit yearly, the younger had the old: priests and deacons had two tunics, two shirts, leather for shoes, and four pairs of hosen annually, and money for wood. Those who had benefices, funds allotted by the bishop, were to clothe themselves. (c. xxix.) There was an infirmary. (c. xxx.) The community was governed by the bishop, archdeacon, and provost. There were also a cellarer, porter, infirmarer, and churchwardens. (c. xxiv.—xxvii.) Canons were allowed assistant clerks, who were not allowed a place either in chapter or hall. (c. i., iii., xxi., xxx.) There were also matriculiers—poor scholars—taught and maintained on the establishment. This rule was adopted by all canons, as S. Benedict's was by monks; and so popular became the new system, that it led to the foundation of collegiate churches, erected out of parish churches. (Mayer, i. 60.) In the year 977, the canons of Tours, who were imitated by the neighbouring chapters, threw off their rule, and became seculars, as Cranz says (Metrop. lib. iv. c. 1), regulars without a rule, and canons without a canon. The Council of Mayence (813, c. ix.) required a common refectory and dormitory. Similar provisions were made in the Councils 4th Arles, 3rd Tours, 3rd Chalons, &c. (Comp. St. of Barcelona. Martene, Thes. Anecd. iv. 600.) Their life in some places resembled that of the Cistercians. (Ib. 1215.) By the Council of Aix (816, c. 114) canons might wear linen, eat flesh, give and receive, hold property of their own and of the church, which was forbidden to monks (c. 117); they were to have a cloister, dormitory and refectory (c. 142), an infirmary, a private house for study, or in case of sickness (c. 135); they were forbidden the monastic cowl, and wore a camail with a hood. (c. 120, 123.) Those who had a patrimony and a prebend or benefice received nothing besides food; those who had a benefice without private means were given also clothing; those who possessed neither one nor the other received a pension, and all had a share in the alms and oblations. (c. 123.) The quality of the food depended on the wealth of the house. Every day (c. 133—137) chapter was held for reading the rule, devout books, for discipline, and church business. (c. 131.) The hours were kept. A canon was, if an offender (c. 134), punished by correction, or actual discipline, or short commons, or bread and water diet; and in extreme cases imprisoned in the cloister jail. (c. 135.) The young clerks and canons were under the charge of a master, and had their own chamber. (c. 139.) The officer next in rank to the bishop was the provost. (c. 140.) The washermen, kitchenmen, and servants were chosen from the serfs of the estates of the house. There was also (c. 141) to be a hospital for the poor maintained by regular funds.

These canons constituted a senate or council of the Bishop. (Frances. c. xiv. n. 93.) The name of canons regular implied a double obligation to a regular life, and having all things in common, unlike seculars. (n. 84.) Pope Nicholas II., in the Council of Rome in 1059, constituted *canons secular*, abolishing the rule of Aix-la-Chapelle. (Mabillon. Ann. Bened. tom. iv. p. 748, lib. lxi. sect. xxxv. p. 586.) In distinction to these were the *canons regular* of S. Augustine,[1] founded by Ivo of Chartres (Ibid. Op. Posthuma, tom. ii. p. 102, 115; Helyot. tom. ii. p. 11; Leg. Longob. l. iii. tit. 1, s. 8; Car. M. Cap. i. c. 57; Thomassini, Disc. Eccl. tom. i. p. i. l. iii. c. xi. p. 657; Muratori, t. v. p. 257), who had their own portions in lieu of prebends, and administered their property, having only its use in common. (Frances. c. xxxi. n. 8, 93.) The canons regular were introduced by Adelwald into England in the time of Henry I., and obtained Carlisle Cathedral, with the right of choosing their bishop. In Spain they held Pampeluna, Tortosa, and Saragossa (now a secular church); in Sicily, Monreale

[1] So called from observing his reputed three rules [Epist. cix.]

and Palermo; in Italy, Milan (ibid. xi. 11). In all respects, except in minor details affected by their rule, they resembled seculars; the bishop exercised complete jurisdiction (n. 21, 22), holding the place of abbot (n. 27), as he did in monastic cathedrals of the order of S. Benedict (n. 41), although they observed their own rule of Divine Service (n. 78). The canons regular were equal to seculars in being permitted to receive pay in service of the church, and act as vicars of the bishop. (n. 95.)

In England secular canons are recognised by the Excerptions of Ecgbright, (740, c. 1.) "We call canons those rules which the holy fathers ordained, and wherein is contained how canons, i.e. regular clerks should live;" and by the Council of Cealythe (785, c. 4,) Canons are expressly distinguished from monks and secular priests, and in the statutes of 1009, c. 1, when the refectory and dormitory of their monastery are first mentioned. The practice of having secular canons living apart is expressly called "the English Mode," by William of Malmesbury, in speaking of Exeter Cathedral.[1]

The cathedral system was established in the larger towns for mutual aid and consolation under trial, and the attainment of greater personal security; and because it furnished a central station for missionary operations, and enabled a community to meet the necessity for daily provisions. The society consisted of monks and clerks, confounded or combined according to circumstances; and, this led to the approximation between their various modes of life which at the close of the 8th century Chrodegang enforced in his archbishopric of Metz, modelled on the Benedictine rule, but attempted four centuries before by Eusebius of Vercelli. Hence came that anomalous designation of secular canons. There were two kinds of churches; 1. Cathedrals served by a composite, or double body of clerks and monks under rule, a sufficient proportion being priests and deacons, to form a chapter and act as clergy. 2. Collegiate churches, served by a body of priests under an archpriest, an office founded at Ely in the 10th century. The bishops, then really fathers in God, lived in a collegiate manner with their clergy, who were called their "family," and acted as parish priests in the city, and itinerated on Sundays and festivals as missionaries in the parish or diocese of which the cathedral was the mother church, (Bede. Hist. Ecc. iii. 7; Flor. Wigorn. s. a. 680,) "the oracle of the whole diocese, and a light unto all places lying nearest." These missionaries became at length permanent parish priests, at Rome, c. 281. (Frances, p. 32.) A trace of the custom survives in the appellation of cursal canons, so called because the incumbents of such prebends were required to circulate through the cylths or circuits into which the parish round the

[1] Episcopatum et canonicos statuit qui, contra morem Anglorum ad formam Lotharingorum, uno triclinio comederent, uno cubiculo cubitarent. (Ap. Savile, p. 256.)

cathedral in Wales was partitioned, as they varied in value. When these missionaries were sent out to evangelise a district, the bishop as universal incumbent of his diocese received the proceeds of the lands, until the landowners built parish churches in remote places, (Wightred's Priv. 692. c. 1; Ina's Laws. 693, c. 6,) with all the revenue, offerings of devotion, and the like, and paid out of them the stipends of his deputed representatives in appointed districts, and of those whom he retained in the episcopium or episcopal missionary college as his capitular council or presbytery. These latter clergy of the original parish became the chapter of the cathedral, constituted as such only after the division of the bishop's jurisdiction into parishes; a system which, whether it denotes dioceses or inferior preaching circuits, has been referred by Jocelyn to P. Honorius. The see of Ramsbury, which had no capitular body, is an exceptional case. The term monastery, or minster, was loosely applied to the community of secular priests as to a convent of monks; and to this day the name is so used at York, Salisbury, Lincoln, Lichfield, Ripon, and Southwell, as secular churches were named previously by S. Augustine (Mayer, i. 167,) and S. Ambrose, and in ancient Councils; and formerly at Ely; and as moutier is used in France. (Roquefort. Gloss. ii. 205.) Sometimes two churches, occupied by the clerks and monks respectively, adjoined each other as at Canterbury and Worcester; whilst at London and Winchester a new monastery was founded. Every early mission-station was a monastery, hence the monastic elements and monastic origin of the cathedral (Scarfantoni, i. 72,) in the 8th century, when the missionary field began to narrow, houses strictly monastic and Benedictine were erected as places of ascetic devotion, penitentiaries, and schools of learning. It is a remarkable fact that the Anglo-Saxon missionaries—probably met by similar exigencies in the conversion of Germany, to those experienced by Augustine in Britain—established monastic cathedrals, a plan adopted in these two countries only.

In the composite foundation of a cathedral church and a monastery, the bishop was not only head of the clerks, but also abbot of the monks, as in the case of Wilfred, Egwyn, and S. Aldhelm. The Benedictine system, introduced by Benedict Biscop, however was brought over too late to be adopted in all its strictness in any existing English foundation, for its true theory was as irreconcileable with an episcopal minster, as the necessity of a secular clergy was with monastic vows. The exigencies of the conversion of Britain combined and amalgamated the two.

In the 8th and 9th centuries a new office was introduced, the vicegerent of the bishop being called a provost, as at Worcester during that period; and at Lichfield, where Bishop Ethelwald in 822 established a chapter composed of a provost and twenty canons, of whom one half were priests, and the rest deacons, with prebends, the bishop himself residing with them.

The invasion of the Danes probably broke up many fraternities; the members having contracted a distaste for the ancient discipline divided the revenues, lived in separate households, and confined their attendance to services in choir. Even this duty they at length neglected, accepted or employed vicarious help, and retired to their prebends. The admission of monks to holy orders, laxity of discipline, troublous times, and the interchange of the names of monk and canon were causes which led to the dissolution of clerical monasteries, and the conversion of conventual and collegiate clergy into secular canons, and finally to the renunciation and ultimate extinction of the Benedictine rule in the 9th century, until its revival at a later period. Alcuin says, that in the monasteries the members of a higher grade, i.e. priests, took the names of canons, whilst the inferior remained monks; and about the same time the colleges of clerks were quietly converted into communities of canons. Until the 11th century all canons were supported out of the common revenues, and benefices were unknown as in the case of monks, the only separation being that the bishop and canons had separate tables; but at that period with the increase of wealth the canons began to live apart, and the cathedral clergy in Germany called themselves no longer capitulars, but lords, (Domini, Domherren,) and like monks and collegiate canons deputed their cure of souls to vicars. The bishops then interfered, and bound all those who had retained the practice of living in common by the vow of poverty, and so the latter were called Regulars, and the others Secular. (Mayer, i. § xxvii. p. 61.) By the decrees of Canute, the exertions of Athelwold, "the father of the monks," and the patronage of Oswald and Dunstan, the Benedictine rule was revived. Generally either new monasteries were raised on entirely fresh ground, or on ancient foundations then entirely reduced to ruins; occasionally even with the consent, or abdication, or extinction by death of the canons, as at Worcester and Winchester. Sometimes, however, Benedictines were ejected for secular canons, as at Exeter, by Leofric. At Canterbury they did not obtain secure footing till the time of Lanfranc, 1080; at Durham, 1083; at Rochester, 1089; and at Norwich in 1081, on the translation of the see from Thetford. Giso "Lotharingus" at Wells, who died 1088, after the manner of his country, built a common hall and dormitory for the canons, (Eccl. Doc. Camd. Soc. p. 19,) which were destroyed by John de Villulâ, his successor, (A. S. i. 560.) At Lichfield, Roger de Clinton in the 12th century, "created the College of Canons," and augmented the number of prebends. (A. S. i. 428—434.)

Before S. Augustine arrived there were in existence sees in Wales, and at York, London, and Lincoln in the 4th century, and at Gloucester, 489—542. Bishops from Somersetshire, Cornwall, and Wales, met the great missionary at Augustine's Ac. Suffragan sees were founded at Canterbury, 597; Rochester, 604; London, 605; Dunmoc, 630; Elmham, 673; Winchester, 635; Sherborne, 705; Lichfield, 655; Dorchester, 636; Sidnachester, 678; Worcester, 680; Hereford, 677; Selsey, 709; York, 625; Lindisfarne, 635; Hexham, 678; Ripon, in the 7th century; Beverley, Taunton, Crediton, and S. Petrock's, or Padstow, in the 9th and 10th centuries; Cirencester, 854; Bath and Wells in 909. But so poor were the three bishops who sat in the council of Ariminum in 359, that they were fain to accept the emperor's offer of journey-money and subsistence.[1]

In accordance with the Council of Laodicea and Sardica, which forbade the residence of bishops in villages, several translations took place from Crediton and Bodmin to Exeter, in 1050; from Sherborne and Wilton to Salisbury, in 1058; and still earlier from Lindisfarne, Chester-le-street and Hexham, to Durham, in 990. At the time of the Norman invasion the sees were suffered to remain untouched at Canterbury, York, Rochester, London, Lichfield, Hereford, Winchester, and Worcester; but from motives of policy, or with the view of protecting the foreign nominees under the shelter of a castle, by Lanfranc's Constitutions, 1075, c. iii. (Gervase, 1654,) the following translations of sees from villages into large towns took place, from Elmham and Dunwich to Thetford, 1066—88, and to Norwich, 1091; and from Selsey to Chichester, 1070. (Wilkins, i. 363.) Constance and Liege, and many others on the continent, were translated sees. The population was at this period 1,250,000; and subsequently Glastonbury was a see for a short time, through a caprice of the Bishop of Bath and Wells. Ramsbury was a see without a chapter. The see of Ely was founded 1109, and that of Carlisle in 1133, because revenues existed in them sufficient to maintain a bishop; the former in connection with a Benedictine monastery, the latter attached to a priory of Austin canons, and in it the bishop acted as vice-abbot or abbot. (Scarfantoni, i. 73.) The other eight were conventual cathedral churches, the prior and monks formed the bishop's chapter, the prior and proctor were members of convocation, and to them the *congé d'elire* was addressed. The sub-prior, sacristan, the cellarer, and chamberlain, were appointed by the bishop, as in the place of the abbot. (Matt. Par. Auct. 237.) At the Reformation these churches were changed into eight chapters, composed of deans and canons, the highest number of the latter being twelve, the lowest four.

At the Reformation there were also thirteen cathedrals of the old foundation, four in Wales and nine in England, composed of deans and canons or prebendaries. Changes were made in them partly by royal ordinances, and partly by statutes agreed upon by the bishops and their chapters, consisting mainly of necessary

[1] Paul III. at the Council of Trent, on similar grounds, entertained the Archbishops of Upsala and Armagh. (Frances, 597.)

modifications of ritual and ordinances: their constitution was not materially altered, while the system of residentiaries was confirmed. These cathedrals were York, Hereford, Lichfield, Salisbury, Exeter, Wells, Lincoln, Chichester, S. Paul's, S. David's, Bangor, S. Asaph, Llandaff.

The bishop, elected by delegates from both churches, was enthroned first at Bath, but the Dean of Wells was the returning officer; both communities formed the bishop's collective chapter, but all grants were confirmed under their respective seals. John de Villulâ, who died 1188, called himself Bishop of Bath only (A. S. i. 560.) Bishop Jocelyn, consecrated in 1206, resumed the joint title. Savaric, his predecessor, transferred the see to Glastonbury, and some say was called Bishop of Bath and Glastonbury (A. S. i. 563; 562, n. 10.) Bishop Peter, who died 1185, transferred his see from Lichfield to Chester; his successor, Lymesey (Matt. Par., 72), removed it again to Coventry; but De Clinton, consecrated in 1128, assumed the title of Lichfield and Coventry. The succeeding bishops, at various times, called themselves Bishops of Lichfield or Coventry or Chester (Ormerod's Cheshire, i. 70; Dugdale's Warwickshire, p. 101), until Bishop Hacket placed the name of Lichfield definitely before Coventry. The latter name is no longer used. By Act 33 Hen. VIII. the dean and chapter of Lichfield were constituted "the entire and sole chapter" of the bishop, "whereof the prior and convent had been the moiety." There were various kinds of union:—1. Incorporation, when the lesser church loses its name (Frances, viii. n. 15). 2. Erection, when two churches are constituted one college, with retention of the respective privileges, as when a church is erected into a cathedral, and united with another cathedral church, both having one bishop. 3. Confraternity; two sees being united under one bishop, but each church retaining its separate endowment (n. 24). A bishop having two cathedrals is considered to have but one church (n. 494); where they are united on equal terms, he has the choice of residence, but otherwise he must live in the one most worthy (n. 394); in cases where there was no ancient precedence, he prefixed the name of that where he was resident (n. 365). For the union of churches the consent of the chapter was indispensable (n. 352), and cogent necessity, destruction of a city, neighbourhood, decrease of population, better government, inconveniences, change of time, poverty, debts, unfitness of site, &c. (n. 38), are the only causes to justify it. In Dublin, at Sisteron, Montauban, Calahorra and Calcada, Mantua and Cremona, and in several other instances in Italy (n. 145), a collegiate church is united in community with the cathedral.

Henry VIII. founded the sees of Gloucester, formed out of Worcester; Peterborough, out of Lincoln; Chester, out of Lichfield; Westminster, out of London; endowing them with part of the estates of the Benedictine monasteries in those towns; and Oseney, removed in 1546 to Oxford,[1] out of Lincoln, which had been until 1525 an Austin Canons' priory; and Bristol, out of Salisbury, which, like Pamiers in France, belonged to the same order. Westminster within ten years ceased to be a see, but it was in contemplation by Stat. 31 Henry VIII. c. 9 to erect bishoprics at Waltham, S. Alban's, Burton-on-Trent, Glastonbury, Colchester, Bodmin, Lancaster, S. German's, and Fountains Abbey. Browne Willis says that Dunstable, Shrewsbury, Bodmin, Colchester, and Southwell were actually endowed for a time (Cathedrals, vol. iii. pp. 402, 403). These five new sees, as well as the eight conventual churches, were refounded by Henry VIII. as cathedrals of the new foundation. By 10 and 11 Victoria, c. 108, the collegiate church of Manchester, and by 6 and 7 Will. IV., c. 77, that of Ripon, became cathedral churches (comp. Scarfantoni, i. 243).

Their statutes and charters, in all their main features, were of uniform character, being designed "for restoration and reformation of true religion and genuine worship of God, after the primitive and pure standard of sincerity, that from henceforth the truths of Holy Scripture may be taught, and the Sacraments of our saving religion rightly administered, good moral discipline be maintained, youth fully instructed in letters, the old and infirm suitably provided for, and lastly, that eleemosynary largesses be given to the poor, bridges and roads repaired, and all other offices of piety may be abundantly diffused unto all the adjacent region, to the glory of Almighty God, and the common advantage and happiness of the realm." According to the Elizabethan statutes of Ely, the dean and chapter were "to act as the bishop's presbytery, to check and expel false doctrine and heresy." The statutes were principally drawn up in 1541 by Bishops Heath, Day, and Cox; at Durham, 1556, by Bishops Heath, Tonstal, Bonner, Thirlby, and Waundstead, king's chaplain; at Hereford, they were altered 27 Elizabeth, and 12 Charles I.; at Lichfield, they were revised by Bishops Hacket and Lloyd; and Ely, by Bishop Mawson, 1663; at Canterbury, by Archbishop Laud, in 1636, who intended to settle the imperfect and unconfirmed statutes of other cathedrals, but meeting with a repulse at Rochester, laid aside his design. At Worcester, Bishop Stillingfleet, for the third time since the Reformation, attempted to revise the statutes. Archbishop Parker mentions statutes completed in 1572 for "newly erected cathedrals," and suggests that they should be sealed with

[1] The original foundation of Cardinal College, 1526, is a remarkable instance of the tendency of the period, comprising the dissolution of monasteries; the constitution of a magnificent collegiate church, containing a dean, sub-dean, sixty canons of the first rank, and forty of the second rank, thirteen chaplains, twelve clerks, and sixteen choristers; and an educational establishment; and Henry VIII.'s original foundation, 1532, was designed for twelve canons (Ingram, i. 442—4).

the great seal and signed by the queen's hand (Letters, ccci., p. 395). At Oxford no statutes were enacted; so that the canons have no fixed rule of residence, and their only diocesan function is that of electing the bishop. The difference of the new foundations from the old consists mainly in the following particulars:—1. No express provision for the bishop to take part in divine service: no definition of his duties regarding the cathedral, except as visitor. 2. The dean to be appointed by the crown; the canons by the bishop, except in some cases by the crown and lord chancellor. 3. Deans and canons to officiate on festival days. 4. Continuous residence enjoined with leave of absence, to the dean of one hundred days, to the canons of eighty days, on condition that one-third or one-fourth of the canons be residing: chapters to be held frequently. 5. Preaching to be frequent. 6. Offices are not permanently distinguished, nor are so various: the vice-dean and treasurer to be elected annually. 7. Minor canons to be equal in number to the canons, and enjoined perpetual residence, and never to absent themselves without the dean's leave. 8. Precentor to be a minor canon. 9. Archdeacons not by office members of chapter or bound to residence; have no right to vote, and no share in the emoluments of chapters, but sometimes have a stall. 10. Deans and canons not restricted from holding parochial benefices. 11. Provision made for education of choristers and poor scholars, and in some cases for maintenance of students at the universities, in conformity with the conventual custom at Canterbury, Durham, Gloucester, &c. 12. Dean and chapter can grant leases of estates, but cannot alienate or mortgage; to visit all the estates annually, and keep a record of all things pertaining to them. 13. Duty of hospitality enjoined, and of benevolence to strangers, and the poor and aged in the precinct and resident on capitular estates. According to the earlier system continual residence was required of the dean and the other three principal officers, and a certain number of the canons. This was modified in the new foundations of Henry VIII., by the permission of a limited term of absence to the dean and residentiaries; a certain number of the body being required to be perpetually present. But between the reigns of Edward VI. and Charles II. the exception became the rule; the term allotted for absence became the term of residence of ninety, sixty, or even fifty days in the year; while in many cases the provision for the presence of one-third or one-fourth part of the canons was abandoned. The canons of 1603, c. 44, and statutes of this period, distinctly recognize the residence of canons on parochial benefices. Canon 42 required from the dean a residence of ninety days continuous or interrupted in the year. By Stat. 1 and 2 Vict., c. 106, he is now forbidden to hold more than one benefice, or to retain preferment in any other cathedral church. Canon 45 required all residentiaries to repair immediately after the expiration of their residence to their benefices, and not to absent themselves for longer than one month in a year from their benefices. The statute 59 Geo. III. c. 99, s. 11, further regulated residence, which by 1 and 2 Vict., c. 106, s. 37, is defined to consist for three months, with a further term of two months' absence from their benefice.

In 1835, William IV. issued a commission, which recommended measures carried out by 3 and 4 Vict., c. 113; 4 and 5 Vict., c. 34; 5 and 6 Vict., c. 26, 108; 6 and 7 Vict., c. 37, 77. These were as follows:—1. The suspension of canonries, so as to reduce the number to four in each cathedral, except where two more are attached to archdeaconries or professorships. Christchurch retains eight. Canterbury, Durham, Ely, and Westminster have six; Winchester and Exeter, five; S. David's and Llandaff, two stalls respectively. 2. Deans to reside eight months (after Aug. 11, 1840), canons three months in the year at least. 3. Deans allowed to hold a benefice not exceeding £500 a year, and only in the cathedral city; canons permitted to hold one benefice without restriction of distance or value. 4. Non-residentiaries retained, but without emoluments. 5. Bishops of cathedrals of new foundations may appoint honorary canons without emolument. 6. Minor canons to be reduced; their number to be six at the most, and two at the least; their incomes not to be less than £150 a year each: they may hold a benefice each within six miles of the cathedral town. 7. Separate and prebendal estates of dean and canons to be transferred to the Ecclesiastical Commissioners. 8. Incomes of deans and canons in future limited. 9. Deans and chapters, with consent of their visitors, may propose alterations in their statutes, to be approved by the sovereign in council. By Act 3 and 4 Vict., c. 113, one-sixth of the entire amount of capitular property, all the separate official and prebendal estates in the old foundations, the incomes of suspended canonries in the new, and part of the incomes of certain deans and chapters have been transferred to the Ecclesiastical Commissioners for the improvement of small benefices and the endowment of new churches. Grants have also been made towards the repairs of the fabric of cathedrals at Carlisle, Worcester, and Ripon, &c. The sums arising from the enfranchisement of leasehold and copyhold capitular property, and from the profits of long leases for mining and building purposes, have been diverted to the same general fund. But a considerable source of revenue has been lost, owing to this wholesale act of interference: an enormous sum of money was abstracted by a fraudulent official of the Ecclesiastical Commissioners; the rewards and dignified studious ease hitherto opened to deserving clergymen, and the inducement to men of brighter talents and in the higher ranks to undertake the duties, were curtailed; no provision was made for residence in case of casualties, when only one canon was left for continuous service of three months; whilst the limitation of the minor canons cannot be carried out where they exist as a corporation, and grave difficulties about their revised rate of income arise, owing to the omission in the Act 3 and 4 Vict., c. 113, of any definition whether the augmented stipend is to be provided from the common fund of the Commissioners or from the chapter property. The chapters of York and Carlisle, for some inexplicable cause, were the first, and those of Chester, Chichester, Gloucester, Peterborough, Salisbury, and S. Asaph also consented, to transfer all their estates to the Commissioners, receiving in exchange an annual payment equal to the amount of their average incomes and ordinary expenditure, until such time as the Commissioners shall convey to the chapters landed property sufficient to produce an equivalent revenue. The incomes at present are of the Dean of Durham, £3000; York, S. Paul's, and Westminster, £2000; canons of those churches, £1000; Dean of Manchester, £1500; canons, £600; deans of the old foundation, £1000; of the new foundation the same, or in some cases between £1000 and £2000; canons £500, or in some cases between £500 and £1000. The deans of the Welsh cathedrals receive £700, the canons £350. At S. Paul's, three canons receive £1000: and the Archdeacon of London, £750. At Durham, four receive £1000. At Winchester, the net revenue, £10,600, is divided into fourteen shares: to the dean two, and to each canon one. At Wells, the net income is divided equally between the dean and canons, and the commissioners. At Chester, Chichester, Salisbury, Ripon, and Lichfield (except one of the value of £341), each canonry is worth £500; at Ely £303, the net revenue being divided into ten shares, two to the dean, and to each canon one; with small separate revenues from £13 to £40 a year; at Hereford, two £587, one £612, and a fourth £637, of the net revenue; at Lincoln, the dean takes $\frac{17}{24}$, the precentor $\frac{1}{4}$ (besides separate estates), the archdeacon and sub-dean each $\frac{1}{8}$, and the chancellor $\frac{3}{24}$. At Manchester the net revenue, £8132, was divided into six parts: to the dean, £2000; the senior canon, one-sixth of dividend; and to the other three canons, £600. At Peterborough each canon has £537; at Rochester the net revenue, £5106, is subject to stipends to minor canons, schoolmasters, &c. The average sum divided is £4809: to the dean $\frac{2}{8}$, and to each canon $\frac{1}{8}$. By 3 and 4 Vict., c. 113, two canonries of Ely were attached to the professorships of Greek and Hebrew at Cambridge; and two at Christ Church to the regius professorships of Pastoral Theology and Ecclesiastical History. The entire average income of twenty-six cathedrals, of Westminster and Windsor, on an average of seven years, was £295,984, and in 1852 £313,000, out of which, exclusive of payments to the chapter, £108,696 were expended in repairs, the stipends, and benevolent contributions.

Bacon, in his "Liber Regis," says that the income of a residentiary in the eighteenth century at Exeter, Chichester, and York, was £200; at Salisbury, £250; Wells, £100; at Hereford, £80; Lincoln, £350; at S. Paul's, £800; and of the deans of Lichfield and Hereford, £600; and of Chichester, £300; but in all cases they had their prebends, and the dignitaries held impropriations or livings, or both. The deans of Carlisle and Peterborough received £300; Durham, £2000; Oxford, £1000; Norwich, Winchester, Worcester, £600; Bristol, Gloucester, £450; Rochester, £400; Canterbury, £900; Ely, £450; York, £700; S. Asaph, £120. Canons of Worcester, £300; Peterborough, £120; Carlisle, £140; Oxford, £150; Winchester, Norwich, £250; Gloucester, £200; Ely, Bristol, Rochester, £160; Canterbury, Worcester, £300; Durham, £400—£800.

Eighteen archdeaconries, out of the total number of seventy, have been endowed by the annexation of a canonry, and three more by a charge on a canonry. The Ecclesiastical Commissioners suggested the extinction of the titles of dignitaries, their offices and revenues; the latter have been, like the prebends of canons, "suspended," and only not "suppressed" through the urgent appeal of the late Bishops of Salisbury and Rochester. The whole evil arose from the acts of ecclesiastics. The superior authorities, alarmed by a passing cry of the day, precipitately suggested that extensive changes should be made. Without a struggle the wealthier endowments of corporations aggregate, by their original intention inalienable, were surrendered without the slightest resistance, or an effort to defend them. The act of spoliation has been regretted too late: the external unpopularity and the expressed personal dissatisfaction of the Commissioners with their work show how signally they have failed in all things but the infliction of injury on the capitular establishments of the country. One day redress—though tardy, yet certain—will arrive. "God seems likely," said the Bishop of London, when dean of that church, whose shrunken establishment has been taken as a model for the rest, "to lay upon our cathedrals a great spiritual charge in these latter days. Help from the centre of the diocese is quite as much wanted as in the old times. A feeling grows throughout the country that some return to the old organization of our cathedrals, without their old faults, might best meet our very pressing spiritual wants. How are the cathedrals, without legislation, reforming themselves? Witness the thousands of working people who assemble at the special services in so many cathedrals through the land."

Members of a Cathedral.

"A rich storehouse, for the glory of the Creator, and the endowment of human life."—Lord Bacon. (De Aug. Scient. Lib. 1.)

The Norman bishops introduced a complete and organized system into the cathedrals, which must have a number of ministers, (Frances, 225,) and an archdeacon and other dignitaries, (Ib. 232,) each body consisting of—1, a bishop; 2, quatuor personæ or dignitaries, the dean, præcentor, chancellor, and treasurer; 3, archdeacons; 4, canons, of whom there should be at least twelve (Ceccoperius, i. 97);[1] 5, vicars. The quatuor personæ were bound to perpetual residence, and each had his respective deputy, subdean, succentor or subchanter, scribe, and sacrist. The canonici simplices had each a vicar. At Lincoln, in 1440, there were thirteen dignitaries besides the bishop, the quatuor personæ, a subdean and eight archdeacons; there were also forty-six canons, non-resident and resident. In France, until the Revolution, the establishment of Amiens, one of the largest in that country, included ten dignitaries, originally prebendal, and conferred by the bishop; the dean (760 livres) elected by the chapter; provost (710 l.) nominated by the archbishop; chancellor (1,380 l.); two archdeacons at 1,700 l. and 1,200 l.; præcentor (230 l.); chanter (260 l.); master of schools (260 l.); penitentiary (550 l.), and treasurer: forty-three canons, "titulaires prebendes," twenty-nine being priests and thirteen deacons, formerly thirty-eight priests serving at the high altar; the official, who attended and buried the town-clergy; cellarer who found the wine for mass, having formerly been the caterer for the common table; theologal; two vicaires prebendes; preceptoriale; seventy-two or sixty-two chaplains, instituted in 1204; and ten choristers (eight in 1224) and six musicians. At Rouen, according to Farin, there were ten dignitaries—a dean, grand chanter, treasurer, chancellor, and six archdeacons; fifty canons, thirty prebendaries of S. Romanus, eight minor canons, thirty-five chaplains titular, for singing low masses, besides habituez, [portionists, candidates for vacant chaplaincies, musicians, canons' servants,] and clerks of choir, and eight choristers in 1471, but only four in 1366 and 1413. There were residences for twenty-six canons. At Paris there were eight dignitaries—dean, chanter, three archdeacons, subchanter, chancellor, and penitentiary, to which, (except the deanery and subchantership, and twenty-two canonries, called servitorian, and conferred on inferior clergy,) the archbishop collated, fifty-one canons, one hundred and twenty chaplains, six grand vicars, besides twenty canons of S. Denis, S. Jean, and S.

[1] At Constantinople there were protopapas, protopsaltes, chartophylax, and sceuophylax. (Goar, Euchol. 268.)

Aignan, and two perpetual vicars, two curés, one hundred and forty chaplains, eight vicars, and one chaplain subdiaconal. At Lima there are five dignitaries—dean, archdeacon, chanter, scholasticus, and treasurer; ten canons, six portionists, six demies, two curates, six chaplains, six acolytes; and inferior ministers, organist, chapter porter, mazero, major domo or chancellor, and the perron, or dog-whipper. In Spain there are usually five dignitaries; a dean, grand archdeacon, two archdeacons, two titulars, a chanter, and twelve canons, occur at Barbastro; and a dean, archdeacon, treasurer, archpresbyter, and twelve canons, at Teruel. (Frances, 232.) At Ratisbon the establishment consisted of a provost archpresbyter, with the right of the mitre and staff, a dean, the chief custos, scholasticus, twenty-four (latterly fifteen) canons, and vicars. (Mayer, ii. 2, 3.) At Barcelona, in 1335, there were an archdeacon-major, dean, cantor, sacrist, scriptor, two archdeacons, and forty canons. (Martene, Thesaur. Anecd. iv. 598.)[1] At Saragossa the establishment included a prior, four archdeacons, chanter, chamberlain (a similar officer was at York), treasurer, chaplain-major, operarius or scholasticus, three archpresbyters, infirmarer, master of the works, charitatarius, almoner, a succentor, vicars, and chaplains. (Frances, xxi. 136.) At Jaca there were an archpresbyter and sacrist minor, or treasurer, (Ib. 231); at Malines twelve canons (Moreri, vii. 34) and at Cologne a provost and canons, called counts (iii. 832).

A canon residentiary, being only a member of delegates of the whole corporation or great chapter, has no precedence except that of his prebend; when hebdomadary, or canon in residence, he is president of choir and chapter in absence of the dean, unless there

[1] I am indebted for the following list to my friend Dr. Jebb's MS. notes from Moreri and Boulainvilliers, &c. :—

RHEIMS. Nine dignitaries: grand archdeacon, archdeacon of Champagne, provost, dean, chanter, vidam, scholastier, penitencier; sixty-four canons, forty chaplains.

SOISSONS. Nine dignitaries: provost, dean, chanter, four archdeacons, treasurer, ecolâtre; sixty prebendaries, thirty chaplains.

CHALONS. Eight dignitaries: dean, præcentor, treasurer, four archdeacons, subchanter; eight demiprebendaries, nine habituez, two vicars, sixty chaplains, appointed by the chapter, except archdeacons and treasurer, appointed by the bishop.

LAON. Five dignitaries: dean, præcentor, two archdeacons, treasurer; eighty-four canons, fifty chaplains.

BEAUVAIS. Six dignitaries: dean, chanter, treasurer, two archdeacons, subchanter; forty-two canons, one of them chancellor and another penitentiary; six demiprebendaries, all (except the dean) collated by the bishop, appointed by the bishop.

NOYON. Dean, archdeacon, chanter, chancellor, treasurer, sixty canons, thirty-nine chaplains.

MEAUX. Five dignitaries: dean, archdeacon, chanter, treasurer, chancellor; forty-four canons, six grand chaplains, twenty-eight petits chapellains, three sacristans, conferred by the bishop, except the deanery.

AUXERRE. Provost (till 1177, when the office was annexed to the capitular mensal), dean, grand archdeacon, chanter, treasurer, archdeacon, penitentiary; the dean, chanter, and treasurer, sixty-three prebendaries, abbot of S. Martin and principal of S. John holding each a prebend; another being subdivided for two persons, is a vice-dean present. In citations the dignitaries precede other canons in the lists of residentiaries and non-residents. In choir the dignitaries occupy the higher stalls; and in the chapter-house of Salisbury (the church whose Use was the model all but universally followed in the three kingdoms, and was modified only in minor details even in the exceptional cases) there were forty-two stalls, seven in each of the seven bays, for the prebendaries, in order of precedence; but at the west end, on either side of the entrance,

the subchanter and reader, and six others subdivided into twelve semiprebends; fifty-one being held by canons, of whom the theologal is one. The chapter conferred the deanery, chancellorship, preceptorial, prebend of S. Martin, and six demiprebends, but the bishop was patron of the rest.

Sens. Five dignitaries: dean, chanter, treasurer, cellarer, archdeacon; four personats-archdeacons; thirty-one canons, four canons of S. Mary's altar, fourteen demiprebendaries, two vicars, twelve chaplains.

Bayeux. Fifty canons, including dean, chanter, chancellor, treasurer, archdeacon, subdean, subchanter, ecolâtre, theologal; twelve vicars, twelve chaplains, and children of the choir.

Avranches. Dean, chanter, treasurer, ecolâtre, two archdeacons, twenty canons, forty-nine other ecclesiastics.

Seez. Forty canons, including provost, chanter, five archdeacons, penitentiary, sixteen canons prebendaries, four demiprebendaries, chaplains.

Lisieux. Dean, grand chanter, treasurer, chefenier (treasurer), ecolâtre, theologal, penitentiary, thirty-six canons, (ninety-three ecclesiastics in all, including the bas-chœur.)

Coutances. Eight dignitaries, twenty-six canons, six vicars, forty-six chaplains, six musicians, fourteen habituez (assistant clergy), six children of choir and their master.

Arras. Six dignitaries, two archdeacons, forty canons, forty-eight chaplains. The king conferred the provostry, the bishop the archdeaconries and canonries, and the chapter the deanery and chantership.

Lyons. Eight dignitaries: dean, archdeacon, præcentor, chancellor, chamarier (chamberlain), sacristan, grand custos, provost. There are also a master of the choir and thirty-two canons; the sacristan and custos nominated by the archbishop, the rest by the chapter, who choose a theologal with the rank of chevalier; twenty perpetuels, who chant the offices, chosen from the twenty-four children of choir; four custodes, and seven chevaliers.

Langres. Dean (elected by chapter), treasurer (nominated by the bishop), six archdeacons, chanter; fifty-two canons, all elected by the chapter; eight demi-canons, elected by the dean; and many chaplains.

Angouleme. Dean, archdeacon, ten prebendaries, four demies.

Bourges. Dean, chanter, chancellor, grand and nine petits archdeacons, forty canons, ninety-six vicars, twenty archpriests.

Montauban. Provost, two archdeacons, chanter, eight canons, twenty semiprebendaries.

Strasburg. Grand provost, grand dean, custos ecolâtre, chamarier (chamberlain), all nobles; portier, six archdeacons; twenty-four canons, twelve capitulars, twelve domicellars; seventy-two vicars, forty chaplains, the former governed by a senior and two deputies, yearly elected.

Auch. Provost, eight archdeacons, four abbots, two priors, twenty canons, thirty-four demiprebendaries, twelve chaplains.

Vienne. Twenty canons, comprising dean, provost, chancellor, and capiscol, the four dignitaries; sacristan, four archdeacons, chancellor; petits clercs appointed by the chapter, two chevaliers, four quaternes, six coadjutors; thirty priests, four deacons, four subdeacons; eighteen clerks, appointed by the dean; twelve clergeons or choristers.

Die. Two dignitaries: dean and sacristan; ten canons, two honorary canons.

Besançon. Forty-three canons, among whom are high dean, grand archdeacon, chanter, and treasurer; four petty archdeacons, all being elective; simple preare two stalls for archdeacons, and at the east end the seven seats for the bishop in the centre, with the dean, chancellor, archdeacon, and subdean on his right hand, and the precentor, treasurer, archdeacon, and succentor on his left. In the register of Archbishop Courtenay, at Lambeth, there is a citation of the clergy of Salisbury Cathedral, including the four principal persons; the four

bendaries, nominated alternately by the Pope and chapter; theological prebendary, elected by the doctors.

APT. Provost, archdeacon, capiscol, sacristan, ecolâtre, theologal, seven other canons, thirteen beneficiati, two curés.

TOULON. Provost, archdeacon, sacristan, capiscol, annexed to priories, eight other canons; *bas-chœur*, eight beneficiarii, two curés, and a master of music.

VALENCE. Four dignitaries: dean, provost, abbot of S. Felix, archdeacon; fourteen canons, eight chaplains, eight children of choir.

ARLES. Twenty canons, including the dignitaries, provost, archdeacon, sacristan, and archpriest; three persons, capiscol, treasurer, and primicier.

At ANGERS there were six archpriests.

MARSEILLES. Provost, archdeacon, sacristan, capiscol, and nine other canons, one being theologal; ten beneficiares, two vicars, two deacons, eight prêtres habitues, four choristers.

SISTERON. Provost, eleven canons, twelve beneficiares, master of the music, four children; in the second cathedral of S. Mary, Forcalquier, in which synods are held alternately, three dignitaries, ten prebendaries.

MILAN. Thirty-one canons, including archpriest, archdeacon, primicier, provost, and dean; and twenty-six cardinals, twelve being priests and nine deacons, and five subdeacons, one cimeliarch, or sacrist; beneficiati, including master of the ceremonies, four notaries, primicierius lectorum; five lectores in feudo, ten minor lectores in feudo, six mazo-canonici, two choral chaplains, four ducales, two perpetual vicars, parish priest of S. Michael's, two chaplains of S. Agnes, two sacrists, sixteen porters, thirty-two stipendiary chaplains, thirty-two præfects of fabric, eight clerks, their servants; twenty-five musicians, one hundred and forty clerks of the seminary.

Basilica of S. AMBROSE. Provost, twelve canons, four chaplains.

TOLEDO. Four dignitaries, forty-nine canons, fifty prebendaries, twenty petticanons, forty-seven priests, and forty clerks for the music; so that there were almost two hundred surpliced ministers. (Moreri, x. 223.)

ELGIN. Seven dignitaries, fifteen canons, twenty-two vicars choral, and as many chaplains (modelled on Lincoln, as Dunkeld on Salisbury.)

ABERDEEN. Dean, chanter, chancellor, treasurer, subchanter, twenty-one prebendaries.

GLASGOW. Seven dignitaries: dean, subdean, præcentor, subchanter, chancellor, treasurer, and sacrist; two archdeacons and twenty-three prebendaries.

A cathedral in Russia, founded by Peter the Great, had eight priests, one being protopapas, and two treasurers; one protodeacon, four deacons, two readers, two vestry keepers, and thirty-three choristers.

S. PATRICK'S. Modelled on Salisbury: most of the Irish cathedrals retain their full complement of dignitaries.

OTRANTO. Archdeacon and præcentor; twenty-three canons, including dean, treasurer, and primicerius; two major chaplains, with cure of souls.

PALERMO. Three dignitaries: chanter (with a prebend), archdeacon (with a prebend), dean; canons, treasurer, and twenty-four called millenarii or centenarii, from their ancient pay of 1,000 or 100 gold "tarens,"—eighteen have options, i.e., right of promotion to a higher canonry; a subchanter, two terminators or masters of ceremonies, four major chaplains, forty vivanderii, or parochial chaplains, &c.

GENOA. Seventeen canons, three priests' chaplains, or mansionarii, and a college of chanters.

TURIN. Five dignitaries, twenty-six canons.

CREMONA. Archpriest, archdeacon, chanter, dean, provost, primicerius, cimeliarch, treasurer, prior.

BERGAMO. United 1575. The archdeacon, provost, archpriest, are dignitaries;

archdeacons; the priest-prebendaries, twenty-four in number, designated variously as dominus, or by the higher title magister; prebendaries-deacons, sixteen; prebendaries-subdeacons, eleven; officials, penitentiary general, subchanter, master of the grammar-school, including twenty-four priest-vicars, with the prefix of dominus, eighteen deacon-vicars and eleven subdeacon-vicars, seven chantry chaplain-priests, two clerks of the sacristy, seven clerks of the altar, two minor clerks of the sacristies. In 1468 there were seven residentiaries, thirty-eight canons non-residentiaries, thirty-one vicars-choral, and thirteen stipendiary priests. The officers at Salisbury were the two masters of the fabric (the dean and a canon), the communar, the keeper of the muniments, the master

primicerius, chanter, cimeliarch (keeper of muniments); two sacrists, six custodes, twelve chaplains. There were forty canons in the first, and twenty-four in the second cathedral.

Padua. Twenty-four canons, four provosts, six custodes, six mansionarii, thirty permanent chaplains, twelve additional for daily masses, thirty junior clerks prebended, a master of music, &c.

Naples. Thirty canons, dean, primicerius, cimeliarch; twenty-two hebdomadaries, eighteen priests' chaplains, two sacrists, twelve deacons.

Nola. Twenty canons, of whom four are dignitaries; the dean and chanter sit first on the right side, and the archdeacon and treasurer next the bishop on the left: twelve numeral priests in the lower stalls, one is sacristan.

Salerno. Three dignitaries: archdeacon, chanter, primicerius; four canons, twenty-four priests with prebends—they use the mitre, as at Lyons, Messina, &c.; ten hebdomadaries.

Syracuse. Eighteen canons, proposed by the bishop, and elected by the canons; chaplains; four hebdomadaries, greater sacrist, two acolyths, a cross-bearer; four dignitaries—dean, præcentor, archdeacon, treasurer, with prebends annexed; twenty canons, a theologal; master chaplain, with cure of souls in the close; four persons, terminator (who ordered processions), subchanter, master of schools, and master of ceremonies, two vivanderii, thirty priests.

Mazzara. Chanter, archdeacon, dean, treasurer, fourteen to eighteen canons, six persons, terminator, chaplains, subchanter, master of the schools, tercenier, twelve chaplains.

Malta. Archdeacon, dean, chanter, treasurer, archpriest, fifteen canons, twelve chaplains.

Lipari. Archdeacon, dean, chanter, treasurer.

Monreale. (Benedictine) abbot, archbishop, archpriest, archdeacon, sitting next the bishop on the right side of the choir; prior, in the præcentor's place, and next him the dean; twenty-five canons, six secular priests, nine officiating priests.

Messina. Dean, chanter, archdeacon, with prebends annexed; eighteen canons, twenty-two tertiary canons, subchanter, two chaplains major, treasurer, six vivanderii, six vicars, &c.

Neti. Prior, chanter, dean, treasurer, twelve secular canons, twelve beneficiati or hebdomadarii. Like Patti, and Cefalu, and Chiemsee, it was formerly an Austin canons' church.

To these I may add the following, from the "Etat Ecclesiastique d'Allemagne." In many instances the canons were to be nobles or doctors.

Minden. Grand provost, grand dean, chanter, treasurer, thirty canons.

Hildesheim. Provost, dean, chanter, treasurer, cellarer, ecolâtre, forty-one canons (four priests, four deacons), five domiciliars, four provosts.

Halberstadt. Provost, dean, chanter, treasurer, ecolâtre, cellarer, vice-dominus, thirty canons.

Liege. Grand provost, city archdeacon, grand dean (the chief of chapter), grand vicaire, seven archdeacons, chanter, ecolâtre, coustre or treasurer, chancellor of the or warden of choristers, and were appointed from among the residentiaries.

PERSONATUS is a generic name, including benefices which require personal residence. According to the institution or custom of a church, the same office may be in one personatus, and in the other a dignity. The word personatus, a barbarous term, came into

prince, sixty canons, called trefonciers, who must be nobles, doctors or licentiates of law.

BAMBERG. Provost, dean, ecolatre, treasurer, cellarer, twenty capitulars, fifteen domiciliars, who must not miss a mass daily during two years.

CONSTANCE. Provost, dean, chanter, treasurer, twenty-four canons, four postulants.

PADERBORN. Grand provost, grand dean, twenty-four canons, graduates of Italy or France.

COIRE. Provost, dean, chanter, ecolatre, treasurer, sextier, forty canons.

FRISINGEN. Provost, dean, ecolatre, treasurer, twenty-four canons.

RATISBON. Provost, dean, archpriest, chaplain, imperial custos, ecolatre, provost of S. John, twelve canons.

PASSAU. Provost, dean, custos, twenty-five canons.

MAYENCE. Provost, dean, chanter, treasurer, ecolatre, archpriest (the three first were mitred 1244), twenty-four canons capitular, eighteen domiciliars.

WORMS. Provost, dean, custos, ecolatre, chanter, twenty-six canons, thirty capitulars, thirty domiciliars.

SPIRES. Provost, dean, ecolatre, custos, chanter, three provosts, fifteen capitulars, twelve domiciliars.

AUGSBURG. Provost, dean, forty canons, among whom are the coustre, ecolatre, archdeacon, cellier, and penitentiary.

COLOGNE. Grand provost, dean, subdean, ecolatre, ancien et nouveau, diacre and treasurer, mitred; twenty-four capitulars, thirty-six domiciliars, all nobles.

TREVES. Provost, dean, treasurer, ecolatre, chanter, elective grand archdeacon, four archdeacons, sixteen capitulars, twenty-four domiciliars, who must be of noble blood.

OSNABURGH. Provost, who is the grand archdeacon; dean, ancien, coustre, chanter, ecolatre, four archdeacons, twenty-six canons.

TOUL. Dean, chanter, penitentiary, ecolatre, coustre, six archdeacons, thirty-six canons.

MUNSTER. Grand provost, grand dean, ecolatre, vidam (vice-dominus), chanter, coustre, forty canons.

VIENNA. Three dignitaries: provost, who is chancellor of the university, dean, chanter, and twenty canons.

LAVANTZ. Provost-archdeacon, mitred; dean, eighteen canons.

TRENT. Dean, provost, ecolatre, ancien, twenty canons.

TRIESTE. Provost, dean, archdeacon, ten canons.

PRAGUE. Provost, dean, ecolatre, chanter, six canons.

OLMUTZ. Dean, provost, four archdeacons, chanter, ecolatre, thirty canons.

BASLE. Provost, dean, archdeacon, chanter, ecolatre, cellarer, treasurer, official suffragan, vicar general, eighteen canons.

GENEVA. Provost, dean, two archdeacons, thirty canons.

SION. Twenty-four canons (twelve capitulars, twelve domiciliars), grand dean of Sion, sacristan, chanter, theologal.

MERSBURG. Provost, dean, senior, coutre (treasurer), chanter, ecolatre, twenty canons.

VERDUN. Dean, grand archdeacon, primicier, sub-archdeacon, chanter, thirty canons.

HAMBURG and BREMEN, joint chapters, each with provost, dean, ecolatre, chanter.

LUBECK. Provost, dean, ancien, ecolatre, chanter, treasurer, thirty canons.

SALTZBURG. Provost, dean, custos, ecolatre, twenty-four canons.

METZ. Primicier, dean, chanter, chancellor, treasurer, four archdeacons, almoner, ecolatre, forty canons.

fashion after the papacy of Alexander III., and, like dignity, is not earlier than the eleventh century. (Mayer, i. 329.)[1] DIGNITY is a kind of pre-eminence in point of degree, and in the canon law includes a personatus. It is used for a superior promotion in the church, viz., archbishops, bishops, archdeacons, and bishops' officials (Dist. 20, Clem. 1, 2, 2), according to its primeval institution and custom observed in that behalf. It is known (1) from the administration of ecclesiastical affairs as being clothed and vested with jurisdiction (28 Dist. c. 2), when the administration is assigned to the dignitary in perpetuum; (2) from the name and preference which the dignitary has in choro et capitulo; (3) from the custom of the place where such dignity subsists. The dignitaries are called "personæ ecclesiæ, personæ principales, and personæ privilegiati." (Dugdale's Monast. viii. 1256, 1200; Mason's Hib. ii. iii.) At Sens the four archdeacons, and at Auxerre the subchanter and lector, were called personats.

In the Decretals the same office is called a dignity and a personatus (x. 1, 2, 8; vi. 1, 6, 1); but these distinctions and different terms, such as that a dignity is 'administration with jurisdiction,' and personatus 'prerogative of a more honourable stall in choir without jurisdiction,' have their rise from a variety or diversity of plans. An office is the administration of ecclesiastical affairs, without any jurisdiction or stall in the choir, as we find by an example in the sacrist or treasurer, who are not dignitaries in the church of common law, but only of custom. (Ayliffe's Parergon, 215, 6.) Dignitaries were instituted for the preservation and increase of church discipline. (Frances, 230.) Wood (MS. Bodl. E. 3, p. 28) calls the dignitaries of Chichester "the four masters of the church;" and at Hereford the special term "parson" was commonly applied to them almost within memory. At Lincoln they were known as "masters of the fabric;" at Exeter, Lichfield, and Lincoln, and formerly at York and Salisbury, they are residentiaries. In Spain dignitaries had a stall in choir, but no voice in chapter. (Scarfantoni, i. 66.) Ceccoperius says that the canons may be said to be quasi in dignitate constituti (Stella Canonic. i. 108), and that coadjutors of dignitaries and honorary dignitaries precede other canons (Ib. 174, 5.) Dignitaries and canons alike are bound to sing Divine Service, even though they maintain vicars (ii. 121). Dignities are given by collation, "libera assignatio canonicatus vacantis;" institution being "collatio non libera beneficii facta ab episcopo alicui præsentato per patronum hujusmodi jus habentem," and præsentatio is "inhibitio personæ canonicè peractæ" (iv. 84, 5.) The Bishop may unite a prebend to a dig-

[1] At Grenoble, Sens, Arles, and Nevers the personats, not being dignitaries, had the principal responsibility of the ordinary Church service. At York, chantry priests of S. William's College were called sacerdotes personæ, and the rectores chorales at Beverley were known as personæ. (Monast. vi. 1307.)

nity. (Frances, c. viii. n. 6, 11.) In processions the dignitaries and canons were to walk in pairs at equal distances, with one pace between those who went side by side and three between each row: if the number were unequal, the junior dignitary was companion to the senior canon. (Ceccoperius, ii. 140.) The right hand side was the post of precedency. (Scarf. i. 72.)

The statutes of Hereford define "personæ in dignitatibus constitutæ" to be the bishop, dean, præcentor, treasurer, and chancellor; and the "dignitates in jurisdictione" the dean and archdeacon. At York the præcentor, chancellor, treasurer, subdean, succentor of canons, and four archdeacons had stalls, and were capable of collation to a residentiaryship, in right of which they claimed the privilege of voting in chapter acts. At S. Paul's the præcentor, treasurer, chancellor, and almoner were officers of the chapter. By charter, 34 Eliz., the præcentor, chancellor, treasurer, three archdeacons, and subdean are dignitaries at Wells.

The canons had the prerogative of precedence and first seats collectively, not individually, with subordination; in consequence of this pre-eminence over the inferior clergy they were called majores. Some members, being more particularly distinguished, were regarded as dignitaries, who, between the thirteenth and fifteenth centuries, although not nobles, prefixed "von" to their names in Germany. (Mayer, i. p. 73.) Beyerlinck says the dean is a dignitary by pontifical right, and the primicerius [præcentor] and archdeacon by common law are also dignitaries. (Theatrum. ii. 790.) The dean's jurisdiction especially depends on custom. By common law he has not jurisdictionem contentiosam, except by custom or privilege. (Mayer, p. 179.) At Mayence there were three dignitaries "prælati," the dean, scholasticus, and cantor; and at an earlier period the provost, as chief, and the summus custos, ranking after the dean: each kept his week as hebdomadary. (Mayer, i. pp. 4, 5.) At Tours the dean robed in the sacristy, the subdean outside the sacristy, the chanter in the chamber, the treasurer in the treasury, the master of the schools in the school.

Dignitas decani et omnium canonicorum est ut alicui in nullo respondeant nisi in capitulo et judicio tantum capituli pareant. (Wells, Lichfield, Salisbury, Chichester.) The dean, præcentor, chancellor, and treasurer at Wells were to reside during two-thirds of the year, continuously or at intervals; they shared in the residue, after the usual deductions for stock, &c. (1321.) They were to receive the order of priesthood (1331) as befitting their office within a year after installation, on pain of losing half the daily distribution. With the archdeacons they received double commons. Each (1259) had to keep eight weeks in each term, which consisted of twelve weeks. At York they resided the greater part of the year. At Lichfield (1197) each resided one quarter of the year, in the order of dean, præcentor, chancellor, and treasurer, and they collectively kept the keys of the seal coffer. At Exeter they were called "the internal dignitaries," and resided for two parts of the year, continuously or at intervals; the office of præcentor being specially endowed with Penyngton, the chancellorship with S. Newlyn's, and the treasurership with S. Probus. The following legends were inscribed over their stalls:—

> "Tardiùs atque manè residens, rege cuncta, Decane.
> Hìc residendo chorum rege, Cantor, dux puerorum.
> Hâc qui sede sedes jura sacra leges (Cancellarius).
> Thesauros conde, residens, pro lumine sponde."

At S. Paul's the order of precedence was, archdeacon, præcentor, treasurer, and chancellor. At Lincoln they resided continuously, the sub-dean being one of the five dignitaries; but if they kept four months, even at intervals, they were not mulcted in the fine for non-residence—one-seventh of their prebend—which went to augment the canons' commune. The archdeacons, in consideration of their diocesan toil, resided only during forty days. At York, contrary to usual custom, they had no seat in the great chapter unless they held a prebend besides; and at Hereford, like the prebendary of Moreton, unless of the number of the twenty-seven prebendaries, were excluded from those who were eligible to become residentiaries.[1]

[1] Qui sunt in dignitatibus vel officiis aut administrationibus constituti, quales sunt decanus, archidiaconus, archipresbyter, præpositus, præcentor, cancellarius, magister scholarium, sacrista, et hujusmodi. (Lyndw. Provinc. lib. v. tit. xvi. n. k.) Archipresbyter idem est quod decanus. (Lib. iii. tit. i. n. d. p. 117.)

Dignitas est præeminentia in ecclesia quoad forum contentiosum gradum tenens. Quæ quandoque dicitur personatus quia honoratur persona. Quandoque dicitur officium, quia officiatur; quandoque habet nomina specialia ut custodia, succentoria, decanatus, præpositura. (Lib. iii. tit. vii. n. b.) Dignitas i. secundùm quòd est quædam præeminentia in gradu comprehendit personatum; ii. strictè sumpta accipitur pro episcopatu et majoribus.

Quicunque habet dignitatem habet personatum sed non è contrario.

Ubi à jure imponitur nomen beneficio, quod sonat in nomen dignitatis, illud beneficium censebitur dignitas, ut in archidiaconis et archipresbyteris propter jurisdictionem et præeminentiam quas habent super alios et præsertim in subditos et in personas ecclesiasticas. (Lib. iii. tit. i. n. e. Comp. Frances. 232.)

Dignitas cognoscitur (i.) quando beneficium habet administrationem rerum ecclesiasticarum cum jurisdictione (quando sibi assignatur pro perpetuo. Ib. tit. i. n. e.); (ii.) quòd habet nomen dignitatis cum prærogativa (et prælatione, ibid.) in choro et capitulo; (iii.) quando constitutio vel consuetudo ecclesiæ habet quòd beneficium habeatur et reputatur pro dignitate. (Ibid. tit. vii. n. b.) Beyerlinck defines dignity, a pre-eminence and administration of Church matters, with jurisdiction. (Theatr. ii. 789.)

Personatus cognoscitur ex prærogativa chori v. capituli in actibus ibi agendis post existentes in dignitate, viz., sedendo, scribendo, &c., (Lynd. tit. vii. n. b.), ille dicatur personatus, qui de institutione vel consuetudine ecclesiæ talis habeatur et reputatur. (Ib.) Propter prærogativam in choro et capitulo in optionibus processionibus et vocibus dandis, plùs quam alii canonici ejusdem ordinis, minùs tamen quàm alii dignitates habentes, qui in eis prærogativis præferuntur eisdem, non dicuntur habere dignitatem sed personatum. (Ib. tit. i. n. f.)

Is cui commissa est dispensatio habet officium, quando qui habet administra-

The Bishop.

By the Councils of Milevi, 402, c. 1, Braga and iv. Toledo, 633, and London, 1075, c. 1, bishops were to take precedence according to their date of consecration, except in the cases of privileged sees. The order of the patriarchates was regulated according to the civil precedence of the cities. (Baron. Ann. 1, A°. 39, § 10.) Pope Gregory (Bede, H. E. i. c. 29) directed the foundation of two chief sees at [London, an error for] Canterbury and York, probably on the ground of still earlier usage, the respective precedency to be determined by priority of consecration, each with twelve suffragan sees. (Thomassin, i. 81.) In 634 the primacy was settled upon Canterbury by Pope Honorius, after Paulinus, in 633, had retreated from York to Rochester. Theodore (Bede, H. E. iv. c. 2) was the first archbishop to whom all England submitted. In 1092 the Archbishop of Canterbury assumed the name of Primate instead of Metropolitan. (Ang. Sac. i. 474.) His privileges were authority (1) to visit his province, (2) to celebrate where he would in England, (3) to hold jurisdiction over his peculiars in various dioceses, (4) to dedicate churches, (5) to consecrate his suffragan bishops, and (6) to administer the see of any bishop elect who was not consecrated within three months after his nomination; (7) the king and queen are his parishioners wherever they may be. (Thomassin, i. 96.) In 1299, at Chichester, Archbishop Robert of Canterbury, in his visitation, was received by the dean and canons on horseback outside the city, who having saluted him, returned instantly to the church; and there, with the bishop in pontificals, the dean, chapter, and choir, with the rest, properly habited, except priest, deacon, and subdeacon, carrying two books of the Gospels, a clerk bearing the cross, one with holy water, two with thuribles, and two with tapers, in processional habits, received him at the east gate of the cemetery, where the bishop and dean censed him. Then they offered the Gospels to him, and having received the kiss of peace, led him to the church, the procession going before with a hymn. Then they prostrated themselves before the high altar. Then the bishop said a prayer over him. Then he arose and gave the blessing, having first kissed the altar. Then he went into the chapter, and having sat down, preached on the text, "Thou art sent to visit Judæa and Jerusalem." (Esdras vii.) It was ruled in 1075 that in councils the Archbishop of York was to sit on the primate's right hand, the Bishop of London at his left side, and the Bishop of Winchester next to York. (Ang. Sac. i. 294.) This order was confirmed by the Councils of London, 1175, 1237, and Westminster,

tionem aliquarum rerum sine aliquâ prærogativâ chori vel capituli ultra alios sui ordinis, sicut sunt præpositi quarundam ecclesiarum, et si quis habet id cui est onus annexum sine honoris prærogativa, ut sunt procuratores. (Ibid.)

1176; but the Archbishop of York contended the point of precedency so late as 1325, and Bishop Foliot of London revived the question of priority for his own see.

The bishops, according to Lyndwood, form a college in the province of Canterbury (Gervase, 1382), in which the Bishop of London is dean, of Salisbury præcentor, of Winchester subdean and chancellor, of Lincoln vice-chancellor, of Worcester chaplain, and of Rochester cross-bearer, holding the crozier when not held by the archbishop. In the time of Gervase the Bishop of Winchester was præcentor; but, out of respect to S. Osmund, the Bishop of Salisbury received the office of ruling the choir at the synod (Provinc. p. 104, gl.), and the Bishop of Worcester still has for arms ten hosts, as he celebrated high mass at the opening of the session. The Bishop of Chichester was confessor to the Queen of England. (Bacon's Liber Regis.) From 1477 until the episcopate of Bishop Denison the Bishop of Salisbury held the chancellorship, now transferred to Oxford, as the Bishop of Winchester is still the prelate of the Order of the Garter. At Mayence the bishop was grand chancellor of the empire. (Moreri, vii. 377.) The Bishop of London, in the absence of the Metropolitan, is president of the synod, receives the mandate for its assembly, and communicates the summons to the other suffragans. The Bishop of Durham ranks next to Winchester, out of consideration to his former high office of Count Palatine, which by 6 and 7 William IV. c. 19, in 1836 was transferred to the Crown, like that of Ely by the same Act, c. 87. The horses, chariot, and chapel furniture of a bishop were forfeited to the clergy of the cathedral in which he was buried. At S. Asaph this custom lasted till the time of Bishop Fleetwood. In Germany several bishops were princes, as at Paderborn, or electors, as at Mayence and Cologne.

Bishoprics, being of the king's foundation, were his donatives, bestowed by the delivery of ring and staff: this privilege was yielded up by Henry I. to Anselm, and by John in Magna Charta, and the latter granted free election of prelates, saving the custody of vacant churches, which was confirmed by 25 Edward III. st. 6, s. 3, 1380, in the Statute of Provisions, and by 13 Rich. II. s. 2. The right of nomination was restored to the crown; and by stat. 25 Hen. VIII. c. 28, confirmed by 1 Eliz. c. 1, the dean and chapter are required to elect the person named in the letter missive which accompanies the congé d'elire, and none other, within twelve days, under the penalties of the Statute of Præmunire. Before the Reformation by mutual composition, in the twelfth century by an equal number of delegates, at Bath and Wells, and in the thirteenth century at Lichfield and Coventry alternately, the monks and canons elected their bishop. The dean and chapter were guardians of the revenues of the see during a vacancy, and elected the bishop; but these privileges were frequently interfered with by the excroachments of the pope and the nomination of the king. The bishop has the chief place in choir and chapter, while the chapter cumulativè holds the government of the church (Scarfantoni, i. 230); but often, as at Durham and elsewhere, when not attending officially, he occupies a stall in the choir. His duty was to celebrate, or assist on the great festivals (Ceccoperius, ii. 178), and he was to be received in procession, with the organs playing (181). At recent enthronizations the Archbishop of Canterbury sat in the dean's stall, and at Ely the bishop in a stall on the north side. His faldistorium or throne, when celebrant, is on the north side of the altar; it ought to have three steps. (Scarfantoni, ii. 48). He has also a right to a similar seat in parish churches. (Ibid. 267.) At Barcelona he sat "in tertio choro." (Martene, Hist. Anecd. iv. 598.) At Vienne, Paris, Rouen, and Chartres he sat on a faldstool (Moleon, 226) on ordinary days, elevated on steps, and placed at the end of the last stall on the south side (p. 8). When the bishop took part in the service, the canons were to receive him and attend him back to the doors. (Scarf. i. 81.) At S. Paul's he sometimes occupied the dean's stall. (Dugdale, p. 238.) At Durham he on ordinary occasions sat in a stall in choir, and at Nola in the usual position of the præcentor.[1] The archbishop has the metropolitical right and duty to visit all cathedral churches within his province. Bangor and Wells have no statutable visitor; the Crown is visitor at Christchurch. In the new foundations the bishop may act as visitor triennially, or when required by the dean and two canons at least: in the old cathedrals disputes about the right were compromised by prescribing the least intervals for its exercise (at Lichfield in 1428, and Salisbury in 1392, septennially) and the time of its duration. He also had the use of the cathedral as his own proper church, took an important part in Divine Service, and exercised general control of the chapter as visitor. At Salisbury, by composition, the bishop was to be received with ringing of bells and in procession. He might celebrate in chapels within the close, receive oblations, and the revenues of the vacant deanery, and had jurisdiction over canons in their prebends. His visitation was not to last more than five days, and was to be announced forty days at least beforehand. The citation was to be affixed to the stalls. The bishop sat daily in chapter as a canon, and was allowed to have his notary and four assessors, being archdeacons or canons. Titles of benefices and letters of orders were to be exhibited by the dignitaries and canons, officers, vicars, chantry priests, chaplains, and conducts. In cathedrals of the old foundation, the bishop might hold a triennial visitation, and with eight persons attendant require two entertainments by the dean and chapter. In some cases he was a canon, and had a vote in chapter (Ceccop. iv. 38),

[1] For the whole allotment of the stalls in choir see my "Interior of a Gothic Minster," (Masters, 1864,) and my "Church and Conventual Arrangement."

sitting near the president (Id. 50); but if he sat as bishop he occupied the first seat, which was handsomer and more ornate than the rest, and having stated the matter under discussion, left the chapter-house to permit the canons free discussion. (Id. 51.) At Salisbury he is prebendary of Potterne, at Lichfield of Eccleshall, at Lincoln of Buckden, and at Chichester bishops were frequently installed as canons previous to consecration. At S. David's he was prebendary and treasurer of Brecon. At Capua the archbishop was a canon. (Scarfantoni, i. 11.) As bishop he is not a member of chapter, to which he is superior. A bishop was not to be absent from his cathedral more than three months. (Frances, 85.) He confers, with some exceptions, all the dignities (except the deanery, reserved to the Crown) and prebends; (2) takes part in the services when present; (3) has in some cathedrals a share in the quotidian or daily distribution, or receives a money payment; (4) may enact statutes with the advice and consent of the dean and chapter, and (5) can exercise jurisdiction over the dean and chapter, but only as a body in chapter assembled. At Lichfield and Salisbury he presided in chapter, which was called his council, and with their advice enacted statutes. At Salisbury he held the extraordinary or pentecostal chapter, consisting of all the members residentiary and non-resident. Archbishop Boniface called the chapter of Canterbury "his chapter." The statutes of Salisbury and Chester designate the residentiaries "the bishop's chapter against heresy and schism;" those of Lichfield denominate them "the bishop's cathedral council." The thirty canons of S. Paul's, with the bishop as their head, form "one body and chapter to treat of the affairs and secrets of the church;" and Bishop Carow, of S. David's, in 1259 assembled the canons in chapter. At Lincoln the Pope in 1245 ruled that the bishop might visit the chapter; but the right of correction resided in the dean. In cathedrals of regular canons, such as Carlisle and Monreale, the bishop held the place of abbot, and more obedience was due to him than to an abbot. (Frances, 577.)

The ancient statutes assigned certain portions of Divine Service to the bishop. Lyndwood says (Lib. iii. tit. iv. p. 131) he was bound to be present on festivals and Sundays, in Advent and Lent. The Reformatio Legum, c. iii., drawn up by Cranmer, 1552, enjoins the bishop, if able, to be present at the Divine offices in his cathedral. The statutes of Henry VIII. are silent on the subject. At S. Paul's he officiated on Christmas-day, Easter, Ascension, and Whitsunday, the feasts of S. Paul and Erkenwald, Ash-Wednesday, and Maundy Thursday, the dean or the next in rank being enjoined to conduct him from the vestry to the high altar or his throne. He bestowed the thirty prebends, and might occupy the dean's stall. Grindal, both here and at York, appointed the order for morning preachers. (Strype's Life, b. i. ch. vi.; ii. ch. ii.)

Hutton, 1708, says the preacher appointed on Sunday mornings by the bishop received forty shillings immediately out of the chamber of lands and bequests. The residentiaries in the afternoons preached in turn. At Hereford he celebrated or did his office on Christmas day, Maundy Thursday, Good Friday, Easter eve and day, and the Assumption. At York he was to be received in procession, with the bells ringing, when returning from the king's council, or business of the church, or from beyond sea. At Wells and Lichfield he received a double share of the quotidian; and in those cathedrals, as at S. Paul's, York, and Salisbury, he, in concert with the deans and chapters, enacted statutes. At Durham, by the Marian Statutes of 1536, on his first coming he was to be received by the choir in procession at the north door, thence to be led by the dean on his right hand to the altar, with the bells ringing. At a visitation no procession was made; the dean and canons on entering the choir were to bow to him, whether seated in his throne or stall. At Lichfield the service was to wait his arrival, and preachers licensed by the chancellor were to receive his licence. At Salisbury the bishop, after his enthronization, is installed in the prebend of Potterne, and admitted canon, with a place and voice in chapter. He issues a mandate for the installation of the dean. He collates to the prebendal stalls, and gives letters mandatory to the dean and chapter for the installation of the prebendary. He also collates a canon to the residentiary house of Ledynhall. He adds his authority to the citation for the meeting of the Pentecostal chapter. In 1740 he presided in chapter at the trial of a canon. He is interpreter of the statutes, and can confirm them when enacted anew. He has the right of celebrating the Holy Communion. He holds visitations, confirmations, and ordinations in the cathedral. His court is held in the part of the cloisters adjoining the church. At Worcester the archbishop, as at Rochester, is interpreter of the statutes; the bishop is visitor, and receives the Worcester College pension of £7. At S. Asaph, until recently, the bishop as archdeacon had a seat in chapter; and at S. David's was prodean, the senior vicar-choral being called the bishop's vicar. At Peterborough the bishop visits triennially and receives procurations; the lord chancellor is interpreter of the statutes. At Norwich, as at S. Paul's still on certain Sundays, he appointed preachers on Sundays until 1850, when the dean and canons undertook the duty. He has his own appointed days of preaching, assists in the celebration of Divine Service, and holds ordinations, confirmations, and visitations in the choir. At Manchester the bishop receives a pension of £3 annually, and may hold triennial visitations. At Llandaff the bishop was prodean, and by act of Queen Anne treasurer (until a dean was appointed 3 and 4 Vict. c. 113). He receives two dividends, one (one-seventh) as bishop and one as treasurer, and a pension of £9. 9*s*. in the latter capacity. At Lincoln he holds visitations, confirmations, and ordinations, and has his consistory court in the cathedral. At Lichfield the bishop, with consent of dean and chapter, may abrogate, alter, ratify old statutes, or enact new: he holds the prebend of Eccleshall. He is arbitrator in disputes among the capitular body, or vicars choral. He collates to all the canonries and prebends. He may convene chapters general or of residentiaries by the dean or president. He has a throne, a chair near the altar, the central stall in the chapter-house, and his consistory court on the south side of the south choir-aisle. He may preach and celebrate Divine offices as often as he thinks fit, and has access to the capitular registry without fee. He receives £20 a year from the chapter. At Hereford he is interpreter of the statutes. At Gloucester the interpreter is the archbishop; the Crown there, as at Carlisle, may change and alter old statutes and enact new: the bishop is the guardian of the privileges of the church, and must see that the statutes are observed. At Ely the archbishop is interpreter. The bishop is required to visit triennially, when the dean (as at Carlisle, at the cost of the church) is to provide two refections for him and ten attendants. He appoints to the canonries, except those appropriated to two Cambridge professorships. Two subsacrists are required to conduct him to his stall on the right of the entrance of the choir. He receives £137 yearly, the amount of tenths and first-fruits due to him from the chapter, and assigned in lieu of manors which he surrendered. He may correct canons after a third offence. At Rochester he received the "great gift of S. Andrew," and two pelisses every year from the chamberlain; and his chaplain was paid forty shillings, or four marks, by the year. At Chichester the bishop collates to dignities and canonries, and holds ordinations in the cathedral. He was formerly required to be installed as a prebendary before enthronement. At Chester the Archbishop of York is interpreter. At Wells the bishop receives a small annual pension. At Bangor he is patron of all the offices. At Winchester he is interpreter, as at Durham, where he appoints canons and honorary canons to officiate in the cathedral in the service, in the preaching, and the burial of the dead, and to give the benediction. At Canterbury he receives a pension of £318 out of the chapter funds. The archbishop of Canterbury has £15,000 a year; the archbishop of York and the Bishops of London and Winchester, £10,000; of Durham, £8,000; of Bangor, Chichester, Llandaff, S. Asaph, Hereford, Manchester, £4,200; of Bath and Wells, Gloucester and Bristol, Ely, Lincoln, Oxford, Rochester, Sarum, Worcester, £5,000; of Carlisle, Chester, Lichfield, Norwich, Peterborough, Ripon, and S. David's, £4,500; of Exeter, £2,700. The estates of the sees of Durham, Bath and Wells, Carlisle, Gloucester and Bristol, and Ripon have been transferred to the Ecclesiastical Commissioners. The Bishops of Chichester, Hereford, Exeter, Wells, Salisbury, Llandaff, S. Asaph, Bangor, Peterborough, Ely, and Chester still inhabit the palaces adjoining the cathedrals; the rest, as Dr. Jebb observes, have only country houses, or modern unepiscopal residences in town, contrary to ancient precedent. (Scarfantoni, i. 8.)

At Chichester, when Bishop Sherborne attended cathedral for pontifical mass, he was preceded by his bell-ringer, and was presented with a quarter part of a bushel of meal, and two gallons of the best wine. According to the ancient form, the dean and brethren, and whole choir in silk robes, were to meet him, and with the usual assistants, a boy with a sprinkler, two taper-bearers, an acolyte with the cross in solemn procession, all vested in albs and amices, to proceed to the east gate of the cemetery, towards the market-place and cross, and then, while the bells were rung, to stand still under the gateway. After receiving the sprinkling, the bishop has to kneel on a cushion placed ready for him, and then the dean and præcentor, or in their absence the two senior persons of the canons resident, were to cense him, and give him the cross to kiss, and then a book with a schedule containing the usual oath. As soon as he had taken the latter, he was led with honour and in procession by the dean on his right hand and by the præcentor on his left through the cloisters to the west door of the church, while the choir sang "Honor, Virtus." The bishop then, being censed, either preached from the pulpit, or went up to the high altar, where a set service was said by the dean. He then rose, and having kissed the altar, and given the benediction to the people, was enthroned, and then departed to the palace with the dean and brethren. Until a recent period the bishop, on his return from Parliament, was met at S. Roche's Hill by the mayor and corporation, and thence conducted to his palace.

At his enthronization the bishop was to be received in procession at the entrance-gate of the monastic precinct by the abbot and higher officers only, where, having put off his shoes, and being conducted processionally to the church (usually taking the oaths in the porch), and then up to the high altar, with the singing of anthems, he celebrated, after being solemnly enthroned.

In the chapter-house he received the profession of obedience from the various members of the body. In some cases he entertained the chapter in the palace immediately after the ceremonial. He is still required to take an oath to maintain the privileges of the cathedral church intact.

"I, ——, by Divine permission, Lord Bishop of ——, elected and confirmed, do promise and swear that I will faithfully observe all the ordinances, and laudable and approved customs, and the statutes of this cathedral church of ——, so far as they concern me. So help me God and these Holy Gospels."

The form of enthronization is the following :—

"I, ——, Dean of ——, by the authority committed to me by virtue of this instrument [holding forth the mandate], do induct, install, and inthrone effectually, and in full episcopal right, you, the Right Reverend Father in GOD, ——, by Divine permission, Lord Bishop of ——, elected and confirmed into the real, actual, and corporal possession of the Bishop of —— and cathedral church of ——, with all and singular its rights, dignities, honours, privileges, members, and appurtenances whatsoever, and do assign this episcopal seat or stall in this quire, usually and of old assigned and appointed to the Bishop of ——, for the time being, to you, and do place you [here the bishop ascends the stall or throne assigned to the bishop] thereon, according to the custom of this cathedral church, and do give you all and all manner of possession, authority, and jurisdiction which to the Bishop of —— do usually belong, in the Name of the FATHER, and of the SON, and of the HOLY GHOST."

The form at Chichester was :—

"Pater noster.
"Salvum fac servum Tuum, Domine, episcopum nostrum.
"Mitte ei auxilium de Sancto.
"Et de Syon tuere eum.
"Domine, exaudi orationem meam.
"Et clamor meus ad Te veniat.
"Dominus vobiscum. Et cum spiritu tuo.
"Oremus. Concede, quæsumus, Domine huic famulo Tuo, episcopo nostro, ut prædicando et exercendo quæ recta sunt, exemplum bonorum operum animos suorum instruat subditorum, et æternæ remunerationis mercedem a Te, piissimo Pastore, percipiat, per Christum Dominum nostrum. Amen." (Ordo Cicestr. Book E, p. 14.)

His oath ran thus :—

"In Dei nomine. Amen. Nos, permissione Divinâ Cicestr. Episcopus, juramus quòd jura, statuta, libertates et privilegia, antiquas etiam approbatas et assuetas consuetudines istius ecclesiæ nostræ Cicestr. observabimus, quòdque possessiones ejusdem ecclesiæ congregatas conservabimus, dispersasque et injuste alienatas pro posse nostro congregabimus, Sicut nos Deus adjuvet et hæc sancta Dei Evangelia. Amen." (Reg. Storey, fo. ii.)

THE DEAN.

(ARCHPRESBYTER, PROVOST, HAUT-DOYEN, GRAND PRETRE, PREPOSITUS.)

In the fourth century, when parish clergy had become common, and a large staff of priests was attached to cathedrals as the council of the bishop, their chief among them was the archpresbyter, as superintendent; although subordinate to the archdeacon in respect of his larger jurisdiction, he sat in a higher stall in church (Mayer, i. p. 163), and was the bishop's vicar in the regulation of worship and services. He was called the urban, in distinction to the rural archpriest. (Mayer, i. § xxii. p. 57.) He generally succeeded as bishop, and exercised episcopal jurisdiction on the vacancy of a see. The ancient jurisdiction and direct internal power of the archdeacon passed to the dean, and his external jurisdiction to the vicar general. (Ibid. § xvi. 179.) "For the guidance of presbyters," says Hooker, "the bishop had under him one of the selfsame order with them, but above them in authority,—one whom the ancients termed usually an archpresbyter; we at this day call him dean:" "as the archdeacon was so termed in respect of care over deacons, albeit himself were not deacon, but presbyter." He corresponds with the protopapas of the Church of Constantinople. Pope Innocent III. (De Archidiac. c. vii.) speaks of "archpriests, who by many are called deans, being subject to the archidiaconal jurisdiction." (Gratian. Decr. dist. xxv. c. 1.) The archpresbyter, who ranked next the archdeacon (Frances, xiv. n. 126; Thomassin, i. 125-8), as the representative of the chapter administered the Sacraments (Frances, c. xix. 127), and marriage (xxi. 123), on behalf of the bishop, as parish priest (xxi. 68) and vicar general of the bishop (n. 99). In Spain, the chaplain major performed the same duties, having cure of souls, and acting by vicars or curates (n. 71). At Osca and Jaca he had precedence of canons, and at Toledo was a dignitary (n. 73). At Saragossa he was curate of the whole diocese (n. 75). A penitentiary was also attached to a cathedral (n. 76). At Seville there was a dean in place of an archpresbyter. (Scarfantoni, 272.) At Bourges one of the city rectors was archpriest of the cathedral (Ceccoperius, i. 175), but at Saragossa there was an archpriest (Frances, 350), and at Cremona. The proper precedence was usually as follows: archdeacon, archpriest, dean, provost, primicerius, treasurer. (Ceccoperius, i. 137.)[1] At Lyons the archpriest (grand prêtre) celebrated in the archbishop's absence, and when the archbishop was present the dean resigned his seat to him, and took that of the archdeacon. (Moleon, 44, 47.) The urban or cathedral dean was the bishop's deputy in the sixth century, but in the seventh and ninth the archpriest superintended the city clergy, saw the bishop's orders carried out, heard confessions of priests, and celebrated; but at length the archdeacon took these duties. (Dansey, Horæ Ruri-Dec. i. pp. 9—11.) At Llandaff the archdeacon was president of chapter, and at S. David's the præcentor. In Norway the provost is the archdeacon.

[1] At Crediton and Warwick there were deans, but at Winchester and Stratford wardens of the collegiate churches. At Haccombe and Dunbar, in the fourteenth century, there was an archpriest. The vicar and dean of Battle was the rural dean of the monastery, and the rector and dean of Bocking was the archbishop's commissary for his peculiars; the rector and dean of S. Burian's is the honorary survivor of an extinct college. (See Gent. Mag. N. S. 1864.) At Middleham, as now at S. Burian's, there was a dean without canons; at Heytesbury, Southwell, Howden, and Wolverhampton there was no dean; but at Southwell and Beverley the archbishop was president. Possibly, deans first appeared in churches remote from the cathedral.

These archpriests also bore the names of deans of Christianity, because their chapters were courts of ecclesiastical jurisdiction for ecclesiastical offenders, and the maintenance of discipline within the precinct. Schneidt identifies the archpriest and provost, and the archdeacon and dean. (Mayer, vi. 339.) When the bishop and his clergy lived together for the performance of Divine service and duties in common, with the convenience of a common maintenance, such a mode of life and of church arrangement was suited only to a contracted sphere and imperfect organization. Increase of labour, the necessity of its division, and the growing sense of some chief governor under them, led the bishops to found the provostry or deanery. Before this the bishop's vicegerent in chapter was the master, primicier (as at Sens), præcentor (as at Exeter until 1225, and at S. David's till 1840), archiclave, treasurer, or provost. The terms archpresbyter and provost are used for the same office in the councils of Autun and Orleans. (Mayer, i. pp. 163, 177.) But in many cases, when sees were in commendam or vacant, in the ninth and tenth centuries, and chapters became independent of their bishops, they chose their own chief. Godfrey de Muschamp, consecrated in 1199, gave the right of election of the dean to the chapter of Lichfield (A. S. ii. 431.)

At Rouen the dean appears first in 990: his election could be annulled, and must be confirmed, by the archbishop, and he was at first removeable. In the Benedictine churches and in the earlier cathedrals the provost ranked next the abbot or bishop respectively. He was a priest, taking care that the constitution and revenues were maintained unimpaired, the statutes observed, and Divine service religiously celebrated; he punished the excesses of canons, saw that the daily quotidian or distribution attached to the discharge of certain offices, the oblations derived from without, and the anniversaries and other funds, were given only to the canons present at service. He was president of chapter, and had precedence in choir and processions. The office gradually expired, except in monasteries, and was afterwards, in cathedral and collegiate churches, merely a dignity next the bishop; the provost only retaining exterior jurisdiction over the common fund, its administration being taken away from him, and the revenues divided among the canons. In some cathedrals the provost did not retain his stall in chapter. In later times he acted merely as a vidam (vicedominus), bailiff, and steward of estates (Mayer, i. 177), charged, as was customary, with the administration of the property. (Mayer, i. 257.) The dean, wherever a provost existed, had the interior charge of the choir and Divine worship (Ibid. iii. 368; Scarfantoni, i. 271), being specially head of the chapter, with the power of convening it, because every morning with the canons he met in chapter, in order to read and explain the statutes. He was elected by the canons, and confirmed by the bishop. He could imprison in case of offences. Where there was no provost, the dean was the dignitary next to the bishop; so that the names of provost and dean were often used for the same office. (Mayer, i. § xxix. pp. 5, 63.) He was to be perpetually resident, and no one was to correct in choir in his presence. (Mayer, i. 7, 14.) At Canterbury there was a provost, like a prior (Thomassin, i. 482), till the time of Lanfranc. At Worcester a provost presided over a college of seven priests and one deacon, though afterwards varying in number of members between fourteen in 872 and twenty-six at its suppression in 972 or 982, by S. Oswald. In 878 a provost and eight priests formed a community at Ely. At Lichfield Bishop Eleutherius (818—22) divided the revenues into prebends, and nominated a provost. (Ang. Sac. i. 431, 463, 465.) At Wells there were four canons in the eighth and twelve in the eleventh century, whom Bishop Giso, who died in 1088, placed under a provost chosen by the canons. (Ecc. Doc. Camd. Soc. p. 19.) When the deanery was erected, owing to the conversion of the canons' revenues to his own use by a provost, the provost by Jocelyn's Statutes became paymaster of the Combe prebends: his office was suppressed in 1547. (Godwin, 363.) At Beverley, Archbishop Thomas, in 1070, appointed a provost to exercise spiritual jurisdiction, to appoint the dignitaries and clerks, and hold the temporal possessions which had been hitherto held in common by the canons. (Poulson's Beverley, ii. 522.) In cathedrals of the archdioceses of Tuam, Aix, Arles, Rheims, Toulouse, &c., there was a provost, as at Amiens, Rotheram, Wye, Wingfield, and Eton collegiate churches. At Wells he corresponded to the chamberlain at York, and in some foreign cathedrals (Ceccop. iv. 13); but at Lincoln he was simply the principal of vicars choral. At Barcelona (1332, st. x.) the provosts served by months, and furnished "nectar et nebulas" to the canons, or money in lieu. (Martene, Thes. Anecd. iv. 614.) The title of provost survives in several foreign cathedrals, but usually in collegiate churches; the dean in such cases looking after the discipline, as a college dean does in our universities, and in some instances, as at Strasburg, convoking chapters. In cathedrals of the new foundation, before the Reformation (as at Catania, Patti, and Cefalu), the prior was head, but in these there were monastic chapters; and in some cases in Italy and Sicily the archdeacon was president. S. Benedict calls the prior a provost (Mon. vi. 1238; Reg. xxi. lxv.), the deans being the permanent council of the abbot elected by the monks. The provosts of cathedral churches (Hospinian, iii. 109), between the close of the eleventh and the middle of the twelfth century, began to be called deans (Ang. Sac. i. 463), the title first appearing in England. In conformity with the system of tythings, dioceses were divided on the decimal system into districts of ten churches or parishes, presided over by deans rural or urban: hence the analogous use of the title in chapters. At Constantinople the canons were called decumans, as a mark of eminence; and at Rome the chief cardinal, and the highest auditor rotæ, is called a dean. (Mayer, i. § xvi. p. 178.) The word was a military title, denoting a subaltern's command of ten men. (Ibid.) S. Augustine (de Mor. Eccl. Cath. c. xxxi.) and S. Jerome (ad Eustoch. Ep. xxii.) apply it to presidents of monasteries or colleges of priests, "called deans because set over ten, præpositi denis," to care and provide food and clothing. (S. Aug. De Mor. Eccl. Cath. lib. i. c. xxxi. 67; Suicer, Thes. Eccles. i. 834; Dansey, 15.) At Oxford and Cambridge there were deans of faculties, like the proctors of Paris and Aberdeen, as officers for discipline and protectors of corporate rights. The dean in Eastern convents was the overseer of the work of ten monks, and made his report to the steward. There were at Rheims and other places many deans, and at length, their number being reduced, and the provostship, owing to an abuse of its powers, abolished, the dean and subdean were substituted in their place. (Thomassin, i. 484.)

The office of dean was founded at S. Paul's, 1086; York, 1090; Old Salisbury, 1091, and again at New Salisbury at the commencement of the twelfth century; Lincoln, 1110; Chichester, 1115; Hereford and Lichfield, 1140; Wells, 1135, reformed by Archbishop Sharp (Life, i. 222); and Exeter, 1225. His stall was that on the south-west of the choir. At Lincoln the dean was a residentiary, and at Wells he was always elected a residentiary. At Lichfield he held the livings of Breewood, Albrighton, and Tatenhall; at Exeter of Colyton Raleigh, Braunton, and Bishop's Tawton; at S. Paul's of Sandon and Lamborne; and at Hereford of Allenmore, Clehanger, and Preston-on-Rye, in his gift. At S. Asaph he was vicar of Henlan. At Rouen the dean, in absence of the archbishop, sat on the first seat to the right on solemn festivals; officiated on the four great feasts; sung the sixth response at matins, and read the ninth lection on fêtes triples; preached two Latin sermons at meetings of the chapter yearly on Easter Eve and the Vigil of the Assumption; addressed royal visitors, and presided in chapter. When he passed to the pulpit to take his cope, the second and third forms rose up; he was censed on all feasts and Sundays at mass and vespers. He paid double money at his reception and installation. (Farin, Hist. de Rouen, iii. 291—3.) The dean of Mayence had the power of correction, and the suspension of the wine and bread given to the canons, and of their suspension from choir; to compel them to take deacons' orders; to correct them if they read ill, and for misbehaviour; and to give the residentiaries three additional days beyond their statutable absence of three fortnights, besides their holidays at autumn (Mayer, i. Stat. Mogunt.), from September 7 to October 28, if present at the autumnal chapter. The dean sat on the north-west stall at Barcelona in 1332. (Martene, Thes. Anecd. iv. 598.) He was to sing mass on great festivals. (Ceccoperius, ii. 157.)

The office of the dean was to preside over all canons and vicars in the cure of souls and the correction of morals (S. Paul's; Salisbury, 1259; Chichester, 1232; Lichfield, 1194), and for ordinary and immediate power (S. Paul's); to hear all causes relating to the chapter, and appeals made in chapter by the canons, and to determine them with the judgment of the chapter (Lichfield, Salisbury, Lincoln, S. Paul's); to correct (with the chapter, York) all excesses of canons, clerks, and vicars (Lincoln, Salisbury, S. Paul's, York), and of clerks in the city of Lichfield, in the parishes of the commune and on the prebends by appeal (Lichfield), and punish justâ animadversione (S. Paul's, Salisbury, Lichfield); to give possession of their prebends to canons (Lichfield, Salisbury); to install canons on whom the bishop had conferred a prebendal house (Lincoln); to institute the clerks and nominate vicars, in the absence of canons beyond the realm (Salisbury, York); to assign vacant places of vicars on the presentation of canons (Lichfield, Salisbury); to admit clerks of the first and second forms (Salisbury, Lincoln). No canon residentiary or vicar might leave the city for three nights without his leave (Lichfield), or one night (Lincoln, Salisbury). At Hereford the dean was required to act in his turn as hebdomadary, or by a vicar, and to be continually resident; to celebrate on all principal and double feasts, except when there was a concurrence of four or five; to furnish water for the washing of the hands of the bishop when present in pontificals; with the præcentor to lead up and conduct back the bishop proceeding to the high altar; to attend the bishop on his side in processions, and to take care that all, great and small, in choir attended matins with devotion.

The dean at S. Paul's was considered to be the first canon, and required to be a priest; to be continually resident; to observe, and cause others to observe, the laudable customs; to exercise his office with care; to defend the liberties; to preserve the church goods intact, and recover what was lost: (these being articles in the oath at installation required in every cathedral.) He gave over delinquents among the majores to the judgment of the chapter, and the minores to correction by the chancellor. He invested canons prebendaries and persons in the presence of the residentiaries. He was elected by all the canons then in England in chapter assembled; the bishop confirmed and led the elect to the high altar, singing Te Deum. He held a weekly chapter for the correction of offences. He read the lection from his stall, and walked between two, last in processions. He celebrated on the greater doubles, and preached on the first Sunday in Advent and on Ash-Wednesday, and could appoint a deputy to lecture if the chancellor did not supply his own turn. He received a double quotidian if resident during two continuous months in each quarter; if present at one hour daily he was paid a quotidian of 2*s.* 2*d.* He had a double collation in the patronage of benefices. His share (£10) in the quarterly distribution was forfeited by absence. When away he selected a locum tenens from the residentiaries; in default, the senior residentiary acted. The dean, if a royal chaplain, or if no royal chaplain is present, presides at the opening of convocation in S. Paul's, and in his absence the Archdeacon of London.

At Chichester the dean was led up to the altar, the bells ringing and the præcentor commencing "Te Deum laudamus." The senior then said a prayer, and confirmed the election. The dean swore on the Gospels to keep perpetual residence; to maintain, and direct others to keep inviolate, the rights ancient, approved customs, and liberties of the Church; to recover its lost possessions, and exhibit humility and patience. He then prostrated himself before the cross in chapter, and the service concluded with three psalms and prayer. He was bound to reside ninety days in the year, as at S. Asaph. He preaches on Christmas, Easter, and Whitsun days.

At Wells, by 1 Edw. VI. and charter 34 Eliz., the offices and estates of the provost and subchanter were annexed to the deanery.

At Salisbury, on every double, in the absence of the bishop, on the first Sunday in Advent, Palm Sunday, Ash-Wednesday, the three days before Easter, Whitsun Eve, and on the anniversaries of bishops and deans, he was required to celebrate or officiate. When he entered or left the choir all the clerks were to rise, and to bow to him when entering or leaving the choir by the west door. The dean and canons were to account to the bishop only in chapter assembled; might hold courts on their prebends, and exercise archidiaconal authority upon them within the diocese. A canon on presentation to a prebend paid the dean an ounce of gold, and was bound to entertain him when passing on a journey through his corps for one, or even three nights, if needful, and, in case of necessity, supply him with horses on his return to Salisbury. He also was empowered to visit in person, or by deputy, all prebends, and correct, make orders, and supply books, vestments, or goods out of the income of the corps. He was bound to continual residence. He is prebendary of Heytesbury, and preaches on Christmas, Easter, and Whitsun days. He is no longer elected a canon residentiary, since 1840. In mediæval times, on his election, he was received in procession at the cemetery gate, near the schoolhouse, and conducted through the west door into the choir, and thence to the chapter-house; on the next day he was installed in full chapter by the chancellor.

At Exeter the dean was required to reside continually, on pain of losing his share in the quotidian, or daily distribution, for one month; or of correction by the bishop. He was bound to note and punish the offences of the ministers, and to delate the excesses of the canons to the bishop. He was to correct and chastise in the chapter-house the vicars and other inferior ministers for neglect, irreverence, indevotion, irregular attendance, and immorality. By

Voysey's Statutes, 1544, he exercised archidiaconal authority within the close, and had the cure of souls within its precincts. Besides his regular turns in the cycle, he preaches also on the mornings of Christmas, Easter, and Whitsun days. He has still cure of souls within the close, and one of the vicars acts as his curate; but he has not archidiaconal authority.

At York he was installed by the præcentor, and when he officiated on the greater festivals was assisted by three deacons and three subdeacons at mass. He was bound to feed forty poor folk daily. He blessed the candles at Purification, the ashes on Ash-Wednesday, the palms on Palm Sunday, and with the canons washed the altars and administered the maundy on Maundy Thursday. He had the power, until the act of 1840, of choosing a successor out of the whole body of prebendaries to a vacant residentiaryship.

At Lichfield, after 1222, the canons elected the dean, but till that year the nomination devolved on the bishop. (Ang. Sac. i. 437.) He heard and decided all causes relating to the chapter; had one month's leave quarterly, like the canons; was archdeacon of the precinct, with cure of souls; visited triennially all the prebendal and capitular churches (a duty now obsolete); corrected all excesses on appeal; was superintendent of all clerks in the city, and prebendal and communal parishes. Canons received institution from the bishop, but possession of their stall from the dean, who, by the præcentor or succentor, allotted to them a stall in choir and a seat in chapter. He resided ninety days in the year. As at Salisbury, he conferred the commune on the newly instituted canon. He officiated on the first Sunday in Advent, Palm Sunday, Ash-Wednesday, the three days before Easter, the anniversaries of bishops and deans, and at the funerals of canons. His duty was to regulate and superintend, in some cases alone and in others with the concurrence of the chapter, the conduct of the subordinate officers and ministers; to preach on the five principal days of the year; to convene chapters of residentiaries, and, in some cases, of non-residentiaries also, and to preside in the absence of the bishop. He had a double share of the commune in the quotidian, and more recently one-sixth of the capitular revenues. The bells for matins and vespers were not to be rung until he had informed the sacrist whether he purposed to attend service, as at Lincoln. He had the first voice in chapter. When he entered or passed through choir and chapter-house, or when they entered or left by the west door, all clerks rose out of respect. If he or a canon passed through a prebend, he might demand hospitality for one night, or require compensation for his expenses. He had archidiaconal jurisdiction in the prebends. By Stat. 1258—95, he was to be continually resident, but might be absent one month in every quarter, receiving 2*s*. a day, on doubles 4*s*., and on four great festivals 20*s*. He was to preach on the first Sunday in Advent and Ash-Wednesday, or appoint by preference an exterior or "extraneous canon," if the chancellor would not take the turn. By Stat. 1296—1321, he was to celebrate high mass on major doubles, or to obtain a canon by invitation through the hebdomadary; but, whether he officiated or not, he was to entertain the customary ministers, the whole choir on S. Chad's Day and the Assumption, and the canons singly, in order to promote cordiality and intimacy, for eight days at least before the chapter dinner. Every Friday the dean or major de capitulo summoned the weekly chapter, after the first peal before prime, or he could give one day's warning for its meeting.

At Lincoln, in the absence of the bishop, he gave the benediction. All members of the choir rose up when he entered or left his stall, passed in choir, or came into the chapter-house. At Chichester the dean was prebendary of Westergate, at Wells of Curry; and at Lichfield of Adbaston.

In cathedrals of the old foundation, from the time of King John by *congé d'élire* from the crown, before the Reformation the dean was elected by the chapter (at Lichfield first in the thirteenth century, A. S. i. 463), and, after the confirmation by the diocesan, was led up to the high altar, the choir singing the Te Deum. But by 3 and 4 Vict. c. 113, s. 27, he is now appointed by letters patent from the crown, just as in the case of those of the new foundation, which were always purely donative; but the bishop confirms and issues his mandate for installation. In 1662 the king issued his letters mandate desiring the chapter to elect his nominee at York, London, Lincoln, Lichfield, Hereford, Wells, Salisbury, Exeter, and the four Welsh cathedrals; in the rest he absolutely nominated by letters patent. (Sloane MS. 856, fo. 36.) The pope has also assumed the right of election. (Ceccop. iv. 24.) His duties were—1, participation in the daily offices; 2, cure of souls within the precinct; 3, care of discipline and morals; 4, archidiaconal jurisdiction over the city churches, and, with the chapter, over the prebendal and capitular churches. When absent, his representative in Divine service was the subdean, or, as at Lichfield, the præcentor and his deputy in chapter, his locum tenens. Before the act of 1840 there was no dean at S. David's or at Llandaff; at the former the præcentor, at the latter the bishop exercised the function, as the warden did at Manchester. By the canons of 1603, c. xii., the dean was bound to reside during ninety consecutive days in each year, but by 3 and 4 Vict. c. 113, §. 3, eight months, at least; and by § 27 no person was declared capable of receiving a deanery or canonry unless he should have been six years complete in priest's orders.

Cathedrals of the new foundation. At Worcester his duties are prescribed, to see that preaching is observed, the boys taught, the services duly celebrated, and alms distributed; to correct canons, and, if himself an offender, to be admonished by the bishop. By Stat. 36 Hen. VIII., at Gloucester and Bristol the dean received £27 a year, and was allowed one hundred days' absence, continuously or at intervals; but if not present at matins, high mass, and vespers, was fined 4*s*. (the amount of his share in the quotidian) for each absence, except he was engaged as chaplain in ordinary, king's almoner, tutor to the prince, or detained by church business, violent detention, sickness, or attendance at a provincial council or convocation. This exemption forms a clause in all the post-Reformation statutes. He, in company with the receiver and steward of the courts, was to visit all the estates, and order new buildings and repairs. The fines were divided by the treasurer among the dean and canons who for twenty-one days consecutively had attended Divine service, and maintained a family apart. At Gloucester he was compelled to keep twenty-one days' consecutive attendance in the cathedral, under forfeiture of his stipend, except by dispensation of a formal licence of the Crown. By chapter articles confirmed 1750 and 1785, he was to reside four calendar months yearly, under pain of losing 10*s*. daily. The precentor noted his absences. He preached on Christmas, Corpus Christi, and Easter days, and twice yearly within the diocese, and celebrated on the great feasts. At Worcester, 1540, he received £32. 19*s*. 2*d*., with 5*s*. 6*d*. daily for attendance at matins, high mass, or vespers. His duties were to see that sermons were preached on the proper days, the boys taught, the services duly celebrated, and alms distributed. He was allowed one hundred days' annual absence. The bishop might correct him, but he was to correct the canons.

By the Statutes of 1556, at Durham, he received at his installation the oath of canonical obedience, invested prebendaries, and could give leave of absence for one week to the ministers, but not extend it without the consent of the chapter. He received a yearly corps of £40. 1*s*. 3*d*. from the treasurer, and 12*s*. 5*d*. for his quotidian in residence or on statutable days of absence, which were one hundred in the year, besides an additional forty days for "repose at Beaurepaire," provided that he attended chapter. A fine equivalent to a day's payment, and forfeited to the common dividend, was levied upon him by the precentor in case of absence or non-attendance before the end of the first psalm. He regulated the place and times of Divine offices, the preaching of stated sermons, the instruction of the boys, alms to the poor. He was to exercise a frugal hospitality, and take charge of the ornaments, plate, charters, and muniments; to take part, in person or by proxy, in all grants of fees, letting lands and farms; in collation of benefices, election of officers, appointment of minor canons, grammar scholars, masters, choristers, and of all officers and servants; and to view and survey yearly, in person or by deputy, being a canon, all the manors, lands, and tenements of the church.

He was to officiate on all festivals, and preach on Christmas, Easter, and Whitsun days. During his eight months of legal residence he is present twice on Sundays and solemnities; twice also every day during his statutable residence of twenty-one days. He officiates on Sundays and festivals when there is no canon in residence, and preaches when the duty is otherwise unsupplied. He presides at the two general chapters, and holds a weekly chapter to transact church business, to consider applications from incumbents of capitular parishes, and receive reports from the agents of the prebendal estates. All stood up when he entered or left the chapter-house, and all bowed to him as they entered or left the choir. In the vacancy of the deanery the subdean and chapter could put the seal to leases, advowsons, or deeds, except letters of attorney and procuration.

At Ely and other cathedrals the fine for absence from high mass or matins was 1*d.*; from vespers or compline, ½*d.*; from prime, tierce, sexts, or nones, ¼*d.*; for coming in after the first psalm, or after Kyrie in the mass, ½*d.*, by the Statutes of Henry VIII. By the Statutes 1666, at Ely, they were reinforced with the necessary modifications demanded by the reformed services. He received quarterly from the receiver £30. 1*s.* 10½*d.*, (by the Eliz. Stat. £29. 2*s.* 6*d.*,) less the deductions and fines, which were distributed among the residentiaries, and of which he received two-thirds. His residence was kept by attendance daily at prayers, and by keeping house during fourteen days in every three months, under fine of 6*s.* 8*d.*; he forfeited 20*s.* each time he omitted to preach on Christmas, Easter, and Whitsun days. He was allowed one hundred days' absence in the year. Until 1845 he also kept a distinct residence of fifty days, as ninth canon: if absent, his consent in granting leases, matters of fees, &c., must be given by his proxy, one of the canons. All officers after his election exhibited and delivered up to him goods, &c., and received them anew under proper indentures.

By the Laudian Statutes, at Canterbury, he was required to reside ninety days at least in the year, twenty-one of which were to be continuous; and every day of his residence to be present at Divine service, except when prevented by the domestic service of the sovereign, ill health, &c.

At Winchester he has charge of the fabric, the property of the church, the library, and distribution of alms to the poor.

At Carlisle he has the same duties, besides the care of Divine offices, the appointments of sermons, the education of the choristers, and the superintendence of all the members of the church. He was to exhibit frugal hospitality, the duties prescribed in all the new foundation statutes, and preach on Christmas, Corpus Christi, and Easter days, in person or by deputy, and to celebrate on all chief festivals. For attendance at matins, or mass, or vespers he received a quotidian of 5*s*., and also for the days of statutable absence; he also, if resident during twenty consecutive days, and present in church, received a share of the statutable dividend. If absent from the November chapter, he forfeited his corps, £29. 2*s*. 6*d*. He is responsible for ten sermons during the residence of each canon, and forfeits £30 attendance money for absence from each June or November chapter.

At Chester his duties are similar, as general guardian of the privileges and property of the church, in the superintendence of Divine offices, and correction of every member of the cathedral, presidency in chapter, and right of consent, if absent, before any matters of grave importance can be determined by the chapter. He is to be hospitable, liberal to the poor, and economical in personal expenditure. He is to attend in choir twice daily, and receive an extra allowance of 4*s*. a day above his fixed stipend. Once in every year, with the receiver and a steward to hold the courts, he is to hold a visitation of all the manors and estates, and to lay before the chapter, within eight days of his return, a register of the state of the manors and buildings, and of orders made by himself and the receiver. He is to preach in person or by deputy on Easter and Christmas days, and Good Friday; he was allowed one hundred days' absence.

At Ripon the dean was bound to perpetual residence, under penalty of losing at least half his stipend, which amounted to £93. 6*s*. 8*d*. a year. He keeps the common seal, and registers, and performs the duties of a parish priest, with the assistance of the two vicars, who act as his curates. If he did not preach once during the annual cycle, he forfeited £3. 6*s*. 8*d*., and by Stat. of 1667 half his stipend, which was divided, £5, one-third to the vicars, one-third to the poor, one-third to the fabric, and any residue to the residentiary. He was to preach on Christmas, Easter, and Whitsun days, and on the first Sunday of every month throughout the year. He is to say the service on the great feasts.

At Norwich the residence of five months was fixed by charter of Edward VI. and James I.; was reduced by Charles I. to one hundred and twenty-two days.

At Peterborough the dean might be absent eighty days. In 1560 his commons were £27 a year, or 4*s*. a day; the commons of a prebendary being £7. 6*s*. 8*d*., or 8*d*. a day.

At Rochester he was required, by Royal Letter, 1785, to reside four months in every year, commencing November 25, and to attend service at least once a day, under a penalty of 10*s*. daily.

At Worcester he was bound to perpetual residence. A dean has no veto, 33 Hen. VIII. c. 27, and 6 Ann. c. 21; no casting vote, and no separate power in the corporation.

Bishop Bancroft in 1610 says, "Concerning apparel of ministers, from the dean to every curate, nothing being left that way to distinguish a bishop from any of them: you shall see deans usually either in velvet damask or satin cassocks, with their silk netherstocks; nay, some archdeacons and inferior ministers." In 1564, deans, dignitaries, and prebendaries were to wear in their common apparel a silk gown with sleeves straight at the hand (without any cuts or falling cape, and with narrow wristbands), and a sarcenet tippet.

The Form of Installation at Chichester.

After his election the dean was led up to the high altar solemnly, while the bells were rung and the præcentor commenced the Te Deum. The senior then said this prayer:

"Concede, quæsumus, omnipotens Deus, ut famulum Tuùm quem ad regimen nostrum eligimus, gratiæ Tuæ dono prosequaris, et Te largiente, tunc ipsâ Tibi nostrâ electione placeamus per Dominum nostrum Jesum Christum. Amen."

After confirmation in the chapter-house, he swore upon the Holy Gospels that he would continually reside and preserve all the rights and liberties of the Church to the best of his power, as well as the ancient, approved, and usual customs, and discreetly teach those set under him to observe the same; that he would gather the possessions of the Church which had been unjustly scattered and the revenues dishonestly alienated, and with the help of God show cheerfulness and patience in keeping this path, and stirring up those subject to him thereto. He then prostrated himself before the cross in the chapter-house, while his brethren sang the Psalms, Deus misereatur, Ad Te levavi, and Ecce quàm bonum. The senior then said this prayer:—

"Cunctorum bonorum Institutor, Domine, Qui per Moysen famulum Tuum ad gubernandas Ecclesias præpositos instituisti, Tibi supplices preces fundimus, Teque devotis mentibus exoramus, ut famulum Tuum, quem convenientia et electio famulorum Tuorum Decanum hodiè instituit, protectionis Tuæ gratiâ munire digneris, sicque regere subditos concedas, ut cum omnibus ille regna cœlorum adipiscatur per Dominum nostrum, Jesum Christum. Amen."

He was then solemnly led up by the "majores" to his stall, and installed therein while the senior said—

"Pater noster.
"Salvum fac servum Tuum, Domine,
"Dominus custodiat te intro et extunc, et auferat a te elationem.
"Dominus custodiat te ab omni malo.
"Mittat tibi auxilium de Sancto.
"Exurge, Domine, adjuva nos.
"Dominus vobiscum.

"Deus, Cui omnis potestas et dignitas famulatur, da famulo Tuo prosperum suæ dignitatis officium, in quo semper timeat et Tibi jugiter placere contendat, per Christum Dominum nostrum.

"Omnium, Domine, Fons bonorum, et cunctorum Dator profectuum, tribue famulo Tuo adeptam benè regere dignitatem, et a Te præstitam bonis operibus corroborare gloriam per Christum Dominum nostrum.

"Actiones nostras, quæsumus, Domine, et aspirando præveni, et adjuvando prosequere, ut interveniente B. et G. Virgine, Dei genitrice, Mariâ, et B. Richardo, cum omnibus sanctis cuncta nostra operatio a Te semper incipiat, et per Te incepta fineatur per Christum Dominum nostrum."

He was sprinkled with holy water by the senior in the name of the Holy Trinity. A place in chapter was then assigned to him by the "majores," and he was then led by them to the dean's manse. (Book vi. E. 178.)

The Præcentor.

(ALSO CALLED CANTOR, KANONARCHES, PRECHANTRE, GRAND CHANTRE, CABISCOL,[1] PRIMICERIO.)

The primicerius (Beyerlinck, ii. 73; Mayer, i. 7), originally the same as the archdeacon in some places (ibid., iv. 460), i.e., the first tabled on the waxen tablets or roll of singers (Mayer, i. 186), or præcentor (ibid., iii. 274), was the bishop's vicar, who governed the inferior clergy, presided at the canonical hours, directed the lections by the clerks, and controlled the order and mode of singing in choir. He gradually succeeded to this part of the old office of the archdeacon, so that at Rome the archdeacon, archpriest, and primicerius were regarded as tria culmina, but in churches out of Italy the duties were resumed by the archdeacons, who with the archpriest and custos were the dignitaries in them (Mayer, i. § 24, p. 59). From a mere office the præcentorship in cathedrals became a dignity (ibid., iii. 274). As there were at first many cantors whom the præcentor actually instructed, at Avignon and other places he was known as magister scholæ, being also scholasticus. At Metz and in other cathedrals also the primicerius had authority over all the city and diocesan schools (Thom., iii. 485). The control of the order and mode of singing in choir according to the solemnity of the season in the cathedral belongs to the chanter (Scarfantoni, i. 106). He presides over the choir, and has the direction of the canons, clerks, and other ministers in the regulation of the singing; and in consequence, in some churches, as at Pisa, Rouen, Angers, Lyons, Catania, Neti, Messina, and Syracuse, on the chief festivals used a silver staff

[1] Scaliger says that in Narbonne and great part of Italy the dean was called capischol, i.e., caput scholæ (Opusc., 393).

(Moleon, 84, 6, 29, 156, 165, 356), and was sometimes mitred (ibid., 29, 84, 147). [But when the precentor holds a simple office, as in cathedrals of the new foundation, without administration, the control of the choir belongs to the dean or president of choir, appointed by the chapter (ibid., 78), as at Haberstadt (Mayer, ii. 48).] To table the ministers, to regulate the order of processions, and other ecclesiastical functions, is the province by right of the chanter (Scarfantoni, i. 95). He only sang on the greater feasts at Vienne and Sens (Moleon, 163, 8). At York, contrary to all precedent, the dean is now præcentor; at Chichester, however, four deans held the præcentorship, at the close of the seventeenth century, to eke out their scanty incomes. The grand chantre at Rouen is the second dignitary in the chapter; and when the grand archdeacon challenged precedence in 1336, the chapter unanimously rejected his claim. He wore a cope, and had the first place on the left on fêtes triples; and whensoever he did the office of chanter on doubles, occupied the seventh, formerly the third place near the gangway as prebendary; his duty was to rule the choir in all relating to the chant on triples and doubles; to intone the anthem, psalm, and hymn; the introit of mass; the sixth response and eighth lection on triples; to give out the copes to the canons and chaplains without regard to their age; to hear the chaplains read, who are bound to recite the psalter; to see that all are attentive in choir and observant of the statutes; to correct faults, and even give a rebuff to offenders; and when he passed through the choir, the bas formiers and choristers (enfans de chœur) rose. His office existed in 1110: he held a prebend, and paid double the petits droits of a canon, and had the presentation to several benefices. No one could open a song school without his leave (Farin, s. v.; Moleon, 356). In Spain he was called sometimes cabiscol, and also, as in some German churches, primicerio. At Braga the primicerio was both chanter and chancellor (Ducange, v. 442; Moleon, p. 23). His duties were by the laws of Alfonso as follows:—"Primero en el coro et en commenzar los cantos et para mandar et ordinar à los otros como canten et anden hasteamente en las processiones" (Leg. Alf., i., t. vi., leg. 5). At Mayence the cantor entitled the readers and singers; tabling their names according to priority of reception into the church, and ordered the chanting (Mayer, i. 7, 11). At Amiens his office was founded in 1219. He installed canons in the upper stalls, ruled the choir, and ordered the chanting; his seat was next the dean; he admitted and dismissed the choristers (Daire, s. v.) At Barcelona, 1338, he sat next the archdeacon, in the second stall on the south-west (Martene, Thesaur. Anecd., iv. 598), and had a house attached to his office (ib., 619) in 1315.

At Seville the chantre was the second dignitary. The ten dignitaries sat thus: on the right the dean, chantre, thesorero, and three archdeacons; and on the left the city archdeacon, matrescuela, two archdeacons, and city prior, who acted as a vice-dean. The chantre commenced all the chants and ruled the choir (regir los clerigos), arranged the services, and delated offenders to the dean and chapter. The treasurer and chancellor had similar duties to those prescribed in England. (Estatutos de Sevilla, 1628.)

The præcentor ranked second only to the dean, from the importance which was attached to the ceremonial of Divine worship, over which he presided. He acted in his turn as celebrant of the week (Martene de Ant. Rit. Eccl., i. 120), ruled the rectors of choir (ibid., 240), and gave the note at mass to the bishop and dean, as the succentor did to the canons and other ministers (ibid., 218). He is the same as the canonarches and protopsaltes in the church of Constantinople. He was appointed at Exeter c. 1080; at Salisbury in 1091; at Chichester, 1115; at Wells, c. 1135; at S. David's, 1224; at Hereford, in the twelfth century, c. 1195; at Lichfield, in 1130; Lincoln, 1097; at York, by Abp. Thomas I., 1090 (Stubbs, 1708); and in S. Paul's, in the reign of King John. His duties were to direct the divine offices as regards the chant (Lichfield, Hereford, S. Paul's, Chichester, Lincoln, Wells, Salisbury), assigning to each person his part (S. Paul's), and leading the choir; to select candidates to supply vacancies among the choristers and singers (S. Paul's, Lichfield, Lincoln, Hereford, Wells, Salisbury, Exeter, Chichester), for whose discipline and instruction he was responsible (S. Paul's, Lichfield, Lincoln, Wells, Salisbury, Exeter); to provide and correct MS. music for the offices; to take charge of the choir-books (Hereford); to direct the rectors of the choir (Hereford); to indicate the lections to canons on the greater doubles, and the chant to the bishop (Hereford), and to rule the choir (Hereford; Lichfield, 1194; Lincoln, 1212; Chichester, 1232; Wells, Salisbury, 1259; Exeter, 1358); to assign his stall to a newly elected canon (Exeter); to lead the chant in processions (Hereford): and to table on the weekly roll the ministers and chanters for the night and day services (Lincoln, Lichfield, Salisbury, Wells, Chichester). At Chichester he introduced inferior clerks into the choir, and at ordinations called over the names of those ordained. At Wells, by Act 1 Edward VI. and 34 Eliz., the præcentorship was attached to the deanery, but is again a separate dignity. At Bangor the office is obsolete. At Llandaff he held a prebend. At S. Asaph the præcentor was prebendary of Vaenol; at Lichfield, of Colwich and Itchington; at York, of Driffield; and at Lincoln, of Kilsby. At S. Paul's he ranked after the archdeacon, and before the treasurer; he examined candidates for choristerships, regulated the services, and distributed the copes. At S. David's he was president of the chapter. The office has been vacant since 1832. He was a prebendary, and held the living of Llandidu. The control of the ritual, the choral service, and music books was allotted exclusively to him. At Hereford, where he held Walford rectory, in solemn processions he commenced the chant, and the sequences at mass and vespers; assigned their office to the rectors of the choir; gave the bishop (when in pontificals) the antiphons, which he began, and Gloria in Excelsis at mass; he was to conduct and bring back with the dean the bishop going to the high altar to be incensed; in processions to attend the bishop on his side (ex parte suâ assistere); to have charge of all the chant and psalmody; to present a succentor to the chapter, and find him; to keep the books of song and psalmody, and, when necessary, repair them. By statute 1637 either he or the succentor, at the end of morning and evening prayer, was to bring up the book to the bishop in his throne (before which two candles were to be burning), in order that he might give the blessing. The succentor was to be always present at the day and night hours, and maintain the divine office zealously and diligently. At Chichester he is prebendary of Oving; he held the vicarage; has three preaching turns; and, as at Lincoln, had a house attached to the office till recently. At York Abp. Thomas instituted the dignity, which was to be collated by the archbishop, the nominee was then presented to the dean and chapter, to be by them admitted in the chapter-house. The præcentor was capable of being collated to a canonry, in right of which he claimed the privilege of voting in all chapter-acts. The prebend of Driffield and rectory of Usborn-parva were attached to the office in the fifteenth century by Abp. Rotherham. The præcentor installed the dean and those who were appointed to any dignity or canonry; was to rule the choir as regards the chant and psalms on doubles; to begin the antiphon after the "Preciosa" at matins and vespers; to direct majors and minors according to the order of their station; to give the antiphon to the archbishop, and walk on his left hand as he went up to cense the altar, and on solemn days to lead the response with procession, and begin the office in the mass; to confer the song-school; to treat and terminate all matters relating to it, reserving the execution after his report to the dean and chapter. At Exeter he held the rectories of Paynton and Chudleigh, and he was one of the four "internal dignitaries," and was required to reside eight months in the year. The estates have been sequestered by the Commissioners, and the functions have wholly ceased. His special duties were to lead the choir, regulate the choral services weekly, to superintend the training of the choristers, not only as regards food and clothing, but also their morals and choral instruction. On great feasts he "ruled the choir," when two canons, robed in the red soutane, were the chanters, whom he followed up and down the choir, regulating the offices, and overseeing the service in rochet and cope, holding a staff in his hand, which was gloved and ornamented with a ring. At Lichfield his duties are (by himself or by his vicar the sub-chanter) to arrange and superintend the musical services of the choir, and to admit and regulate the choristers. In the absence of the dean or vacancy of the deanery, the præcentor represents him as president of the chapter. He also installs the bishop, dean, and canons; he has three preaching turns as præcentor, and two as prebendary of Colwich. He arranged the processions, and made out the weekly services on Saturdays. On the greater doubles he took part in ruling the choir, and on doubles instructed and led the chant at mass for the rectors of choir, and gave the chant to the bishop. He enjoined the lections to be read by the canons, and changed the paschal table (chronica paschalia) yearly. He, or in his absence the succentor, assigned the stall in choir and place in chapter to a newly appointed canon. At S. Paul's, where he held the impropriation of Bishop's Stortford, he observed that all in choir sang with proper modulation, and that various and proper chants, according to the day and festival, were used. He began the antiphons of Magnificat and Benedictus, the processional chant, sequences, and Gloria in excelsis. He gave the note to the canon celebrant at the altar, distributed the copes in choir, and left correction to the dean and chapter. At Wells he gave the chant to the bishop. At Lincoln he had the same duties as at Salisbury and Lichfield, ruling the choir at the bench in choir, with the other persons and rectors of choir. He corrected the song books, and gave them their second binding, and superintended the writing of new books—the provost of canons finding the money—and corrected all faults or discord in the song and psalms. He installed canons. (MS. Harl. 6953, f. 5, 6.) The prebend of Kilsby (£184 a year) is attached to the office, which is held by a residentiary canon. At Llandaff he receives no emolument from the cathedral revenues. At Salisbury (1259), where he held Westbury rectory, he was one of the "Quatuor Personæ." His duties were to regulate the pitch of the singing; to table ministers and chanters; to instruct, discipline, and admit choristers; to apprise the rectors of the choir of the chants on doubles, and on greater doubles "to rule the choir" at mass with the rectors of the choir; and to inform the bishop of all the chants which were to be commenced by him. He now makes the scheme of the services, anthems, &c., attends the music school, and regulates business connected with the choir. He has two preaching turns.[1]

[1] See for Salisbury, MS. Harl. 1001, f. 117; 6985, f. 1, 10; 6127, f. 215; Lichfield, ib., 57; Wilkins, i. 457; Chichester, 6973; Lincoln, 6954; Wilkins, i. 537; Wells, 1682, 6968; Exeter, 1027; York, 4200, 6971-2; Hereford, Hargrave MS. 246, 357, 4343, 2983; Benet Coll. cxx. 485; and for S. Paul's, Dugdale's History.

The Chancellor,

(CALLED THEOLOGAL IN FRANCE, AND MAGISTRAL IN SPAIN, AND SOMETIMES SCHOLASTICUS.)

The bishop held a double chair: one as the parish priest in preaching; the other, as the instructor of youth, in consequence of the want of public schools after the fifth century. The younger canons, by the Council of Aix la Chapelle, A.D. 816, were required to be taught by a clergyman known as the magister or scholasticus. A similar master of the schools existed in conventual houses; with a cloister school for monks, and a canonical school for young lay persons. The canons, as his vicars, or the bishop himself, instituted cathedral schools, which became numerous in the ninth century; and from the more famous of these arose the universities or academies and universal schools, as those of Paris in the thirteenth century, Cologne, and Ratisbon. (Mayer, Nov. Thes., i. § xii. p. 47; § xvii. 152). The scholasticus was formerly the teacher, but afterwards the superintendent of teachers (ib., § xxx. p. 63; vi. 347—9). At Paris he was also chancellor of the university (see Du Boulay's History), while the præcentor had charge over the lesser schools.

It is far from improbable that the colours of the hoods of the universities, which resembled each other both on the continent and in this country, were derived from the colours of the lining of the almuces (Scarf., i. 28) of the dignitaries and canons, as the cathedral school was the germ of the university, the name given to ministers and chapters (Frances, c. xxiii. n. 27). At Orleans, with the master of the school, he led the processions on annual feasts (Moleon, 184). He was sometimes called cabiscol, like the præcentor (ibid., 23), and at Rouen made out the paschal table, and tabled the ministers; whilst he also performed his proper function of hearing the lections read over by the children and clerks (356). At Mayence he appointed the lections, and had under him magister disciplinæ to teach the domicellares (Mayer, i. pp. 4, 9, 194), and pointed out the lessons (p. 11). At York, when Archbishop Thomas founded, in the eleventh century, the deanery, chantership, and treasurership, the office of master of scholars already existed (Paulson's Beverley, ii. 522). At Amiens the chancellor, whose office (founded 1219) was simply to seal documents issuing from the bishop's office, became a merely honorary dignitary almost from the first, as the bishop chose his own officials in the thirteenth century. The escolâtre, who ranked after the chanter, was founded in 1219. He sat next to the archdeacon of Amiens, appointed lessons at matins and mass, ruled schools and registered readers (Daire). There was also a theologal established 1469, who read lectures once a week, and preached on Sundays and festivals. At Barcelona there was a scriptor in

1315, whose title appears to be misprinted præcentor in 1332; the cantor having been already mentioned, who sat next the sacrist (Martene, Thes. Anecd., iv. 598, 691). He corresponds to the Greek chartophylax. His office was declared in Convocation, 1562, to have been instituted for preaching. It was founded at Wells for the instruction of junior canons by Bishop Robert before 1091, and revived 1135; at Salisbury, in 1091; Chichester, 1115; at Exeter, 1225; at Lichfield, c. 1222; at S. David's, 1287; and in S. Paul's, 1310: and at York, 1090, as master of the schools, by Abp. Thomas I. (Stubbs, 1708); Hereford, 1217. His duties were to preside over the department of theology and learning (Lincoln, S. Paul's); as archiscola (Wells); to inspect schools (Chichester, Lincoln, Lichfield, Exeter, York, Wells, Salisbury); to superintend the readings of the lections and Holy Scripture in choir (Chichester, Salisbury, Lichfield, Wells, Exeter, Lincoln, Hereford); to correct bad readers; to preach, and, with the bishop's sanction, arrange the cycle of preachers; to table the readers for chapter and choir (Lichfield, York, Salisbury, Wells, Lincoln) ad populum and ad clerum; to act as theological lecturer (comp. C. Florence, 1573, c. xx.), librarian, and secretary of the chapter (Salisbury, Lichfield, Exeter, Wells, Chichester, Lincoln, Hereford); to nominate schoolmasters; to provide, correct (Salisbury, Lichfield, Wells, Lincoln), and repair (Hereford, Salisbury), and keep (S. Paul's, Hereford) the books, and keep the capitular seal (Wells, Salisbury, Lichfield, York, S. Paul's, Lincoln); sometimes with the treasurer or a faithful brother (Chichester). At S. Paul's he administered oaths, and exercised a jurisdiction like that of a college dean over the ministers; he superintended the city schools, and the ordination of clerks in minor orders for the service of the church; and was called master of the schools. At Lincoln, where he held Stoke prebend, he showed that the books were in proper condition, on the first week in Lent yearly. At Lichfield he held the prebend and living of Alrewas; by Wolsey's statutes he regulated the regular exercises of devotion in the church; he is a residentiary, with three preaching turns as chancellor, and two as prebendary of Weeford. At S. Asaph he was prebendary of Llanufyd. At Salisbury he has two preaching turns, and is prebendary of Bricklesworth, and held the livings of Brixworth, Odiham, and Swinbrook. His duties were those of secretary to the chapter, and keeper of the archives; the superintendence of chapter and sometimes diocesan schools; delivery of lectures in theology and canon law; care of the chapter library; supervision of readers of lessons in church, and the appointment of the courses of preachers. At Salisbury he was bound by S. Osmund's Constitutions, 1096, to continual residence. He ruled the schools, and corrected the books; heard and determined readings; kept the seal of the church; wrote letters, and read them in chapter;

tabled the readers, and enjoined the lections at mass; read theology, or appointed lecturers at his own cost; and had the oversight of all the scholars in the city, frequenting schools under a permanent teacher. By the statutes of Peter of Savoy he was responsible for the binding of the books of the library, choir, and high altar. By statutes of 1319 he was directed to dictate, write, read, and seal in chapter, every letter which was to receive the chapter seal, at his own cost; but if copies were to be multiplied, they were to be paid for out of the common fund. By Queen Elizabeth's Injunctions, 1558, an enlargement of those of Henry VIII. in 1535, the chancellor was to pay £20 a year to find some learned man to read a divinity lecture twice a week at 9 A.M., which all the canons, prebendaries, and other common members were bound to attend, under a fine of 4d. for the former, and for the latter of 1d., to be devoted to the fabric fund. In the statutes 1096 he is called scholarcha, chief schoolmaster, or master of the schools, and receives a fee of £10 a year. In 1348 he made arrangements for ordinary readings in the close; the reader to be D.D. or B.D. Neither the præcentor, chancellor, or treasurer had residences; they lost their double commons in 1547; they were bound, however, by S. Osmund's statutes, 1096, to perpetual residence. At York the prebend of Laughton was attached to the chancellorship by Archbishop Rotherham. He was not a member of chapter in right of his dignity, but could be collated to a canonry, in right of which he claimed to vote in all chapter acts. The dignity is in the collation of the archbishop: it has no emoluments, and admission is given by the dean and chapter in the chapter house, according to ancient custom. At York he was anciently called master of the schools; he was required to be a master in theology, and read actually near the church; the schools in York he passed over to a regent in arts; he preached to the people on first Sunday in Advent, first Sunday in September, and in synod ad clerum; he licensed readers, and heard them before the office of the vestibule; composed the church chronicle; he appointed preachers in chapter and church on Sundays and Rogation days (Dugdale, viii. 136.) B. Willis says that he had the supervision of the divinity lecturer and grammar school. At Wells he held Ringbury rectory. The duties of this and the other dignitaries have fallen for the most part into desuetude. He receives £12 a year. At Chichester he held the livings of Chittingley and Pevensey; ruled or taught the schools; was the choristers' schoolmaster; heard and determined lections; composed letters, and, with a "faithful brother," kept the seal of the church. At Exeter he held the livings of Newton and Stoke Gabriel, with an income of £200 a year; he was lecturer on Holy Scripture and chapter secretary; recently he has delivered lectures to candidates for ordination during Ember weeks in the cathedral. He had a house at Lincoln (as formerly was the case at Chichester), and holds the prebend of Stoke; he preached either in person or by a deputy—a member of the church, or, with the consent of dean and chapter, a stranger—in the presence of the choir; on Sundays to the people, and to clerks in chapter on the three days after Christmas and Easter, Epiphany, Holy Trinity, All Saints, the Assumption and Nativity of B.M.V., which might be done by a canon or approved person. He rebound and made fresh copies of the legendaries, at the expense of the provost of canons. He kept the smaller, and the treasurer the larger key of the treasury, which in their absence were entrusted to a canon or the dean. He kept the books of theology and others in the aumbry, which he showed in the first week in Lent to commissioners. No one might read in Lincoln without his licence, and he conferred all schools in the county, except those in the prebends. B. Willis says that he preached on all Sundays in Advent and in Lent, except the Sunday next before Easter. At S. Paul's he held the livings of Boreham and Ealing; read the sixth lection on the greater festivals; his scribe acted as church annalist. At Chichester he had a notary and letter writer (1232); he heard minors of the second, and boys of the third form, read the lections over before vespers; and saw that the books, if faulty, were properly corrected. At S. David's the chancellor, in 1348, was required to give lectures: he has a residentiary house; he held Llanwhaddon rectory, and the prebends of Llanwhaddon. At Hereford he held the rectory of Hereford Parva, and at Llandaff a prebend.[1]

[1] The chancellor of the diocese, who is too commonly confused with the capitular chancellor, must be M.A. or B.C.L., of the age of twenty-six years, and is to hold the bishop's court for him, and assist him in other matters of ecclesiastical law. All causes triable in the bishop's consistorial court are triable by him as judge. The limits of his jurisdiction are those of the diocese of the bishop, whose chancellor he is. His office includes those of principal official and vicar-general. The judge of the archdeacon's ecclesiastical court is called an official, a title first used in 1250 by Innocent IV.; and of the bishop's court in a peculiar a commissary. Their offices and duties are the same as a chancellor's. The commissary has also jurisdiction in such parts of the diocese as he holds the bishop's licence for. By 21 Hen. VIII., c. 13, he may grant licences, prove a will, but only in the name and during the lifetime of the ordinary who appoints him. The official principal and vicar-general was the executor and administrator of jurisdiction purely spiritual, by authority of the bishop; such as visitations, probate of wills, letters of administration, institutions, sequestrations, corrections of manners, &c. These were not stated officers of the bishop till about the Reformation. Their patents for life were granted much later, but possibly remained only valid during the life of the bishop who granted them. Usually the offices were united to that of chancellor. Chancellors do not occur earlier than the reign of Henry II., and then were granted as substitutes to bishops during their attendance at court or in parliament; or, if burdened with large dioceses, as chief judge of the ecclesiastical court. The name of official was first used at the end of the thirteenth century, and was then applied to the administrator of religious justice; the vicar-general had spiritual authority; the commissary was appointed by the bishop to exercise authority over parts of the diocese too remote for the chancellor to summon the subjects thereof to the bishop's principal consistory. Appeals lay to the principal official of the Archbishop of Canterbury, whose office has been united to the limited jurisdiction of the dean of the Arches.

THE TREASURER,

(COUSTRE, CHEFICIER, CHEVICIER, CIMILIARCHES.)

THE custos (Mayer, i. 194; iv. 433) had the charge of the cathedral and all that it contained, but at length became the superintendent of deputies discharging his personal duties. The sacrist, matricularius, keeper of the inventory and roll, or treasurer, the cimiliarches of the Greeks, had charge of the plate, vestments, and furniture kept in the sacristy, whence his former name; but owing to the multiplication and splendour of the treasury, he became a dignitary. The distinction between the custos and sacrist gradually merged, and the names became synonymous. (Mayer, i. § xxiv. p. 59; § xviii. p. 153.) At Berne he was next in rank to the dean (ibid. 433.) At Rouen this officer, who existed in 1036, was the third dignitary of chapter, and previously to 1469 furnished lights, paid expenses, found bells and books and their repairs, ornaments, fire, incense, hosts, and cleansing. In that year, by composition, the chapter undertook these duties, and the treasurer resigned his rights to certain offerings and profits. In 1470 his income was fixed at 120 crowns of gold. He occupies the first place on the right au bout des chaises on solemn festivals, and attends the audit of fabric accounts. He held a prebend, and presented to certain benefices (Farin.) The constitution of this cathedral was adopted as his model by Remigius at Lincoln (Ang. Sac., i. 415.) At Amiens, the office in 1149 was united to the bishopric. At Barcelona, 1332, the sacrist sat in the next stall to the dean on the north-west (Martene, Thes. Anecd., iv. 598.)

He is called at Lichfield perpetual sacristan; was the guardian of the fabric (Stat. Lichfield, York, Exeter), of all furniture and ornaments (Stat. Salisbury, Chichester, S. Paul's); he furnished lights (Stat. Lichfield, York, Exeter, Wells, Salisbury, Chichester), candles, the paschal taper, bells, bread, wine, incense, coals; all the requisites of divine service; bell-ropes, straw, hay, rushes, mats; was keeper of palls, curtains, relics, vestments, crosses, books; made an inventory of the church goods, which he could neither lend nor change without the sanction of the dean and chapter. He controlled the chiming and tolling of the bells (Stat. Chichester), and was keeper of the treasury and sacristy. He corresponds to the Greek sceuophylax, the Saxon cyrcweard, and the monastic sacristan. The office was founded at Chichester, 1115; Lichfield, 1140; by Abp. Thomas I. at York, 1090; at Wells, by Bp. Robert of Lewes; Hereford, 1173; at S. Paul's, in the reign of King Stephen: at Llandaff, 1280; at S. David's, 1287. The office does not exist now at York, where it became obsolete after the Reformation; or at Lincoln, being dissolved at the same period; or at Lichfield. At Exeter and Llandaff it is merged in the bishop's office, and in the former cathedral, on the next avoidance, the stall will be suspended. At York he was prebendary of Wilton; at Salisbury, of Calne, annexed in 1231 (MS. Harl. 6985, fo. 25); at S. Asaph, of Meliden; and at Lichfield, of Sawley. At Exeter he held the living of Proby; at Hereford, of Bockleton; at Chichester, of Eastbourne; at Wells, of Martock; at S. David's, of Llandisilio; at Salisbury, of Figheldean, Alwardby, and Pilton; at S. Paul's, of Brent Furneaux Pelham, and Aldbury. The oversight of the church servants, the custody of the furniture and sacred plate, and the charge of the fabric, to which a strict architectural knowledge was indispensable, were his duties. At Lincoln, in the fourteenth century, he was master of the works; he found straw for the chapter-house; and mats, and on great days rushes, in the choir. At Exeter, where he was bound to eight months' annual residence as an internal dignitary, he had a house near the church; received the wax candles and half the oblations made at the altars, except in case of special bequest for special purposes; half the pentecostals (a fee of one farthing given yearly at Whitsuntide by every householder in the city towards the fabric fund); and half the fees for the use of the bells; and three marks yearly for the hire of four keepers of the church. He superintended the cemetery, and had all burial-fees over 12d. In addition to his prebend he found mats in choir, both in the upper books (superiori gradu) and the second form, in the chapter-house, and before the altars. New mats were laid in the upper books on the vespers of S. Andrew's Eve. He paid the sacrist and one other servant half a mark, to keep the church and mark the hours. The other servants were paid from S. Andrew's prebend. At Lichfield, by the Statutes of 1699, his duties are to celebrate marriages, administer holy baptism, and perform burials in the cathedral, receiving all the fees; to keep the registers; to superintend the times of ringing bells and opening the doors; the cemetery; the fabric; to find oil and ironwork for the bells, and provide the sacramental elements; mats; coals; and see that the church plate and furniture are kept decently and in repair. He held the prebend of Sawley. He gave out the silk copes for processions on doubles, and provided custodes ecclesiæ and for the opus ecclesiæ. At Chichester, 1232, he provided the various lights, a sacrist and custos ecclesiæ, with a clerk under him to attend to the lighting, &c., and two servants as bell-ringers, who swept the church with brooms before Easter and the feast of dedication; and hung the church with curtains, palls, and veils at proper seasons. He also regulated the times for opening and shutting the doors. At Lincoln he had charge of the clocks, provided necessaries for the altars, mats for the choir, straw or hay in the chapter-house, kept the building in repair, and paid wages to the servants. At York Archbishop Rotherham attached the prebends of Wilton and Newthorpe to the office, to which the treasurer was collated and admitted like the two other dignitaries. He took notice of all irregularities in church, and corrected all but those of the choir, who were punished by the dean and chapter. He paid the sub-treasurer 50 marks; and for the food of the minister, the two clerks of the vestibule, and three sacrists quarterly 12½ marks; to the clerks of vestry, as their salary, 20s.; to the three sacrists each, to the laundryman of vestments, and to the church cleaner, 8s. He repaired copes, vestments, cloths; found charcoal, thread, incense, salt for holy water, hay for the choir; mats at Easter and Christmas; wine and bread for masses; wine to wash the altars on Maundy Thursday; wood and furnace to bake the hosts; ropes for the clock, and repairs of the bells; and had the church, sacristy, and canons' houses swept out thrice a year. In 1360 he kept two vicars. At S. Paul's he appears to have had charge of the common chest. At Hereford he found all the lights: three burning day and night before the high altar; two burning there at matins daily, and at mass, and the chief hours on festivals; three burning perpetually, viz., in the chapter-house, the second before S. Mary's altar, and the third before the cross in the rood-loft; four before the high altar on "Minùs Duplicia," and five tapers in basons; on principals and doubles, at mass, prime, and second vespers, four tapers before the high altar, five in the basons, thirteen on the beam, and seven in the candelabra; the paschal and portable tapers for processions. He kept the keys of the treasury, copes, palls, vestments, ornaments, and the plate, of which he rendered a yearly account to the dean and chapter. He found three clerks to ring the bells, light the candles, and suspend the palls and curtains on solemn days. He found hay at Christmas to strew the choir and chapter-house, which at Easter was sprinkled with ivy leaves; and on All Saints' Day he provided mats. He brought out the books at matins and vespers. The treasury was locked with three keys, which were kept by the dean and two canons. At Llandaff the office and prebend annexed by Stat. 12 Annæ were attached to the bishopric. At Manchester he acted as bursar. At Salisbury he holds the prebend of Calne, and has two preaching turns. He provided ornaments, and was keeper of the treasury; and found the sacrists, the paschal candle, and lights, four for mass on Sundays; two on the super-altar, and two on the step before the altar on Advent and Palm Sundays, Easter and Whitsun Days; on Christmas Day and great doubles, when there was procession, Easter and Whitsun Eves, eight round the altar, two before S. Mary's images, and six elevated on the beam in front of the relics, the crucifix, and images; and five in the corona before the step; and five on the wall behind the pulpit for the lections; from Whitsun Day to the Nat. B.V.M., and on Christmas Day, seven lights in the brass candlestick; two lights for mass on Good

Friday, and two round the sepulchre; the great paschal taper; and every night during matins a light at S. Martin's altar, and another before the west doors of the choir. He furnished also necessaries for every altar except "the parish altar;" rushes on Whitsun and Ascension Days, the feasts of S. John Baptist, the Assumption, and Nat. B.V.M.; straw on All Saints' Day, Christmas and Easter Day, and Purification; and mats on All Saints' Day. He also took charge of the bells. At S. Asaph he held the prebend of Meliden. At S. David's he has a house, and held the prebends of Llandisilio and Llanmarnmarch. At Wells he receives £130 a year; at Chichester, £200.

In cathedrals of the new foundation, the treasurer is a canon, and elected annually, but not a dignitary; acting as the paymaster, the sacristan, and master of the fabric. At Gloucester he had charge of the effects of the church, and kept in repair the church roofs and the houses of all the ministers; and if the dean and chapter were defaulters in this respect, caused their houses to be repaired out of their stipends, as at Bristol. He was elected annually in November; paid all stipends, fines, and common table money quarterly; divided, at the close of the year as dividends, the fines for absence, two parts at Michaelmas being paid to the dean, if resident; and had charge of the vestry, ornaments, robes, and muniments. At Ely, in 1666, his office was merged in that of receiver. His statutable fee was at Gloucester, Ely, Rochester, Chester, £2: at Durham and Canterbury, £2. 13s. 4d. At Chester his duties were to pay the monthly allowance for table and commons to the inferior church officers; annual stipends of members; annual dividends at Michaelmas; to have guardianship of the fabric; to keep it in good repair, as well as all the official houses, except those of the dean and chapter; to provide all requisite material for the furniture and fitting of the church and choir; to take care that a sufficient supply of timber for building be kept in store; to see that the dean and canons keep their houses in repair, and, in case of their neglect, to repair them at their expense; to have charge of the vestry, sacred vessels, vestments, and records. He was yearly accompanied by the seneschal or steward, to hold the courts, and to make a register of all the incomes, buildings, and orders of the dean or receiver, which was to be laid before the chapter within eight days of his return. The custom was the same at Gloucester; but there he was empowered to direct repairs, and his assistant was called the steward of the lands. At Durham the treasurer's chest had three keys, severally held by himself, the dean, and sub-dean; his accounts and inventory were audited and inspected at Lady Day and Michaelmas; and a canon was appointed to collect arrears, which were paid over to the treasurer. At Canterbury he is elected annually on Nov. 25, as at Rochester, Durham, Peterborough, and Norwich. By the Reformed Statutes his duties are to pay the stipends; to take charge of the muniments; to supply the church with necessaries for divine services; to keep the church and capitular buildings in proper repair; to provide ornaments for the church. By the Laudian Statutes of Canterbury and those of Ely, of the time of Charles II., he is to have a double treasury, containing in the outer room a money chest for daily expenses; the compotus; rolls of court; rentals and terriers; and in the inner chamber the statutes, chapter seal, and chest for the reserve fund. At Durham he must provide materials for church repairs; and repair between March 1 and Michaelmas the houses of the dean and canons out of the party's stipend, if neglectful, with the sanction of the dean and chapter. At Carlisle the offices of vice-dean, treasurer, and receiver are held in rotation. A canon is also librarian. At Winchester he pays the monthly and quarterly stipends, the yearly dividends, and for the repairs of the fabric and the houses. At Durham the office, like that of the receiver, is nominal. At Canterbury he was bound, like the receiver, to reside three-fourths of the year. At Worcester he kept extra residence in the months of June and November, when the audits were held. At Christchurch the office is retained.

The Archdeacon.[1]

Besides the four persons or dignitaries, the archdeacon of the archdeaconry in which the cathedral stood, and occasionally others of the diocese, were regarded also as dignitaries of the body, ranking after the former. Next in succession was the sub-dean, at Salisbury and Wells, but with precedence above them at York. At Lincoln he was a canon, ranking after the chancellor. Next in order came two officers. The sub-chanter of canons at York and Salisbury, after the sub-dean; and the prælector of Hereford following the archdeacons; while a penitentiary, holding a prebend, occurred in several cathedrals, whose precedence was after the archpriest (Molanus, ii. c. 9.)

Deacons were specially appointed as assistants of the bishop, as his eyes in his diocese, and protecting him from the crowd in preaching (Const. Apost., ii. c. 57; Origen, Tract. v. in Matt.) At length they were immediately attached to the cathedral, their chief being called the archdeacon. Being attached to his person and executing many of his duties by deputy,[2] he was regarded as

[1] Sozomen, l. vii. c. 19; Socrates, l. vii. c. 7; B. Hieron. ad Evang. Ep. ci. Op. iv. ii. c. 803; Comm. in Ezek. xlviii. Ep. iv. ad Rust.; Libr. Pont. Damasi. ap. Labbe Conc. i. c. 719, 817; Opt. Milev. de Sch. Don. i. c. 16 (Molanus, ii. c. 7.)

[2] By the canon law the archdeacon's duties in church were to keep the plate; to read the Gospel, or direct a deacon to do so; and to hear and provide for reading or singing the lections and responsals; and govern deacons and subdeacons; arch-presbyters, "by many called deans," and the primicerius being subject to him

his vicarius natus, and included among prelates, but held only the position of "person," honour without actual administration in the chapter (Mayer, i. 56.) Importance was first given to the archdeacon, owing to the jealousy of the growing power of the priests, which was felt by the bishops. The grand archdeacon of Rouen, whose office existed in 680, was the fourth person in the chapter, and archdeacon of Christianity. His seat was the first on the left au bas du chœur. The second archdeacon (d'Eu) was the second in order on the right, immediately after the dean, on solemn days. The third archdeacon (du grand Caux) held the second place on the left, and on grand days sat next the grand archdeacon. The fourth was on the right, next the treasurer. The sixth sat in the third place on the right; and the fifth on the left, next the præcentor, on great days.

The archdeacon was a necessary officer in a cathedral, because his duty was to attend the bishop, and assist at a pontifical mass as the first deacon (Frances, 232.) The treasurer and sacrist were subject to him (ibid., 334.) He is one of the dignitaries with cure of souls (Scarfantoni, ii. 121.) At Barcelona, 1332, he occupied the south-west stall as major in ecclesiâ, the dean sitting on the north-west (Martene, Thes. Anecd. iv. 598.) At Gerona, during the vacancy of the see, he acted in place of the bishop (Scarfantoni, i. 227.) At Llandaff he was president of chapter.

The office was founded in the third century. In the time of S. Jerome the archdeacon appears to have been chosen by the deacons, but under the direction of the bishop. In time he became the minister and vicar-general of the bishop; providing for the order of divine service; presenting candidates for orders; directing the ministers in their functions; assisting the priest at the altar, and ministering the chalice; announcing fasts and festivals to the people; providing for the ornaments and repairs of the church, if there was no economus or steward; and distributing to the clerks their daily maintenance. In the sixth century his authority, as the bishop's vicegerent was established, even over an archpriest; and after the year 1000, he was regarded no longer as the bishop's vicar, but as an ordinary, having jurisdiction from his chief, with power in himself to delegate other judges at the same time. The

also (Decretal. l. i. tit. xxiii. xxiv. xxv.) He provided incense and the sacred elements; saw that the altar was vested; and regulated the reading of the Gospel and Epistle; appointed the readers and singers of prayers and responsals on Sundays and festivals; and published notices of fasts and solemn days. 2. The archpresbyter celebrated in absence of the bishop, had charge of all the priests, and was to be constant in attendance in choir. 3. The primicerius regulated the order and mode of singing in choir according to the season; the carrying of processional lights, and the duties of the inferior clergy in their ministrations. He also appointed basilicani or servants, kept the register, and could correct defaulters. In his absence, his vicar was the next in position or learning. 4. The treasurer had charge of the church, the lights in the choir and sacristy, the baptistery, and doorkeepers (Decret. i. dist. xxv.)

custom crept in of conferring priest's orders on archdeacons, without depriving them of their office. In 1200, the bishops growing jealous of their power, forbad their interference in certain important matters. In England, in many places, they still visit and can suspend, excommunicate, prove wills, and institute to benefices. The archdeacon who resided in the cathedral town was called the grand archdeacon, a name given at Constantinople to an officer who read the Gospel when the patriarch officiated.

Their name and function were suppressed at Rome, Liege, and Constantinople, and in some French provinces, owing to their arrogance. At first they were merely almoners and administrators of the temporalities (Conc. Neoc. c. xi.; Chalc. c. xv.; Aix, c. xxv.; Rome, sub Sylv. c. vi.; Onuphrius, l. iii. tit. xxiii.; S. Greg. Ep. xxiv. xlix.; S. Leo, Ep. xcii. xix. xv.)

The dates of foundation are as follows, according to Bacon:—Bath, 1106; Cornwall, 1098; Barnstaple, 1143; Hereford, 1120; Salop, 1175; Stow, 1213; Salisbury, 1086; Wilts, 1157; Merioneth, 1280; Chichester, 1120; Lewes, 1184; S. David's, 1128; Bangor, 1166; Anglesea, 1268; Worcester, 1089; Durham, 1080; Oxford, 1092; Norwich, 1200; Sudbury, 1120; Suffolk, 1127; Norfolk, 1124; Rochester, 1089; Winchester, 1114; Canterbury, 798; Northumberland, 1092; Llandaff, 914. The archdeacon of Salisbury held Rothfen prebend; the archdeacon of Stow, Liddington rectory; and the archdeacon of Wells, Huish and Brent prebends, and Barrow rectory; at S. David's he was prebendary of Meidrein; at S. Paul's he held the living of Shoreditch in his gift. In the old foundations the archdeacons are always members of the cathedral.

The Ecclesiastical Commissioners introduced the rule that archdeacons of the district in which the cathedral stands should have stalls, being the bishop's minister and commissary (as at Lincoln, Peterborough, S. Asaph, Rochester, Carlisle, Oxford, Durham, and Canterbury), if they did not possess them previously. At Lincoln Remigius founded seven archdeaconries; at S. Paul's they ranked next to the dean; at York their residence was prescribed to consist of three months and thirty days; and at Salisbury of three weeks, "the lesser residence" on forfeiture of one-fourth of their prebend. They were required to maintain a vicar, but were allowed long intervals of non-residence to attend to their diocesan duties. The archdeacon of Brecon has a house at S. David's. At Exeter the archdeacon has a house annexed; he pays one-third of his income as canon to the archdeacon of Cornwall. The bishop of Bangor, since the Act of 1840, is no longer archdeacon of Bangor and Anglesea. At S. Asaph, from 1574 until recently, the bishop was archdeacon. The archdeacon of London receives £750, two-thirds of a canonry, and £25 as archdeacon; of Middlesex, £400, one-third of a canonry of S. Paul's: of Northumberland and Lindisfarne (endowed with the vicarage of Eglington), each a stall,

£1000, at Durham; of Surrey, £30; of Winchester, £40, and each a stall with one share of the net revenue of £10,600 at Winchester; of Merioneth, £350, at Bangor; of Wells, £81, with a stall at Wells; of Taunton, £150; of Bath, £5; of Carlisle, a stall at Carlisle; of Chester, £189; of Liverpool, £185; of Chichester and Lewes, each £200; of Hunts, £30, and a stall with one share of net revenue of £6000, about £300, at Ely; of Exeter, £114, with a stall at Exeter, £488; of Cornwall, £300; of Totnes, £200; of Barnstaple, £89; of Gloucester, £328; of Bristol, £200; of Salop and Hereford, each £200; of Derby, £200, with the prebend of Offley and Flexton, £500, at Lichfield; of Salop and Stafford, each £200, at Lichfield; of Lincoln, £161, with one-sixth share of the net revenue of Lincoln; of Nottingham, £210; of Stow, £157; of Monmouth, £32; of Llandaff, £30; of Manchester, £200; of Norwich, Norfolk, and Suffolk, each £200; of Oxford, a stall at Christchurch, Oxford, subject to a payment of £300 per annum to the archdeacon of Buckingham; of Buckingham, £450; of Berks, £200; of Northampton, £144, with a stall, £537, at Peterborough; of Leicester, £200; of Craven and Richmond, each £200, the latter having a stall, £500, at Ripon; of S. Alban's, a stall, one-eighth of net revenue of £4800, at Rochester; of Colchester, £847; of Essex, £45; of Salisbury, a stall, £500, at Salisbury; of Wilts and Dorset, each £200; of S. Asaph, a stall, £350, at S. Asaph; of S. David's, £200; of Brecon, £92; of Caermarthen, £200; of Worcester and Coventry, each £200; of Canterbury and Maidstone, £59. 16s., each a stall at Canterbury; of York, £200, with a stall, £700, at York; of Cleveland and East Riding, each £200 a year.

The Sub-Dean,

(subdecanus, subdiaconus, sous-doyen.)

The dean's vicar ("vicarius et substitutus," Thomassin, i. 485), was the sub-dean, who represented him in his duties in choir when absent, as his substitute, and was his deputy or assistant when resident. He corresponds to the Greek deuteroon of Constantinople, and acted as a sub-officer under the dean, and vicariously performed the duties properly belonging to the dean, and originally performed by him in the cathedral and its precincts, in the occasional services and cure of souls, being technically called vices gerens. The vice-dean, on the contrary, was in Germany a senior, that is, a canon according to priority of installation, and in England a member of chapter and the representative, locum tenens, of the dean in his absence, and during a vacancy president of chapter and choir. Lyndwood thus contrasts the offices of a sub-dean and vice-dean. Decanus ea quæ pertinent ad officium suum potest aliis committere per se, nec requiritur consensus capituli, istud de jure speciali. Dicitur "locum habet," quando persona constituta ad supplendum vices decani in absentia suâ habet in eâ parte officium perpetuum, cujus officii institutio ab initio potest fieri per solum decanum, sed requiritur consensus capituli; pone exemplum in subdecano, cujus officium in quibusdam ecclesiis est perpetuum, et stat in hoc ut suppleat vices decani absentis. Contraria loquuntur in eo, quem deputat decanus loco suo ad tempus, et est remotivus ad libitum. In ecclesiis illis quibus locum tenens decani est perpetuus, habet locum, quod hìc dicitur. Ubi vero non est, habet locum, quòd dicitur in contrariis (Provinc. lib. v. tit. 16, c. i. in v. Decano.) Frances (p. 200) says personal delegation differs from real, because in the former it is made to an individual named, but in the latter to an office.

The office was founded at Salisbury, 1091; at Wells, by Bp. Robert of Lewes, 1135—65, where he held Wotley rectory; Lincoln, 1140; at Exeter, 1284, where it was united to the office of penitentiary; at York, 1228, where he held the penitentiaryship of the church and city, in 1400; at S. David's, 1287. At Chichester no such office is mentioned in the Consolidated Statutes of 1247, but he occurs among vicars choral in 1481 (Storey's Reg. p. 70), and appears at a later date as holding the vicarage of S. Peter's in the cathedral; the senior canon acted as president of chapter. At York he ranks next to the chancellor; at Exeter and Salisbury after archdeacons; and at Wells, before prebendaries. At Lincoln he is a canon, but his prebend of Kirton has been taken from him by the Commissioners, who also sequestered the estates of the office at Exeter. At Salisbury he did not preside in chapter when a higher dignitary was present, but was to be perpetually resident. He had a preaching turn by Osmund's Statutes; he was to supply the absences of the dean, and to exercise archidiaconal authority in the city and suburb, but not in the close, which belonged to the dean, and over all clerks and students not frequenting schools under a permanent master, except clerks and vicars of the cathedral, over whom he had jurisdiction with the chapter, only in absence of the dean. At Exeter the functions have wholly ceased, and the estates have been sequestered by the Commissioners. At York the dignity is in the gift of the archbishop; it has no emolument, and admission is given to it by the dean and chapter in the chapter-house. At S. Paul's the dean, in his absence, constituted one of the residentiaries whom he deemed most fit his locum tenens. If the latter was absent, then the senior residentiary acted. At Glasgow he acted in absence of the deanery, and during a vacancy. The sub-dean of Hereford rendered an account in chapter of the amerciaments of spiritualities within their four manors; but in the absence of the dean, the hebdomadary installed canons. At Lichfield he supplied the dean's place in church, A.D. 1194. At York he was to reside perpetually, c. 1390. His office was a dignity, and he was the penitentiary of the archbishop. His precedence was after archdeacons. At Lincoln he ranked next to the treasurer; was one of the quatuor personæ and required to reside, being bound in his turn to celebrate on major doubles, and taking his oath on the south horn of the altar at his installation. In the dean's absence he installed the canons. At Wells, in the absence of the dean (1241), the sub-dean gave permission of leaving the town or of being bled, and of transferring any one into the first grade or second form; he supplied the dean's place, and exercised archidiaconal power in city and suburb about a century earlier. His place was between the treasurer and succentor, and he was bound to assiduous residence. At Lincoln, Exeter (founded 1284, as penitentiary also), Salisbury (as other dignitaries) the sub-deans had estates held of them. The penitentiary, like the theologus, was found in all cathedrals (Thom. i. 135). At Chartres the sub-dean ranked between the præcentor and succentor (Ducange, ii. 753). There was a sub-dean at Elgin and Glasgow. At S. Paul's he was a minor canon, elected by the dean and chapter, 1280, who governed the ministers, presided in a chapter in the dean's absence for the correction of non-capitular members, especially on Saturdays: he had no jurisdiction over major canons. In 1400 he was permitted the use of the grey almuce, and received additional commons, or in lieu, money. At S. David's he is a minor canon, and officiated as the bishop's deputy in the college of vicars choral, and instructed the choristers. At Lichfield the præcentor, and at Llandaff the archdeacon, discharged the duties. At Ripon he was nominated by the dean, and received an annual stipend of £35, of which he forfeited one half if absent from his duties in the annual cycle; besides a mulct of 10*s*., raised in 1805 to £1, if he did not supply his ordinary turns of preaching.

Vice-Dean.—This "officer" occurs in the cathedrals of the new foundation, being instituted at the same time as the other office-bearers, the treasurer and receiver, and like them appointed annually. He is vicegerent of the dean in his absence, or in the vacancy of the decanate, being a canon, and called an officer at Canterbury, where he exercised decanal powers in church and abroad, and ranked next to the dean, being regarded with him as "paterfamilias." At Rochester, by Stat. 1541, the canons hold the office in rotation. At Canterbury, Ely, Chester, Bristol, Peterborough, and Gloucester, he is annually elected in the general chapter, held Nov. 52; at Carlisle, Nov. 23. At Chester his official stipend was £2. At Westminster and Christ Church the office is permanent. At Canterbury he was bound to reside three months at least in the year, but was relieved from this necessity by order of William IV., who also permitted him to be absent even when the dean was also from home. In his absence here and at Winchester the senior canon present or residentiary acts. At Durham, where he was appointed besides the dean and twelve prebendaries, he is to represent the dean except in matters requiring his special consent or his proxy. At Chester he ranked next to the dean, and in his absence presided over the canons and all the officers of the church; and his duties are defined to be the execution of the decanal office in absence of the dean, to sit next him when present in choir, being nearest to him there and elsewhere. He was elected annually on Nov. 25. At Ely, if the dean is absent from the kingdom, and at Carlisle and Chester during the vacancy, he exercises full decanal power. At Norwich, Durham, and Canterbury, the office is annual. In every cathedral of the new foundation he is a canon and member of chapter, and acts as the dean's representative in his absence. At Carlisle the office is held in turn, but the residentiary, in absence of the dean, acts as vice-dean. The vice-dean usually occupies the north-west stall.

Ayliffe calls the sub-dean (i.e. a vice-dean) a deputy dean to exercise decanal jurisdiction, but incapable to charge the possession of the church, and generally speaking he cannot confirm grants and join in the making of leases. (Parergon. 203.) His proper stall would appear to be the first on the left of the entrance, but this seat was sometimes appropriated to the hebdomadary, or, as we should say, canon in residence (Ceccop. ii. 47.) A bishop, holding a canonry, would sit next the dean (ibid., 51.) In the absence of the dean, the presidency of choir, that is, the correction of offences in choir, and the office of choragus or director of the choir, belongs to the second dignitary or senior canon (ii. 199.) At Seville the prior of the city, the senior dignitary, or senior canon, acted as vice-dean. At Pistoia a deputy of the dean as præfect of choir was annually elected from among the canons. (Ceccop. lib. ii. lit. v. § 2.)

The Prælector or Theologal

existed at Vich, Bayeux, Sens and Lisieux. The theologal-prebendary, and penitentiary were not to precede elder canons except by provision of statute (Scarf., i. 45), but all canons were bound to attend his lectures (117). He could appoint a deputy (ii. 128), but was required to be a graduate. At S. Paul's, as at Hereford, divinity lectures were appointed to be read on Wednesdays and Fridays by nominees of the chapter (Strype's Whitgift, b. ii. ch. iii. 4). In 1394 Bishop Gravesend instituted a lecturer B.D., in conformity with other cathedrals (Dugdale's S. Paul's, p. 17), to read daily. At Chichester the prebendary of Wittering, by the foundation of Abp. Boniface, 1259, as theological lecturer, was to give readings in the cloisters. He now lectures in Lent. At

Hereford, the prælector, who ranks after archdeacons, and succeeded, Bacon says, to the first vacant residentiaryship, except the golden stall or bishop's prebend, is a prebendary elected by the chapter, who preaches sermons on certain saints' days, and on every Tuesday during several months in the year, and delivers two lectures weekly in Lent. By Stat. 1583 he was to deliver two sets of lectures on the Holy Bible, each an hour long, on Wednesdays and Fridays during ten weeks in each quarter, and to be paid out of the bishop's prebend. Bacon says he received £40 a year.

At Westminster a canon is term lecturer. At Canterbury there are six preachers appointed by the archbishop, with a stall in choir, and originally a house, ranking after the canons, and originally directed to preach twenty sermons in the city, neighbouring towns, or capitular parishes yearly, and on eleven Sundays in the cathedral, a duty which they still discharge. Their statutable fee is £25. They also receive about £32. 10*s.* as compensation for their loss of houses in the close.

At Valencia a pulpit stands in the Chapter House for the theological lecture. (Villanueva. I. 31.)

The Penitentiary

was a necessary officer of the cathedral (Scarf., i. 117), he heard confessions (ibid., iii. 148), and regulated penances throughout the diocese at Salisbury, at York, and at Hereford, where he was called the golden prebendary; and other cathedrals, as at Orleans (Moleon, 185) and Amiens, where he held an office founded 1219, and received 550 livres. He ranked next the archdeacon of Ponthieu, and was the bishop's deputy to hear all confessions, except of vicars-nobles, which were reserved to the diocesan. At Rouen he reconciled penitents, and preached on Holy Thursday (ibid., 357.) The penitentiary at Rouen was also preacher and divinity reader, and after 1480 held a prebend annexed to his office, and if engaged in the confessional, conferring with heretics, or studying with respect to his office, was excused attendance in choir. At Worcester, by command of the bishop, he heard confessions and distributed ashes to the people (A. S., i. 512.) At Salisbury, after nones on Maundy or Shier Thursday, he or the archdeacon besought the bishop, in the name of the penitent, at the church door, to readmit them to favour. At Exeter the sub-dean as penitentiary sat in the third stall on the dean's right hand, and visited those sick of the diocese annually who could not come up to the cathedral church. His office was founded July, 1284. The sub-dean was usually the penitentiary. There were two penitentiaries: 1. The external, who was the confessor for the diocese, or a certain district in it; and, 2. The internal, who regulated penances, and conferred absolution in cases referred to the bishop.

At S. Paul's the prebendary of S. Pancras was penitentiary, and confessor to the Bishop of London from 5 Edw. IV. (Newcourt's Repert., i, 193.) A penitentiary, appointed by the bishop or dean and chapter, confessed canons. (Lyndw. b. v. c. xvi. p. 327.)

Sub-Chanter of Canons.

At York the office is in the patronage of the archbishop, and has no emolument. Admission to it is given by the dean and chapter in the chapter-house. The succentor major, or sub-chanter of canons (as at Glasgow, Bayeux, Paris, and Chalons), or the succentor of the vicars in the absence of the præcentor, installed canons, on the mandate of the dean and chapter, and gave the antiphon on doubles. The succentor major, of York, c. 1396, was to attend matins, vespers, and mass on feasts of nine lections (f. 134, MS. Harl. 6972.) At Wells the office was suppressed by Act of Parliament in 1547: at Salisbury, where he ranks before prebendaries and after the sub-dean, being regarded as a dignitary, Bishop Burnet relieved the succentor from residence in 1695. He has one preaching turn.

The Chapter.[1]

"Potior et nobilior pars et quasi cor ecclesiæ."—Schubert.

Chapters are sacred congregations, set apart for the more solemn, frequent, and magnificent worship of God in the principal churches, and also in a certain sense the councils of the bishops. Chapters

[1] The following additional instances of the constitutions of foreign cathedrals will form a useful supplement to the list given on a former page :—

Embrun. Four dignitaries, provost, nineteen canons.

Gap. Dean, thirteen canons, three personats, twelve beneficiarii.

Riez. Eight canons, including two dignitaries, twelve beneficiarii.

Toulon. Provost, archdeacon, sacristan, capischol, eight other canons.

Grenoble. Bishop, dean, eighteen other canons, theologal, sacristan, twenty habituez.

Oleron. Six canons, eight prebendaries.

Lescar. Six canons, eighteen prebendaries.

Dax. Ten canons.

Conserans. Archdeacon, three dignitaries, twelve canonries, twenty-four semiprebendaries.

S. Bertrand. Grand archdeacon, four petit archdeacons, præcentor, fourteen canons, sacristan, twenty-four semiprebendaries.

Lectoure. Four archdeacons, præcentor, twelve canons, fourteen semiprebendaries.

Vabres. Three dignitaries, ten canons, four semiprebendaries.

Rodez. Four archdeacons, sacristan and receiver, chanter, eighteen canons, four hebdomadaries, twenty-five vicars, twenty-seven choristers.

Cahors. Thirteen canons, including four dignitaries; four hebdomadaries, twelve demiprebendaries, twelve chaplains.

Senlis. Three dignitaries, twenty-four canons, twelve chaplains.

Boulogne. Four dignitaries, twenty-one prebendaries.

Orleans. Fourteen dignitaries, sixty prebendaries.

were formed when the common table was divided into separate prebends. Till then the word "congregation" was used as by S. Benedict (Reg. viii. cap. 3), and Julian Pomere, Bp. of Marseilles, in 480; but about the seventh century, chapter was commonly substituted, and occurs in the Capitulars of Charlemagne, and the Councils of Aix-la-Chapelle, ch. 115, and Mayence, ch. 21, 22. In secular churches the origin of the name is found in its existence at a corporation assembled under one head, ab ejusmodi capite capitulum dicitur, and in monasteries from the daily reading of a capitulum, a little chapter, a portion of the rule. It must consist

Blois. Six dignitaries, eighteen canons.

Chartres. Seventy-six canons, including seventeen dignitaries.

Troyes. Eight dignitaries, forty-one canons, five archdeacons.

Nevers. Dean, archdeacon, four other dignitaries; two personats, forty prebendaries.

Cambray. Eight dignitaries, forty-three canons.

S. Omer. Six dignitaries, thirty-four canons, twenty-four chaplains.

Tournay. Eight dignitaries, forty-two prebendaries.

Autun. Ten dignitaries, fifty prebendaries, twelve to fifteen chaplains.

Chalons-sur-Saone. Seven dignitaries-canons, twenty-three prebendaries.

Maçon. Six dignitaries, twenty canons, four appointed by the bishop; four archdeacons, thirteen chaplains.

Tours. Eight dignitaries, forty-nine canons, sixteen personats, one hundred chaplains.

Le Mans. Nine dignitaries, including two archdeacons; thirty-eight canons, four semiprebendaries, one hundred chaplains.

Angers. Eight dignitaries, three archdeacons, twenty-eight canons.

Bourdeaux. Dean, three archdeacons, six other dignitaries, twenty-three canons.

Agen. Two dignitaries, nineteen canons.

Clermont. Provost, abbot, dean, chanter.

Limoges. Twenty-eight prebendaries, eighteen vicars.

S. Flour. Archdeacon, treasurer, chanter, seventeen prebendaries.

Lombez. Provost, three dignitaries, twelve canons, twelve demiprebendaries.

Pamiers. Six dignitaries, canons; twelve canons, twelve demiprebendaries.

Vienne. By the foundation according to Le Lievre, provost, dean, archdeacon major, four archdeacons, scholasticus or capiscol; officers, sacristan, mistral chancellor; personats, præcentor, and chanter; one hundred priests, twenty deacons, twenty subdeacons, forty clerici formerii, and twenty-four clerici.

Belley. Four dignitaries, fourteen other canons.

Milan. The basilicas of S. Lawrence, S. Nazarius, and S. Stephen, have each a provost.

Bologna. Four dignitaries, one archdeacon, and sixteen canons.

Placenza. Archdeacon, provost, vice-dominus, nineteen canons, eighteen prebendaries or mansionarii.

Cesena. Provost, archdeacon (Græv. Ital. xxx.)

Forli. Archdeacon; provost, founded 1466; archpriest, 1519; primicerius, 1562; nineteen canons, nobles (ibid.)

Tarento. Twelve canons (ib. xxvii.)

Rieti. Archdeacon, forty canons (ib. xxii.)

Girgenti. Dean, first on the right hand; præcentor, first on the left hand; archdeacon, second on the right hand, the chanter's deputy, all holding prebends; treasurer; seventeen other canons, three being priests, five deacons, and three subdeacons; a theologal prebendary; four personati, terminator, the marshal of procession, subchanter; schoolmaster; master of the ceremonies; two vivanderii; four sacrists (Græv. Sic., iii. 769.)

Patti. Prior, archdeacon, chanter, treasurer, eight chaplains, four sacristans, six clerks, an œconomus, a secular priest (Græv. Sic., iii. 872.)

Cefalu. Prior, archdeacon, two personati, master of the ceremonies, and treaof three at least. Collegium in uno retinetur et non nisi in tribus constituitur (Næratus, l. lxxxv. de verb. scatione). The Councils of Verné in 755, and Aix in 789, required the canons to live in community under the bishop (comp. Meaux, 845, and Pont-sur-Yonne, 876). Qui ad clericatum accedant quod nos nominavimus canonicam vitam. Volumus ut illi canonicè secundum suam re-

surer; two priests communerii, two deacons, two sacristans, two melinglerii, or church keepers (ib. 921.)

CATANIA. Prior, chanter, who acts as vice-prior; dean, treasurer, twelve canons, twelve hebdomadaries. Two dignitaries and six canons attend weekly.

NICE. Provost, prior, archdeacon, sacrist, præcentor, infirmarer, twenty-four canons.

AICHSTADT. Provost, dean, custos, chanter, ecolatre, cellarer, and provost of a collegiate church; sixteen canons, eleven domicellaries, must be of noble birth.

WURTZBURG. Provost, dean, ecolatre, custos, cellarer; twenty-four canons, thirty domicellaries, must be of noble birth (Mayer, iv. 361.)

BRIXEN. Provost, dean, ecolatre, coustre, provost of Notre Dame, ten canons of noble birth, and ten canons, doctors or licentiates of divinity or law.

BRANDENBURG. Provost, prior, archdeacon-provost of Liezeke, and a chapter of Præmonstratensian canons, like Havelburg.

SALTZBURG. Austin canons, founded 1048, became twenty-four seculars in 1514. The provost-archdeacon, elected by the canons, like the dean, wore the ornaments of a bishop (Hansizius, ii. 236, 332, 906.)

LITTOMISSEL, 1343. Abbot, prior, chanter, custos, ecolatre, procurator, canons regular of Premontré.

LEITMARITZ, 1655. Provost, dean, canons.

CAMIN. Provost, dean, treasurer, five archdeacons, fifteen prebendaries.

PEDENA (Istria). Four canons, including an archdeacon and sacristan.

[*Spain*, from Vayrac.] LERIDA. Dean, two archdeacons, chanter, two archdeacons, twenty-five canons, twelve hebdomadarii, twenty prebendaries, one hundred and ten beneficiarii.

VICH. Dean, archdeacon, sacristan, chanter, twenty-four canons, one hundred and sixty beneficiarii, of whom some are prebendaries. [Three prælati, archdeacon, sacristan, and primicerius, or capiscol, as early as the twelfth century; twenty-three to thirty canons, a reader of theology founded 1354, and lectoral in 1596 (Villan., vi. 63.)]

URGEL. Dean, sacristan, four archdeacons, chanter, twenty canons, one hundred and sixty-three beneficiarii. [Prior or provost, succeeded by a dean in 1299; forty to forty-five canons prelados, operarius (Villan. 180.)]

GERONA. Four archdeacons, abbot of S. Filiu, dean, sacristan, chanter, thirty-six canons, seventy-six beneficiarii.

ELNA. Three archdeacons, twenty-four canons, eighty beneficiarii.

SOLSONA. Dean, archdeacon, treasurer, twelve canons, twelve prebendaries, forty chaplains.

SEVILLE. Dean, archdeacon, treasurer, chanter, two archdeacons, ecolatre, two archdeacons, prior, archdeacon, all mitred on solemn feasts; forty canons, forty prebendaries, twenty semiprebendaries, twenty chaplains nominated by the chanter, twenty chaplains who assist at the hours, five keep silence in the church during divine service, and there are two vergers. [Dcan, chanter, treasurer, matrescuela, three archdeacons, and city prior, who acted as vice-dean (Estatutos, ii.) Statutes published 1610.]

CADIZ. Six dignitaries, ten canons, twelve prebendaries.

GUADIX. Six dignitaries, six canons, eight prebendaries.

CANARIES. Eight dignitaries, sixteen canons, twelve prebendaries.

COMPOSTELLA. Thirteen dignitaries, including seven cardinals, who serve at the high altar since 1114. All are mitred, and use the pluvial on feasts. Thirty-four canons, eleven prebendaries.

ASTORGA. Dean and archdeacon of Astorga, chanter, ecolatre, treasurer, five archdeacons, prior, fifty canons, ten prebendaries; master of the chapel, a pregulam vivant, et episcopus illorum vitam regat sicut abbas monachorum (Capit. Car. M.) Decrevimus ut canonici clerici canonicè vivant, observantes Divinæ Scripturæ doctrinam, et documenta S. patrum (Counc. Mayence, 813, c. 9.) The Benedictines are sometimes called canons (Anast. in vitâ Greg. IV., c. ann. 827.)

bendary, organist, who is a prebendary; twenty-four chaplains, twelve chaplains called nona, sixteen enfans de chœur or seyses, fourteen others. The Bishop and Pope nominate alternately the dignitaries and canons except four, and the ecolatre, who are appointed by the chapter.

LEON. Eleven dignitaries, eighty-four canons, twenty prebendaries, twelve bachelors. The king is first canon, and sits in choir, so does the Marquis d'Astorga.

OVIEDO. Thirteen dignitaries, twenty canons, twelve prebendaries, ten chaplains.

PALENCIA. Dean, five archdeacons, treasurer, chanter, master of schools, procurator of the chapter, four abbots of collegiate churches, prior, fifty canons. In the bishop's choir sat three archdeacons, treasurer, and master of schools; in the dean's choir two archdeacons, chanter, two abbots, and prior. All the revenues belonging to the Messa Capitular were divided into eighty prebends. Twelve belonged to twenty-four racioneros or portionists, who sat in the lower stalls, maintained hebdomadaries, and had a place, but no vote in chapter. There were forty (formerly eighty) chaplains, twelve removable choral chaplains, a chapel master, and organist and choristers. Two prebends went to the fabric (Pulgar's Teatro, ii. n. iii.)

CALAHORRA. Dean, five archdeacons, chanter, treasurer, twenty-four canons, eighteen prebendaries, twelve semiprebendaries, three curés, thirty-four chaplains.

S. DOMINGO (1234). Four dignitaries, eight canons, eight prebendaries.

PAMPELUNA (Austin Canons). Chamberlain, prior, seven archdeacons, infirmarer, hospitaller, abbot of S. Michael, twenty-two canons, six prebendaries, vicar of the parish, twenty-four chaplains.

BURGOS. Dean, six archdeacons, chanter, treasurer, seven abbots, prior, forty-five canons, of whom the king is first; twenty prebendaries, twenty semiprebendaries, forty chaplains, five acolytes, five chaplains of king's chapel, thirty-three chaplains of parish chapel, two curez, three beneficiarii.

MALAGA. Three archdeacons, chanter, ecolatre, treasurer, dean, twenty-four canons, fourteen prebendaries, twelve semiprebendaries, twelve acolytes.

ALMERIA. Four dignitaries, eight canons, six prebendaries.

GRANADA. Seven dignitaries, twelve canons, twelve prebendaries.

ORIHUELA. Six dignitaries, six canons, twelve prebendaries.

SEGORBE. Six dignitaries, twelve canons, twelve prebendaries. [Dean, chanter, treasurer, two archdeacons, and six canons. In 1358 the offices of obrero (master of the fabric), almoner, succentor, escolastre, and infirmarer were added. The dean sat on the north-west, and the grand archdeacon on the south-west, and the bishop between them (Villanueva, iii. 13, 25, 246.)]

VALENTIA. Seven dignitaries, twenty-four canons, twenty-four prebendaries.

TERUEL. Six dignitaries, fourteen canons, eight prebendaries.

BALBASTRO. Seven dignitaries, twelve canons, twelve prebendaries.

JACA. Nine dignitaries, seventeen canons, sixteen prebendaries.

ALBARAZIN. Four dignitaries, eight canons, eight prebendaries.

HUESCA. Six dignitaries, twenty canons, twelve prebendaries.

SARAGOSSA. Twelve dignitaries, twenty-four canons, twenty-four prebendaries.

ZAMORA. Nine dignitaries, twenty-four canons, eleven prebendaries.

LUGO. Eleven dignitaries, six canons, twelve prebendaries.

CIUDAD RODRIGO. Dean, archdeacon, chanter, treasurer, three archdeacons, ecolatre, twenty canons, three prebendaries, four semiprebendaries, master of chapel, and twenty-four chaplains.

ORENSE. Eleven dignitaries, eighteen canons, twelve prebendaries, fourteen chaplains.

MONDONEDO. Eleven dignitaries, twenty-six canons, six prebendaries, twelve chaplains, twelve enfans de chœur, and sochantre.

TUY. Eight dignitaries, twenty-seven canons, fourteen prebendaries.

BADAJOZ. Dean, archdeacon, chanter, archdeacon of Xerez, treasurer, ecolatre,

[For the cathedraticum paid to the cathedral, see Ep. Gelasii Fabiano, ann. 494, Canon V. q. 3, causa 10. In 580, two shillings were allowed in Sicily. It was sometimes one-third of the offerings. See also Counc. Braga, 592, and Paul's Hist. of Benef., p. 32.] The common life, according to Trithemius, died out in Germany, c. 977, but it lasted at Rheims till about 1200. In 1068, at Rome, Pope Alexander in council reinforced the duty. Besançon was in 1300 the last French cathedral which abandoned the common

prior, fifteen canons, fourteen prebendaries, ten semiprebendaries, twenty chaplains, sochantre, master of chapels, and twelve enfans de chœur.

PLACENCIA. Dean, archdeacon, chanter, archdeacon of Truxillo, treasurer, two archdeacons, ecolatre, six canons, nine semiprebendaries, twenty-four chaplains. Statutes published 1704.

CORIA. Dean, five archdeacons, chanter, treasurer, nine canons, six prebendaries, seven semiprebendaries.

SALAMANCA. Ten dignitaries, twenty-six canons, thirty-one prebendaries.

AVILA. Six dignitaries, twenty canons, twenty prebendaries, twelve semiprebendaries, master of the chapel, two chaplains major, twenty chaplains ordinary, two sacristans, two minors, twenty-four enfans de chœur.

TOLEDO. The archbishop has the right of carrying the cross throughout Spain. Two archdeacons, chanter, treasurer, archdeacon, abbot of S. Leocadie, vicar of choir, dean, archdeacon, ecolatre, two archdeacons, abbot of S. Vincent, chaplain major; the first seven sit on the right, the rest on the left in choir; forty canons; twenty extravagants, who assist on certain anniversaries; bas-chœur, fifty prebendaries; forty-eight chaplains; twenty-four clerks maytinantes, who assist at the night hours; four ordinary readers; ten singers; forty enfans de chœur, of whom sixteen are called seyses. The archbishop nominates to thirty-seven canonries, the extravagants, thirty-eight prebends, and forty-four chaplaincies; the chapter nominates to the rest. Two canonries are reserved to two doctors or licentiates in law, and one in theology. Eight prebends are allotted to the chanters, a ninth to the master of chapel of clerks, and two others to the two subchanters, and other inferior beneficiarii and enfans de chœur.

SEGOVIA. Eight dignitaries, forty canons, twenty prebendaries.

VALLADOLID. Six dignitaries, twenty-two canons, eighteen prebendaries.

OSMA. Prior, sub-prior, three archdeacons, chanter, treasurer, sacristan, ecolatre, and two abbots; ten canons, twelve prebendaries, curé, archpriest, chaplains, ten enfans de chœur, two of whom are called infantes mayores, because they recite only the martyrology, and mark the offices in the choir books; four seminarists; six clerks messarii, who assist at mass; master of the chapel, and organist. The præcentor appoints the subchanter and eight enfans de chœur; the treasurer nominates a chaplain of the treasury; the sacristan, two subsacrists; and the ecolatre, a curé and vicaire. The pope and bishop nominate dignitaries, and the bishop and chapter canons alternately. The cathedral is associated with Toledo, Palencia, Segovia, and Cuença.

SIGUENÇA. Dean, five archdeacons, treasurer, chanter, chaplain major, archpriest d'Atiença, ecolatre, abbe major, and prior; forty canons, twenty prebendaries, penitentiary. Six canonries are reserved—four for theologians, and two for doctors of other faculties.

CUENÇA. Thirteen dignitaries, twenty canons, ten prebendaries, twelve enfans de chœur, four psalmites, two succentors and musicians.

CARTAGENA. Six dignitaries, eight canons, twenty prebendaries.

JAEN. Dean, three archdeacons, chanter, ecolatre, prior, twenty-one canons, twenty-four prebendaries.

TARRAGONA. Three archdeacons, sacristan, chanter, prior, dean, treasurer, infirmarer, hospitaller, archdeacon, twenty-four canons, twenty-four prebendaries, sixty-nine beneficiarii.

BARCELONA. Archdeacon major, dean, chanter, sacristan, five archdeacons, succentor, treasurer, twenty-four canons, twelve prebendaries.

TORTOSA (Austin Canons). Prior, major archdeacon, major chamberlain, salife, having till that period read the rule of the Council of Aix-la-Chapelle daily after the martyrology.

S. Augustine directed his community, besides their duties of living in common, teaching youth, and observing the hours, to read and comment on a chapter of the Bible, or a smaller portion (capitulum), daily, whence they were said to go to chapter, and each individual was called a capitular, and the whole society a

cristan, claustral prior, chanter, dean, hospitaller, three archdeacons, twenty canons, twenty-four prebendaries.

LISBON. The patriarch wears the robes of a cardinal; the canons use the mitre and pontificals, and rank with grandees (Moreri.)

EVORA. Eight dignitaries, twelve canons, four demiprebendaries, four quartenarii, i.e. ecclesiastics having the fourth part of a canon's income.

ELVAS. Five dignitaries, ten canons, twelve demiprebendaries, four quartenarii.

PORTALEGRE. Five dignitaries, seven canons, six demiprebendaries.

COIMBRA. Eight dignitaries, twenty-five canons, six demiprebendaries.

GUARDA. Seven dignitaries, twenty-two canons, four demiprebendaries.

LAMEGO. Seven dignitaries, four canons, six demiprebendaries, six tercenarii.

VISEU. Nine dignitaries, eighteen canons, ten demiprebendaries.

PORTO. Eight dignitaries, twelve canons, six conegos.

LEIRIA. Five dignitaries, ten canons, four demicanonigos, seventeen quartenarii.

ALGARVA. Seven dignitaries, twelve canons, six demiprebendaries, ten quartenarii. (Descripçao de Portugal, 1788.)

Holland (Hist. Episc. Fœd. Belg., 1719.) UTRECHT. Originally a major provost and forty canons, founded 1088, and monks under an abbot. It had also four archdeacons or provosts in the city, and four archisubdiaconi or chorepiscopi, fifty perpetual vicars or chaplains, twelve priest vicars for the choir service, founded 1447. The capitular body is called dean and chapter in some old documents.

HAARLEM, 1559. In 1479, provost, vice-curator, and four chaplains; in 1559, nine canons graduates, three of theology, three of canon law, and three nobles of the diocese, licentiates of either of those faculties.

DEVENTER. Dean, provost, or archdeacon, twenty canons, with nineteen prebends and fifteen supplements. The dean holds two, the bishop one; nine are "affectæ," being allotted in equal partitions to graduates of theology, law, and noble birth; the rest are free "liberæ." One belongs to the parish rector.

LEUWARDEN, 1565. Dean and ten canons, including two archdeacons and a penitentiary.

GRONINGEN, 1561. Dean, ten canons, and chaplains or vicars.

At GHENT the Benedictines became seculars in 1536, the abbot was changed to a mitred provost, the prior to a dean, the provost to præcentor, the provost of Papingloo to ecolatre. The treasurer remained, but ranked before the ecolatre. Besides these dignitaries were an archpriest and twenty-four canons: seven were royal prebendaries, sixteen graduate prebendaries in theology or law. Eight were libres. There were three vice-curés or desserviteurs (Hellin. Hist. de S. Bavon, pp. 5—400.)

At Lunden, Abo, and Upsala, the chapters consist of the bishop, dean, always primarii professors of divinity, and other professors; at Wisby, of the bishop and neighbouring clergy. Lunden was the metropolitan church (Miræus, Not. 21.)

At Bergen there were twelve prebendaries (Registr. præd. Episc. Berg., p. 2.)

RÖESKILDE. Provost, canons, sacristan, theological lecturer, vicars (Paludanus.)

LUNDEN. Provost, dean, præcentor, founded c. 1320; archdeacon, twenty-four prebendaries, c. 1250; priests, deacons, and subdeacons; cellarer, procurator fabricæ, master of schools, vicars, poor scholars. There were canonical residences, and a common table (Langebeck, ii. 27, 469; Soderström, Alleg. 1.)

DRONTHEIM. Dean and canons. Cardinal Breakspeare, in the twelfth century, formed resident chapters in Norway on the English model (Munch, 14; comp. Torfæus, 173.)

UPSALA. Founded 1063, with Scara and Wexio. 1595, Provost, custos (Fant. i. 70), dean, penitentiary, all readers of theology in the cathedral school (Baazius, chapter (Mayer, Nov. Thes., i. § 26, pp. 60, 175.) Scarfantoni says, because canons were minora, as bishops are majora capita. Lyndwood says, "Propriè loquendo capitulum dicitur respectu ecclesiæ cathedralis; conventus respectu ecclesiæ regularis; collegium respectu ecclesiæ inferioris ubi est collectio viventium in communi." Capitulum denotes the place of meeting. 2. The place of discipline. 3. A paragraph (a lesson from the Bible), a statute under one rubric. 4. An assembly of persons for con-

112, 563.) Between 1225 and 1234 the monastery was converted into a college of secular canons, with four persons, the provost, archdeacon, and two ancient canons. Between 1281 and 1289 the deanery was instituted, with a new prebend annexed. Thirteen canonries were afterwards founded. There were five vicars and eight prebendaries (Benzelius, 38, 61.) There was a provost at Aarhus, and with a dean also at Lincoping with prebendaries (Kröningwald's Diplom. Dalekarl.)

England. Old Foundation. YORK. Three dignitaries: no treasurer since the Reformation; subdean, succentor of canons, three archdeacons, four canons residentiary, twenty-four prebendaries appointed by the archbishop, subchanter, and five vicars choral with a subchanter.

S. PAUL'S. Four dignitaries, two archdeacons, four canons residentiary, three recommended by the crown, thirty prebendaries appointed by the bishop, divinity lecturer, twelve minor canons, with subdean, succentor, two cardinals, librarian, gospeller, epistoler, almoner, and warden.

BANGOR. Dean, two archdeacons, three canons residentiary, two prebendaries, two vicars choral.

WELLS. Four dignitaries, three archdeacons, subdean, subchanter, forty-four prebendaries, three (formerly four) priest vicars.

CHICHESTER. Four dignitaries, two archdeacons, four canons residentiary, twenty-four prebendaries, four Wiccamical prebendaries held by clergy educated at Winchester; four vicars choral with a principal.

EXETER. Four dignitaries, four archdeacons, six canons residentiary, subdean, twenty-four prebendaries, three (formerly four) priest vicars, with a custos.

HEREFORD. Four dignitaries, two archdeacons, four canons residentiary, prælector, twenty-six prebendaries, five (formerly twelve) vicars choral, with a custos and succentor and subtreasurer.

LICHFIELD. Three dignitaries, no treasurer since the Reformation, three archdeacons, four canons residentiary, twenty-five prebendaries, divinity lecturer, five priest vicars, with succentor and sacrist.

LINCOLN. Four dignitaries, a subdean, but no treasurer since the Reformation, three archdeacons, seventy prebendaries, four vicars choral, with a provost.

LLANDAFF. Four dignitaries, two archdeacons, nine prebendaries, including seven cursal canons, two (formerly four) vicars choral and parish vicars.

SALISBURY. Four dignitaries, three archdeacons, four canons residentiary, subdean, succentor of canons, forty prebendaries, four vicars choral, with a proctor.

S. ASAPH. Dean, two archdeacons, four canons residentiary, nine cursal canons, four vicars choral.

S. DAVID'S. Four dignitaries, four archdeacons, four canons residentiary, fourteen prebendaries, including six cursal canons, three minor canons, with subdean and bishop's vicar.

New Foundation. CANTERBURY. Dean, two archdeacons, six (formerly twelve) canons appointed by the crown, six preachers, six minor canons, with precentor.

WINCHESTER. Dean, two archdeacons, six (formerly twelve) canons, five minor canons, with precentor.

DURHAM. Dean, three archdeacons, seven (formerly twelve) canons—two are professors of Durham University—six minor canons, with precentor and sacrist.

CHESTER. Dean, two archdeacons, four (formerly six) canons appointed by the bishop, four minor canons, with precentor.

ELY. Dean, four archdeacons, six (formerly eight) canons, four appointed by ference on common business (lib. i. tit. 2, n. a.; Ceccoperius, iv. 1.) At Rouen the chapter met on the feast of the Assumption; at Mayence four times a year. Every canon has a voice or vote in chapter (Scarf., ii. 103), and a dignitary who holds a canonry had, according to some, two votes (ibid. 94.) A proxy had but one vote, except when the merits of two candidates were equal, and then he might use his own vote (94.) In cases of dispute touching priority of voting, the bishop is to decide (98.) The chapter forms the members, and the bishop the head of a college body or corporation (Frances, 206; Scarfantoni, i. 69); but in corpore representing the episcopal chair, it demands equal respect with a bishop (ibid., Frances, 603.) It is the bishop's council (ibid. 230): "by birthright counsellors to the bishop, and assistants in his whole office" (Thorndike, Plea, § 5, p. 5.) At Worcester the prior and archdeacon exercised episcopal jurisdiction on the vacancy of the see (Chron. Evesh., 227.) The chapter has jurisdiction in all causes and over all persons of the cathedral church, and can enact statutes (the particular and domestic rule binding every member of

the bishop; two are Cambridge University professors—four minor canons, with precentor, and sacrist.

Bristol. Dean and archdeacon, four (formerly six) canons appointed by the crown, three minor canons, with precentor.

Gloucester. Dean and archdeacon, four canons appointed by the crown, one master of Pembroke College, Oxford, three (formerly four) minor canons, with precentor.

Manchester. Dean, two archdeacons, four canons, five minor canons, with precentor, clerk in orders, and curate.

Norwich. Dean, three archdeacons, four (formerly six) canons appointed by the crown—one is master of S. Catherine's College, Cambridge—four (formerly eight) minor canons, with precentor and sacrist.

Oxford. Dean, three archdeacons, seven (formerly eight) canons—five are Oxford University professors—six chaplains, with precentor.

Peterborough. Dean, two archdeacons, four (formerly six) canons, three (formerly four) minor canons, with precentor.

Ripon. Dean, two archdeacons, four canons, two minor canons and parish vicars, with precentor.

Rochester. Dean, three archdeacons, four (formerly six) canons appointed by the crown—one the Provost of Oriel College, Oxford—four (formerly six) minor canons, with precentor.

Worcester. Dean, two archdeacons, four (formerly ten) canons appointed by the crown, four (formerly eight) minor canons, with precentor and sacrist.

Carlisle. Dean, two archdeacons, four canons, three (formerly five) minor canons, with precentor.

Ireland. (See my learned friend Dr. Jebb's "Choral Service.")

Armagh. Four dignitaries and archdeacon, four prebendaries; three vicars choral, the successors of the colidei, who, under their prior, survived to Queen Elizabeth's reign. The residentiaries had houses. The capitular members share the duties equally. There is a daily choral service.

Clogher. Four dignitaries, five prebendaries. Duty done by the parochial incumbent.

Christchurch, Dublin. Four dignitaries and archdeacon, three prebendaries attached to certain churches, and three vicars. The preaching turns are divided between the dignitaries and prebendaries. All had formerly houses.

S. Patrick's. Four dignitaries, twenty prebendaries. The dignitaries for-the body) for the advancement of Divine worship, and matters not affecting the privileges of the church or bishop (Frances, 234), which must be confirmed by the bishop (Mayer, i. 176, 179), who is head of the chapter (Frances, 206.) It is a congregation of canons (Scarfantoni, i. 17, 333), having a seat in choir and vote in chapter, with proper revenues, a chapter-house, a steward or chamberlain, the right of a syndic and proper seal, endowed with common property, and assembled under a president, and able to be convened by the sound of the bell (Frances, 372; Ceccop., i. 61.) Deans, archdeacons, cathedral chapters, &c., were required to have their seal, by the Constit. of Otto, A.D. 1237, c. 28. The bishop technically is called the principal head, and the dean the numeral head of a chapter (Scarf., ii. 81.) A close chapter was one in which the number of members was rigidly defined (Mayer, vi. 340.) The appointment of organist and singers belongs to the chapter, who provide the salaries and pay, and the bishop cannot

merly were residentiaries. All are answerable for preaching turns. The prebendaries had a common residentiary house. Choral service only on Sunday afternoons.

KILDARE. Four dignitaries—the dean was elective—and archdeacon: four canons responsible for residence and duty, eight prebendaries.

MEATH. Dean of Clonmacnoise and archdeacon. The see was formed out of the reduction into a regular diocese of many ambulatory bishoprics.

DERRY. Dean and archdeacon, three prebendaries. A parish church.

RAPHOE. Dean and archdeacon, four prebendaries. Duty done by the parish incumbent.

CASHEL. Four dignitaries and archdeacon, five prebendaries. There were formerly residences. The duties are performed by deputy.

EMLY. Three dignitaries, no treasurer, four prebendaries. A parish church.

WATERFORD. Four dignitaries and archdeacon. There were residences.

LISMORE. Four dignitaries and archdeacon, nine prebendaries.

CORK. Four dignitaries and archdeacon, twelve prebendaries. There were residences. There is a Sunday choir.

CLOYNE. Four dignitaries and archdeacon, fourteen prebendaries. There is a choir.

ROSS. Four dignitaries and archdeacon, five prebendaries, one vicar choral.

DOWN. Four dignitaries and archdeacon, two prebendaries. Duty done by the parish incumbent.

CONNOR. Four dignitaries and archdeacon, four prebendaries. Church in ruins.

DROMORE. Four dignitaries and archdeacon, one prebendary. Duty done by the parish incumbent.

KILLALOE. Four dignitaries and archdeacon, six prebendaries. Duties performed by deputy.

KILFENORA. Three dignitaries, no chancellor, and archdeacon. Duties performed by deputy. A parish church.

CLONFERT. Dean and archdeacon, six prebendaries.

KILMACDUAGH. Three dignitaries, archdeacon and provost, two prebendaries. Church in ruins.

KILMORE. Dean and archdeacon. Had formerly twelve prebendaries.

ELPHIN. Dean, præcentor, archdeacon, eight prebendaries.

ARDAGH. Dean and archdeacon.

LIMERICK. Four dignitaries and archdeacon, eleven prebendaries, a residentiary preacher, five priest vicars. There is a regular daily choral service. The dean is rector of the parish. There were residences formerly for the dignitaries.

ARDFERT. Four dignitaries, two archdeacons; the duty is performed by deputy.

AGHADOE. A mere parish church; probably never had a corporation.

OSSORY. Four dignitaries, archdeacon, and seven prebendaries, three vicars compel them to hire or engage any such persons at his will (Scarfantoni, i. 106.) The punishment of all the inferior members rests with the chapter (280; ii. 291.) The bishop ought to forbid the employment of any other instrument than the organ (ibid.), or the use of unsuitable music. He has no vote, and is not a member of chapter (ibid. ii. 94), except he be also a canon (81.) A chapter confirms elections in place of the bishop (Frances, 198), and in the vacancy of a see gives licence to the nearest bishop to administer episcopal acts and functions (ibid.), and retains the power of government (p. 199) and jurisdiction properly its own. It has all the rights and privileges of a parish (p. 348.) Where it delegates the charge of the parish to a person nominated by itself, it exercises the power of control in all that relates to the cure of souls (361; Scarf., iii. 51.) Its members the canons can perform the burial office to the exclusion of the parish priest (Frances, 293.) It can administer the Holy Communion (351.) In matters of difficulty, as in alteration of statutes, the bishop should consult

choral, dean's, præcentor's, and archdeacon's vicars. The dignitaries had houses. There is a choral service in S. Canice's, Kilkenny.

FERNS. Four dignitaries and archdeacon, ten prebendaries.

LEIGHLIN. Four dignitaries and archdeacon, four prebendaries. A mere parish church. There were formerly residences.

TUAM. Dean, provost, who is vicar of Tuam, archdeacon, eight prebendaries. Choral service on Sundays and holidays.

KILLALA. Dean, rector of the parish, præcentor and archdeacon. Five prebendaries and capitular members preach twice a year.

ACHONRY. Dean, præcentor, and archdeacon, three prebendaries.

Scotland. Ross. Dean, præcentor, treasurer, chancellor, archdeacon, subdean, subchanter, all with prebends; sixteen canons, seven found priest vicars, five deacons, and five subdeacons. The bishop held a prebend (Registrum Episc. Moraiensis, xvii.); founded on Lincoln, the statutes of which occur pp. 45, 51.

(*From Dr. Jebb's MS. notes.*)

S. ANDREW'S. Twelve canons regular of S. Austin, Culdees, established 1140, with a prior, and vicars for Divine service. Until 1255 they joined with the secular canons of the cathedral in the election of a bishop. There were two archdeacons, but in 1606 a dean, prior of Portmollock, archdeacon, and twenty-four vicars.

EDINBURGH, 1630. Dean, twelve prebendaries.

DUNKELD, 1127. Like Glasgow, modelled on Salisbury. After the Reformation, dean, præcentor, archdeacon, chancellor, treasurer, subdean, three prebendaries, and eight parish rectors and parsons.

DUNBLANE. Culdees with a prior, who appointed a chaplain. In 1220 there was a chapter of prebendaries with a dean founded.

BRECHIN. Culdees with a prior, till the beginning of the thirteenth century, when a dean, archdeacon, and chaplains were appointed.

LISMORE, 1200. There were prebendaries and a præcentor.

ABERDEEN, 1157 and 1256. Modelled on Lincoln. Dean or archpresbyter, principal of King's College; præcentor, anciently primicerius; archdeacon, chancellor, treasurer, subchanter, twenty-two prebendaries. Twenty vicars choral added 1506; eleven choristers, two deacons, two acolythes, a master of music, and sacrist. There were residentiaries' houses in the close.

CAITHNESS, DORNOCH, 1223—45. Like Elgin and Aberdeen, modelled on Lincoln. Five dignitaries, three prebendaries.

KIRKWALL. There was an archdeacon, with prebendaries and choristers.

GALLOWAY, WHITHERNE. Canons regular. There were nine prebends.

THE ISLES. IONA. There were prebendaries and a dean, vicar of Icolmkill.

it (506; Scarf., iii. 11.) The chapter can correct by deprivation of a share in the distribution and funds, and of the privilege of voting (Frances, 567.) It can enact statutes, both when the see is full and when vacant, touching the state of the church, provided they are capitularly made for the increase of Divine worship and in due form, with discreet judgment, and without prejudice to the bishop (234.) Where there were two regular chapters in one church, as in S. Ambrose's, Milan, and S. Augustine's, Pavia, each had its own superior (579.) The oath of obedience was made to the chapter of residentiaries by the newly installed canon latterly in England.

There are two kinds of chapter:—1. Ordinary, held monthly or weekly, according to custom, and assembled by sound of the bell. 2. Extraordinary, convoked by mandate or cited by summons (Ceccop., iv. 8.) The bishop, if to be present as bishop, or the matter touches his dignity or church service, convenes and presides as ordinary, unless the power of convocation by custom and right resides in the first dignitary or dean (11); and in that case, in his absence, it passes to the second dignitary or to the senior canon. At the instance of the canons, or even of one canon, if the matter be of moment, and the president refuses or neglects to convene the chapter, two parts of the canons may convoke "the chapter convoked by itself," and appoint the senior canon present its president (Ceccop. iv. 14.) A minority may carry a matter, if the term for its transaction draws near, and they warn the majority. The bishop cannot forbid a chapter, nor compel a revelation of the matter discussed. The dean must convene a chapter at the usual hour, and only for suitable business; not during Divine service, nor except in the chapter-house (16, 17.) Three canons constitute a chapter (19), and for an extraordinary chapter all canons resident must be summoned (22), and two-thirds of the number appear to carry a measure. An absent canon might appoint another canon, and him only (44), his proctor (42), who in open voting, but not in secret, might also give his own vote. Chapters are to be opened with prayer, and all present to wear the same habit as if in choir (48.) The dean or any canon proposing any private matter affecting his own interest, should leave the chapter until it had been discussed (52.) The senior canon should speak first, and the junior last, the dean not interfering (54.) Canons arriving late may discuss the matter still before the chapter, but not any questions previously decided (58.) The dean first, and then the canons in their order, are to propose any question (59) which is definitely settled by the majority, that is, by the casting vote (61.) When the vote is made vivâ voce, additional weight must be given to the dean, a canon who is a bishop, or who is one of the seniors, owing to his experience, or one acknowledged to be superior in learning (69.) Silence implies the assent of a canon (74.) Elections to canonries and benefices are made by silent votes (83), or by (1) postulation, addressed to a superior for confirmation of the elect; by inspiration, when all unanimously, without previous concert, name a person; by (2) compromission, when a delegate of the whole chapter nominates him; or by (3) scrutiny, election by the majority, made by means of the ballot, or voting papers, sealed and written in a feigned hand, or open vote. The chapter by a majority, and without the bishop, can enact statutes touching the good order and government of the chapter, the administration of their property, the assembly of chapters, the ordering of the choir, the division of duties among canons, and the choral vestments, and make them binding by oath, with penalties for their non-observance (133), if not contrary to the ecclesiastical law; but it is fitting and safer that they should be confirmed by the bishop (134.) If unconfirmed, they can be repealed by the chapter itself (177.) His consent is necessary to all new statutes of graver importance (135.) An appeal lies to the archbishop in case of his refusal (138.) The customs of the church should be written (140) in a book. Like statutes they may be altered by new enactments, but ten years' usage is required to confirm them (145.) The bishop at his installation must swear to observe the statutes (153.) The chapter, which should assemble on the morrow, if the usual day fall on a feast (Scarf., ii. 82) cannot without the bishop's authority alter old statutes (Scarf., iii. 10.) The consent of all the members in matters touching all as individuals must be unanimous (ii. 136, 144, 153; iii. 11.) The bishop may be present, except in matters touching himself or his (14.) Statutes are only to be made for the augmentation of divine worship and the edification of the faithful (ii. 135), and must be made in chapter and committed to writing (134.) They cannot be carried by a majority, to the prejudice of the minority, for the latter have an appeal to the archbishop (144.) One vote makes a majority (103.) All canons ought to attend ordinary and extraordinary chapters (89, 97), and honorary canons, when the statutes to be promulgated will bind them (93); and non-resident canons ought to be cited for the election of the first dignitary of the church, when the divine service is to be suspended with the bishop's leave, and in the collation of prebends, and in any special and important business (88.) When the bishop convenes the chapter (82), he presides, takes the votes, regulates the time, and proposes business (36.) He who convenes the chapter, need not state the business to be discussed, but the citations must be duly issued and a bell rung (84.) In the extraordinary chapters, canons going out lose their right of protesting against the votes of the residue; but in ordinary chapters, if the majority goes out, no business can be done (88.) No important business was to be sealed except in presence of the dean, or his locum tenens, and all the residentiaries, and their proctors; and then, after mature deliberation (Praty's Reg. 1441), the consent of the dean and major part of the chapter was sufficient to confirm matters relating to the cathedral (ib., Storey, 1480.)

At first canons lived in common, or in the one canonical house (Scarfantoni, i. 8; Thomassin, l. iii. c. 9, § 7, &c.) called a minster (Counc. Aix, 816, c. 138), and were maintained out of the common stock, from which the necessaries of life, the quotidian, and daily allowances of food were afforded (præbebantur). Hence the word prebend (provender). Their rents were the portio canonica. But when the common life was given up, each canonry having its own fixed revenues or prebend became a benefice, although the name of prebend in a secondary sense was retained (Mayer, i. § 37, pp. 74, 259.) They hold these endowments, and are required to be in holy orders, because they are the bishop's council (Frances, 230.) In consequence of this primitive community of revenues, the collation of canonries resided in the bishop and chapter (Scarf., i. 16.) At S. Paul's, the apportionment of prebends began, if it was not completed, before the arrival of William I. In the Exchequer Domesday some canons hold land, afterwards made prebendal (Domesday of S. Paul's, iii. iv. xcv.) Robert Bloet, of Lincoln, added twenty-one prebends to an equal number appointed by his predecessor. Giso at Wells enlarged the estates for the sustenance of the brethren; and those whom the want of the necessaries of life previously compelled to live among the people in a mean manner, being thus enriched, he brought to adopt canonical obedience (Eccles. Doc. Camd. Soc., p. 19.) Prebenda differt a canoniâ, nam canonia est jus spirituale, quod aliquis assequitur in ecclesiâ per receptionem in fratrem et assignationem stalli in choro et loci in capitulo. Præbenda est jus spirituale recipiendi certos proventus pro meritis in ecclesiâ competentes percipienti ex divino officio, cui insistit et nascitur ex canoniâ tanquam filia a matre. Præbenda est nomen juris quia non constituitur tantum ex possessionibus sed ex jure canonico cui annectitur, quæ sine reditu non potest constitui quia sic non esset quid præbendario præberetur (Lyndwood, lib. iii. tit. 7, n. e. p. 144.) The names of the prebends are derived from (1) their corps, as Pratum minus, Consumpta per mare, &c.; or (2) their prebendal church, e.g. S. Decuman's, Nova Ecclesia, &c.; or (3) from their reputed or actual founder, e.g. prebenda episcopi, Arthur Bulkely, David ap Howell, Richard Harrison; or (4) the altar from which they derived the oblations, e.g. Holy Cross, S. Dubritius, S. Nicholas, S. Andrew's, major et minor pars altaris; or (5) their portion—Combe first, second, &c.; Llanfair Portio, secunda; or (6) their stipend—LX. and centum solidorum, X. librarum, like the canons of fifteen marks at Rouen, founded in 1190, &c. In some cases they are attached to a dignity; or to a cure, as at Lincoln, to Gainsborough vicarage; or to the mastership of a school, and a theological lectureship, as at Chichester; to the regius professorship of civil law at Oxford, at Salisbury; at Oxford, Dec. 21, 1635, to the office of public orator. "A canonry," says Ayliffe, "is an ecclesiastical benefice in some cathedral church, which has a prebend or stated allowance out of the revenues of such a church commonly annexed to it. The canonry has of necessity a prebend, and a prebend of necessity has a canonry belonging to it" (Parergon, 139; Mayer, iii. 275.) P. Symmachus, in a letter to S. Cesarius, allowed a bishop to give a glebe to clergymen for their life; and the Council of Agde, 506, directed a special subsistence to be allotted; and the Councils of Orleans, 538 (cxvii.), and Lyons, 567 (v.), directed bishops to confirm to clergy the gifts of their predecessors. In the twelfth century prebendaries were allowed to bequeath property. One of the earliest prebends at Rouen, that of Bretagne, was founded in 1184 by Geoffrey, Duke of Brittany, who attached to it an income of twenty livres; the most ancient, however, was that of Neaufle, which was founded in 1095, by Robert II., Duke of Normandy. As the revenues were attached to certain duties, the connection between the benefice and sacred office was regarded as so intimate, that by the Council of Lateran, 1179, no person was to be admitted canon unless there was an actual vacancy. But, however, there were in fact besides (1) the capitulars, ordinary, simple, or major canons, in actual possession[1] (Scarfantoni, i. 49; ii. 141); (2) supernumeraries appended by the bishop, with consent of the chapter, called domicellares or minor canons, supported on small prebends (at Strasburg one-fourth of the prebend of a capitular canon), expectants of vacancies. They were usually regarded as students, and ranked after the vicars, until their emancipation or promotion to a stall (Mayer, i. 17, 175; vi. 340.) They were intended to augment the efficiency of the choir (p. 260.) These were again distinct from (3) canons elect, but not as yet installed. The domicelli were so called as if non domini or lordlings, in distinction to the canons major or dom. herrn (ib. 258.) Their vicars were called chorales (iii. 42.) The curious ceremonial of emancipation is given by Mayer, iv. 363. (4) Honorary canons were canons exempt from the observance of the canonical hours. The emperor was canon of Strasburg, Liege, Bamberg, Cologne, and Utrecht,

[1] Canons that are obliged to perform the Communion Service, and other solemn parts of divine worship, in their turns weekly, are sometimes called hebdomadal canons, and are in one degree before ordinary prebendaries (Ayliffe, 140.) At Hereford the hebdomadary ranks first only in absence of the dean. All members of the chapter are to be called canons except the dean (3 and 4 Vict., c. 113, s. 1), and each in respect of his office is a corporation sole. All canons were required to be learned and able to sing (Frances, 230, 372; Scarf., i. 77), to be in orders (Scarfantoni, i. 54), and are personæ graduatæ, brothers of the bishop, and one body with him (ii. 304) and the church senate (i. p. 256.) On solemn days they were to walk two and two from the sacristy into the choir (80.) Pre-eminence in choir is founded on the prebend (19.) In some places juniors went before seniors (59).

Spires and Aix-la-Chapelle, and of S. Peter's and S. John's in the Lateran at Rome. The King of the Franks was custos of S. Quentin's, the King of the Romans at Nivelle, the king at Ratisbon (Mayer, iv. 48, 50, 55.) The King of France was abbot of S. Hilary, and canon of Poictiers, Chalons, Sens, Anjou, and Tours; the King of Spain canon of Burgos, Toledo, and Leon (Frances, 80; Scarf., i. 12); and the queen is first cursal at S. David's. This prerogative was due to the unction, which was supposed to equal that of a priest (Mayer, i. § 33, p. 68.) At Bourges, the archpresbyter, a city rector, during the life of the bishop who collated him, took precedence of all canons (Scarf., i. 49.) Honorary clerical canons were said to have their right in the wind, and their canonry in the air (62), and were only appointed in order to increase the efficiency of the church service (p. 63), being merely ficti canonici. The coadjutors of canons were regarded as ficti canonici (Scarf., i. 50), but succeeded to the vacant canonry (51.) At Lyons there were chanoines comtes and chanoines perpetuels (Moleon, 44); and chanoines bas-formiers at Angers, Sens, and Rouen. From their right of electing the bishop and president of chapter, they were called electionarii, electors; and as a mark of honour, domini, as the masters of arts and doctors are styled in universities (Scarfantoni, i. p. 11.) The bishop holds a stall at Lichfield, Salisbury, Deventer, and Limerick, and the archbishop at Cashel and S. Patrick's. At Lyons, the Dukes of Bourges and Burgundy; at Utrecht, the Duke of Brabant; at Autun, the Counts de Chasteluz; and the Counts of Anjou at Tours, were honorary canons. At Strasburg four prebends were allotted to princes of Mecklenburg. In Germany a canon on his admission paid sixty Rhenish florins to the fabric (p. 95.) The oldest title was senior or brother; then succeeded canon and lord; and lastly, capitular, as being a member of chapter (ibid. 258.) Molanus thinks that Domheeren is a corruption of Bisdom Heeren, canons of the see (lib. iii. c. 3; i. c. 3; Minsheu, 61.)

At Exeter, when the present chapter was fixed, 1225, lesser chapters, called parliaments, were held every Saturday, but not during high mass. The services for the week and celebrants (hebdomadarii, Fr. semainiers) were tabled, and the defects of the previous week corrected. All canons, vicars, and annuellars present at prime were to attend the daily chapter for the despatch of business. The collector of rents exhibited his accounts annually before the chapter. There were monthly chapters in 1287. At Salisbury the dean, in 1222, instructed in chapter the vicars to summon their canons into residence. The extraordinary or Pentecostal chapter was held annually until 1813 by the bishop, attended by the dean, chancellor, two archdeacons, and subdean, on his right; and on his left the precentor, treasurer, two archdeacons, and succentor; and in due order canons residentiaries and the rest of the prebendaries; the notices being fixed upon their respective stalls. At S. Paul's every canon was bound to attend on Easter Monday, two parts forming the majority present being competent to decide matters. At S. Paul's a servant summoned residents to attend. At York, in 1542, all canons, whether residentiaries or not, were required to be present after summons. At Lichfield, in 1260, there were weekly chapters after prime, a custom confirmed in 1420. The primate was enthroned in the chapter-house of Canterbury, which, like the refectory and cloister, was strewn with rushes and seated with cushions on great days. At Salisbury the dean and residentiaries form the lesser chapter; and with the dignitaries, archdeacons, subdean, sub-chanter, and all the prebendaries (thirty-two, c. 1092; afterwards fifty-three) constitute the large or Pentecostal chapter, which used to meet every Whitsuntide, and was only suspended in 1813. At Llandaff, Bishop Henry, who died 1218, founded fourteen prebends. At Lincoln the lesser chapter included the dean, dignitaries, and subdean; and the great chapter comprised them, with the arch-deacons and fifty-two prebendaries. At York a non-residentiary canon preaches in person on certain allotted Sundays and holy days appropriated to his stall, or finds a deputy, who must be one of the cathedral body. If present, he takes part in the Communion office. At S. Paul's the thirty canons constituted with their head the bishop the body and chapter, and managed the business and secret affairs of the church, with the right to elect the bishop and dean. They now receive only a small sum for preaching sermons. At Hereford all canons non-resident are summoned at the audit and to the installation of a prebendary. At Salisbury all canons non-resident are summoned on a bishop's visitation of the chapter, the election and enthronization of the bishop, and installation of the dean; at Lichfield, under the authority of royal and episcopal letters, on certain statutable occasions, such as concerning the prebends and commune, and the election of a divinity reader and chapter clerk, when the election by the residentiaries is not unanimous; at Exeter, for the election of a bishop and proctor for convocation, on the archbishop's mandate, and any statutable occasion; at Chichester, for the election of a bishop. At Bangor the dean issues his mandate for chapter fourteen days previous to all members of the chapter, who may vote by proxy or in person.

At Gloucester, by Act 36 Henry VIII., chapters were to be held fortnightly, and general chapters on Nov. 30 and on the eve of S. John Baptist. At Ely, by the statutes of 1566, on Nov. 25 and June 4, under penalty for absence of twenty shillings for the dean, and ten shillings by a canon. The chapter is represented by one half the entire number of canons; at Gloucester by one third; at Peterborough, non-residents are warned of chapter, but personal attendance is not required. At Durham there were to be fortnightly chapters, and general chapters July 20 and Nov. 20, when the dean and chapter were required to be present, under pain of losing the proceeds of their corps for the year. Two annual chapters are ordered in all the post-Reformational statutes. For these statutes see Cardwell, Doc. Ann., ii. 259.

Monastic Chapters in winter were held after Tierce, but after Prime in summer; at the sound of a bell rung by the prior, the monks assembled, walking two and two; and on entering the chapter-house, bowed towards a cross in the centre of the room, to the superior's chair, and to one another. The ordinary business comprised,—1, reading the martyrology; 2, announcement of the coming festivals; 3, prayer followed by reading the Rule, or on Sundays and feasts, a homily of the Fathers; 4, commemoration of the departed; 5, and living benefactors; 6, nomination of Hebdomadarii; 7, public confession of faults and judgment thereon, with discipline; and 8, once a year recital of charters. Strict silence was observed regarding capitular acts. (Martene de ant. Mon. rit. iv. c. v.) Before the collation (Ib. i. c. viii. Anecd. p. 1226) which consisted in reading devout books from the pulpit by the lector who had read in the refectory during the past week, followed by an exposition given by the superior; and after the maunday or washing the feet and hands on all Saturdays, the sacristan standing before the pulpit, near which two candles were burning, announced the hour, and the prior having beaten a stroke on the drum (tympanum) the convent proceeded to the refectory to drink the caritas, a measure of wine. On Cœna Domini a general absolution was given in chapter. (Ib. iv. 128.) A taper burned before the doors until a dead monk was buried. (P. 256.) A sermon was preached on Christmas Eve and on the first Monday in Lent. (Ib. xciii. 115.) The candidate for the cowl petitioned in chapter. A monk on recovery from sickness received absolution. Corporal punishment was administered, and an inventory taken in Lent of all the books of the library in it. The superior was elected here, and received the words of obedience from the convent; and before a general chapter and an election of a bishop or prior, the Mass of the Holy Ghost was said. A light was kept burning in the room after the bell rang for collation until the termination of matins.

The duty of residence, and the emoluments attached to it were confined to a portion of the whole body of canons; and non-residents were compelled by statute to pay a certain portion, a fifth, sixth, or seventh of the income of their prebends for the benefit of the resident canons. And from this cause arose the name of Residentiaries. The chapter was, however, still considered to comprehend all the canons, the right of being summoned to its meetings and of voting still remaining, but by degrees the residentiaries acquired the chief management of the capitular property and the enjoyment of the privileges and principal revenues of the Church. No person can be appointed canon until he has been six years complete in priests' orders, except in the case of a stall attached to a University office. (3 and 4 Vict. c. 113, § 27.) He takes his title from the prebend or corps, an endowment or revenue usually the tithes of some parish, a stipend or rent paid for his individual maintenance as distinguished from the communa or manors appropriated to maintain all the members of the foundation. A prebend was sometimes allotted to a dignitary who had thus a separate endowment of land or tithes. In the old cathedrals all the prebendaries appear to have enjoyed originally the same capitular rights and privileges, but in most cases the small body of residents acquired the greater part of these benefits for themselves. Their duties are now confined to attendance at the cathedral for the election of a bishop and of a proctor in Convocation, and for preaching in the cathedral, for which they receive in a few cases a small stipend. Reginald of Durham, speaking of Durham at the close of the 10th century, says, "Clerici (Lindisfarnenses) præbendas, de more canonicorum qui nunc dicuntur secularium, de ecclesiâ possidebant et exercitia monastica in officiis ecclesiasticis persolvebant." (c. xvi. p. 29.) And in the year 822 Ethelwald at Lichfield clericis sæcularibus certas prebendas consignavit, et Huictam, titulo Præpositi Canonicorum, præfecit. (A. S. i. 463.) R. de Clinton, 1128—48, augmented their number. (i. 434.) At Lincoln Remigius, 1070—92, Canonicos xxi. adhibuit datis præbendis et assignatis, cunctorum etiam altarium totius ecclesiæ oblationibus canonicis eisdem perpetua largitione concessis, after the constitution of Rouen. (Ibid. i. 415.) R. Bloet, 1092—1123, added twenty-one more, endowing or founding them. (Godwin, 232.) At Wells Bishop Robert, 1136—59, distinxit præbendas quæ fuerunt primitùs in communâ, ordinavit Decanum sub-decanum, Præcentorem succentorem, Thesaurarium et archidiaconum quem vocavit archiscolam in statutis. (A. S. i. 561.) See also Maillane, i. 434, iv. 449.

At Salisbury the bishop is prebendary of Potterne, and at Chichester Moleyns and Praty before installation as bishops were elected prebendaries. At Durham and Carlisle the bishop on ordinary occasions, such as evening services, occupies the dean's stall, as formerly at S. Paul's.

At Lincoln the bishop holds the prebend of Buckden. At Lichfield, of Eccleshall. In 1343 all the prebends at York were declared to be sacerdotal. At Bangor the præcentor, chancellor, and three canons held nihil prebends, i.e. unendowed and maintained by corrodies, pensions, and oblations; allowances to canons whose places were vacant were sold and converted into money.

At Lichfield there are 27 prebendaries. At Hereford, 24. At Exeter, 24 (1050;) Lincoln, 46; Salisbury, 32—53; at Chichester, 24: besides four Wiccamical prebends founded by Bishop Sherborne, 1520 and 1523. At Wells, 49; at S. Paul's, 39; at York there were 36, but 6 were dissolved at the Reformation—there are now 28. Abp. Thomas divided the lands of S. Peter's, York, into prebends, allotting to each canon a portion, so that they no longer lived in common; and establishing a resident chapter. Abp. Grey augmented the prebends in number, and Abp. Romaine instituted the last stall, both in the 13th century. Between this period certain prebends were attached to the dignities. At S. Asaph there are six prebends besides seven canons cursal, (curâ salutis, says Edwards,) who have a stipend of £6 per annum, two having also corps. The prebendaries have reserved rents and corps of impropriated tithes.

As a canonry, according to Innocentius, is much more honourable than a simple benefice, canons are styled clerks of the first degree, and other beneficed men clerks of the second degree. The canons even of a cathedral church have not properly a dignity. (DD in c. 11, c. vi. 1, 3.) But in a large sense as they are collateral to bishops they are men of great honour in the church, and thus they have a dignity, (Felin. in c. 28, x. 1, 29;) and if there be not a custom to the contrary, they have precedence of abbots and such other principal clergy in a cathedral church, and walk before them in all processions, because they are not divided from the bishop. (Ayliffe, Parergon, 139.)

Giles Bellamera says that the bishop has the sole collation to canonries and prebends. (Consens. 10, n. 58.) In England sometimes the crown, sometimes the bishop collates, and in some cathedrals the chapters, as long as a canon survives who was one previous to 1840, in the old foundations, choose their canons, but of common right in collegiate churches vacant prebends and canonries are disposed of by way of election and presentation made by the dean and chapter, and it belongs to the bishop to give institution hereunto, (Fed. de Sen. Cons. 34,) except there be a custom to the contrary. The number of canonries and prebends may be restrained by the bishop with consent of the chapter, if the rents and revenues are not sufficient to maintain the canons and prebendaries in a fit and convenient manner. (Ibid.) The right of election to all elective dignitaries in the church was confirmed by Statute of King John, 1215; Edw. II. Art. Cleri, 1315; 25 Edw. III. 1350, de provisionibus; 13 Rich. II. § 2, but repealed 25 Hen. VIII. c. 20, and 1 Eliz. c. 1. At Lincoln the dean was always collated to a prebend in order to become a residentiary, the præcentor and chancellor having their own prebends, and the sub-dean who always holds a prebend, constituting with him the lesser chapter; the dean of Wells was elected a residentiary and chose a brother out of the dignitaries or prebendaries having houses. Every residentiary canon has his own house now. At York and S. Asaph, there is only one residentiary house. At Exeter by Stat. of Bronescombe, 1268, residence of forty-six days was required in every quarter; in 1544 this was reduced to thirty-six days; in 1560 to thirty; and in 1712 to twenty-three days. All the canons have residences, as at Wells, Lichfield, S. Paul's, Salisbury, and S. David's. At Exeter in 1560 there were to be nine residentiaries. For two centuries the Crown had occasionally recommended its nominee; the bishop gave him a vacant prebend, and he was elected residentiary. At S. Paul's the same custom prevailed, and by 3 and 4 Vic. c. 113, § 24, the appointment of three canons there was vested in the Crown, like all deaneries of the old foundation, excepting Wales; but all residentiaryships at Chichester, Exeter, Hereford, Salisbury, Wells, York, Ripon, and Manchester, were to be in the diocesan's gift, § 25. At Hereford the prælector became residentiary; at Lichfield the prebendary who had a residentiary house given to him by the bishop was admitted residentiary. At Chichester and Exeter the dean and lesser chapter elected; and at York the dean appointed, but the first prebendary whom he saw after a vacancy had a right to claim the promotion. By Stat. of George III. the dean had the power of deliberating for three months before making his choice; by Stat. of William III. there were to be five residentiaries, —there are now four. Their nomination is in the archbishop. Formerly there was a major residence of twenty-six weeks and a minor residence of twenty-four weeks; the former was remitted by Statute of George III., and the latter changed to three months. At Seville the president of choir was the dean, in his absence the city prior; and in their absence, the next dignitary; or in the absence of dignitaries, the senior canon. A dignitary paid 2000 maravedis, if holding a canonry 800 maravedis, a canon 600 maravedis, and gave a cope and clasp to the fabric at installation. (Estatutos de Sevilla, p. 25, &c.) The new canon was to give a cope to the "fabric," at Treves in lieu of a banquet to the value of 100 grossi of Tours, (1310, Martene, Anecd. iv. 239;) £10 at Barcelona, (c. xxi. 1317, Ib. 611;) a processional cope at Urgel, 1287, (Villanueva, xi. 104;) canons who were absent as students or pilgrims were excused from fines, 1338, (Ib. 597, 604,) and no one was to occupy two prebendal houses. (1315, Ib. 619.) At Strasburg residence within the diocese for three months in the year was regarded as capitular residence. (Etat de l'Allem. i. 80.) At Constance a new canon had to wait five years before receiving the fruits of his prebend, (Ibid. 98;) and at Bamberg, was to attend the daily mass for two years under pain of losing his seniority. (Ib. 194.) The new residentiary (or Stagiarius, from stagia, a residence) at S. Paul's had to spend in his first year in entertainments between 1000 (as at York, Monasticon, iii. 166) and 700 marks. The consequence was in the 22nd year of Richard II. there were but two residentiaries, who absorbed all the revenues and did not give the statutable bread and beer common to the non-residentiaries, and the king directed the custom of Salisbury as regards residentiaries to be thenceforward followed under penalty of a payment of £4000. (Dugdale, 254.)

Archbishop Jean d'Avranches at Rouen, required the canons to wear black copes in church with a furred hood to protect them from the cold. They also wore the camail, a hood or domino lined with sheepskin behind and before; for the camail or cloth hood was worn in warm countries and the aumusse of sheepskin in cold climates; in the 15th century the hood was worn no longer on the head, but on the left shoulder like Graduates. It reached at first only to the knees, but at length was changed to white, edged with black, to distinguish canons from the blackhooded canons regular, and Benedictines, and again was exchanged for grey for canons, and red for chaplains. By statute, 1477, the new canon without his habit presented himself in chapter and requested the canon to admit him, exhibiting at the same time his letters of orders, promotion and capacity, with the collation. He then retired. After awhile he was recalled and prostrated himself at the president's feet, and putting on his habit took the prescribed oath, and was admitted to spiritual and temporal position by the delivery of the Gospels and two loaves. He was then led into the choir and installed by the president in the lower stall if not in holy orders, in the chaplain's stall if a subdeacon; but in the upper tier, if deacon or priest, in the seat allotted to his dignity or prebend. He was then received to the kiss of peace, and nominated two proctors to represent him in his absence, but had no voice or place in chapter unless at least in subdeacon's orders. In ancient times he presented himself in a violet habit like a bachelor's cope with a fur hood and a square cap.

Within two months after obtaining possession of his prebend a canon was to make a profession of faith before the bishop and chapter under pain of losing his revenue. (Scarf. ii. 129.) A single member of chapter can instal him (126) with the proper ceremonial (126:) he was to swear obedience to the statutes (129) then observed, and previously read over by him. (137.)

At Salerno the cardinal canons wear rochets and crimson tunicles, but violet in Lent, and then the hebdomadaries used black and red, and at other times red. (Græv. Ital. xxvi.) At Otranto the canons wore violet amesses edged with crimson silk, and the other priests black amesses with violet silk at the ends, (Ibid. xxvii.,) like the Vivanderii (clergy who received the vivenda or commons) of Palermo. Those who are curious in such matters may search with success for information about the choral habit in the pages of Grævius, and Villanueva, i. 33, 44. At Vienne (de Lievre de Can.

c. 26, p. 192,) it was in winter a black cope over a surplice, and in summer a surplice with a green almuce. The subalterns went bare-headed and in black amesses. At Chichester (1197) canons wore a surplice or rochet under the black cope without corsets and open (fissa) according to custom.

In England the choral habit of canons consisted of the almuce, or hood of grey, formerly worn on the head over the hood of the cope, and a close or sleeveless cope. (Canons 1222, § 30; 1237, § 14; 1268, § 5.) The vicars choral of Lichfield wore surplices with black copes and stoles. At Astley, S. Elizabeth's, Winchester, Stoke, the choral habit was also a surplice and black cope, with the grey amess. At Rieti there were formerly a chamberlain, œconomus and proctor. (Nandæus ap. Græv. Ital. Ant. xxx.) At Strasburg they wore red velvet lined with ermine, with boutonniers d'or, at Catania a rochet and monzetta of black cloth. Vicars in England wore a black amess, like those of Monteregale, or the ordinary canons of Mazzana, or the insigniti of Cefalu, but the Tertiarii of Messana had them of violet. At Syracuse the canons wear a black or violet amess, rochet and violet mozetta (Grævius Sic. ii. 649.) At Besançon they wear a mitre, cross, rochet and camail of blue silk, lined with red taffeta. (Etat d'Allem. ii. 182.) At Langadoc the amess was purple and the hood of lamb's fur. Canons wore at Setabis (Villanueva, i. 8,) the almuce de variis griseis sive dossis mucetas de pieles de arminos u otro color; at Valencia a white rochet with sleeves, a great cope with tails, a hood of violet with ermine in winter, and crimson armesino serico in summer, (Villanueva, i. 178, 32;) at Tortosa, 1414, a cloth cassock, or surplice and black cope, (V. 621;) and at Gerona, (xii. 164.) At Urgel the robes were red, (ix. 186.)

Martene says that the following words were to be read frequently by all canons, and they concisely state the original design of a cathedral. (De Ant. Rit. Eccl. i. 183, Ordo Paris. comp. i. c. viii. 8, p. 120.) "Canonici omnes in ecclesia perpetuo residere debent in obedientia, castitate, caritate, oratione, lectione, psalmodia, contemplatione, et sobrietate: aliqui eorum presbyteri aliqui diaconi aliqui subdiaconi semper existentes; ad altare Dei sacerdotes vicissim per septimanam ministrant, diaconis et subdiaconis pariter vicissim inservientibus. Hi communi consilio omnia ecclesiæ negotia tractant, et in victu eorum sit justa rerum distributio, ideò non debent abesse a sua ecclesia et in aliis locis degere, nec debent amare mundum nec cursum sæculi sequi, quoniam in eorum manibus tota ecclesia est posita ut in gratiâ Dei eam regant et gubernent." A canon who was to be of the age required for the orders in which his prebend was to be held, (Scarf. ii. 115,) on his election was to apply to the bishop for confirmation within three months. (Ceccoperius, iv. 104.) The prefix of canon is to be given to canons (i. 44.) At Syracuse, Naples, Orense, Ravenna,

Milan, and Compostella, the canons were called cardinals (Ibid. 45.) They were in turn to be hebdomadaries (Martene de ant. Rit. Eccl. i. 120,) were to hear the canons read daily in chapter (ii. 182,) and if tardy at divine service to lose their communa, (iii. 233.) They ought to be able to chant. (Ceccop. iv. 120.) A new canon must make a confession of faith before the bishop and chapter, (121;) and swear to observe the statutes as far as they are observed, (124,) and are lawful, (125.) This oath does not apply to statutes thereafter to be enacted, (127.)

The following prayers were used at the installation of a dignitary or canon at Paris:—

"Ecce quàm bonum.
"Memor esto Congregationis Tuæ quam possedisti ab initio.
*"Salvum fac servum Tuum Deus sperantem in Te.[1]
"Mitte ei Domine auxilium de sancto.
"Et de Syon tuere eum.
*"Nihil proficiat inimicus in eo.
"Et filius iniquitatis non appropinquet nocere ei.
"Domine Deus virtutum converte nos.
"Et ostende faciem Tuam.
*"Domine exaudi orationem nostram, et clamor noster ad Te veniat.
*"Dominus vobiscum, et cum spiritu tuo.
"Prætende, Domine, famulo Tuo dexteram cœlestis auxilii, ut Te toto corde perquirat, et quæ dignè postulat assequatur per Christum."

He was then sprinkled with holy water.

The statutes of the cathedrals of the old foundation, unlike those of the new foundation, which are codified under chapters, form a common law of usage founded on ancient ordinances, confirmed by the bishop, and old capitular statutes recorded as acts of chapter. At York these have been supplemented since the Reformation by a statute of Henry VIII., a statute of William III., and a statute of George III. At Chichester by statutes of Bishop Curteys, Harsnet, and others. At Wells by charter of 34 Elizabeth. At Lincoln the statutes were embodied before 1440, and with Bishop Alnwick's Award or Laudum constitute the code. At Exeter they were made by Bishop Bronescombe, 1268, and confirmed by Cardinal Othobon, the papal legate. Bishop Voysey in 1544 gave a complete digest of them. At Hereford the statutes were reformed by Queen Elizabeth, and by Charles I. in 1636. From these various documents I have made such extracts as will now appear in the following pages, having found them in various MSS. in London and the two Universities.

The 12th century was an age of non-residence. Richard of Devizes (De gestis Ricardi, c. 84, 85, comp. Fitz-Stephen, Vit. Tho. Cant.) describes the canons as building houses which they did not

[1] These suffrages marked with a * and Esto ei Domine turris fortitudinis a facie inimici were used at S. Paul's. The forms were identical. (Moleon, 250.)

occupy, spending their revenues where and how they pleased; hangers about the houses of great men; leaving their houses to be filled and their duties discharged by ill-paid vicars, and seeing their cathedral perhaps once in their lives. If absent for only one-third of a year the canons did not provide substitutes. To correct this flagitious neglect the commune system was introduced, the residents being paid an additional income in proportion to their attendance at Divine Service, with a distribution of the residue among them. The constant presence of some few at least of the capitular members was thus secured; but gradually and universally in the 14th century heavy expenses amounting to a prohibition and contrary to law, (Scarf. 149,) were laid upon those protesting residence, obstacles interposed, and non-residence encouraged in order to share a larger residue, until at length the Old Foundations either by private arrangement or formal statute, limited the residentiaries to the slènderest complement,—(at S. Paul's to four by Wolsey, owing to reduced revenues, at Chichester in 1574 to four, at Exeter in 1560 to nine, at Hereford in the 17th century to four,) and absorbed all the duties of the collective chapter so that the other prebendaries or canons non-resident were reduced to merely titular membership. The next step recently was in a period of great excitement to rob these titulars of their prebendal emoluments, and almost with a play of words it hung in the balance whether the abolished stalls of residentiaries and dignitaries were suspended or suppressed. At Berne (Mayer, iv. 433) the new residentiary had to contribute a cope to the fabric: and Archbishop Warham in Convocation, 1531, strongly reprobated the cost of entertainments imposed upon the residentiaries. Canons ought to reside nine months in the year, and two-thirds of their number at one time. (Scarf. iv. 148, i. 125.) The canons of Rouen paid fifteen livres for their cope, and in the fourteenth century their installation fees were ten livres, but in 1420 the latter were raised to fifteen livres, and the former to twenty livres. The dignitaries paid double. They also paid in 1612 twelve livres for a dignity without a prebend, and the dean gave double, while the canon with a prebend paid to the receiver forty livres, and to the messenger six livres; to the tabler, the distributor, the tavellion, and the choristers collectively, three livres each, and for wine for the dean twenty sols, and for bread for the choristers, five sols. If in the lower stall he paid a crown to the basformiers or inferior ministers, and the same if a subdeacon to the two chaplains at the mass of his reception. The great residence was for eight months in the year, each month estimated at twenty-eight days, in two terms between Michaelmas and Easter, and Easter and Michaelmas. The little residence was for fifteen days before or immediately after each term. By the greater residence he had a share in the gross receipts or commune of the chapter. The "manual" was delivered only to those actually present, and was increased by the forfeitures of absentees; and the residue was similarly divided at the end of the year. Canons sick or absent on chapter business were considered resident. Residentiaries' houses were of two kinds: 1, those of the chapter, and 2, those of the fabric. To the first, the canons, if in priests' orders, succeeded in rotation on the death or resignation of the last tenant; the second were leased to the highest bidder. Changes could only take place by licence of the chapter and under many restrictions. If a canon refused his option he must then wait his next turn, or the cession of the canon who took it. A prebendary could devise the produce of his prebend for one year after his decease. At Catania, two dignitaries and six canons attend weekly. At Malta, all canons attend on feast days, ten weekly, and one-third in summer: with twelve chaplains or sacellani. At Lyons, the chapter is divided into three corps, and each corps into three orders, the first corps of thirty-two canons called counts, is divided into dignitaries, hoteliers, and batcheliers. At Verdun, the canons were strictly bound to "assist at the Divine Office;" and the four juniors were to attend the choir service daily, but did so by deputy. (Causes Célèbres, viii. 345.) At Meissen, the Emperor claimed the right of nominating one canon by jus primarium precum. The oath of a canon at Bergen may be seen in Registr. præd. Episc. Bergen. p. 7.

A canon was to wear in all places the insignia of his rank, (Scarf. iii. 25;) in England now a broad scarf instead of the narrow stole; but was never to occupy the vacant stall of a dignitary, (142.) A canon who was a priest had precedence of even a senior canon in lesser orders, (66, 130.) In order to share the residue at the end of the year, A.D. 1242, at Wells, the canons were required to reside in the town either continuously or at intervals during half the year, and to receive the quotidian, A.D. 1351, to be present in choir, and not merely come for the day into the city and remain in their houses. Like the persons, officers, and dignitaries by Foxe's injunction, 1493, they were to be installed only by the dean or subdean, or in their absence by the president of chapter and chapter. Each was to pay regularly, A.D. 1241, to his vicar at least two marks, A.D. 1340. Residence, 1241, on their part was optional; if they came into residence they were, A.D. 1259, to keep six weeks and four days in each term consisting of thirteen weeks, and could not make up in a subsequent quarter the time they had missed in a previous term. There was, A.D. 1273, an audit of accompts on Jan. 2, April 1, July 1, and October 1, when the money due to each canon was announced, but if neither he nor his vicar attended the payment stood over till the end of the next quarter. If absent on chapter business, A.D. 1321, he received his emoluments. When intending residence, A.D. 1331, he was to protest before the chapter and "initium in esculentis et poculentis juxta facultates suas honorificè faciat procurari;" when resident he was to exhibit hospitality (onera ecclesiæ.) If he died between Annunciation and Michaelmas his estate received all the "fruits" sown within that period, A.D. 1252. Two weekly masses and the Psalter were said for the dead canons. At Lincoln a daily mass was said by the canons in succession, and a particular psalm by each individual. Two-thirds of a vacant prebend, 1242 and 1295, for one year devolved to the dean and chapter, and one-third to the estate of the last incumbent; the former was divided among the residents and vicars thirty days after his death by the escheator of the chapter, (Comp. Martene de Ant. Mon. Rit. iv. 251, 255, 259,) masses being said for him during this period. By the charter of Elizabeth, out of the forty-nine prebendaries not more than eight, nor less than six were to be elected residentiaries, the dean at his pleasure to be one of the number at Wells.

The old cathedrals had a common property from which the expenses of the fabric furniture and other necessary outgoings were defrayed, and from which the dean, resident dignitaries, and canons received a quotidian or daily portion according to their times of residence and regularity of attendance at Divine worship, the decanal share being twice that of a canon. Besides this communa the dean, dignitaries, and canons, had each a separate estate or prebend, from the produce of which they were expected to maintain a vicar. At Exeter the whole property was communa, and each canon, whether resident or not, received quarterly as his prebend 20*s.* and his vicar 5*s.*, the residue being divided quarterly among the residentiaries. At Salisbury all holders of prebends had to contribute to the communa which belonged exclusively to the residentiaries. Sometimes the estates belonging to the communa were farmed by individual canons, who paid an annual rent to the common account. The communa was divided into prebends at York by Archbishop Thomas I., when he founded the dignities, (Stubbs, 1708,) and by Bishop Robert of Lewes, at Wells, (Godwin, p. 363.) At Lichfield, Adelwald, c. 847, is said by Chesterfield (A. S. ii. 431,) but Bishop Peche (consecrated, 1117,) by others (Willis, 1, 425) to have established the prebends. At Wells previous to 1242, the bishop received on every day of presence, arrival or departure, as quotidian distribution of the commune 6*d.* and four white loaves, but after that date, 8*d.* and 5*d.* for bread, fruits, rents, or moneys arising from the lands assigned to the chapter in common, in contradistinction to the rest; out of which was allotted to every canon a portion by the name of a prebend. The five persons,—dean, præcentor, archdeacon, chancellor, and treasurer,—then received 8*d.* a day, with 4*d.* for bread in lieu of 6*d.*, two white loaves, and two of black bread; and all other canons received 4*d.* and 2*d.* for bread, instead of the former allowance of 3*d.*, one white and one black loaf, (Stat. Wellens.) Robert of

Lewes, 1136—74, first distinguished the prebends at Wells, which had previously formed a common fund, (A. S. 1. 561,) when he founded the dignities, subdeanery and subchantership. By charter, 1582, dignitaries were to be preferred to residentiaryships, (Phelps, 52,) and at Exeter the præcentor had a similar claim. At Exeter, under pain of forfeit, canons were to attend matins, prime, mass, or vespers, daily; if resident, they received the dividend of the quarter, and the quotidian of forty-six days. In 1282 only those present at high mass were to receive the wine quod ratione sequentiæ debetur. The canonical bread in 1266 was to be white of pure wheat and weighing 73*s.* and 4*d.* Immediately upon installation the canon received his commons, 12*d.* a day and three loaves, c. 1200. In 1387 they were to be warned of chapter, which if they did not attend they forfeited their commons, as they did if not present at matins or prime, or vespers and high mass, in their choral habit. The ordinary chapter was held after prime. At S. Paul's the Stagiarius might be absent for seventeen days in each quarter without loss of his quotidian or with the forfeiture during seven weeks in one quarter. In 1290 residence was defined to consist in attending mass or one of the hours daily. The chapter assigned the residentiary houses. At Chichester all the dignitaries had houses, and the bishop conferred houses on the residentiaries, (Reg. Storey, fo. 71,) as now still at Hereford. At Salisbury the commune was distributed only amongst the residents or those absent on chapter-business. At Lincoln residence was kept in two halves of the year for thirty-four weeks and four days continuously or at intervals. The præcentor, chancellor, treasurer, and subdean, were bound to residence. In 1596 a residentiary was allowed an absence of two hundred and sixty-one days yearly. In the time of Bishop Sutton the communa was raised from 8*d.* to 1*s.* a day. At a later period the chapter property was divided into six parts of £95. 17*s.*, to each residentiary, a portion, £56. 4*s.* 2*d.* being reserved for the fabric. The prebend of Corringham was annexed to the vicarage of Gainsborough by act of Parliament, 1704, and Bugden to Buckden vicarage 4 and 5 Annæ. The dean was usually prebendary of Welton Painshal. In 1218 canons non-residents, except two living with the bishop and students of theology, were to pay a seventh of their prebend to augment the commune of the residents, unless they resided continuously or at intervals one-third of the year, and paid 40*s.* a year as wages to their vicar, except prebendaries of S. Botolph, All Saints, c. sol. and lx. sol. excused for their poverty. By 3 and 4 Vict. c. 113, the archdeacon of Lincoln is the fourth residentiary but has no house. At York one portion equal to a canon's distribution was given to the fabric. By the statutes of Henry VIII., if there were two or three residentiaries, one at least must reside the whole year, the others for half the year; if four or six, then two; or if five, then three or two must be perpetually resident. In 1796, residence for two calendar months was required of a residentiary at Lichfield under pain of losing his share of the whole dividend. The commune before the Reformation was 12*d.* daily and 2*s.* on doubles. At Chichester, 1197, besides bread the canon received 12*d.* every Saturday on condition of having attended mass and vespers in his habit throughout the week, or of forfeit according to his absences. On the six feasts of highest dignity, 1232, he received 12*d.* instead of the wine which hitherto had been distributed in choir; and on other feasts of the first rank 6*d.* If when employed on chapter-business his expenses were paid out of the commune, he forfeited his quotidian. At S. Paul's in 1283 (Domesday, lii.) the commune of the year was £24. 6*s.* 7½*d.*, and for the quarter, £6. 1*s.* 7¾*d.*, the residentiaries in the several quarters had £9, £8, £10, £7, and the distribution for residence of one quarter was £13. 6*s.* 0½*d.*, two quarters, £1. 9*s.* 6½*d.*, three quarters, £2. 10*s.* 0¾*d.*, and for a year £2. 18*s.* 4½*d.* Each of the thirty canons had three loaves and thirty gallons of ale daily; three minor canons, a chaplain, and scriptor librorum, each two loaves and six gallons; nine canons and custos bracini one loaf and three gallons; and the sacristan one loaf for hosts, so that 40,463 loaves and 67,814 gallons were yearly consumed.

At Lichfield by Hacket's Statutes the general chapter was to be summoned only by royal diploma or episcopal mandate, for the election of a prælector, for the consideration of matters touching residentiaries and non-residents alike, and financial affairs of the commune or prebends. The citation was to be affixed to every stall twenty days before the meeting. The fine for non-attendance was 40*s.* The chapter of residentiaries was to be held after morning prayer on Fridays, and to be attended under penalty of 10*s.* One residentiary could suffice at the installation of a prebendary, admission to a canonical house, or to be vicar-choral or a benefice. Other chapters were to be summoned by the dean or a president (designated by the dean as *locum tenens*, or in default the senior residentiary,) and to be held and concluded between the end of matins and dinner-time. Their privileges were to instal prebendaries, admit to prebendal houses and choral vicarships, appoint officials and servants, visit all dwellers in the close, punish or remove vicars choral; exercise archidiaconal authority in the prebendal parishes, settle all disputes between capitular members; to regulate the treasury library and works, and inspect and audit the accounts.

Bishop Hacket says in his statutes that all the canons at first served in four courses, as the assistants, satellitii, of the four dignitaries, but that when they became secular in time, certain of the number, seven in all, including the dean, were admitted as residentiaries; but that Everton on account of the diminution in the revenues reduced them to five. The election of these was given to the dean and chapter, and in case of dispute, by Bishop Lloyd to a general chapter summoned after notice of twenty days. The dignitaries took precedence; and other residentiaries by seniority, but were to rank higher than all other canons. The new residentiary received a key to the great coffer, containing the chests of the common seal and hundred marks, letters patent and privileges of the church. The senior residentiary present acted as vice-dean and president in chapter. Each was to reside ninety days, under pain of a penalty of 5*s*. for every day of absence: but one might exchange duties with another, but could not at the same time be residentiary for himself and another. The courses were: 1, between the vigils of Michaelmas and the Circumcision; 2, those of the Circumcision and Ascension; 3, those of the Annunciation and S. John Baptist; 4, those of S. John Baptist and Michaelmas. Residence was to consist in attendance at matins and evensong, to assist the bishop and dean in the Holy Communion on Sundays and festivals, under penalty of 2*s*., and to attend chapter; before admission, he was to pay 100 marks to the use of the church; and after admission, to entertain canons or their deputies coming to preach; to entreat hospitably all clerks of the choir, and be liberal to the poor. The dean was to receive 16*s*. 8*d*., and each residentiary 8*s*. 4*d*. a week with shares in the dividend. The order in chapter was the bishop in the centre, with the dean, chancellor, and residentiaries on his right, and the præcentor and treasurer on his left, the other canons ranking by seniority. The residentiaries had no jurisdiction or authority over non-resident canons. By statute 1752, three non-residentiaries were added, one of the old foundation to reside two months, and one of the new foundation to reside during one month in each "course." In 1796 there were to be by act of Parliament six residentiaryships,—the 1st, the præcentorship and prebends of Itchington and Colwich; 2nd, chancellorship and prebends of Alrewas and Wreford; 3rd, treasurership and prebend of Sawley; 4th, prebend of Rinton and Prees; 5th, prebend of Offley and Flexton; 6th, prebend of Freeford, Hansacre, and Armitage: the prebends of Tervin and Stotfield being appropriated to the fabric fund.

At Hereford after collation the canon presented himself with the bishop's letters to the dean and chapter, and the dean or hebdomadary with the chapter led him into the chapter-house, and thence having said the Miserere and being clad in his canonical habit, in procession to the choir, where he was installed in his proper stall, and prayers said over him while in prostration. His place in chapter was afterwards assigned to him and the dean or hebdomadary invested him by the Text or Gospels for spirituals, and with bread for temporals. He then swore to observe the statutes, not to reveal chapter secrets, and not to suffer detraction at his table, and afterwards received the kiss of peace. His quotidian distribution consisted of bread, grain to make ale, and a penny for presence at mass. The prayer is as follows:

"Omnipotens sempiterne Deus, respice ad preces nostras et da huic famulo Tuo, qui Tui Nominis honore, in nostram hodiè fraternitatem convenit, fidem rectam, spem inconcussam, humilitatem veram, devotionem sanctam, caritatem perfectam, boni operis sedulitatem, et perseverantiam. Et concede ut sit in corde ejus simplex affectus, patientia fortis, religio munda et immaculata, consummatio irreprehensibilis ut viriliter currens in Tuum regnum obtineat fideliter introire per Christum Dominum nostrum. Amen."

All the prebendaries are summoned to attend an installation.

At Hereford there were three kinds of communia.

I. Parva communia, consisting of wheat, mixtill, and oats issuing from four manors, and of 20*s*. a year payable to every canon who had taken the statutable oaths.

II. Magna communia, or quotidian, consisting of wheat and pence payable to the residentiaries only, paid weekly or monthly, as might be most convenient to them. Twice in the year the stewards or bailiffs rendered their accounts of rents, perquisites, and oblations on the three first days of Whitsuntide, at Michaelmas, and Lady-day; and every canon who was to share in these funds, constituting the greater commune, was required to be personally present. The delivery of the wheat in seams from Mora and Maddeley was made according to turns, and in equal proportions or tallies. The forensic rents were payable on Annunciation and All Saints' day, and the Nativity of S. John Baptist, to residentiaries. The perquisites accruing at different times of the year were paid according to the period of residence, besides one mark at the Assumption and Nativity of the Blessed Virgin Mary, if these funds were adequate. The yearly pennies were raised from the four manors of the canons, perquisites, and tithes of the granges of Mora and Maddeley, oblations at the high altar, tithes of the bishop's mills; from the canons' lands at Eglitone and Hame, the canons' churches of S. Mary Magdalene, with the tithes of the fair, and Lydney, and three marks from Ledbury Hospital.

III. Quotidian, consisting of bread, grain for beer, and the mass pennies; the former being paid for appearance at matins, whether the canon was or was not a residentiary, except he succeeded to the prebend of a dead canon, who was presumed to retain it for a year and a day. The quotidian was not forfeited by absence of the dean, or by the canon if absent one night in the week, or if employed on chapter business, or if ill, or if let blood during three nights. The bailiffs received even if absent from matins; but the canon could not be away at night at Easter, on feasts of nine lections, or of three lections when the choir was ruled. The mass pennies, the Pentecostal oblations, and distributions at anniversaries and on S. Laurence's day, accrued only to residentiaries. A canon absent for study received the quotidian, which was furnished in kind or rents from various sources, prebends, churches, granges, and tithes.

The canon who was installed produced the bishop's letters of collation or mandate for admission; the dean or hebdomadary then led him (being in his canonical habit and present in chapter) with the psalm Miserere and in procession to the stall assigned to him in choir, and said a prayer over him in prostration. He then returned to the chapter-house, where his place was assigned to him, and he was invested by the dean or hebdomadary, by the text for spiritual goods, and for temporals by bread. He then took the oath on the Gospels, "I will henceforth be faithful to this church, and observe as I best may (pro viribus) its ancient and reasonable customs, and abide by its statutes." He then received the kiss of peace from all present. Certain customs and the principal statutes were then explained to him; the remainder were to be learned by experience. He did not receive the parva communia unless he took the oath in person. He might then offer residence or not at will. The statutes explained were—1, that he should not reveal chapter secrets; 2, that he should not reveal the name of a canon who had spoken ill of another, to the latter, although he might mention the subject of detraction; 3, that he would not suffer detraction of a canon to pass at his table; 4, that he would not sue for his commons through the superior (bishop); 5, that in questions affecting the commune he would abide by the decision of the chapter; 6, that if justice was not done by the dean and chapter in a case of dissension between two canons, appeal was to be made to the superior. Installation was made by the dean, or hebdomadary in his absence, and the chapter. If there was any scandalous report affecting a canon, the dean was to admonish him privately; for the second offence before two or three other canons; for the third offence in open chapter; and in an extreme case the dean and chapter delinquenti pœnam infligent.

The statutes of Hereford were altered by Archbishop Whitgift, who "corrected abuses and added what was wanting." (Lans. xxxvii. No. 20, c. 1583.) The principal points are the following: No one except in deacon's orders at least was to be admitted prebendary, nor, except of the degree of M.A., to receive the diary or petty commons. Before admission 40*s*. were to be paid to the library, and a caution put in for repairs of the prebendal house. No one was to be admitted to major residence except being M.A., at least, and a preacher, having a house and possessed of £40 a year of his own; nor if he had received the profits of any benefice in any cathedral or collegiate church during that year; nor unless he first preached four sermons, each one hour long, in the cathedral on four Sundays and holy days, and delivered four lectures in the chapter-house. In the major residence he was to provide a table during forty days, pay £5 to S. Ethelbert's hospital, 40 marks to the residentiaries, and £5 to the fabric. There were to be six residentiaries, each to reside six months at least (the bishop's prebendary during four months), and of these three months continuously, with an absence of only six days together. By the Laudable Customs sixteen weeks' absence yearly was allowed. He might yearly be absent on pilgrimage in England for three weeks; and once in his life, for seven weeks to visit S. Denys: or for sixteen weeks to visit Rome and Compostella, or eight weeks to visit S. Edmund's, Pontigny, or for one year at Jerusalem; and after three years' residence, might be absent for study during three years in the universities. Three canons were always to be ready to perform the duties. The canon who neglected to say prayers twice and celebrate once every year was fined 40s. The hebdomadary was the preacher of the week. [At Rouen he slept during the week in the sacristy. Moleon, 357.]

They have rotatory turns of preaching, and a vote at the election of a bishop. One is called the bishop's or golden prebendary, (so called like that of Leighton at Lincoln and of Mathry at S. David's,) having formerly acted as his confessor and diocesan penitentiary. By the Caroline statutes, 1636, thirteen weeks constituted residence, two months being kept together, with permission to be absent not more than thirty days together or at intervals, the duties of which were to be supplied by some other residentiary at his cost, two canons being always resident. In 1534 there were only six canons. One residentiary house is attached to the bishop's prebend, which was anciently held by his confessor. The bishop also confers four houses in his gift within the close, for the respective uses of the four residentiaries.

A canon, petticanon, and vicar going into the town was to take his servant, scholar, fellow, pupil, or some other decent person with him, and wear decent apparel with a tippet. (Inj. 1556, stat. 1583.) The senior in age or excellence, or a graduate of divinity was to be preferred, after the dean and bishop's prebendary. In 1636, in lieu of giving entertainments for forty days after admission, he was to provide a simple table for the poorer ministers of the church, and to pay five pounds of silver to S. Ethelbert's Hospital; and in lieu of 100 marks hitherto given, to pay £40 to the use of the residentiaries, and £5 to the fabric. There were to be only six residentiaries. The bishop's prebendary paid no entrance fee, but was to give £20 a year to the prælector, and kept only a residence of four months. All others kept a residence of six months together, with intermission of six days only. Three were to be always resident. All fruits of the prebend between Annunciation and Michaelmas, if a prebend became vacant in the interval, went to the heirs of the dead canon. (c. 3.) A residentiary was to be chosen librarian yearly, (c. 5,) and each was to be a celebrant once in the year, and twice to say the prayers in church. (c. 7.) Regent masters in arts were not to wear furred hoods, but silk linings, and to give up "linea fragmenta quibus quidem colla amiciunt."

At York a prebendary was capable of being collated to a canonry. Besides the rectorial estates appropriated with prebendal churches to each prebend, there were others held in common in reserve for the residentiaries and for the fabric, which was entitled to a share equal to that received by a residentiary. These estates were farmed by individual prebendaries, who paid an annual rent to the common account. Henry VIII. by statute enacted that the proceeds of the common estates should be equally divided among the residentiaries, and no longer let to farm as heretofore; he likewise corrected the irregular method of admission to residence, which was as follows: any prebendary might give notice to the dean, or in his absence to the senior residentiary, that he would appear on a certain day and protest his residence, on which he was admitted to the office, which he held for life, or so long as he maintained canonical residence. William III. reduced the number, including the dean, to five, and George III. permitted the dean to nominate a canon from the existing prebendaries; the patronage now is in the archbishop. There were two terms, the major and minor, the former being residence after protestation of twenty-six weeks, the latter of twenty-four weeks: the major was remitted, and the minor commuted for three months by George III. There is only one residentiary house, which is occupied in turn. The canons now receive stipends in lieu of their commuted estates from the Ecclesiastical Commissioners. The residentiary assists the dean in the government and duties of the church, the services, Holy Communion, and sermons, in the care of the fabric, the superintendence of the organist and choir, and the supervision and control of the music and services. In the absence of the dean he is president of the chapter. By statute 1221 the canonici simplices resided continuously a whole half year, or during one quarter in each six months, receiving each day 6*d.*, on feasts of nine lections 1*s.*, on doubles 2*s.*, being bound to attend at least mass and the chief canonical hours. Henry VIII. in 1542 required twenty-four weeks of residence, but released the canon from the customary entertainment given to the minor canons "in red mantles," four in their greater and two in their lesser residence. By Stat. 1238 the "residue" was distributed among the residentiaries on S. Martin's day and Pentecost.

The canon nominated by the archbishop was received by the chapter, by the book and bread invested by the dean and chapter, and installed on their mandate by the præcentor, having promised to observe the liberties and customs of the church, and not to reveal the secrets of the chapter. In 1365 the treasurer was installed per librum et morsum panis. A cope (or 20 marks) and a palfrey (or 10 marks) were paid at the acceptance, vacancy, cession, or change of a prebend. There were two residences, the winter beginning at Martinmas and the summer ending on All Saints' day. A canon intending the major residence waited on the dean, or in his absence the major, and said that he proposed to protest residence. He then on a fixed day after the "preciosa" in chapter and in his choral habit, protested and resided for twenty-six weeks, being present at every canonical hour except when blooded or ill, entertaining at table double the usual number of vicars and ministers; never sleeping out of the city for a night, nor being from his house after curfew, under pain of forfeiting all his previous residence. All this time he received no communia. Minor residence lasted during twenty-four weeks, and necessitated presence at all matins, vespers, and high masses, and specially on doubles. Twelve weeks at least were to be kept between Martinmas and Pentecost in the winter residence. In 1221 archdeacons, if also canons, resided through three months; simple canons kept half a year continuously, or a quarter in each half year. Every day they received 6*d.*, on feasts of nine lections 1*s.*, and on doubles 2*s.*, and were required to sleep in York, and attend matins, high mass, and the hours (a night's absence in a week, if of rare occurrence, was overlooked). On the days of arrival and departure they received the quotidian. The residue was divided among residents either at Martinmas or Pentecost. To have the communia canons must have resided half a year; those absent on study by Pope Honorius III.'s ordinance received their portion. For one year all rents and commons went to the dead prebendary's estate: if a canon resigned, one-third of the prebend for the year passed to the fabric. In the statutes of Wells it is said, in the fourteenth century, that in all the great churches priest-canons celebrated the solemn or major mass by weeks, the bishop only officiating on the principal feasts. (Comp. Martene, de Ant. Mon. Rit. iv. 66.) At Lichfield no "stationary canon" was to leave the city for three nights without the dean's leave. The residences were quarterly, at least five out of the twenty-five canons being resident together. At Exeter the canons wholly maintained the choristers at table. (Comp. Ann. of Burton, p. 280.) They might dispose by will of the proceeds of their prebends for one year after their death to any pious uses. They were not to detain their vicars from church. The duties of non-residents now consist only in the attendance of two of them at assizes and sessions, and preaching on Sunday afternoons. They are members of the great chapter which meets for the election of a bishop or convocation clerk, and to advise with the bishop. The right of election of a dean has only recently lapsed.

At S. Paul's a canon was to profess residence within a fortnight before Michaelmas, Christmas, Easter, or the Nativity of S. John Baptist, in the chapter-house, the residence to commence on one of those feasts. He was to maintain two clerks who were not already serving in the cathedral; to give three refections daily to two parvi canonici, two chaplains, four vicars, two boys of the almonry, the vergers and bell-ringers who woke him for matins, and received bread and ale and a livery from the kitchen for that service. Once in every quarter he gave a breakfast to the minors after matins, and at prime every day entertained the squires of canons (armigeros canonicorum stagiorum), and all qui chorum sequuntur. Every quarter he gave a special dinner (specialia communia) to the canons resident, and two great feasts at the beginning and ending on his residence, to which all the residentiaries, the canons in town, the bishop, the mayor, aldermen, justices, and majores curiæ were to be invited, in order to keep up good relations with the city; and on the morrow all the rest of the choir were to be invited. (Camb. MS. E. c. 5, 21, fol. lxxxv., and Rawlinson MS. 371.) Residence was not to count until one year after the late canon's death. The stationarius, if absent for study even for three years, was regarded as resident, and received 40*s*. a year for books; but if resident, and absent for a month, he lost 4*s*. of the 13*s*. due for the quarter, 5*s*. for absence of five weeks, and the whole quarter's stipend for any longer absence. (Tanner MS. 145, fo. 54—8.) The Bishop of London still appoints most of the preachers in S. Paul's, as the successors of the Paul's Cross lecturers; and at Norwich, till 1850, the bishop exercised the same power, as there had been an open-air preaching cross on the north of the cathedral.

At S. Paul's the canon nominated by the bishop presented his letter of collation to the dean and chapter, and their scribe read it. The form of admission by the dean was:

> "Nos admittimus te in canonicum et fratrem, et tradimus tibi regularis observantiæ formam in hoc volumine contentam pro cibo tuo spirituali: item tradimus tibi istum panem in refectionem tui corporalem."

The bread was given to the poor by the almoner. A canon deputed by the dean performed the act of installation, saying, "Dominus custodiat introitum tuum et exitum tuum ex hoc nunc et usque in sæculum." The new canon then said the LORD's Prayer, suffrages, and this collect:—

> "Deus . . . tribuas ei sic in hâc domo tuâ per veram charitatem cum fratribus conversari, ut post decursum præsentis vitæ stadium, Te donante, speratum incorruptibilis vitæ bravium comprehendat."

He was then told the psalm which he was to recite daily for benefactors: its title is still written up over the stall. He then in the chapter-house took the lowest place, and swore—1, to obey the dean and chapter; 2, to be faithful to S. Paul's; 3, to defend the rights and liberties of the Church; 4, to preserve the laudable customs of the Church; and 5, not to reveal chapter secrets. He was also bound to attend chapters, or to send a written excuse. He then said a mass for his predecessor. After any long absence, within three days after his return he was to visit the dean and his brethren. When another canon died, if a priest, he said ten masses in person or by deputy; if a deacon or subdeacon, ten psalms. He was then admitted to the kiss of charity in chapter, but if appointed to a dignity also, the dean said to him, "Friend, go up higher;" and he received a new place. Without a prebend, a dignitary did not enjoy full privileges. As often as his prebend was changed a fresh installation was required. The canons personally or by deputy were required by weeks to celebrate at the high altar, and took the oblations, deducting one-third for the deacon and subdeacon. In summer he wore white and in winter black in choir. For one year he was to learn his duties, and then to receive the fruits of his prebend, being ready to obey with alacrity when warned by the chancellor for reading, or for singing by the præcentor, or to rule the choir or assist the dean at mass on the greater festivals, when the canons ruled the choir at prime in antiphons and psalms, and began the hymns. They were not to enter choir after Gloria Patri of the first psalm; and on entering the choir were required to bow eastward to God and westward to the dean. They were not to smile, or talk, or laugh in choir; not to idle about in the nave during divine service. They wore black copes and surplices, and were to shave clean before officiating. If they misbehaved they were to stand in a place of penance appointed by the dean in choir. Two canons were always in residence.

The form in case of a dean was as follows. All the canons, summoned by letter or by citation affixed to their stalls, made the election. The dean was then led up while Te Deum was sung to the high altar, where he prostrated himself. The Lord's prayer was said, and the bishop added the suffrages, as in the case of a canon, and said,

> "Miserere, quæsumus, Domine, famulo Tuo et dirige eum secundum Tuam clementiam in viam salutis eternæ ut Te donante Tibi placita cupiat, et quæ Tibi placita sunt totâ dilectione perficiat per Christum Dominum nostrum."

If he was confirmed elsewhere, he was received with solemn procession at the church door, and led up to the high altar, and installed by the major present. The bishop or his deputy otherwise installed him, saying,

> "Dominus custodiat introitum tuum et exitum tuum, ex hoc nunc et usque in sæculum."

He then prostrated himself in his stall while this prayer was said:

"Dominus omnipotens, officiorum dispositor et honorum omnium distributor, qui ad gubernandas Ecclesias diversorum graduum dignitates institui voluisti, devotis mentibus Te suppliciter exoramus ut hunc famulum Tuum ad regimen decanatus hujus ecclesiæ deputatum, protectionis Tuæ gratiâ munire digneris, eique Spiritus Sanctus cœlestium charismatum divisor assistat, ut sicut doctor gentium Paulus instituit, proficiant ei honoris augmenta, ad incrementum meritorum, sit exemplum et forma justitiæ ad gubernandum fideliter ministerium sibi deputatum, sicque sibi commissos regere concedas ut cum vel omnibus regnum promereatur eternum, per Christum Dominum nostrum. Amen."

He was then led into the chapter-house and set in his place, and on the Gospels swore to preserve the approved use (morem), rights, and liberties of the Church; to maintain its ancient and laudable customs, and see they were maintained; to keep inviolate the Church goods and possessions, and recover what was alienated, as far as in him lay. He then received the oaths of obedience from majors and minors.

A residentiary or stagiarius, if resident also in any other cathedral, could not become residentiary of S. Paul's, where he was bound, by statute of 1290, to attend all the hours on principal feasts and solemn days, and on other days to attend (1) matins and lauds, or (2) vespers and compline, or (3) prime with preciosa in chapter, or (4) high mass, including chapters, and to bear the public burdens, duties, and labours of the church. If he required leave of absence, it was to be asked of the dean and chapter. In 1518 there were to be four residentiaries, appointed by consent of the dean and majority of the residentiaries. The new residentiary paid the income of his first residence to furnish ornaments to the church, and 200 marks, according to Pope Martin's ordinance. If no one came forward, one of the worthiest canons was to be desired, for the honour of God and the Church, to reside under pain of a fine. If residents quarrelled, the dean's decision was to be abided; if the dean and residents, then the bishop, as upon appeal in causes affecting prebendaries and persons. By Wolsey's statute the senior prebendary had the choice of residence. The residentiary of the quarter appointed to vacant chantries and benefices, but the dean had two turns. In cases of chapter, a minister was appointed and paid to summon resident canons by the dean's order; the absent were notified by their vicars and by a paper fixed on their stalls. The dean and "saner part" of the residents decided matters in chapter. Money arising from fines, perquisites of courts, legacies, burial fees, and sales of wood went to the treasury, but pittances and obits to the residents present. The quotidian was 13*d.* to each residentiary present in his habit at one of the four principal hours, by the chamberlain daily or weekly: 5*d.* additional was paid on the feasts of S. Paul, the whole quotidian for the year reaching about £20. If absent, the 12*d.* went to the residentiaries present, and 1*d.* to the informer. The quarterly distribution was £5 to those resident and attending one hour of the day: in case of absence the money fell to the treasury, and if non-resident during a whole quarter, the canon had to protest residence again, and if away for a year to pay 100 marks. Residence was protested in one of the following eves, of Nativity, Easter, S. John Baptist, and Michaelmas.

At Lichfield the best ornaments were used on days when the bishop, dean, or a canon was celebrant. The new canon exhibited the bishop's letters patent to the dean and chapter in chapter, and the dean or president admitted him, having put on his habit and taken the oaths of—1, defence of the rights and liberties of the Church; 2, concealment of chapter secrets; 3, observance of ancient, laudable, and other customs approved by the dean and chapter; 4, obedience to the dean and chapter. The præcentor or succentor then installed him, saying, "Dominus custodiat," &c. After the LORD's Prayer had been said he went into the chapter-house, and was led to his place, according to seniority, by the dean, who afterwards gave him corporal possession of his prebendal house. Every residentiary received daily 12*d.* on doubles. (The bishop and dean received double commons.) If he was absent for thirty days in any quarter, he lost the commons; but if not absent longer shared in the distribution at the year's end. Five canons, called chaplains, served in turn at the high altar on all doubles by the hebdomadary; if they could not officiate they nominated some "gravior persona." Their vicars were required to be priests, and their deacon and subdeacon at mass received 6*d.* For one year the fruits of his prebend went to a dead canon's estate. Each canon had his own light and book in choir. By stat. 1300, when he intended to reside, he gave forty days' previous notice of his intention at least, in person or by letter, before the course on which he would serve, to allow the dean and chapter, if circumstances required, to delay his coming; and no one was to be admitted who could not spend £40 a year, either of his own or "CHRIST's patrimony." On his first residence he was required to pay 100 marks, to be spent partly in ornaments for the church, and partly upon the fabric. By Butler's statute canons who would not submit their grievance to the decision of the dean and chapter, or the bishop, within two months, forfeited commons; and if they claimed them, incurred excommunication. By Halse's stat. a copy of the statutes was made for the use of all canons, resident or non-resident. A canon entering choir without his habit forfeited 4*d.* Bobenhall, Dorset P^a, Flinton, Rinton, Sandiacre, Tervin, Wellington, and Wolvey were archidiaconal prebends, because under episcopal and archidiaconal jurisdiction, and Breewood and Adbaston were decanal.

Forms of Prayer at Installation at Lichfield.

FOR A BISHOP.

A prayer before the throne, to be said by the præcentor or senior canon:

Oremus. Deus honorum omnium, Deus omnium dignitatum, quæ sacris gloriæ Tuæ famulantur ordinibus, huic famulo Tuo, quem throni hujus episcopalis præsulem et sacerdotem primatem, ac ecclesiæ Tuæ tutorem dedisti, et ad summi sacerdotii ministerium elegisti, hanc, quæsumus, Domine, gratiam largiaris ut cathedram episcopalem, ad regendam ecclesiam Tuam et plebem unitam ascendat, per Dominum nostrum Jesum Christum. Amen.

Here shall he be enthroned, and then shall be said,

Authoritate decani et capituli hujus ecclesiæ (mihi sufficienter in hac parte commissa et ex officio meo) assigno tibi, reverende Pater, istum thronum seu sedem episcopalem in choro Lichfieldiensi ad episcopum pertinentem, et in corporalem et realem possessionem ipsius episcopatus cum suis juribus et pertinentiis universis, te induco; Dominus custodiat introitum tuum et exitum tuum ex hoc nunc et usque in sæculum. Amen.

Then the Lord's Prayer and the Apostles' Creed shall be said, with these prayers following:

Omnipotens Deus, Pater Sancte, Deus Æterne, Tû omnem ordinem dignatus es in sedibus cœlestibus ordinare: in cœlo Domine in æternum manet Verbum Tuum, ubi angelos et archangelos suo quemque ordine constituisti, et modo veteris Testamenti privilegio Mosen et Aaron in sacerdotibus Tuis et Samuelem inter eos qui invocant Nomen Tuum, Patriarchas et Prophetas ad consulendum populo Tuo ordinâsti; et in Novo Testamento Filium Tuum Jesum Christum unxisti; et Apostolos Sanctos et Matthiam eorum consortem in apostolatum atque cathedram honoris evexisti: quæsumus, pro Tuâ immensâ misericordiâ, in nostris temporibus, da gratiam servo Tuo humillimo patri vero nostro in Te reverendo, ut, ad instar Sanctorum Tuorum Apostolorum in cathedrâ honoris et dignitatis sedentium in conspectu Majestatis Tuæ dignus honore appareat per eundem Dominum nostrum Jesum Christum. Amen.

Oremus.

Domine Jesu Christe, Tu præelegisti Apostolos Tuos ut doctrinâ suâ nobis præessent; Tu etiam vice Apostolorum hunc episcopum doctrinam docere et erudire digneris; et ut immaculatam vitam et illæsam conservet gratiâ fac Tuâ, qui vivis et regnas cum Patre et Spiritu Sancto, unus Deus in sæcula sæculorum. Amen.

Benedictio.

Populus te honoret, adjuvet te Deus; quicquid petieris præstet tibi Dominus; cum honore, cum castitate, cum scientia, cum largitate, cum charitate, cum humilitate dignus sis: justus sis, humilis sis, patiens sis, sincerus sis, Angelus Christi sis, accipe benedictionem quæ muniat te in die istâ et die futurâ; Angeli Dei te custodiant: ecclesia sit tua Mater; Deus Pater tuus; Apostoli exempla tua; confirmet te Deus in justitia et in sanctitate; pax tecum inseparabilis, per Redemptorem Dominum nostrum Jesum Christum. Amen.

Benedictio Dei omnipotentis, Patris, Filii, et Spiritûs Sancti, super te descendat et semper maneat. Amen.

Then shall begin the Te Deum, to be sung by the choir going to the chapter-house; and the hymn ended, the highest place of all in chapter, that is to say, the seat in the midst or centre, shall be assigned to him by the dean or principal canon present, who shall say,

Pater, accipe locum in capitulo Lichfeldiæ; Dominus custodiat introitum tuum et exitum tuum ex hoc nunc et usque in sæculum. Amen.

INSTALLATION OF A DEAN.

Before the beginning of Morning or Evening Prayer, all the canons present being met in the chapter-house, the Royal letters patent shall be read by the chapter clerk, and the principal canon shall administer this oath following to the dean elect:

Ego, N., decanus ecclesiæ Cathedralis Lichfeldiensis, in ecclesiâ eâdem residentiam per nonaginta dies continuam quotannis faciam; fidelis ero eidem ecclesiæ; secreta ipsius capituli non revelabo: statuta ejusdem et statuenda necnon antiquas approbatas et assuetas consuetudines cum ea vel eas scrivero observabo; omniaque jura et libertates ecclesiæ præfatæ contra universos pro posse meo servabo et defendam, mihique subjectos ut id facient instruam: possessiones ejusdem ecclesiæ injuste dispersas, facultatesque prave alienatas pro posse meo congregabo. Humilitatem et patientiam in memet ipso custodiam, et ad hoc custodiendum subjectos meos excitabo. sic me Deus adjuvet et hæc Sancta Dei Evangelia.

The præcentor, or in his absence the principal canon, shall lead up by the hand the dean to his stall in choir, viz., the first on the right hand of the western entrance; and in the midst of Divine Service, for which a convenient pause shall be interposed, shall thus say,

Authoritate sufficienti mihi in hac parte commissâ, assigno tibi, N., illuc stallum in choro ecclesiæ cathedralis Lichfeldiensis ad decanatum ejusdem pertinens, et te induco in corporalem possessionem ejusdem, cum suis juribus et pertinentiis universis. Dominus custodiat introitum tuum et exitum tuum ex hoc nunc et in sæcula sæculorum. Amen.

Sta in justitia et sanctitate, et retine locum a Deo tibi delegatum, sanctus Deus augeat tibi gratiam, dignetur nos hodie sine peccato custodire; miserere nostri Domine, miserere nostri; fiat misericordia Tua in nos, Domine, sicut speravimus in Te.

In Te Domine speravi, non confundar in æternum.
Salvum fac Domine servum Tuum,
Deus noster, sperantem in Te.
Esto ei, Domine, turris fortitudinis
A facie inimici.

Nihil proficiat inimicus in eum.
Et filius iniquitatis non accedat ad lædendum eum.
Memor esto congregationis Tuæ,
Quam possedisti ab initio.
Domine exaudi orationem nostram.
Et clamor noster ad Te veniat.

Oremus.

Pater noster, &c.

The dean shall add,

Sed libera, &c.

Then the præcentor, or he who does his office, shall say,

Deus cui omnes potestates et dignitates famulantur, da famulo Tuo prosperum suæ dignitatis effectum, Te semper timeat, Tibique jugiter placere contendat, per Christum Dominum nostrum. Amen.

Then shall the hebdomadary proceed to the end of the office for that day, and, after the Benediction, the choir shall begin Te Deum, and all shall go in procession to the chapter-house, where the president shall set him by the hand in the proper seat of the dean, viz., that next after the bishop on the right hand.

Authoritate hujus capituli assigno tibi locum hunc decanalem capitulo, et vocem primam in omnibus capitulis ejusdem.

OATH OF A RESIDENTIARY

[*who has paid his* 100 *marks as "entrance money," and will, after dignitaries, rank according to seniority of installation, but before all non-resident canons.*]

Ego, N., residentiam in ecclesiâ cathedrali Lichen. debitam juxta statuta ejusdem faciam, aut pœnam pro non residentia per statuta impositam non diffugiam, residentiarii loco et munere in eadem per tempus residentiæ meæ fideliter defungar, tam residentiariorum capitula quàm generalia, quod possim accersitus frequentabo; secreta eorundem celabo, nec reclamantis in aliquo negotio inibi tractando nomen revelabo; jura et libertates ecclesiæ dictæ defendam contra universos, ejusdemque bono et honori et diligenter studebo, et ea pro virili in omnibus promovebo. Sic me Deus adjuvet.

INSTALLATION OF A CANON.

During the time of Divine Service, morning or evening, being assembled in the chapter-house, and the letters patent of the bishop having been read, the dean or president shall administer the oath following to the canon, who shall put on his choral habit:

Ego, N., ero obediens et decano, et capitulo Lichen. in canonicis mandatis, jura et libertates ecclesiæ Lichfieldiensis defendam contra universos pro posse meo; statuta et statuenda et consuetudines antiquas et approbatas cum ea vel eas noverim, observabo; fidelis ero ecclesiæ Lichfieldiensi; secreta capituli non revelabo. Sic me Deus adjuvet, et hæc Sancta Dei Evangelia.

Then shall the canon put in a caution to keep his prebendal house in repair, &c., and the præcentor or succentor, before the end of Common Prayer, shall lead him up by the right hand to the stall assigned to his prebend, and say,

Authoritate sufficienter mihi in hac parte commissâ, assigno tibi istud stallum in choro ecclesiæ cathedralis Lichfieldiensis ad præbendam de N. ab antiquo pertinens et te induco in corporalem possessionem ipsius cum juribus suis et pertinentiis universis. Dominus custodiat introitum tuum et exitum tuum, ex hoc nunc et usque in sæculum. Amen.

Then shall all kneel and say the Lord's Prayer. After Common Prayer is ended, the dean or president shall assign to the new canon, being led in by the præcentor or succentor, his proper place in the chapter-house, and set him therein.

THE OATH OF A VICAR CHORAL.

Ego, N., fidelis ero ecclesiæ cathedrali Lichen.; servitium in eadem pro posse meo rationabili sustentabo; decano et capitulo obedientiam in canonicis mandatis exhibebo; statuta quoque ejusdem me meumve officium aliqualiter concernentia religiosè observabo. Sic me Deus adjuvet.

Then shall the dean command the succentor, or in his absence some other vicar, to lead the new vicar choral by the right hand to his stall, and set him therein, saying,

Authoritate decani (aut præsidentis) et capituli residentiariorum mihi in hac parte commissâ assigno tibi istud stallum vicarii choralis præbendæ de N. in choro dictæ ecclesiæ existens; teque in vicariam ejusdem stalli induco, cum suis juribus et pertinentiis universis; Deus custodiat introitum tuum et exitum tuum ex hoc nunc et usque in sæculum. Amen.

Pater noster, &c.

At Lichfield the form of installation is now—

Immediately before the First Lesson in the Morning Service, the dean or canon in residence and Mr. ——, with the subchanter or his deputy and the chapter clerk, go out of the choir at the west gate into the chapter-house.

Mr. —— will present to the dean or canon in residence the mandate, which being read by the chapter clerk, Mr. —— will put on his habit. He will then take the oaths of allegiance, supremacy, of simony, and of obedience, and subscribe to the Thirty-nine Articles and Declaration of Conformity.

The dean or canon in residence will then take him by the right hand, and deliver him to the subchanter or his deputy to be installed, saying,

In obedience to the mandate of the Lord Bishop of Lichfield just read, I deliver to you, the Reverend ——, clerk, ——, for the purpose of being installed into the stall belonging to the prebend of ——, founded in this cathedral church.

The parties will then return to the choir, and the subchanter or his deputy will take Mr. —— to the stall belonging to the prebend of —— in the cathedral, and, both standing, he will say,

By virtue of sufficient authority committed to me in this behalf, I assign you this stall in the cathedral church of Lichfield anciently belonging to the prebend of ——.

Then, setting him down in the stall, he will say,

I induct you into the real, actual, and corporal possession of the same, with all the rights, members, and appurtenances thereunto belonging; and GOD preserve you at this your entrance and at your going out, and even unto your life's end. Amen.

Then the subchanter or his deputy shall say, Let us pray, and, all kneeling, shall repeat the Lord's Prayer.

Mr. —— will then be left in his stall, and remain until the conclusion of the service, when all return to the chapter-house; the subchanter or his deputy certifies the installation, and the dean or canon in residence will then say,

I assign unto you a place and voice in the chapter, according to the seniority of your prebend.

The composition with the bishop touching the right and term of visitation is dated, at Lichfield, Sept. 27, 1427, (Tanner MS., clii. 5, b,) and at Salisbury, August 30, 1392, (Ib. cxliii. 35.) Residentiary houses were built at Lichfield, 1459—96. (A. S. i. 454.)

The installation at Exeter to a dignity or canonry is by order of the dean and chapter given in chapter, on the person appointed presenting the mandate of the bishop for that purpose. This is done in the chapter-house during the time of morning service, after the psalms, whereupon the chapter appoint two of the body installers, who thereon place the person to be installed in the proper stall in the choir, in somewhat this form of words:—By virtue of a mandate of the Lord Bishop of Exeter, we install you, A. B., into the dignity or canonry (as the case may be) founded in this cathedral church, and we assign you this stall in the choir. And then afterwards they assign to him the accustomed seat in the chapter.

At Exeter, according to Izaake, Bp. Brewer (c. 1236) instituted twenty-four prebends, each prebendary receiving £3. 12*s.* yearly for "bread and salt." The allowance was increased by Bp. Gauden in 1660 to £20. On March 28, 1663, Bp. Ward reduced the attendance of prebendaries to the times of the assizes and quarterly sessions, and their duties to preaching in turn on Sunday afternoons. The whole property was held in common, and each canon received always quarterly as his prebend, whether resident or not, 20*s.*, and each vicar, 5*s.* The residue was divided quarterly among the canons, according to the times wherein they had kept residence. Ecton says (p. 27) there were twenty-four prebendaries. In 1266 there were twenty-four canons who had not distinct prebends, each receiving six marks; the residue of the commune became quotidians, distributed amongst the residents, who bore onera ecclesiæ, the duties of hospitality, entertainment of vicars, and attendance at matins, high mass, prime, or vespers. A canon was to keep an honest household, with open doors for honest guests, but might interchange dinners and suppers with his brethren, except on feativals, great refections, and at sessions and assizes. He might be absent for study for two days in the week; but if absent on greater doubles forfeited the quotidian of 18*s*. Absence was permitted on the day of arrival, and on the score of illness, of chapter business, and discharging the duties of steward. A canon on admission paid £40, of which £24 was given to the vicars choral, 40*s*. to secondaries, 6*s*. 8*d*. to choristers, 6*s*. 8*d*. to the annuallers, and 56*s*. 8*d*. to the clerks of the chequer, at the rate of 40*d*. apiece. The residue went to the common use of the church. But no canon could be admitted residentiary unless one of the residentiary houses was vacant. (Rawlinson, MS. 63.)

At Exeter they were called simple canons and residentiaries, and after the year 1050 were twenty-four in number, all of whom were to be nominated as vacancies might occur by the bishop. After the lapse of some centuries the revenues were found insufficient for the maintenance of so large a number, and in consequence the bishop consented that it should be reduced to nine, including the dean, who were to be elected by the residentiaries out of the whole establishment of twenty-four, provided that preference should be given always to the præcentor, chancellor, and treasurer, who were to be absolutely nominated by the bishop. In 1219 Bishop Simon required the chapter to dine at a common table, with the steward as caterer. The internal officers or dignitaries were bound to keep a yearly residence of eight months. By the Custumal and Bishop Bronescombe's statutes the residence was fixed at forty-six days in each quarter; the other six months in the year were spent on their benefices or the chapter estates, which for many generations were farmed by the canons. In 1544 the quarterly residence was reduced to thirty-six days, for the purpose of allowing longer residence on their benefices; again, by Bishop Alley, in 1560, to thirty days, and by Bishop Blackhall, in 1712, to twenty-three days—three months in the whole, but so that two residentiaries should always be in residence. Residence originally implied presence "in mensâ quàm in choro," the former implying hospitality to "honourable guests" at festivals, the gentry at assizes and sessions, as well as general hospitality and the gift of food from their table to the secondaries and choristers, until a composition was made of a money payment in lieu, and the "obsequium familiare" given up. One night's respite weekly was allowed, but attendance at high mass, and at one of the hours, matins, prime, or vespers, was required. The canons choose their residentiary houses by seniority. Each canon received six marks as his prebend yearly, and a part of the quotidian or daily distribution, which was made out of the common stock or surplus revenue, after the payment of the prebends by the steward, if he was resident, and had attended at one of the chief canonical hours and high mass; being permitted, however, to have one night's indulgence or respite weekly. The distribution on ordinary days amounted to 1*s.*, on days when the choir was ruled to 15*d.*, and on doubles to 1*s.* 6*d.*, with canonical loaves. The surplus was divided on the last day of each quarter. A canon, when "bled," was allowed three nights' indulgence. He might bequeath his "common" for one year following his death to any legatee. If he did not appoint a vicar within a month after his installation, the dean supplied the vacancy. He was bound to bow to the dean in choir or in passing. In order to participate in the daily distribution he was to be a priest. He received wine allowance if he assisted at high mass. He forfeited a day's share in the distribution for every offence or absence, but was permitted to sleep without the city one night weekly. He was allowed to hold one farm. Bishop Grandison rebuked their want of hospitality, mean housekeeping, irregular and indevout attendance at church, and their habit of retiring before the service was ended. They wore a double almuce, of black material, lined with red or green sarcenet. All the rents of houses, lands, and churches were brought by the stewards or farmers of rents quarterly, who distributed to each canon 20*s.* and to each vicar 5*s.*, the residue being reserved for wheat, and the weekly allowance of diet, white bread and wine. They made a reserve fund out of the profits of lands and churches not set to farm, for necessary expenses, collectors' dues, and with the residue a distribution to the canons. Bishop Oldham suppressed the customary installation-feast given by each canon, and bestowed its estimated cost, £40, among the inferior ministers. No canon was to claim dilapidations. All burial fees above 1*s.* accrued to the canon whose vicar officiated. On Feb. 22, 1560, owing to the depression in the revenues, the number of canons was reduced to nine. There are now six, two stalls being attached to the archdeaconries of Exeter and Barnstaple.

At Salisbury, the chapter being assembled in the vestry of the cathedral church at the time appointed for the purpose, the dignitary or prebendary to be installed will exhibit to the dean or president of the chapter attending on the occasion the mandate from the bishop for his installation, which being then read by the chapter-clerk, the oaths of allegiance, supremacy, and dignitatum s. canonicorum are administered. The dean or president of chapter will then decree the said —— to be admitted to the dignity or prebend, and direct two of the vicars choral attending for the purpose to install the said —— into the stall assigned to the dignity or prebend, with its rights, members, and appurtenances thereunto belonging, in the Name of the FATHER, and of the SON, and of the HOLY GHOST, and to certify to the chapter then assembled their having done so. The dignitary or prebendary is then to be conducted by the vicars choral going on either side of him, and preceded by a verger, into the choir, who then install him in the manner directed, immediately before the Te Deum in the morning, or the Magnificat in the afternoon, which is to follow the ceremony. The vicars choral then return with the dignitary or prebendary to the chapter-house as before, and certify in form the installation in the manner before described. The dean or president of the chapter will then assign the said —— a place and a voice in the chapter. Then the following prayers are to be said by the dean or president of the chapter: Ps. cxxxiii., the LORD's Prayer, "Ostende nobis Domine misericordiam Tuam, et salutem Tuam da nobis," and instead of "Domine Deus," "Esto ei Domine Turris fortitudinis. R. A facie inimici." The other suffrages and the prayer are the same as at Wells. The installation now takes place during the chanting of the psalms; when it is over, the new dignitary or prebendary returns to the chapter-house, whilst the first lesson is being read in the cathedral. The service in the chapter-house is then concluded, and the whole chapter proceed to the choir, where the Te Deum or the Magnificat is forthwith commenced.

All canons at first were to be residentiary. From 1319 until the Reformation the law of obligatory residence was relaxed. The dean and twelve "residentiaries" and principal officers, who (as the statutes say) bore the heat and burden of the day, and in distinction to the dignitaries and the rest of the viri canonici prebendarii, were called residents, managed all the ordinary capitular business, and shared the communa amongst themselves. In 1340 their name was full canon and residentiary, and thirteen houses in 1447, including the deanery and two houses of the bishop, were attached to their stalls. In 1448 there were six, in 1468 seven, residentiaries. In 1500 and 1538, owing to the loss of oblations, there were only seven residentiaries, including the dean; in 1584 there were five houses besides the deanery, and another belonging to the bishop. In case of default of residence, they paid one-fifth of their prebend to the common fund; but from 1232 it was reduced to half of this sum. They received 40*s*. for residence in any quarter, with leave for twelve days. Thus the obligatory residence was at first modified for a time; then fifty-two were desired to reside in turns during the year, the same thirteen members always keeping residence, until at the Reformation the number was reduced to seven. In 1637 the dean's residence was fixed at one quarter, and two canons at a time out of the whole number were to reside during each of the other three quarters of the year. In 1672 one of the dignitaries, in turn, was to reside during one quarter.

On obtaining a prebend the canon paid an ounce of gold to the dean and 40*s*. to each canon, or one day's procuration: if he attended the bishop at a consecration or other office, he received a fee as his chaplain. On the death of a canon, two parts of his prebend for one year were paid to the other canons, and a third to the poor, with the oblations at his funeral except half the gold. The expenses of constant hospitality, and the entertainments they had to give on entering residence—which in 1385 amounted to invitations to the bishop for forty days, the dean for thirty days, and each canon for twenty days—deterred prebendaries from becoming residentiaries. Their duty was to act as the bishop's council against heresy and schism, preaching in the cathedral, hospitality, maintenance of the fabric, the charge of the lands, chapters, vicars, and choristers, the government of ministers and officials, and the ordering of Divine Worship. In 1637 residence was defined to imply attendance at matins and evensong in person; or, in case of sickness or lawful impediment, by proxy, to be indicated to the sub-communar for insertion in his list. The year, by stat. 1319, was divided into quarters, and certain prebendaries, consisting in each course of priests, deacons, and subdeacons, were required to reside together. They received the offerings at the consecration of their prebendal church or chapels on their prebend, and were bound, whether absent or resident, to find entertainment for one night to the dean or any canon travelling through their prebend. Queen Elizabeth, in her Injunctions, 1588, desired that not more than £20 should be required from any prebendary who would come into residence, being able to preach and to spend £40 yearly, and had "a convenient mansion-house." Any prebendary having £40 a year from his prebend was to rent a house in the close, and those who had not so much as that were to lodge in the city, under pain of forfeiture of 6*d*. on each default to the fabric fund. The residentiaries preached the morning sermon within the lower altar rails, but the prebendaries to whom Sundays were allotted preached in the afternoon in the nave.

At Salisbury (Constitutions of S. Osmund, 1096; confirmed, 1214; and re-affirmed, 1319) the canons were not to be excused from residence except to teach school, or service for the king's chapel, or of an archbishop or bishop, or for the common advantage of the church, or for residence on his prebend; and then he was allowed an absence of three parts of a year. The dignitaries received a double share of the communa. Canons, if convicted of disobedience, were to be degraded from their stall, and remain at the choir door behind the dean or among the choristers until they had done penance. The four personæ were always to be resident, and one-fourth of the whole number of canons in 1214. (MS. Harl. 6985, fo. 10, 11.) In 1091 two-thirds of a dead canon's prebend were to go to the canons' use, and one-third to the poor, for one year (fo. 8); but afterwards the entire prebend for one year might be devised by a dying canon (fo. 23), as at Barcelona, 1332. (Martene, Anecd. iv. 604.) In 1222, non-residentiaries were to pay one-fifth of their prebend to the residentiaries (fo. 28), who were to maintain constant residence for forty days in the year (fo. 28, b. 29), the archdeacon keeping only three weeks (fo. 22). In 1389 it was declared to be an ancient custom for the new residentiary, on his "entry," to entertain the bishop for forty days, the dean for thirty, and each canon for twenty days, a duty afterwards commuted for a sum of money. After the customary oath of obedience, the canon prostrated himself in choir while a psalm was sung: he then received the kiss of charity, was installed, and received 6*d.* for his commons of that day. By statute of Bishop Jewel, the non-resident canon who did not reside thirteen weeks in every year within the close, was, according to S. Osmund's constitution, to pay one-fifth of his prebend. The residents were reduced from fifty-three (the prebendary of Potterne being bound, in 1214, to residence) to twelve, and at length to six; and by statute, 1672, a residentiary might compound for non-residence of three months in the year by a payment of £15. The fine for residence, besides customary fees, was at first 40*s.* in 1319, but was raised to £105 for dignitaries, and £71. 13*s.* 4*d.* for canons by statute 1428, confirmed by P. Eugenius 1442. In addition, every resident for his first year received no commons which were bequeathed by his dead predecessor. The dean received an ounce of gold from each canon whom he installed, and could demand one day's plentiful entertainment for himself and his retinue from every canon by whose corps he should pass in any journey. The four dignitaries (1305) were always to be resident; one-fourth of the canons were to reside quarterly, under forfeit of one-third of their prebends, in four defined courses of canons, but might be absent twelve days in each term. (Tanner MS. 327, fo. 27, 29. A Vindication, &c., by the Dean of Sarum, ch. iii. § 6.)

At S. Paul's the suffrages are the same as at Salisbury, and the following prayer was prescribed (1300) in the installation of a dean (Tanner MS. cxlv. fo. 5):—

"Miserere quæsumus Domine famulo Tuo, et dirige eum secundum Tuam clementiam in viam salutis eternæ, ut Te donante Tibi placita cupiat et quæ Tibi placeant totâ dilectione per Christum perficiat."

At S. Paul's major canons kept perpetual residence, ministered at the altar, and each maintained his vicar. They were either priests, deacons, or subdeacons. They afterwards took the names of seculars and prebendaries, which led to non-residence; and then those who remained staunch to their duties undertook a solemn engagement to reside, and so were designated residentiaries, acting as delegates of the whole capitular body of prebendaries. The number of residentiaries was latterly reduced to four, "because of the slender patrimony of S. Paul's" (Dugd. 258); the dean afterwards, till a recent period, being counted as one.

At S. Paul's no prebendary on his admission to a stall was required to undertake a residence. It was a voluntary act followed by a very severe year of probation, accompanied by much outlay of money, at the end of which he became a Stagiarius, and in that capacity was overseer of the chamberlain and pantryman. The number of such residentiaries therefore fluctuated. In 1290 residence was defined to consist in attendance daily at mass or one of the canonical hours; the residentiary had a house assigned, he might be absent for seventeen days in each quarter without losing his share in the commune, and seven weeks in each quarter with forfeiture in proportion to his absence. Residence by usage consists in attendance at service, and preaching sermons on Sunday afternoons. There are three residentiary houses. Every prebendary coming into residence was to apprize the dean and chapter on the eve of Christmas, Easter, S. John Baptist, or S. Michael, of his intention; and this statute was confirmed 22 Rich. I., as there were only two canons resident. The residentiary was bound to announce at which of the hours he would be present on weekdays; and to attend at every service on Sundays, major and principal feasts: he received 13*d.* daily from the Chamberlain for attendance at either matins, or prime and chapter, or high mass, or vespers and compline, to be paid on Saturday: or forfeited in case of absence, 1*s.* to the canons present and 1*d.* to the officer who noted his absence. On S. Paul's day he received £5, so that the whole annual quotidian would amount to £20; besides this sum, if he had been present at one of the hours daily for two months continuously, in each summer and winter quarter, he received for each £5; for residence of two weeks after S. John Baptist, and for one week after Michaelmas he was paid as much for each, so that he might make an additional sum of £20.

The appointment to a prebend at Wells is by collation, and the form as follows, after the usual commencement:—

"I do collate thee to the prebend or canonry of ——, in the cathedral church of S. Andrew, in Wells, in the county of Somerset, now vacant by the —— the last prebendary or canon thereof, and to the donation and collation of the said ——, in full right belonging by reason of the bishopric. And I do rightly and canonically admit and institute you in and to the said prebend and canonry, and invest you with all and singular the rights, members, and appurtenances now belonging thereto, you having first, in my presence, made such oaths, declarations, &c., as are by law required in this behalf; and I do by these presents appoint and assign unto you the accustomed stall in the choir and place and voice in the chapter of the said cathedral church belonging to the said prebendary or canon, and hitherto usually assigned to the same, saving always to the said Lord Bishop and his successors, &c., &c., &c., episcopal rights, and the dignity and honour of the cathedral church of S. Andrew in Wells aforesaid. Given under my hand and seal, &c., &c."

In the case of installation simply, notice is given of the day when the prebendary intends to take his stall; then, at the beginning of divine service, the dean and canon in residence go with the prebendary to the chapter-room, where certain oaths are taken, and during the psalms the procession enters the choir, and the prebendary is conducted to his stall. The suffrages and prayer are the same as those already given as used at Paris.

At Wells, by Bishop Jocelyn's statutes, 1242, the four dignitaries were required to reside half the year, continuously or at intervals. For the rest of the residentiaries there was no precise rule. By charter 34 Eliz. not more than eight nor less than six residentiaries (including the dean, if he so pleased) were to be chosen out of the forty-nine prebendaries. Each canon has a house; the order of each residence of three months is settled by private arrangement.

At Lichfield the non-resident canons have a vote in chapter, by 37 Geo. III. c. 20. There were formerly four residentiary stadia of three months each; this, before the passing of the Act 4 and 5 Vict., had been curtailed to two months, but the former period has been now re-affirmed. Each has a house, and receives one-fourth of the corporate revenues. The duties are, attendance daily at the services, business of the church, hospitality to the canons, vicars, and farmers of the chapter estates, and liberality to the poor. These duties might be performed by proxy, and the service of the king, attendance at convocation or synod, imprisonment, inevitable detention, business of the church, or sickness, to be proved to the chapter, formed grounds of exemption. By the statutes of 1194 and 1260, one-fourth of the twenty-one canons were to be resident, five at a time together at the least, and to be present at the hours. Every day each residentiary received 1*s.*, on doubles 2*s.*, and on the Assumption, S. Chad's day, Christmas, and Easter, 10*s.*; the dean, like the bishop, receiving a double share of this quotidian. Every canon was to celebrate at the high altar with deacon and subdeacon, and if not a priest, to find a priest vicar. By stat. 1260 two canons were appointed annually on the Friday after Michaelmas to distribute, according to their terms of residence, the residue of that year among the residentiaries. By stat. 1300 canons were not bound to reside unless possessed of £40 a year clear income, [at York 1,000 marks, and at S. Paul's 700 or 800 marks.] Bishop Overton, owing to the poverty of the church, reduced the number of residentiaries to five instead of seven. The number eight was prescribed by 4 and 5 Anne c. 32, and six 37 Geo. III. c. 20. There are now four canonries, two of which are attached to the dignities of præcentor and chancellor, and a third to the Archdeacon of Derby.

Admitting a Dignitary or Prebendary at Chichester.

Upon receiving and reading the bishop's letter, the dignitary or prebendary is to be thus questioned:

Will you promise and swear to perform due fealty to the church of Chichester, obedience to the dean and chapter, and that you will observe the ancient and approved customs of this church?

He shall answer,

I promise.

Then shall be administered the oaths of allegiance, the Queen's supremacy, and denial of any simoniacal contract.

This done, the dean or residentiary is to deliver him a book, with the rule, and a loaf of common bread placed over it, saying,

I receive you to be a canon, and invest you in this office or dignity, or prebend of ——, by this book as to spirituals, and this bread as to temporals.

Being thus constituted, he shall say before the dean and brethren,

I swear that I will perform canonical obedience to the dean and chapter of this church, and their successors, and that I will rightly observe the statutes and ordinances, and approved decrees and customs of the said church, as well the ancient, as those newly set forth, so far as they affect me, and I am bound by law.

Then the bond is to be signed.

Here followeth the 133rd Psalm, to be sung or said.

Lord, have mercy upon us, &c.
The Lord's Prayer.
The proper suffrages.

Then shall the dean, or in his absence the residentiary, say,

Almighty and everlasting God, look graciously upon this Thy servant, and according to Thy mercy lead him in the way of everlasting life, that he, desiring those things which are acceptable in Thy sight, may daily proceed in all virtue and godliness of life, through Jesus Christ our Lord. Amen.

Prevent us, O Lord.

The new dignitary or prebendary shall proceed to the choir where a stall or place shall be assigned to him in the following form:

By virtue of this mandate of the Lord Bishop, I assign you a stall in this choir, and a place in the chapter due of old and of custom belonging to the prebend of ——.

Then shall be sung the Te Deum.

The form of protestation was as follows:—

In Dei Nomine, Amen. Coram vobis ven. viris, dec. et cap. . . . ecclesiæ cathedr. S. Trin. Cicestr. ego —— canonicus sive præbendarius præbendæ de . . . in eccl. cath. Cic. prædicta protestor et protestationem facio in his scriptis me jam primo et proximo corporalem residentiam facturum et eandem in festo . . . quod erit proximum post mortem naturalem liberam resignationem cessionem vel deprivationem cujuscunque residentiarii moderni in hac ecclesia cath. Cicestr. inceptarum, cum continuatione, juxta statuta ordinationes et laudabiles constitutiones hujus ecclesiæ in ea parte editas constitutas et observatas, promittens hic coram vobis venerabilibus viris me observaturum omnia et singula statuta ordinationes et laudabiles consuetudines hujus ecclesiæ cath. ritè et legitimè editas, constitutas, ac per canonicos residentiarios ejusdem ante hæc tempora observatas. Supplicans vestris residentiariis hujusmodi protestationem acceptare et admittere supplendo defectus si quos in eadem invenietis prout convenit.

This protestation was followed by the acts called ratification, consent, admission, and signing of the office of residentiary.

Lecta fuit hujusmodi protestatio per Dom. mag. . . . in dicta domo capitulari eccles. cath. Cicestr. coram ven. viris . . . unde dicti ven. viri eandem protestationem acceptarunt et admiserunt die et anno prædictis juxta tenorem et effectum ejusdem in præsentia mei . . . notarii publici suprascripti.

At Chichester four additional prebendaries were added to the original twenty-eight canons in 1523. The dignitaries were bound to nine months' residence in 1573. If their absence exceeded three months in the year, they forfeited their share in the quotidian. There is only one residentiary house, as at York, which is occupied in turn, the second residence having been given up to the principal of the theological college. The communia or maintenance included bread paid for out of the corn-rents derived from lands: in one year 12,496 loaves were baked, including 240 of thirty-two oz., and 120 cob-loaves each of twelve oz.; these were subsequently commuted for a money payment. Each canon admitted to residence paid £33. 6*s*. 8*d*. to the fabric fund. The right of calling a prebendary into residence rested with the dean and chapter at the first establishment; the incumbents upon their prebends or endowments were called into residence according to seniority.

At Chichester the nine priests said mass, the eight deacons read the lections, gospel, and epistle, and ten subdeacons carried the processional cross. A canon absent from the duty to which he was tabled was corrected by the dean in chapter (1247). He could not share in the commune unless present at vespers, at matins, or high mass in his habit in choir. The quotidian was 3*d*. a day, and 1*d*. for wine on great festivals. Residents divided the residue of the commune, those being regarded as residentiaries who resided the whole year, being absent only three weeks in every quarter, by permission of the dean or his vicegerent; but they might for their private convenience arrange their absences, so that the whole term should not exceed twelve weeks in a year. But in case of great worth by special grace half the portion due to full residence might be given to absentees who had not been away altogether six months. The residents also shared in the anniversaries, obits, legacies, and half of a dead canon's prebend for one year, and half a mark each at Easter. The only excuse for non-residence was teaching school, the service of the king's chapel, or the bishop or archbishop. A canon, if a priest, was to say thirty masses—if in minor orders ten psalters in the year—for a dead canon. In the night hours silk copes without embroidery were used, except on the eves of Christmas, Easter, Pentecost, and Trinity, or by order of the dean or other major ecclesiæ, to do honour to the bishop or other eminent person. In 1574 the number of residentiaries was reduced to four, owing to reduced funds. A canon who intended residence was to pay twenty-five marks to the fabric—meaning (Frances, xx. n. 48) the work and material structure, and also ornaments and necessaries for Divine worship—and twenty-five marks to the dean and chapter, and attend, for the first year, all the day and night-hours; and if absent from any one, to recommence his residence. Every day he was to entertain his vicar, two other vicars of choir, the porter, two sacrists, and one chorister; to entertain the dean and chapter and ministers of the church, and strangers of Sussex visiting Chichester. The canon on his institution swore, in chapter, to observe fidelity to the church, secresy with regard to chapter business, to observe the ancient and approved customs of the church.

At Lincoln (Stat. in Hist. Epist. Moraien. pp. 45—51) the residentiaries, the præcentor, chancellor, treasurer, and subdean, were required, in 1440, to reside thirty-four weeks and five days continuously or at intervals. The Archdeacon of Lincoln is now a permanent canon by Act 3 and 4 Vict. c. 113, in place of the treasurer, whose office became void in the time of Henry VIII. Before the Reformation there were at least six residentiaries elective; but since 1541 the subdean, who held the prebend of Welton Westhall, became the fourth of the four residentiaries whose stalls are fixed to their dignities. In 1439 the four personæ, three archdeacons, the subdean, and three canons were residentiary. It was then objected to the dean that he introduced, in lieu of a single verger, his friends and armed lay persons into chapters. Every canon was to maintain a chaplain, not being a vicar of choir, to attend him in choir. No one was to be admitted to the "lesser" who had not kept the "greater residence" during three years. Every non-residentiary canon, if his prebend was worth £4 a year, was to maintain a vicar. The chancellor, provost, and one residentiary kept the chapter-seal. Stoke prebend in the fifteenth century was attached to the chancellorship. Residentiaries were to be present during two-thirds of the year. Their duties comprise the superintendence of the services, the care and repairs of the fabric, inspection of the national schools, attendance twice daily at the services, and preaching on the days assigned to them. At the audit in September, since 1603, they select their residences (as at Chichester) according to seniority. In 1596 each canon was allowed an absence of two hundred and sixty-one days in the year. The fourth canon has no house.

Form of Installation of a Prebendary at Lincoln.

The canon shall present the mandate in the chapter-house, saying,

Dom. Decane vosque domini capitulares, præsento vobis literas mandatorias rev. dom. Episcopi, obnixè rogans ut juxta tenorem eorundem me in canonicatum et præbendam de ——, admittere installare et inducere dignemini cum favore.

He then shall give the mandate to the clerk of the chapter to read them; then the installer [the dean or in his absence the subdean or subdean's deputy, Reg. Episc. Morai. 45] *shall say,*

Literas rev. Patris Episcopi cum humili observantiâ acceptamus iisque statim debitum præstabimus obsequium, juramento de statutis hujus Ecclesiæ observandis per te priùs præstito.

The oath was as follows:—

Ego, canonicus hujus ecclesiæ cathedralis, B. M. Lincoln. et præbendarius præbendæ de ——, in eadem, juro, quòd decano ejusdem ecclesiæ ejusque successoribus obediens ero, et capitulo hujus ecclesiæ in licitis et canonicis mandatis; fidelis ero ecclesiæ huic Lincoln. et ejusdem capitulo; statuta consuetudines et ordinationes in novo registro conscriptas et alias legitimè editas vel edendas observabo; onera præbenda meæ incumbentiæ præsertim in solvendo septimas decano et capitulo debitas supportabo; et pro juribus istius ecclesiæ defensandis opem et operam præstabo efficaces. Secreta capituli quamdiu sint secreta celabo. Laudum s. arbitrium ven. quondam patris Gul. Alnewick, Ep. Linc., ac omnia in eo contenta, quantum in me erit, inviolabiliter observabo; nec personis quibusvis volentibus vel intentibus laudum illud violare vel infringere seu eidem contraire assistentiam consilium v. favorem dabo. Sic me Deus adjuvet et hæc Sancta Dei Evangelia.

The installer shall then invest him, saying,

In Dei Nomine, Amen. Nos decanus hujus ecclesiæ cath. una cum confratribus hisce meis te recipimus in fratrem et canonicum hujus ecclesiæ [here he takes him by his right hand] atque canonicatum et præbendarium de ——, omnibus suis juribus et pertinentiis admittimus et investimus. [*Here he shall give him the book of the Gospels.*] In Nomine Patris, Filii, et Spiritus Sancti. Amen.

Then the canon was led into the common chamber to seal the bond for the payment of sevenths to the dean and chapter, and of dues to the vicars and choristers, and preaching of a sermon on the appointed day. The installer and canons then received the canon at the door of the vestry, vested in his habit, and led him into the choir and placed him in his stall, the installer saying,

Dominus custodiat introitum tuum et exitum ex hoc nunc et usque in sæculum.

Nos te installimus, frater, in stallum præbendæ tuæ assignatum, inque realem actualem et corporalem possessionem ejusdem, cum suis juribus membris et pertinentiis universis inducimus cum effectu.

Pater noster.
Salvum fac servum Tuum,
R. Sperantem in Te, Deus.
Esto ei turris
R. A facie inimici.
Nihil proficiat inimicus in eo,
R. Et filius iniquitatis non apponat nocere ei.
Domine exaudi orationes nostras,
Et clamor noster veniat ad Te.
Dominus vobiscum,
R. Et cum spiritu tuo.

Oremus.

Deus omnium bonorum principium et finis, virtutum dator et meritorum benignissime largitor, obsecramus immensam Tuæ largitatis abundantiam, ut tribuas huic famulo Tuo, quem nostro dignatus es ascribi collegio, Tibi tam piè famulari, itaque in hac Domo Tuâ per veram charitatem cum fratribus suis conversari, ut post decursum præsentis vitæ stadium, Te donante, speratum incorruptibilis vitæ brabeion comprehendat, per Christum Dominum nostrum. Amen.

Then he said to the installed,

Respice titulos Psalmorum quos singulis diebus, impedimento cessante, recitare debes.

Then he was led into the chapter-house, and was received to the kiss of peace by the canons, in their order, on the right hand and on the left, the installer first saying,

Præstat ut in symbolum amicitiæ et fraternitatis tuæ admittamus ad osculum.

Meanwhile the vicars choral said the psalm antiphonally,

Ecce quam bonum.

Then the installer said,

Nos te recipimus, frater, ad locum et vocem in capitulo.

Oremus.

Actiones nostras, &c.
Gratia Domini, &c. (Cole MSS. xxxi. 184–5.)

Form to be used at the Enthronement of an Archbishop at York.[1]

A procession will be formed from the chapter-house to the west end of the nave, in the following order: proctors, clergy of the diocese, vergers, dean, residentiaries, canons, vicars choral, songmen, choristers.

On arrival at the west door the proctors and clergy will file off to the right and left, and form a passage for the cathedral clergy and choir to pass through.

The procession will then move up the nave in the following order (the choir chanting the 121st and 122nd Psalms): vergers, choristers, songmen, vicars choral, canons, residentiaries, dean, archbishop, chaplain, clergy of the diocese, and proctors, two and two.

The chapter pass within the altar rails, having conducted the archbishop to his chair.

The clergy pass to the seats on the altar steps.

The archbishop petitions and takes the usual oath administered by the registrar.

The president inducts the archbishop, and reads a schedule.

The Litany, with the prayers, is then chanted by the subchanter.

The canons conduct the archbishop to the throne; the president goes into the throne with the archbishop, again reads the schedule, and declares the enthronement completed.

The Te Deum is sung by the choir, after which the subchanter and choir chant the following suffrages:

O Lord, save Thy servant our bishop,
Who putteth his trust in Thee.
Send him help from Thy Holy Place;
And evermore mightily defend him.
Be unto him a strong Tower
From the face of the enemy.
O Lord, hear our prayer;
And let our cry come unto Thee.

After the suffrages will follow the prayer:

Almighty God, the Giver of all good things, Who by the Holy Spirit hast appointed divers orders of ministers in Thy Church, mercifully behold Thy servant, who is now admitted to the high office and dignity of Archbishop of this Province, and so replenish him with the truth of Thy doctrine, and adorn him with innocency of life, that, both by word and deed, he may faithfully serve Thee in this office, to the glory of Thy Name, and to the edifying and well governing of Thy Church. Grant, we beseech Thee, that he may long live happily to rule this Church, and that, having worthily fulfilled his course, at the latter day he may receive the crown of righteousness laid up by the Lord, the Righteous Judge, Who liveth and reigneth with the Father and the Holy Ghost, one God, world without end. Amen.

The Hallelujah Chorus.
The Blessing by the Archbishop.

At Salisbury two prebends were held by the abbeys of Sion and

[1] There are no special suffrages or prayers used at the installation of a dignitary or canon. For the form at Worcester, see Green's Worcester, ii. p. xxxvii.

Sherborne (Ecton, 515). At York two belonged to Nostell Priory (p. 663); at Wells two, in 1200, Long Sutton and Ilminster, were annexed to the abbots of Athelney and Michelney (Phelps, 43); one at Chichester, Wilmington, was held by the abbot of Grestein.

The Welsh cathedrals: At Bangor the chapter consisted of the dean, the archdeacon of Merioneth, the prebendary of Penmynydd and the treasurer; no residence is required, and there are no statutes. In 1561 there were three archdeacons, three dignitaries, and three canons. The members perform their duties according to a cycle prepared by themselves. By the new act there are to be four canonries, two of them annexed to the archdeaconries of Bangor and Anglesea, and of Merioneth. There is no residentiary house at Llandaff, as no residence was required. In 1218 and until the recent act, the bishop was dean, the archdeacon was subdean, and with the chancellor, treasurer, præcentor, and nine prebendaries, formed the chapter. All were non-resident. By acts of parliament and orders of Council there are now a dean and four canons, two of the stalls being annexed to the archdeaconries of Llandaff and Monmouth, the others are held by the chancellor and præcentor: residence is to be kept for three months, in a residentiary house to be occupied in turn. At S. Asaph there were no residentiary houses nor statutes. The chapter consisted of the dean, the archdeacon (since 1574 until recently the bishop) the three dignitaries, three prebendaries, and seven cursal canons. In future it will consist of a dean and four canons, two of the stalls are attached to the archdeaconries of S. Asaph and Montgomery: residence is kept for three months in a residentiary house which is occupied in turn. At S. David's canons were called canonici nati as forming the standing chapter. By the statutes of 1112 and 1224 there were twenty-two canons, including the bishop and four archdeacons; the number was augmented by the creation of præcentor, 1224; treasurer, 1259; chancellor, 1287; a subdean and subchanter, 1287; the three officers were always resident: the distinction between resident and non-resident canons dates from 1287; and in 1332 the archdeacons and beneficed canons were required to reside more than twenty-six weeks in the year. At the Reformation the chapter was restricted to the three dignitaries, and three residentiary canons chosen from the archdeacons or prebendaries. There were then four archdeacons, and eight prebendaries, and eight cursal canons, all formerly were cursal, so called from the cycle by which the canons took their tithes by a rotatory system of allotment. Residence became neglected, and one canon was paid to reside for the rest until 1822, when each canon was required to reside two months in the year. The chapter now consists of a dean and four canons, three of the stalls are annexed to the chancellorship and treasurership, and the archdeaconry of Brecon, each having a house. Residence is kept by preaching and living within the precinct for two months. Canons hold the offices of Proctor Communar and Master of the Fabric.

In Ireland the system of residentiaries never prevailed, although traces of it may be found at S. Patrick's, Armagh, Kilkenny, Cork, Limerick, and Waterford.

The cathedrals of the New Foundation had a corporate property from which were paid the statutable stipends of dean, canons, minor canons, other members, all the expenses of the fabric, and other outgoings.

The following form is used in cathedrals of the new foundation: The ceremony of institution having taken place before the bishop in person, and in his own house, the dean or canon robes in the vestry before Divine Service, and is attended by his proper verger (mandate in hand) and the chief officiating priest to his stall after the Second Lesson. The mandate is then read, and the oath out of the statutes is administered; after which the priest who installs descends from his seat, and takes the new dean or canon by the right hand, and pronounces certain words of installation while assigning to the new dignitary the seat which he is henceforth to occupy. The document containing the above particulars is afterwards signed in the vestry by the officiating priests who attend the dean or canon to the residentiary-house, and give him lawful possession of the same. The corpus prebendæ in these cathedrals means the dividend.

The arrangement of officiating was as follows: the dean on principal feasts, the subdean on greater doubles, and the canons on other feasts in their order; the bishop when he pleased. Each canon was to keep four servants, and preach four sermons.

In the matter of residence it must be observed that there were four kinds. I. Statutable residence by a canon throughout the year, with a holiday varying between eighty and ninety days, for the purpose of visiting his benefice or on private business: with absence by exemption under circumstances already mentioned under the head of dean. II. Statutable residence of a term of (generally) twenty or twenty-one days continually. III. Ordinary residence required by by-laws. And IV. Legal residence of three months required by act 3 and 4 Vict. By the Council of London, 1597, c. iii., prebendaries were not to absent themselves beyond the necessary time from their cures on the plea of their cathedral duties. At Ely (1666) the canon was to be corrected by the dean, but on his third offence by the bishop; he was paid by the receiver £5 (by Eliz. stat. 1541, £7. 16*s.* 8*d.*) quarterly, he had eighty days' leave of absence, (by Eliz. stat.) all but the fourteen days' statutable residence in every quarter. His share in the quotidian was 3*s.* 4*d.* daily, to be forfeited by absence. For omission to preach on three Sundays in his month of residence he was fined 10*s.* He was allowed to commute his statutable residence by attendance at the two daily services and preaching on Sunday by a yearly residence of fifty days continuously. One canon was always to be in residence: a house is attached to each stall and kept in repair by the chapter-funds. At Winchester the canon was required to reside ninety days at least, of which twenty-one must be continuous, one-fourth of their number to be always resident. At Bristol the canons by custom confirmed by Queen Anne divided the terms of residence among themselves. Each has a house. At Carlisle a canon was to preach in person or by deputy four times yearly in English to the people: to officiate on all major doubles: to receive a quotidian of 10*d.* for attendance at matins and mass or vespers, and on days of statutable absence. His statutable residence was for twenty days together, and if kept, entitled him to a share in the common dividend. Canons were required to be in residence the whole year with the exception of eighty days; as in the dean's case (and at Chester) they were allowed absence of one day of preaching within fifteen miles, or of two days if at a distance over fifteen and less than twenty-four miles from Carlisle. One third of the whole number was always to be resident. Absence from either the June or November chapter subjects him to the loss of attendance-money, £15. Every canon has a house and preaches on Sundays when resident. At Chester canons are to preach four sermons in English, one in each quarter, in the cathedral: to officiate on all doubles: to be present at the November chapter or to lose the entire amount of their prebend: to attend the daily services under pain of a "perdition" of 8*d.*, the amount of their quotidian. They were allowed eighty days' absence in the year. One third of their number —two canons—was to be resident. The residentiary house is occupied in turns. At Gloucester the canons might have eighty days' absence, and absence for preaching as in other cathedrals: one-third of their number was to be resident under pain of losing their dividends and the money due to the corps of each prebend. Twenty-one days continuously kept constituted residence, and entitled them to a quotidian of 8*d.* By various chapters' resolutions approved by the bishop and confirmed by the king, 1750 and 1785, each canon signified to the chapter-clerk on June 23, in the year preceding the term of residence, that he was about to keep a residence of two months, one of six terms beginning in October, into which the year was divided; the choice being made in order of seniority; for every day's absence he forfeited 10*s.*, to be reserved by the treasurer for the fabric fund in case his proxy did not appear to receive it; he was also to signify to the præcentor his entrance on residence for twenty-one days continuously, and attending at least one daily service. Every canon has a house. At Norwich by the statute of James I. and charter of Edward VI. the residence was fixed at five months; reduced by Charles I. to one hundred and twenty-two days, and by letter of Charles II., 1674, fixed at two months' close attendance at the two daily services. A house is annexed to every stall. At Peterborough by stat. 1541, the canons were bound to constant residence with dispensation for half the year: one half of their number always to be resident: the residence was until 3 and 4 Vict. c. 113, reduced to two months. Each canon has a house. At Rochester, a canon was required to reside two months, with attendance at one daily service, under fine of losing 10*s.* daily: after the first twenty-one days of residence a canon might be absent one day in each week. A house is attached to each stall. At Worcester, the canon resided two months, two being always resident together. Each stall has a house. He might be absent eighty days in the year: his statutable stipend was £7. 16*s.* 8*d.*, and 8*d.* daily for attendance at matins, high mass, or vespers. To be considered a residentiary he was to reside twenty-one days together in the year and maintain a household. The dean received double of a canon's share in the dividend at Peterborough. The canons were allowed to preach within fifteen miles, and be absent one day or during two days if within twenty-four miles; but they were each to preach four times a year in the cathedral.

At Ely and Durham exceptionally the dean and canons held each a portion of property annexed to their separate stalls. By the statutes of Henry VIII. the canon was required to maintain a house and establishment with hospitality; if he was not possessed of more than £40 private income over his prebend, he might diet at the dean's or another canon's table; but several thus clubbing together to form a mess were to reckon only as one person in the share of the daily distribution, or at the minor canons' common table. A fine was levied on want of hospitality. The prebend or corps was usually worth £7. 17*s.* 8*d.* (at Durham, £8. 4*s.* 9½*d.*) a year: and the share in the daily distribution or quotidian, 8*d.* (at Durham, 16½*d.*) which was forfeited by non-residence. Residence was defined by an attendance of twenty-four, sometimes twenty-one days together, at Divine Service and maintenance of house-keeping. The treasurer distributed the fines, so that the dean should receive double a canon's share. At Gloucester, Rochester, (by stat. 1542,) &c., he was to be present at matins and mass, or vespers daily, under fine of 8*d.*: he had a holiday of eighty days in the year: he was to preach four sermons in the year, and to celebrate on the lesser doubles: but was excused for absence if preaching within twenty-four miles of the city. Three parts of the whole body of canons were to be resident. At Gloucester he was to signify his intention to reside in chapter, which was registered by the notary. At Durham (by stat. 1556) the canon coming to reside was to produce in chapter the bishop's presentation, and then was admitted by the ceremonial of the delivery of a white loaf (which was given to the poor) upon the statutes: he was then installed by the dean or præcentor, and on his return to the chapter-house took the oaths. He was to preach four times yearly in the cathedral, and twice in the year out of it. He was to officiate on all festivals, to be present at the general chapters, July 25, and Nov. 20, and constantly to advise with the dean on the management of the property and the general government of the church. His quotidian was 16½*d.*, which was granted for every day of absence beyond eighty days in the year. The dividend of the communa was made at Michaelmas. The residentiary was required to entertain once yearly the choir, besides showing hospitality to strangers and citizens. Notice of the commencement of residence, which was to consist of twenty-one days kept continuously, was to be entered in the registry. Those who resided throughout the year were to entertain the choir twice, and the bedesmen at various times. This custom has been commuted for a money payment. The new canon succeeded to his predecessor's house. If he preached within twelve miles of the city he had one day's absence, if within double that distance leave for two days; but never more than three days. A third part of the canons were to be resident. Each had his corps in lands or farms, besides a share in the product of woods, mines, quarries, and tithes, a reserve being made for the necessaries of the church. Two canons now are always in residence, they compose the weekly chapters, officiate on Sundays and festivals, and attend at least one daily service. Each more recently observed the three appointed weeks of "statutable residence," residing, officiating, and giving alms; and an "ordinary residence" of seventy days by the by-laws; being subject to forfeits to be paid to the canon who supplied their absence. Each now keeps three months of "legal residence" and has a house.

At Canterbury (by Laudian stat.) the statutable residence was ninety days, twenty-one to be kept continuously; on their expiration he was to repair forthwith to his benefice: one-fourth of the canons were to be resident. At Ripon the chapter consisted of a dean, subdean, and six prebendaries, including the præcentor and two residentiaries: by charter 1604 there were only five prebendaries, and now there are only four canons; the dean, and two canons form a chapter: the canon has to reside in the residentiary house during three months; and preaches on Sunday mornings not allotted to the dean: they choose their term of residence, according to seniority. At Manchester the residence was perpetual, with the exception of eighty days in the year, under pain of forfeiture of a fixed sum of money daily to the bursar, to be distributed to the poor. Houses for residence are now rented for the canons, who each will have an incumbency in the parish of Manchester allotted to him,—these are, S. George's, Hulme, £350; S. Andrew's, Manchester, £120; and S. Matthew's, Manchester, and S. Philip's, Salford, each £200 yearly.

At the Reformation five out of six stalls at Norwich, at Durham five, at Canterbury eight out of twelve, at Worcester five out of ten, and at Gloucester two out of six, were filled by late monks: and at Rochester four were retained in inferior offices. Certain stalls are annexed to offices: at Durham to the Professorships of Greek and Divinity by Act 3 and 4 Vict. At Ely, to the Regius Professorships of Hebrew and Greek at Cambridge by 3 and 4 Vict. At Gloucester to the Mastership of Pembroke College, Oxford, by Act 12 Anne, stat. 2, c. 6. At Norwich to the Mastership of S. Catherine's College, Cambridge, by 12 Anne, stat. 2, c. 6. At Rochester to the Provostship of Oriel College, Oxford, by the same statute: and formerly at S. David's to the Principalship of Jesus College. At Christchurch, where there are neither statutes nor a fixed rule for residence, to the Regius Professorships of Hebrew, by Charles I., 1630; Divinity, by James I., in 1605; Pastoral Theology, and Ecclesiastical History; and the Margaret Professorship of Divinity in the University of Oxford, formerly held with a canonry at Worcester by letters patent dated July 5, 1628, till 1853. Their only diocesan function consists in electing the bishop; the see having been moved to the cathedral in 1546 after the foundation of the college. The earliest annexation of a stall to an archdeaconry occurs at Rochester by patent of Charles II. Queen Mary, in 1555, resigned the patronage of the stalls at Durham and Peterborough to the bishops. Since the act of 1840 stalls have been suppressed in the following number. At Wells, Exeter, and Salisbury, two; at Hereford and S. David's one; four being preserved. The bishop of Winchester in Parliament in 1859 said that 204 residentiaryships had been reduced to 72, and 340 non-residentiaryships to 317, so that the entire number was reduced to 150, and half their revenues lost. (Hansard, lv. 991.) There were 104 canons left with an income ranging from £300. (Ibid. 1011.) The act 3 and 4. Vict. provided for the suspension of 65 canonries residentiary, and 360 prebendal stalls; and 300 vacant stalls were calculated to furnish £78,000 a year.

Out of the existing 134 stalls the crown has the patronage of 27 stalls (Worcester, 4; Westminster, 6; Oxford, 7; Canterbury, 3; and S. Paul's, 3); the Lord Chancellor, of 12 (Gloucester, Bristol, Norwich, and Rochester); the bishops, of 90; the University of Cambridge of 2 (at Ely); and Oriel and Pembroke Colleges, Oxford, and Catherine College, Cambridge, of 3. By 3 and 4 Vict. c. 113, stalls have been suppressed in the following proportions. At Canterbury and Durham, Worcester and Winchester, six; at Ely, Exeter, Gloucester, Bristol, Norwich, Peterborough and Rochester, two. At Chichester and Manchester the dean and chapter elect residentiaries. The suspended stalls may be restored by an endowment of £200 a year. But there is no definition wherein residence consists.

The bishops may in the fifteen New Foundations nominate honorary canons, who may be called upon to take duty in the cathedral, to the number of twenty-four. They are not to be considered cathedral preferment, and there is no obligation on the bishop to fill up vacancies. (3 and 4 Vict. c. 113, s. 23; 4 and 5 Vict. c. 39, s. 2, 3.) They now preach, and occasionally supply the place of residentiaries. In the scandalous abuses and low estate which befell the Church in the time of Elizabeth laymen were installed at York, at Salisbury one and at Norwich two serving men were prebendaries: James I. also confiscated a stall at Salisbury to endow a lay professorship at Oxford.

By the present law the proceeds of a vacant canonry devolve on the dean and chapter; but if the late canon was a corporation sole, they fall to his successor. A statute to bind successors only is invalid, but a chapter can make by-laws; and the bishop can enforce a proper performance of church duties on their part. A majority of existing canons constitutes a chapter (4 and 5 Vict. c. 39, § 16); and, by a preposterous infraction of precedent, three residentiaries can be appointed at S. Paul's without the old qualification of a prebend (Ibid. § 5); and by 1 and 2 Vict. c. 108, the canons of Exeter were forbidden to elect a new residentiary; and by 3 and 4 Vict. c. 113, § 1, all residentiaries were to be called canons.

The following account of the constitution of a Scottish cathedral, 1489, will form an interesting supplement to this chapter, and I will only add the hope that once more, under God's good providence, the Scotch Church may see it revived conformably with the reformed ritual in every diocese. On the side of the dean sat as canon priests, the subdean (hebdomadary) a canon hebdomadary, the bishop; a canon hebdomadary, and the chancellor hebdomadary. Then two canons deacons; and four canons subdeacons; and thirteen chaplains, including the prior of S. Thomas M. On the cantoris side, were the hebdomadary priests, chanter, archdeacon, succentor, a canon, and treasurer; two deacons canons, and four subdeacons, including the sacrist, and twelve chaplains. All non-residentiaries paid one-seventh part of their prebends to the commune. The four excellentiores personæ or dignitaries were to reside perpetually. The præcentor had charge of the tabling of singers, the instruction and discipline of the choristers, to keep a song-school and appoint a master; the chancellor was to appoint the master of the general school; the treasurer was to have charge of the clock. Hebdomadaries were to celebrate in turns vespers, matins, and high mass; and deacons and subdeacons to assist at the offices; all being bound to reside according to the order of foundation of their prebends: each was to give a silk cope to the church: if a prebendary did not reside within forty days after his monition he was mulcted of the choral distribution. If three months elapsed he lost the third of his prebend for that year; and if he was absent for a year he was deprived of all the fruits of his prebend. The new residentiary was to signify his arrival in chapter and sign a paper declarative of his term of residence; to attend one hour daily and two hours on greater feasts; and to appear at the Saturday chapters. The chaplains received from ten to five marks according to the revenue of their masters. (Registr. Epis. Morai. 253—271.)

At Aberdeen were thirteen prebends, held by the bishop, dean, chanter, chancellor, treasurer, archdeacon, and seven canons. In the close the houses were arranged as follows: the bishop, the chancellor, chanter, dean, (who was rector of the church,) treasurer, five canons, the archdeacon, and the two remaining canons. The dean was elected by the canons. A dignitary or canon was installed by the dean, or in his absence his deputy or canon, with the Gospels, and these prayers:

Ps. cxxxii. Kyrie eleison. Pater noster.
Salvum fac servum Tuum,
Deus meus, sperantem in Te.
Esto ei Domine turris fortitudinis,
A facie inimici.
Nihil proficiat inimicus in eo,
Et filius iniquitatis non apponat nocere ei.
Domine exaudi,
Et clamor meus ad Te veniat.

Prætende Domine misericordia Tua famulo Tuo dexteram cœlestis auxilii ut Te de toto corde perquirat, et quæ digne postulat assequatur.

Actiones nostras, &c.

Dominus custodiat introitum tuum et exitum tuum ex hoc nunc et usque in sæculum. Amen.

The dean was to reside for the greater part of the year; the other three persons during half the year. The archdeacon was bound only to attend when the bishop was present. There were seven priest-vicars of choir, two of them at a time acting as hebdomadaries; they represented the bishop and dignitaries, and the prebendary of Balheluy. There were also three deacon-vicars and three subdeacon-vicars for the other canons. They were to be nominated within forty days after a vacancy. Black copes and surplices formed the choral habit. The dean provided two parish chaplains, and two sacrists-clerks, who with one of their chaplains lighted the candles and served water. There were also four boys, two serving as taper-bearers and two as thuriblers. (Registr. Aberdon. Sæc. xiii. i. pp. 39—50.) At Dunkeld, established 1127, in place of Culdees, there were in 1480 a dean, præcentor, chancellor, treasurer; archdeacon, subdean (the rural dean of the diocese); ten prebendaries, four Abernethy-vicars, ten others, one being vice-penitentiary, and six choristers. (Vitæ Episc. Dunkeld.)

In the newly-erected cathedral of Cordova, 1577, the constitution included a dean, archdeacon of Cordova, matrescuela, chanter, two archdeacons, treasurer, prior, (who had no voice or place in chapter nor duty in choir,) twenty canons, ten racioneros, and twenty having medias raciones. The officers included a canon magistral, a doctoral, a lecturer, penitentiary, subchanter, and sacristan major. Any dignitary might be president of choir, and in their absence (the dean excepted) the custos chori. There were also chaplains, perpetual sacristans, a chapel master, two muchachos, trebler, contralto, tenor and counterbase, organist, four minstrels, and twelve choristers. (Estatutos. Bodl. Libr. Oxford.)

Officers and Inferior Ministers of the Church.

Cathedrals of the Old Foundation.—In cathedrals of the old foundation each dignitary, and canon and prebendary, found his respective vicar, to whom he paid stall-wages; the subordinate servants were appointed by the dean and residentiaries. The establishment at Chichester included dignities, personages, canonries, prebends,[1] officers, and ministries (Reg. Rede. fo. xxv. Praty, fo. 73); or, as it is given in 1675, the dean, dignitaries, canons residentiary, prebendaries, vicars choral, lay vicars or clerks, and all ministers and servants of the Church. (Reg. Brideoake, 127.) At S. Paul's the following offices existed:—Minor canons, including two cardinals of the choir; master of song school; 2. choristers; 3. master of grammar school; 4. grammar boys; 5. chamberlain; 6. collector of rents or receiver-general; 7. auditor of accompts; 8. keeper of new fabric; 9. keeper of bakehouse; 10. steward of courts; 11. almoner; 12. vergers; and with the following fees, 1. chapter clerk, £31; 2. clerk of the works, £36. 6*s.*; 3. senior verger and church sexton, £156; 4. junior verger, constable of the close, and porter, £46. 13*s.* 4*d.*; 5. belfry sexton, £1. 19*s.*; 6. beadle and pulpit verger, £14. 6*s.*; and, 7, church pricker [punctator, the marker of absentees from the choir services], £3. 6*s.* 8*d.* At S. David's there are a communar, sub-treasurer, parish clerk, verger (£6), and dog-whipper, (£3. 18*s.*) At Ripon there are a parish clerk (£39); organist (£56); organblower (£5); the dean's verger and sexton, who has charge of the belfry and the fires and lights (£69. 10*s.*); canon's verger; the chapter clerk, who is also the registrar, paymaster of choir salaries, steward of the courts and manor, receiver of rents and payments, except tithes, and legal adviser (£190);

[1] Dignitas et personatus pro eodem accipiuntur, sed fortasse pro loquendi consuetudine alibi vocatur dignitas, alibi personatus. Præbenda erigitur (1) fundatione, cùm de novo fundatur, (2) restitutione cùm beneficium extinctum vel suppressum in pristinum statum restituitur, (3) cùm forma beneficii et qualitas mutatur. Beneficia adipiscantur collatione [libera præbendæ concessione] vel institutione, cùm in aliquorum sunt tutelâ aut patrocinio. (Corvinus, tit. xxviii., xxix.)

bailiff of the court leet, court baron, and customary court (£3. 10*s.*); tithe collector (£85), ringers (£15. 10*s.* and fees), clock keeper (£10); dep. sexton, who cleans and shows the church (£27). In the reign of Henry VIII., an. 27, there were 6 vicars choral, being parish vicars and chaplains of the six altars at a stipend each of £6. 2*s.* from their prebendaries and £4 from the common, and having a house; 9 chantry priests of the nine altars, or petty canons, who supplied the places of the vicars when ill, to be present at matins, high mass, and vespers, and in processions, and in principal and double feasts to do service at the high altar; 3 deacons, 3 subdeacons, 6 choristers, 6 treblers, 1 organ player, and 1 clerk of the works, 1 clock keeper, 1 auditor, 1 sub-treasurer, and 1 chamberlain. In 1604 there were 7 vicars or clerks choral and singing men, 1 organist and 8 choristers; in 1635 there were 2 vicars choral, 6 chanters, 1 organist and master of the boys, 6 choristers, 1 parish clerk (£3), verger and sexton (£3), steward of the canonical court (£4), 1 auditor and 1 receiver of the king (£8), 1 registrar (£2), £19 being reserved to the fabric fund. At Lincoln the statutable officers are—chapter clerk, receiver general, clerk of fabric, sacrist, succentor, organist, master of choristers, vice-chancellor, lay sacrist, senior and junior vergers, 2 porters, 2 stall keepers, surveyor of chapter estates, and surveyor of fabric. At Lichfield there are a chapter clerk and registrar, a sub-sacrist, senior verger (£120), junior verger and dean and chapter's apparitor (£60). At Exeter there are a lecturer (£30), 2 custodes or vergers found by the treasurer, who show the church, and 1 inferior custos. When Bishop Grandison visited Exeter Cathedral in 1337, there were 24 canons, 24 vicars, 21 annuellars, 12 secondaries, and 4 sacristans.

Cathedrals of the New Foundation.—The cathedrals of the new foundation contain a dean, canons, minor canons, deacon and subdeacon, lay clerks, master of choristers, choristers, two grammar masters, grammar boys, poor bedesmen, sub-sacrists, porter and barber, butler and cooks. Appointments to the choir and nomination to preferments are vested in the dean and chapter (3 & 4 Vict. c. 113 § 45), except where the right of appointment in the choir rests in the dean (4 & 5 Vict. c. 39 § 16) as in many cathedrals of the old foundation, as Carlisle (Burns, II. 97), Rochester (Rawlinson, p. 14), Norwich (Tanner c. 34 MS. 136 Bodl. Lib.), Worcester (Rawlinson MS. 102, Benet Coll. MS. 120), Durham (Hutchinson, II. 104), Oxford (Rymer, VI. P. iii. 82), Chester (ibid. 68), Bristol (ib. 7, MS. Harl. 6127 fo. 43), and Gloucester (ib. 102 and Rymer 71), Ely (Cath. Comm. Rep. App. 60), Westminster (ibid. 92), where he constitutes, admits, and accepts all and singular inferior officers, ministers, and other persons; he in all cases chooses the doorkeepers and cooks; and, with the consent of the chapter, elects from the canons the annual officers, vice-dean, receiver, and treasurer, and also the auditor, steward, and bailiffs, and the butler. The qualification of minor canons, gospeller, and epistoler and clerks, is that they shall be men of good fame, upright conversation, and skilled in singing. At Peterborough, if there is any dispute about the right of nomination to any office or ministry between the dean and chapter lasting over two days the election devolves on the bishop (ch. xvi.); but in other cathedrals the dean has no casting vote; neither can he give a veto (33 Hen. VIII. c. 27, 6 Anne c. 21). The rule appears to have been that if the dean stood alone against the united residentiaries, his dissent was void; but if the votes were equal, the arbitrement lay in the bishop. A curious circumstance is connected with the statutes of Peterborough, which prescribe the use of S. Paul's as its model, whilst all the statutes of the other New Foundations speak only generally of the "mode and rites of other cathedrals of England." At Chester the foundation consisted of 71 members (now 67)—6 *bedesmen, 2 *sub-sacrists, 2 porters, 1 butler, 2 cooks, 2 seneschals, and for the temporalities, 1 *steward, 1 *auditor: all these officers but those marked * are obsolete since 1669, owing to the disuse of the gates and the suspension of the common table. At Durham (MS. Harl. 4343) there were 96 (but now 139) offices: these included 8 *bedesmen, 2 *sub-sacrists or vergers, 2 bell-ringers, 2 porters, 2 bakers, 2 butlers, 2 cooks, 1 auditor, 1 bailiff or clerk of court. There are now 8 bell-ringers, 8 sub-sacrists or under vergers, land and colliery agents, a constable, gardener, and woodman, and a clerk of the works. At Canterbury (Ben. Coll. MS. cxx. 15, MS. Lambeth 728) there were a manciple (£3. 11*s.* 4*d.*), 2 *sub-sacrists (each £3. 11*s.* 4*d.*), 2 *vergers (£2. 18*s.*), 4 *bell-ringers (each £2. 18*s.*), 2 *porters (each £2. 11*s.* 4*d.*), 2 butlers (each £2. 18*s.*), 1 cook (£2. 18*s.*), 12 *almsmen (each £6. 3*s.* 4*d.*), under cook (£2), *steward or clerk of lands (£6. 13*s.* 4*d.*), *auditor and clerk of accounts or registrar (£6. 13*s.* 4*d.*) The offices not marked with a * are obsolete, like those of the sackbuteer and corneteer; their stipends have been added to the pay of the choir; the common table seems to have been disused in the reign of Charles I. At Carlisle (Hutchinson's "Cumberland") there were 1 verger, 2 sub-sacrists, 1 porter and *barber, 1 *butler, 2 *cooks and 6 almsmen, and 1 seneschal and clerk of the lands. The offices marked * are obsolete. At Ely (Benet Coll. MS. cxx. 207, 407, MS. Harl. 6885, 7049) there are 6 almsmen (£6. 13*s.* 4*d.*), 2 sub-sacrists (£6, one has a house), 1 purveyor (£6), 1 cook (£6), 1 barber (£6), 1 bell-ringer, 1 clock keeper, 1 bridgereeve, who has a house. By the statutes of 1666 there were also appointed 4 chaplains for Trinity and S. Mary Ely, Stuntney and Chettisham, 1 registrar, 1 steward of the courts, 1 auditor and 17 bailiffs of manors. At Gloucester (MS. Harl. 6127 fo. 1) there were 4 bedesmen, 2 sub-sacrists, 2 porters and vergers, 1 butler and 2 cooks, an auditor, a chapter clerk, and steward. There are now, also, a surveyor, and 1 bailiff and woodward. At Bristol there were 4 almsmen, 1 sub-sacrist, 1 doorkeeper (called the verger), 1 butler and 2 cooks. At Peterborough (MS. Benet Coll. cxx. 523) there were 2 sub-sacrists (now sextons), 2 doorkeepers (now porters), and a cupbearer and 2 cooks (now obsolete). Besides these are the surveyor of the works (£5), steward and chief clerk (£40); bailiffs of the manors (£18. 2*s*. 10*d*.) At Rochester (Rawlinson's Hist.), there were 2 sub-sacrists (£6 each), 1 porter and barber (£6), butler (£6), 2 cooks (one £6, the other £1. 15*s*.), steward (£2. 15*s*. 4*d*.), auditor (£2. 13*s*. 4*d*.) At Worcester the establishment (Benet Coll. MS. cxx. 409) included 10 bedesmen, 2 vergers, 2 sub-sacrists, 2 now 3 porters, 2 bakers, 1 caterer (obsolete), and 2 cooks.

In the French cathedrals the chaplains were frequently called habituez, from wearing the choir habit.[1] Their other names were perpetuels, at Lyons, portionists, demi-canons, semi-prebendaries, beneficiarii[2] (in contradistinction to conducts, i.e. conductitii, stipendiaries) being substitutes and coadjutors of dignitaries and canons. These must not be confounded with the non-præbendati, coadjutors, or expectants, canons in herbâ, as they were called, who were canons without a prebend. (Molanus, i. c. v.) At Hereford there were frequentantes chorum, who served no canon, and received no certain payment. In the Spanish cathedrals, in place of the arch-priest, there was a capellanus major, a dignitary with cure of souls, which he delegated to vicars, as at Siguença, where he was curate, at Barbastro, Saragossa, Osca, and Jaca, where he was an officer, and Toledo, where from an officer he was constituted a dignitary in 1476. (Frances, 348.) The master or major-chaplain at Palermo had cure of souls in the precincts, being assisted by three chaplains and two clerks, and taking precedence of all parochi. He was the fourth persona in inferiori choro, ranking after the sub-chanter, terminator, and schoolmaster. (Pirrus de Ecc. Panorm. p. 166 ap. Græv. xxix.) At Girgenti a canon was yearly chosen to be master chaplain (Græv. Sic. iii. 769). He appears to have been the same as the pastor mentioned by Molanus (lib. ii. c. xii.), who was a parish priest and the plebanus of Louvaine. His assistants

[1] The almuce was a distinctive part of the choral habit; it was anciently worn on the head; and afterwards by the secular canons on the arm, and by regulars on the shoulders. The word has been derived from eleemosyna; from alden mutsen, "the ancient cap;" and from amiciendo. Canons wore the almuce of black in choir (Bayfius de Re Vest. c. xvi.), but in summer of fur: the vicar's almuce was unornamented. The birrus appears to have been a head-covering or hood of red fur. It has been supposed that the mitres worn by some canons in certain churches were merely the mitre-shaped end of the almuce which hung next the arm; these episcopal ornaments, however, in some churches were permitted to the canons.

[2] Præbenda est jus percipiendi reditus ecclesiasticos, ratione divini officii, cui quis insistit. Præbendam, beneficium, et titulum nihil reipsâ interest, usu tamen loquendi in aliâ ecclesiâ vocatur præbenda, in aliâ beneficium s. titulus. (Corvinus, tit. xxviii.)

were the vice-pastor and primissarius, the singer of the first mass (ib. c. xxxvii.), the chaplains and matricularii; the keepers of the church were called mansionarii, because always resident, (ib. c. xxxviii.), in distinction to the chanoines forains, who served by vicars. At Kilkenny, Ely, Bangor, Norwich, Chester, Salisbury, Hereford, and Carlisle, as formerly at Lincoln, and Chichester till 1840, there was a parish church in the cathedral. In foreign cathedrals, there is frequently a parochus with subordinate cure of souls (Frances, 223) as the deputy of the dean in the close, the dean being actually charged with such a cure (Coke, Inst. ch. lxxi. p. 155) by statute. At Chichester there was "a præcular or orator" of Bishop Sherborne, called also Lord Robert's bedeman, who celebrated his mass of requiem at the four altars in the choir, and had charge of his tomb, the cloisters, and cemetery (Ordin. Rob. iv. fo. xi.) At the same time there were 6 clerks, 2 chaplains of the King's and Lord Mortimer's Chapel, 4 other clerks, 2 sacrists, 2 vergers, 8 choristers, 18 vicars choral, and a principal of vicars, and 12 residentiaries (Reg. Ib. fo. xxxi.)

The Almoner at S. Paul's was to distribute the alms, and bury paupers dying in the close; he was to have charge of eight boys to be trained free of cost for the church services, in singulis etiam quarteriis chori stent ij pueri, nec alternent loca, nisi ministerio sub necessitate postulante; they received the ends of the candles (MS. Camb. E.e. 521, fo. xl. 6.) A minor canon still bears the name. At Winchester the choristers were called in Wykeham's statutes "boys of the almonry." At Lincoln he was called the hospitaller (Ecton, p. 232); and auditor, in the Caroline statutes of Canterbury; he is called also the clerk of accompts and registrar; his fee was £6. 13*s*. 4*d*.; he receives now £209, with fees for leases and a house. At Chester he received £4. 10*s*., and is a minor canon. The office also existed at Durham, Ely (where he is a minor canon), at Gloucester and Rochester, where his fee was £2. 13*s*. 4*d*. a year, and is now, including his salary as chapter clerk, £39. 3*s*. 4*d*. per annum.

The hospitaller (the English ostler, as hostiarius became usher), was a Spanish dignitary or officer, and occurred at Pampeluna and Saragossa, but mostly in cathedrals of the regular orders. At Saragossa there was a hospital (Frances, 470-473) in which pilgrims were maintained from the commune during three days. At Tournay there was a hospitaller for the charge of the sick and poor. Molanus attributes the foundation of the two offices of the almoner and hospitaller to the time when the canons received separate portion, and then no longer one as in the early times attended to the duty (Lib. ii. c. xix. xx.) At Segorbe the offices of almoner, succentor, escolastre, infirmarer and obrero, were founded in 1358 (Villanueva, iii. 13).

Annuellars, or chantry priests, by the Council of Gloucester

1378, c. l., were allowed seven marks a year as stipend, or diet, and three marks for celebrating annuals or anniversaries, masses for the souls of the dead, without holding a parochial charge. They correspond to the foreign chaplains, beneficiarii, and semi-prebendes. At Exeter, being twenty-one in number in 1337, and in 1358 twenty-four, (Stat. fo. 57 b,) they were bound to say matins and the hours in the nave, and also the matin or Bratton mass, and then their own masses, (Rawlinson's MS. fo. 24-6); to attend choir like the vicars; to act as sub-deacons, and to serve under the superintendence of two "stewards of obits," a canon and a vicar, being fined 1*d.* for every neglect of duty. In 1337 there were twenty-one living in a College on the north side of the subdeanery, they ruled the choir on Doubles. At Wells (MS. Harl. 6968,) they were secular stipendiary priests, fourteen in number, called "Annuellars of the new hall." Bp. Ergham founded S. Anne's College on Mounterey for the accommodation of fourteen chaplains, (A. S. i. 570,) they were to say the hours after prime in the Lady Chapel. So late as 1575 the name of Annuellar was retained at Llandaff. In foreign churches they were called Sacellani and Capellani. The chaplains of S. Paul's who lived in S. Peter's College, (Dugd. 253,) were attached to particular altars and chantries, and were required to go to their altar in a surplice and their robe; they attended on the principal feasts at matins, prime, high mass, and vespers. Some who were called coadjutors, secutores, or assistants of the choir, attended the chief services, officiated at burials, received an additional stipend, and also lived in S. Peter's College. Fuller mentions that there were seventeen chantries, and only fourteen altars. At Lichfield the chaplains who had a college, 1411, (Monast. vi. 1254,) celebrated between the hours of 6 and 10 A.M., the small bell beginning before each mass; they were bound to attend matins and compline in summer, and sing a mass for travellers, which began after the consecration in high mass. The S. Chad's chaplain sang matin mass at 5 A.M. No private mass was allowed to proceed during high mass, or in time of processions. Some of the chantry priests were supported merely on the bequest of the founder. These must not be confounded with the five canons chaplains, the priest-canons, who celebrated at the high altar, or the five deacon canons who were called principal chaplains, and if not actual priests appointed a priest vicar to serve for them. On S. Matthias' Day at York, where they lived in S. William's College, temp. Henry VI. (Monast. vi. 1183,) they came and made oath that they had fulfilled their founder's will, and were required to attend matins, masses, the hours, all festivals of nine lections, and great feasts. A relic of these old special services may be traced in the early morning prayers maintained in several cathedrals; the statutable short service with one lesson at Canterbury, and the 6 A.M. prayers enjoined at Lichfield for the convenience of servants, labourers, and small traders. The Collect retains the phrase, "the beginning of this day," which plainly alludes to the early hour at which it was formerly used. Several cathedrals retain their Morning Prayer chapels. At Hereford the early service was at 5 A.M. in winter, and at half-past 6 in summer by the Caroline statutes. At S. Paul's the early or Apostle's Mass was sung at 4 or 5 A.M. in the Jesus Chapel in the shrouds, an early morning service was substituted for it. At Chichester there was an early mass before 5 in summer and 6 in winter, in the Guild chapel of S. George, which was attached to the cathedral. At Exeter the Queen's commissioners in 1559, confirmed the 6 A.M. service in the choir, and the right of the congregation to sing a hymn. At Winchester on Sundays the Morning Prayer is said at 8 A.M., and the Litany and Communion Service follow at 10. At Westminster and S. Paul's there is an early service at 8. There was an early service at Salisbury at half-past 6 at the beginning of the century, and at 6 at Winchester. At Verdun the chaplains were first employed by the four minor canons, who had to maintain hitherto the choir services. (Causes Célèbres, viii. 345.)

Archpriest.—As the archdeacon had charge of the deacons and subdeacons, the urban archpriest presided over the city priests, as the rural archpriests, deans rural, (Kennet, Ant. 636,) or deans of Christianity did in regard to the priests of their districts, from which they took their titles; and made their reports to the bishop. (Decret. l. i. tit. xxv. For archpresbyters, as deans of decaniæ, see Morinus, p. iii. p. 215, exerc. xvi. c. ii.) At Padua and Turin they still precede archdeacons. (Ib. s. x. 217.) In 1476 the "dean of the city" is mentioned at Worcester.

Bailiff of Manors.—This officer was appointed 1666 at Ely. There are now seventeen. At Manchester he issues summonses, and attends courts of the chapter held by them as lords of the manor; he receives £2 with fees. At Durham he was called clerk of the courts. There is one at Gloucester. At Ripon he is bailiff of the Court Leet, Court baron, and Customary Court, receiving £3 a year, and some very small fees. There is also a tithe-collector with a salary of £65, and an allowance of £20 for expenses.

Bedesmen.—In cathedrals founded by Henry VIII. the number of these almsmen varies from six to twelve; they were usually in the patronage of the crown (which appointed at Ely till 1670), they were to be poor aged or wounded soldiers, to attend daily service, to act as bell-ringers, sweep the church, and to receive wages, usually about £6. 13*s*. 4*d*. a year, with an allowance of clothing. Their numbers and stipends now are as follows:—Canterbury, twelve, £6. 13*s*. 4*d*., 10*s*. and a gown yearly. Durham, eight, £2. 12*s*., and 10*s*. a week. Carlisle, six, £5; almsmen of S. Nicholas who assist the vergers, £2; and two pensioners, one receiving £2, the other £1. 10s. Chester, six, £6, who receive a livery gown with a red rosette on the left shoulder. The Tudor rose refers to the re-founder of these cathedrals, Henry VIII. Ely, six, £6. 13s. 4d., with allowances for duties performed. Gloucester, four, £10, and a gown occasionally. Bristol, four, £6. 13s. 4d., a gratuity of £8. 16s. 8d., and clothes. Norwich, six, £10 a year, Peterborough, six, £6. 13s. 4d. Rochester, six, £6. 13s. 4d., now fourteen, £18. 4s. Worcester, ten, £9, and from the Hurd bequest, £6. Westminster, twelve, £154, divided among them, wearing a rose on the breast. At Chichester, fifty poor still receive a weekly dole of bread. At Durham there are thirty, at Bristol ten, and Peterborough eight church widows who receive weekly alms. There are twenty-four old soldiers at Christ Church who are bell-ringers.

Bell-ringers.—There are two at Durham to ring the bells, clean the church and cloisters, attend to the clock, and open the doors at 6 A.M. in summer, and close them after curfew, but in winter after evensong; they were to search the church after the doors were shut. At Canterbury there are four who received £2. 18s., but now £20 a year, £1 for curfew, and small fees for knells. At Durham there are eight with stipends of £47, at Winchester three at £24, and one at Gloucester at £10 a year. At Ripon they receive £12 a year and fees.

Cardinals.—There are two minor canons at S. Paul's, so called from serving at the matin or cardinal mass, celebrated at the high or cardinal altar. (Martene de Ant. Mon. Rit. iv. 66.) They with two other minor canons had charge of the choir, and presented defaulters on Fridays to the dean. (MS. Camb. E. e. 525, fo. liii. liv.) They preserved order as rectors of the choir, administered sacraments, enjoined penances, heard confessions, buried the dead, and received the oblations. At Ravenna, Milan, Syracuse, Naples, Orvieto, Salerno, (Scarfantoni, i. p. 12,) Oviedo, Seville, Compostella, and Milan, Canons are called Cardinals. (Frances, xxxiii. 130.) There were four at Seville (Moreri, ix. 388.) Paul III. forbad the practice. Pope Leo IX. in 1084 appointed seven canons, called Priest Cardinals, who had the right of officiating pontifically in S. Stephen's Cathedral, Besançon, as he had done at Cologne, Rheims, and Aix-la-Chapelle, (Etat de l'Allem. ii. 181); the other canons wore the mitre and cross. Didacus Gelmerius, Bishop of Compostella in the eleventh century, obtained the right of having in his cathedral seven cardinals, as at Rome, with the sole privilege of celebrating at the high altar. (Mariana, lib. x. ch. vi. p. 416.) Father Paul, in his History of Benefices, shows that a cardinal was a strange clergyman transplanted (incardinatus) into a church at Rome or Ravenna, when expatriated or exiled. (Lib. Diurn. Summ. Pont. tit. xi. cap. 3.) The idea of the church "hinging" on cardinals is not earlier than the Council of Basle, Sess. xxiii.

(See also Cohelius, Notit. Cardinal. 1653.) At Milan there were twenty-four cardinal canons, twelve priests, nine deacons, and five subdeacons who officiated weekly. Fleury suggests that cardinal meant permanent or stationary, instead of temporarily employed clergy.

Chamberlain.—The paymaster and receiver of rents, (Scarfantoni, ii. 161,) in his time of office was superior to other canons, (ii. 82.) At S. Paul's (Camb. MS. fo. xl. E. e. 521) he distributed the notices of summonses of prebendaries to their vicars for transmission or posting upon their stalls. He received money due to the chamber, inspected the lights, and paid stipends and pittances; bread, wine, oil, and wax for the church; under him was the collector of rents, who rendered him a quarterly account. There was a similar officer at York, 1290, who noted absences of vicars, delating them in the Saturday chapter, and paid them for attending on the greater feasts. He is the chamalier of foreign cathedrals. He kept an account of the revenues, superintended the pantry-man and meal-man, and transferred to the sacrist the fees paid by new canons for their copes. At Passau the marshal, chamberlain, server, and butler, were hereditary officers. (Hansizius, Germ. Sac. i. Coroll. xiv.) At Ripon he received the rents from the sub-treasurer, and acted as paymaster of the stipends of minor ministers, and of the common dividend to the residentiaries. At Paris the chambrier was a kind of churchwarden. (Fleury, cxvii. p. 179.)

Chapter Clerk.—He keeps accounts usually and transacts law business; he ought to be a notary. (Frances, 378.) At Lichfield he was appointed in 1699, and acted as a notary public, and registrar, with a stipend of 40*s*. He is first mentioned in 1526, and acts also as registrar, receiving £230 a year. At Carlisle he is steward and deputy treasurer; at Chester he is also steward, with a bailiff under him: at Winchester he has the privilege of making out leases, with fees for business done; at Gloucester he acts as legal adviser, steward of the manor, and holds courts, transacts land business, and acts as receiver of rents with the treasurer; at Ely he is steward; at York he receives £200 a year; at Salisbury £31; at Ripon £190, where he is registrar, attends chapter, records acts, pays the choir salaries, receives all rents, profits arising from renewal of leases and copyholds, transacts law business, and payments, except tithes, and has on an average also £40 as steward of courts and manors. He corresponds to the Notary of the Chapter (Molanus, ii. c. liii.)

Chorepiscopus.—The præcentor in the Cathedral of Cologne, who used on solemn occasions a bishop's staff; but at Utrecht the Archsubdeacon, or chief dean rural, called at Lincoln, Arles, and Poictiers simply subdean. (Molanus, ii. c. xxxii.)

Choristers.—Called also "Clerks of the third form," from their seats in choir; were termed "boys of the almonry" at S. Paul's, and lived in the Almonry at Canterbury. At Tours there were twelve *enfans de chœur* (De Moleon, 115) a large number in a continental cathedral. Their annual wages vary between £26 at Durham, and £3. 6*s*. 8*d*. in less wealthy cathedrals, with other small allowances. They all receive education under the master of the choristers, who has usually an under-master, and have in most cases an apprentice fee on leaving. At Hereford the succentor provided five boys or clerks out of his school, in the first form, to begin the antiphons on week days and at funerals, and carry the cross, censers and tapers. At Lincoln, Bp. R. de Gravesend made a statute that the twelve choristers of Lincoln who hitherto had subsisted on the canons' alms should live in a house under a master, and made provision for their maintenance. (Schalby, MS. Harl. 6954, fo. 6.) The choristers at Lichfield, four being added to their number, were placed in one house by Dean Denton and Bp. Blythe 1486—1510. (A. S. i. 455.) At Exeter there were never more than fourteen, and all received the first tonsure, they were instructed (1540) by the chapel clerk, and appointed by the præcentor, (Rawlinson MS. fo. 40); their number is now ten, and they receive education and clothes, and £13. 10*s*. each; they were in the thirteenth century maintained wholly at the canons' tables. At Chichester there were eight in Bp. Sherborne's time, and twelve in 1342; there are now ten, and their wages vary from £6 to £12 a year. By Stat. 1232 there were ten, and those who misbehaved, were either expelled, or received seven or fourteen stripes from their master or the chanter's vicar. At Lichfield there were four in 1522, but twelve at the Reformation; by Stat. of 1699 there were to be eight, each receiving 20*s*. for robe and surplice, and £4 as stipend; there are now eight receiving from £7 to £20 with their education. At S. David's there are six who divide £19 yearly. At Salisbury they were endowed with the tithes of Preshute in 1322 by Bp. Mortival, and are boarded, clothed, instructed, apprenticed, and lodged in houses in the close under the charge of one of the canons, called "Custos xii. puerorum;" they were in 1448 instructed with the altaristæ; in 1314 there were fourteen; their number was fixed at eight in 1580; there are now eight with wages varying between £8 and £12, and receiving clothes. For the origin of the Boy Bishop, Molanus may be consulted, lib. ii. c. xliii., and Phelps' Wells, p. 54. At York there are ten receiving from £8 to £14 a year; in the thirteenth century they were required to have a good voice and sing well, and then if found worthy, were permitted to be thuriblers, subdeacons, deacons, and vicars. (Stat. c. xviii.) At S. Paul's there are twelve receiving from £5 to £15, with a quotidian of 1*s*. At Hereford in 1637 there were seven who were required to play the lyre and harp; there are now eight with wages of £6. 5*s*. and clothes. At Wells eight with wages of £4 to £10. At Bangor eight received £6 to £8. At Lincoln ten, four being boarded and lodged, with wages of £1. 2s. 8d., and six receiving £1. 13s. 4d. At Manchester four, receiving £20, instead of the statutable £5. At Ripon eight, (since 1604, but previously only six, with six trebles,) with wages varying from £4 to £7, and small fees on an average about 16s. per annum. At Canterbury ten, with wages £6 to £12, instead of the statutable fee of £1. 5s. At Durham ten with wages £17 to £27. At Winchester eight, with wages £4 and clothes. At Carlisle six, with wages £3 to £7. At Chester eight, with wages £3. 6s. 8d., and further allowances amounting to £33. At Ely twelve, originally eight, with wages £4 (instead of £4 among the entire number), and £3. 6s. 8d. if in the Grammar School. At Gloucester eight, with wages for four £10, for four £8. At Bristol six, with wages £4. 10s., with augmentations, instead of the statutable 18s. At Norwich ten, (two being added to the original number of eight in 1784,) with wages £5, and £10, divided at Christmas. At Peterborough ten, with wages £7 for six, and for four £4. At Rochester eight, with wages, dividends of £84. At Worcester ten, with wages £6. 19s. 2d. At Westminster six, with a dividend of £135 between twelve. At Christchurch there are eight boys who receive college allowances, and are sometimes appointed servitors.

Claviger.—Four offices are held by the Residentiaries of Hereford in rotation, elective for three years,—the senior and junior Clavigers, Master of the fabric, and Master of the library. The duties of the former were to keep the keys of the chest, and accounts. At Rouen the clavigers were canons, keepers of the chapter seal and chest. By the Legatine Constitution of Otho, Lynd. App. 69, seals were to be kept by Ecclesiarum cathedralium capitula et cætera quæcunque collegia et conventus, simul cum suis rectoribus, aut divisim, juxta eorum consuetudinem vel statutum. The clavigers of the new foundation are the dean, vice-dean, and treasurer.

Clerks.—The Clerk of the Works at Ripon superintends repairs of the church and tenements on the lands forming the commune, with a salary of £36 a year; he is the same as the surveyor of Peterborough, where he has a fee of £5; at Canterbury he received £6. 13s. 4d., but now £352; at Gloucester he inspects the estates before the renewal of leases, and makes other surveys. Clericus denoted a scholar, and in the University any one enjoying the privilege of a clerk or scholar. (Ashmole MS. 8489, fo. 40.) The Clerk of Accounts, also Registrar and Clerk of Lands, at Canterbury, is, like the Chief Clerk of Gloucester, also Steward: the Clerk of the Chapel was the Master of Choristers at S. Paul's. The Clerk of the Sacristy at York receives £2. 4s. yearly.

Common Table.—The cathedrals of the new foundation had a common table enjoined by the Council of London, 1554, c. viii., for canons and other unmarried ministers, which was discontinued within a century, at Canterbury, c. 1561, at Worcester, 1580, at Ely before 1604, at Lichfield in the civil war, at Gloucester, 1634, and a payment in lieu was sanctioned by some recent statutes. It was usually maintained in the ancient monastic refectory, and provision made at it for the ministers and officers of the cathedral and the boys of the school and choir. The persons attending it were divided into three classes. To the first belonged the præcentor, who acted as censor morum, the head grammar master, and minor canons, and master of the choristers: to the second table were assigned the deacon, subdeacon, lay-clerks, and sub-grammar master: to the third the grammar boys and choristers. One of the priests was appointed annual steward of the hall at the general audit in November, provided coal, salt, charcoal, &c.; and examined the accounts of the monthly steward, who was required to check and examine the accounts of the butler and purveyor and accompany the latter to market. The steward of the hall exhibited his account at the end of the year to the members of the first and second tables. The dean might order money-allowance to married or sick members of church in lieu of commons. Queen Elizabeth ordered that no priests' wives should be allowed in cathedrals; Bishop Cox and Archbishop Parker inveighed against this injunction in 1561 as unscriptural and impolitic; the consequence was that only one prebendary resided at Ely and at Norwich. With the restoration of wives to the close the disuse of the common table was probably simultaneous. Until 1828 the vicars at Hereford lived in common in their college. A cook and under-cook, a pantryman and manciple held appointments connected with the table; their usual payment was £6 each.

Communar at Chichester is a residentiary, and was bursar and paymaster of stipends and deputy of the master of the fabric. At Lichfield by Bishop Meyland's Statutes, 1197, there were two canons communars who acted as bursars paying the canons their quotidian on Saturdays, and at Michaelmas rendered an account of receipts and expenses. In 1526 he is mentioned as distributing their portion to the residentiaries, and by stat. of 1699 is a residentiary elected by the dean and chapter on the Friday after Michaelmas to collect and audit all the capitular revenues, forming the communa (whence his name) [the Spanish Maza and Italian Massa Communis] except those arising from matters connected with leases for the year past. He was receiver and paymaster of salaries, corresponding to the receiver-general and treasurer in other cathedrals. At Catania there were two priest communars. At Salisbury the sub-communar looks after the repairs of the capitular houses and keeps the perdition book of fines. The communar was an annual officer who visited as capitular official certain parishes within the jurisdiction of the chapter.

Conservator.—In foreign churches the advocate, patron, or defender of their rights (Molanus, l. ii. c. xliv—vii.)

Custos Fabricæ at S. Paul's was an officer, the same as the mayerdomo de la fabrica at Seville; he had charge of the gutters, roofs, and windows, seeing that they were weatherproof; and of the gates of the close; he was not to sleep in the belfry. (Camb. MS. E. e. 521, fo. xli.) At S. David's he is a canon: at Salisbury there are two, the dean and a canon: at Lichfield this officer was appointed in 1699 to see that the church library, chapter-house and vestry were in repair. At Chichester the residentiaries were masters of the church. At S. David's he was the proctor and supervisor fabricæ, and at a later period master of the fabric and keeper of the works. The office of Magister Fabricæ is found at Lincoln and York; and at Exeter, &c., as Œconomus. (Frances, 305.) The residentiaries formed the Corporation of Custodes Fabricæ at Lincoln. This officer managed the estates, being usually assisted by two receivers of rents and two administrators of the fabric fund. He is the "obrero" of Segorbe. At Rouen the superintendents of the fabric were two canons who had charge of repairs and ornaments of the church (duties formerly of the treasurer), and the servants' wages. The custos of York noted vicars' absences and paid certain additional stipends. In foreign cathedrals there was frequently an operarius. It must be remembered, however, that fabrica commonly included vestments, as the ordinary gift of a cope at installation is often said to be made to the fabric. At S. Canice's, Kilkenny, and in other Irish cathedrals the economist is master of the fabric or economy fund. In some foreign cathedrals the masters of the fabric were ecclesiastics and lay persons (Molanus, ii. c. xxi.) called Operarii (Ceccop. ii. 69.) At Lyons there are four custodes. At Urgel the operarius was instituted in 1175, (Villaneuva, ix. 298.) At Lunden the economist was procurator fabricæ, (Langebek, ii. 27.) At Patti there was an economist. The name of the mediæval architect in France was Maitre Maçon (Chartres), maistre ès œuvres en maçonnerie (Rheims and S. Ouen), maitre de l'œuvre qui dirigeait tous les travaux (Cologne), cementarius (Dunkeld), at Winchester, Hereford, and Rouen, ædificator principalis, 1405; but in Spain lapicida, maestro mayor; superintendent of masons, fabricator, 1203; magister operis, 1251; architecto, 1415; these names properly designating the actual architects, most of whom were ecclesiastics and all educated necessarily in the only schools of art of the period by ecclesiastics; whilst the canon in charge of the works was known as operarius, custos operis, magister fabricæ, canonigo fabriquero, obrero or œconomus. (See also under the word *steward*. This appears to be the only satisfactory solution of an obscure question of names.) Under him was the clericus (v. solutor) operum. At Exeter there was a distinct custos operis, from 1274 to 1439. At Lichfield by Pateshall's Statutes he was to render a yearly account and not begin new or great works without leave of the dean and chapter; by statute of 1699 he is a canon elected yearly and has charge of all the buildings. Abbot Horton of Gloucester had been supervisor operis, (Chron. 54.) In the 13th century Walket was procurator and custos fabricæ at Chichester. At Messina and some Italian cathedrals the præfecti fabricæ were laymen chosen by the citizens. At Malta there are two æditui. In the new foundations the treasurer has the charge of all capitular buildings. Custors or keepers at Exeter in 1276 (MS. Harl. 1027,) were four in number and were to have (1176) the two principal clerks and their two assistants who kept silence in the church, according to the Council of Lyons; in surplices with staffs in their hands cleared the way for processions, strewing carpets along the floor on solemn occasions, kept the vestments on perches in the sacristy and acted as bell-ringers. They were the treasurer's subordinates at Durham; there were four who rang the peal of bells, two of them belonging to the revestry had charge of the vestments and censers and slept in a chamber over the west end of this chamber: the other two lay in a chamber of the north alley, over against the sacrist's chequer; swept the church, filled "the holy water stones" on Sunday morning before the hallowing, and shut the church doors at night. At Worcester and Lichfield the watchers' gallery remains. (For their chambers in other churches, see my "Interior of a Gothic Minster.") At York the custodes chori delated absent vicars in 1294. (MS. Harl. 4200, fo. 24.) The chief custos under the pastor was one of the chaplain priests called the matricularius, from his charge of the church-registers, or mansionarius [residentiary]. (Onuphr. de obsc. verb. eccles.; Greg. Dial. l. iii. c. 25.) He had charge of the church cemetery, baptistery, and belfry; and had an inferior custos, a layman who acted as grave-digger (Molanus, ii. c. xxxvi.) The vicars were also called mansionarii (c. xxxviii.) The King of France was hereditary custos or treasurer of S. Quentin's (c. xlix.)

Custos Puerorum at Salisbury is a canon in charge of the choristers.

Dean.—By the Benedictine Rule, c. xxi., deans in monasteries presided over ten monks; and they are mentioned by S. Augustine, (de Morib. Eccles. c. xxxi.,) and Cassian, (de Inst. Cœnob. c. vii.) Canons adopted the arrangement, which finally resulted in the appointment of a single dean with cure of souls. (Counc. Lat. c. iii.)

Distributor or præsentiarius, the officer who paid the quotidian (Molanus, ii. c. li.)

Dom, or domnus, a title of canons, to distinguish by the contraction the word from Dominus, which was applied only to the Deity. Dom-heeren is a contraction of bisdom-heeren, applied to canons only of a cathedral. A canon of the cathedral church of Liege, the "Paradise of Priests," being saluted as brother by a canon of the collegiate church of Hoxemen, replied, "Brother, yes, as flies are birds!" (Molanus, i. c. 3.)

A Grammar School was appointed in every cathedral for the instruction of poor clerks, youths, and others, by the Councils of Lateran, 1179, c. xviii., 1215, c. xi. Nearly every foreign cathedral had its seminary and school, (Molanus, ii. c. xli., xlii.) At Louvaine the provost was Chancellor of the University, (ibid. c. xxxi.) At S. Paul's the master was appointed by the chancellor to teach the grammar boys; in the absence of the chancellor to table the lections in choir and the readers; to wear his habit in choir, and read the first lection on great festivals. At Hereford the head master received £20, and the under master £10, besides the dianomæ or distributions on certain feasts, symnells or S. Milburga's bread, and the pennies at certain masses. (Stat. 1583, c. vi.) The Welsh and some cathedrals of England, Ripon and Manchester, have no grammar school. The greater part of the new cathedrals have grammar schools, had statutable payments, a common table, and allowance for clothing. The number of king's scholars and their payments are as follows: at Canterbury, fifty, £1. 8*s*. 4*d*., and 8*s*. 4*d*. for gowns; at Durham, eighteen, £39; at Chester, twenty-four, £3. 6*s*. 8*d*.; at Peterborough, twenty, £2. 13*s*. 4*d*.; at Ely, twenty-four, £3. 6*s*. 8*d*.; at Rochester, twenty, £16. 13*s*. 4*d*.; at Worcester, forty, £2. 13*s*. 4*d*.; at Westminster, forty, with board and lodging; at Ely, Chester, and Peterborough, four divinity studentships were founded, in conformity with the monastic practice of sending novices to Oxford, with a fee of £6. 13*s*. 4*d*. a year, but the funds have been diverted by the crown. At Worcester there were twelve similar students to be sped to the Universities with a bursary of £6. 7*s*. 4*d*., but these are also obsolete. At Canterbury, Henry VIII. revoked his provision for the maintenance of twenty-four students at the Universities. The funds or estates for scholarships at the Universities founded at Ely and Worcester have been resumed by the crown, but at Rochester two exhibitions of £5 each at either University remain. At Peterborough there are three exhibitions at S. John's College, Cambridge, attached to the school. The statutable payments severally to the head master and ushers were as follows:—at Ely, (i.) £11. 5*s*. Hen. VIII., £16. 6*s*. 8*d*. Eliz., £18, 1666; (ii.) £4. 5*s*. 10*d*. Hen. VIII., £10, 1666. At Gloucester (i.) £8. 8*s*. 8*d*., with black cloth for livery, £1, and commons; (ii.) £2. 19*s*. 2*d*., with cloth, 13*s*. 6*d*., and commons at second table. At Durham, (i.) £5. 2*s*.; (ii.) £2. 19*s*. 2*d*. At Rochester, (i.) £8. 8*s*. 8*d*., commons, £3. 18*s*., and cloth for livery, £1; (ii.) £2. 19*s*. 2*d*., commons, £3. 8*d*., cloth for livery, 12*s*. At Bristol, (i.) £8. 8*s*. 8*d*.; (ii.) £2. 19*s*. 2*d*. At Carlisle, (i.) £8. 17*s*. 4*d*., with allowances, making in all £29. At Chester, (i.) £6. 15*s*. 4*d*.; (ii.) £4. 5*s*. 10*d*. At Canterbury, (i.) £15. 2*d*.; (ii.) £6. 5*s*. 10*d*. At Ely, the masters are to obey the rules which the dean and chapter prescribe; are removable after three admonitions; and are to attend services on all festivals (as at Chester) in the cathedral: the boys are to attend matins and take such part in the services as the præcentor shall direct, with consent of the head master: deserving choristers are admissible to the school. Now the (i.) head master receives £120, and a house; (ii.) the usher, £40. At Gloucester, (i.) £20, and a house; (ii.) £10. At Canterbury, (i.) £97. 10*s*., the value of an acre of underwood, and a house; (ii.) £60, the value of half an acre of underwood, and a house. At Durham, (i.) £200, and a house; (ii.) £80, and a house. At Bristol (choristers' school), (i.) £60. At Peterborough, (i.) £71. 13*s*. 4*d*., from Magdalene College, Cambridge, £10, and capitulation fee of £1. 10*s*. from each boy; (ii.) £18. 6*s*. 8*d*. At Rochester, (i.) £150, and house, and £10. 10*s*. from every boy not on the foundation; (ii.) £100, and £3. 10*s*. from every boy not on the foundation. At Worcester, (i.) £113, and a house; (ii.) £55, and as writing master, £80. At Westminster, (i.) stipend, £20, allowances, £19. 6*s*. 8*d*., and house; (ii.) £15, and house. At Chester, (i.) £62. At Carlisle, £29, with rents of an estate given by Bishop Smith in 1700, £94 per annum. At Durham, (i.) £200; (ii.) £80. Generally the masters are appointed in general chapter but always by the dean and chapter. In the new foundations in choir the head master sits before and the under master after minor canons. By 3 & 4 Vict. c. 113 sect. 44, preferment may be given to "a member of the chapter, or one of the archdeacons of the diocese, or a non-residentiary prebendary or honorary canon, as the case may be, or to *any* spiritual person who shall have served five years at the least in the office of minor canon or lecturer of the same church, or of master of the grammar or other school (if any) attached to or connected with such church, or as incumbent or curate," &c., &c.

Gospeller and Epistoler, terms used since the Reformation for deacon and subdeacon, are minor canons at S. Paul's. In the cathedrals of the new foundation they are usually called deacon and subdeacon, being distinct from minor canons. At Canterbury, York, and Christchurch, Dublin, the eagle formed the Gospel lectern on the north side of the altar. In the Statutes of Ely a deacon in 1666 was appointed to read the Epistle. In the old cathedrals there were sometimes, as at Exeter, a deacon and subdeacon for the month; or, as at Salisbury, a certain number detailed for each quarter. At Norwich the gospeller is eligible for the office of precentor, and the epistoler for that of sacristan. (C. xxxiv., xxxv. Tanner MS. 136, fo. 27.) At Carlisle they are now merged in the lay clerks. At Worcester a canon acts as deacon or gospeller, and the sacristan as subdeacon or epistoler; the statutable stipend of each was £4. 5*s*. 10*d*. At Rochester they each received £6. 11*s*. 10*d*., but originally £2. 19*s*. 2*d*., the pay of a lay clerk; at Ely, £4. 5*s*. 10*d*., and later £8; at Durham, £2. 14*s*. 8*d*.;

at Chester, £4. 5*s.* 10*d.*; at Canterbury, £5. 2*s.*; at Peterborough, £2. 19*s.* 2*d.* In the rubric of 1549, "he that is appointed shall read the epistle" is by Alesius translated subdiaconus. By the Advertisements of Q. Eliz. 1564—5, Art. 4, in Cathedral and Collegiate Churches, the "principal minister," "using a decent cope," is to be attended by "a gospeller and epistoler." (Comp. 2 Zurich Lett. p. 361.) The 24th Canon of 1603 requires the same assistants "agreeably," i.e., in copes; and by Act of Unif. 2 Edw. VI. c. 1, "so many priests and deacons shall be ready to help the priest" (who is to wear a white alb plain, with a vestment or cope) "in the ministration as shall be requisite, and shall have upon them the vestures appointed for their ministry, that is to say, albs with tunicles."[1] At Milan, six mazo canonici (canons supported on the massa communis, or common fund) acted as gospeller and epistoler at certain times. It would be most convenient to restore these two officers, who are required to be skilled in singing, as assistants in choir and parochial charge of the precinct. At Lichfield, by Bishop Hacket's Statutes (App. Rep. Cath. Com. p. 40), one clerical vicar acts as epistoler and another as hebdomadary for a week.

Hebdomadary (Septanéer), a name taken from the monastery to

[1] As some misapprehension exists on the subject, I may mention that the distinctive habits of the canons of cathedrals consisted of three dresses, almuce, cope, and surplice. The almuce or amess, a hood of grey fur, originally of a similar form to the stole, and worn like it in England; but occasionally on the head or over the arm. It was, probably, introduced about the thirteenth century, and in the fifteenth century a cape with pendants, also of fur, was added to it. The vicars wore an amess of Calabrian fur, or of a black material. (Bayfius de re. vest. c. xvi.) The word has been derived from eleemosyna; alden mutsen, the old cap; and amiciendo. The birret (whence the birretta) was a hood for the head of red fur (πυῤῥος). The mitre-shaped end of the almuce has by some writers been suggested as the origin of the mitre worn by certain canons. 2. The cope (cappa), a dress worn over the rochet, semicircular, worn like a cloak, and fastened across the chest with a brooch (morsus). Behind it was a hood (caputium), which in the fourteenth century was simply an ornamental appendage, the almuce superseding its use. The ordinary choral cope in England was black; the processional or precious cope was of the colour of the festival, with orphreys or embroidered edges, whence the term "festa in cappis." Copes are still preserved at Durham, Ely, Westminster, and Carlisle. In 1197, at Chichester, the cope was to be sufficiently open in front, and without collars. 3. In England, the surplice, as at Burgos (Ceccop. ii. 304) and Vienne (Le Lievre, stat. c. xxvi.); but in foreign churches often a mozzetta, or rochet, was worn. Canons regular only in this country wore the rochet. The surplice, with deep hanging sleeves and closed in front, without girdle or apparel, was worn over a fur pelisse or tunic: hence its name, superpelliceum, sobrepelliz, &c., which is not earlier than the eleventh century in England. It occurs first in the laws of Edward the Confessor (de Latron. c. xxxvi.) It corresponds with the subucula or subumblem of King Edgar's reign. Lyndwood says the rochet was worn by the clerk assisting the priest. (Prov. 252.) The rochet, said to be derived from the German "rock," or the French word "richa," common at Avignon when the Popes resided there, was formerly called "linea," or "camisia Romana," and was like a diminished albe, with tight sleeves, or mere apertures for the arms (Lyndw. 252), resembling the mantillettum. (Cær. Episc. l. i. c. 1.) Chaucer uses the word "rockette." The canons, when celebrating, originally wore the same dress as bishops, a trace of which may be found in the mitres still worn by those of Lucca, Naples, and other places. (Ceccop. i. tit. vii.)

denote the priest for the week who sang the daily high mass and commenced the Hours. At Louvaine the treasurer was perpetual hebdomadary. At Lichfield there were five permanent hebdomadaries or perpetual chaplains. There were also weekly hebdomadary deacons and subdeacons. At Hereford he gave leave of absence to vicars. The three ministers of the high altar (hebdomadary priest, deacon, and subdeacon) received daily from the offerings 9*d.*, the priest 4*d.*, the deacon 3*d.*, and the subdeacon 2*d.*, the priest had also from the feast of dedication to the feast of S. John Baptist 1*d.* a day: every canon present in choir received also a penny, and on great festivals an allowance of wine. The hebdomadary inflicted discipline on the bare back of a delinquent deacon or subdeacon, a priest had to ask pardon on the morrow in chapter. The vicars often kept the hebdomadary standing ready to commence the service for half an hour or more. Canons who could not sing and canons in deacon's and minor orders were of necessity obliged to find such demi-prebendaries as the canonicati of Utrecht, who were vicars wearing a canon's habit and acting as hebdomadaries. (Molanus, ii. c. xv.) The hebdomadary canon sang mass and the offices for the week at S. Paul's (Dugdale, 249) and Lichfield (Mon. Angl. vi. 1255.) But all canons were bound personally to recite the canonical hours in choir (Scarf. i. 87, 103, 110, 121) and to act as hebdomadary in turn (94) the junior canons supplying the absence of their seniors. At Cefalu twenty-four insigniti prebendaries were always as hebdomadaries present in choir to supply the canons' absences; there were six others who were only semi-prebendati. At Catania the hebdomadary one of twelve beneficiati, on solemn feasts occupied the prior's seat, and the præcentor was vice-prior.

Lay Clerks.—So called in the Statutes of Worcester, representing clerici de stallo v. de choro in the elder statutes. In some of the old cathedrals they form a corporation either singly or jointly with the priest vicars, having formerly been in minor orders at the least, until the emoluments became depreciated in modern times, and have a common estate. In the new cathedrals they do not form a corporation, but are mere stipendiary singers, in some cases having a common estate given to them subsequently to their foundation, besides their statutable payments from the chapter. Up to the period of the civil wars most of the singing men were in orders. Thus, in 1634, at Hereford there were twelve priests and four deacons; at Bristol, four out of ten singing men were in orders; at Lichfield, six out of sixteen; at Wells, six out of fourteen. A trace of this clerical character survives at Lincoln, where two laymen, and at Exeter and Lichfield, where a priest and lay vicar sing the former part of the Litany; at Chichester in 1700 two lay clerks "read the Litany." At Exeter and Chester there were sixteen; Canterbury, eighteen, with forty singing boys; at Rochester, sixteen; at Wells, fourteen; at Durham, thirty singing men at that period. In 1635 there were various instruments used in the choir at Lincoln; two sackbuteers and two corneteers were appointed by the Laudian statutes at Canterbury, and musicians were employed at Durham in the time of Cosin and Lord Crewe. The singers were at Rouen simple clerks, called in the tenth century clerks of choir; about 1433 they received the definite title of chaplains, and in 1311 were constituted a college. At Lichfield, in 1241, "secular clerks, commonly called clerk-vicars, were paid quarterly, attending the Lady mass, singing common canticles, which all or most knew, and on solemn days hymns without the organ." In 1613, at Exeter, the laymen were dissociated from the priest vicars. At S. Asaph they were called parvi v. minores vicarii; at Salisbury and Exeter laici secundarii, clerks of the second form, from their position in the second range of seats. At S. Paul's, originally thirty in number, but latterly six, they lived in a common house after the collegiate manner, under the charge of two priests, and wore a surplice and black cope. Each vicar was presented by his master, and admitted by the dean and chapter, being on probation for a year to learn the psalter by heart. On admission he took deacon's or subdeacon's orders, and attended all the hours, Mary mass, &c., as a singer, and waited on the resident going to and coming from the church, and if absent warned him for chapter. Six live on the proceeds of a corporate estate. Until the Great Fire the six vicars choral, organist, and master of the boys lived in houses in Ave Maria Lane and on Ludgate Hill. One bore the title of pittanciary.

The term lay choral vicar occurs first at Salisbury, alongside the annuellars, in 1551; at Ripon, in 1635, they were called chanters; at York, songmen. At Exeter there was a vicar to every canon, whom he was bound to attend when going to church, or leaving it. Besides these were twelve secondaries, admitted at eighteen years of age, and serving as probationers, in the order of acolyths, to learn their duties, the psalter and its use, during one year: they were required to become subdeacons and deacons, and so rose to be priest vicars. They were excused attendance in choir while attending the grammar and song schools. In 1547 their number was reduced to twelve, each receiving £12 and a gown, and paying 1*s.* 4*d.* to be allowed in commons with the priest vicars. In 1563 they were reduced to ten. In 1613 they received £100, still paid by the priest vicars, and a moiety, now one-half, of the net proceeds of the tithes of Woodhay. Eight lay clerks, appointed by the chapter, receive about £70 a year, made up from a moiety of the tithes of Woodhay, about £40; £12. 10*s.* from the priest vicars; a stipend of £10 from the dean and chapter; and the rest from fees and rent of a vicarial house. Four secondaries or probationers appointed by the dean divide £110, originally £15. 6*s.* 8*d.*

At Salisbury seven receive wages: £20 from the vicars choral, as their substitutes; a daily gratuity from the chapter amounting to £23; Sunday gratuity, £7; dinner money, 7*s.*; introitus and funeral fees about 7*s.*: in all about £52. There is a fine of 10*s.* 6*d.* for absence on Sundays, Christmas and Ascension day, or the anniversary of the infirmary, and of 1*s.* 6*d.* on other days. In 1605, when they were called "church laics," they were seven in number, and had their wages increased from £8. 13*s.* 4*d.* to £12. At S. David's there are three supported on estates and tithes; one is organist. At Lichfield they were called, as they were in orders or laymen, clerk vicars and secular vicars, or secundarii (Dugdale's Monast. viii. 1259); they wore the almuce, black cope, and surplice, acting in turns as "rectors of the choir," except on simple feasts, when the hebdomadarii were in course. Seven form a corporation, with the vicars choral and subchanter. Their income is derived from leases, reserved rents, stall wages, commons, and houses; as vacancies occur the wages will rise to £100 a year. They are allowed absence on three days or six half days in each month, called sine days; the fine for absence is 2*d.* to the fabric fund, loss of commons, and 1*s.* for distribution among the rest. They may read the First Lesson or sing the Litany, as far as the LORD's Prayer, if appointed in the hebdomadary table, by the Stat. of Charles II., if the priest vicars could not sing; and must, if required, report on the qualifications of candidates. At York there are fourteen, with wages varying between £45 and £50. The four lay clerks of Bishop Sherborne's foundation at Chichester wore his initials, R. S., embroidered in gold and black thread, on the back and front of their "plain" (i.e., without apparel) "surplices." There are seven (in 1800 four) at wages varying from £40 to £50. At Wells there are seven, forming a corporation, founded 1349, and confirmed 1582, receiving in the very highest average £50, but usually far less. At Bangor six, as comportionists of Llandenam, receive between £25 and £30. At Hereford there are six, with an income each of £60; at Lincoln five, at £60, with certain fines and rents for houses in the close, on an average, £5.

In cathedrals of the New Foundation their annual wages vary from £114. 12*s.* at Durham, £40 at Peterborough, and £30 at Christchurch. They have not, in general, houses of residence. At Canterbury there are twelve, receiving £24 (instead of the statutable £4. 5*s.*), with a quotidian of 2*s.* 6*d.* for two daily services, and 1*s.* for attendance at one service, the fines being paid to a benefit fund; two others are at £60, without a quotidian, and the other at £24, with the lesser quotidian. One who is master of choristers receives also £20 (instead of the statutable £5. 10*s.*), and another £30, as instructor of choristers in singing. At Durham there are ten who divide £1,147; for three years they are on probation, at £100 a year. They must attend two services daily. One is master of choristers, receiving £25. At Winchester there are sixteen (instead of the statutable ten); three receive £73. 10*s.*; three £69. 10*s.*; three £57, and one £37: the supernumeraries have £5. At Carlisle there are eight: two are substitutes for the deacon at £50, and subdeacon £10; two, who attend daily twice, receive £50; one has £30, and another £25, and two represent the subsacrists, one at £51, the other at £26. At Chester there are six at £50, three to be always present at the services; one, as master of the choristers, has £50 and house. At Ely eight divide £400 from funds bequeathed in 1667 and 1714; they have also each £10 by statute, £3 in lieu of dinners, £12 by grant of chapter, 1812, with a fine of 1*s.* for absence at either daily service or the two weekly practices: one, as second master of the school, receives £40. At Rochester six receive £50, two being substitutes for the deacon and subdeacon; one, as master of the choristers, receives £20. There are no fines, but leave is granted by the dean and chapter. At Christchurch eight, at £20 a year, receive a gratuity of £10. At Gloucester there are six at £40; at Bristol six, in addition to the statutable £2. 19*s.* 2*d.*, receive a gratuity of £40; five supernumeraries are paid £40. At Norwich eight receive £30, by statute £18, and a gratuity of £12, added since 1808, a quotidian of 1*s.* for attendance, a house, or lodging-money. At Peterborough six (originally eight) receive £40, two being substitutes of the deacon and subdeacon. At Worcester eight have a stipend with corn rents equivalent to £50; one, as master of the choristers, receives £30 in addition. At Ripon six at £40 (in 1635 £4); one, as master of the choristers, receives £10. At Manchester four, with £50 (by charter £10). At Westminster twelve divide £105 to £122; attendance is required at the two daily services for six months.

Lecturer.—At Vienne the sacrist and chancellor were only officers. (Le Lievre, 192.) When the chancellor was not a divinity lecturer, he appointed a deputy, who at S. Paul's as divinity lecturer receives £185 a year, to be ready to preach on all saints' days and holidays, and on Wednesdays and Fridays in Lent, whenever the canon whose turn it is does not appear. Knight says that Dean Colet instituted a lecture, to be read three times a week by the chancellor, or his sufficient deputy (p. 116). At Salisbury a vicar choral is paid for preaching on saints' days. At Llandaff the junior vicar receives £9. 6*s.* 8*d.* for preaching money. At Lichfield the lecturer preaches on certain saints' days. At Exeter a lecturer who preaches the morning sermon on feast days receives £30 a year.

In all cathedrals of the New Foundation, from 1604—43, he was a recognized officer, receiving a stipend varying from £30 to £10 a year, and was a minor canon. At Carlisle for some time a lecturer was maintained, as the deputy of the dean and chapter. At Chester Queen Elizabeth appointed a lecturer, at a salary of

£40, to preach certain sermons in the year; but the dean and canons performed the duty, and divided the stipend. At Ely, as prælector theologus, appointed by the statutes of 1666, he receives a stipend of £80 for "guarding the pulpit," or for preaching on Sundays, fasts, or festivals, whenever the dean and canons are unable to do so. In 1570 a divinity reader was appointed at Winchester, who examined the major and minor canons weekly on the subject of his lectures. The theological lecturer is mentioned by Innocent III. in the Council of Lateran, c. xi. Decret. lib. v. tit. de magistris. An ecclesiastes, a prebendary, at Tournay, preached in Flemish to the people. (Molanus, ii. l. xxv.) Sometimes the ecolastre or scholaster was a dignitary superior to the theologal, because for a long time he did not instruct personally, but merely superintended schools. (Durand de Maillane.) In some places he or the capiscol executed his functions. There is a theologicus prælector at Sion, and a theologal prebendary at Girgenti. (Grævius Sic. iii. 769.) At Lyons the scholastique is one of the twenty perpetuels, with a submaster of choir next in rank; the theologal is an officer. The theologal of Valencia was founded in 1345. (Villaneuva, ii. 100.) The prebendary of Wittering, the theologal lecturer, is like the master of the prebendal school, prebendary of Higham, elected by the dean and chapter of Chichester. If the bishop's prebendary at Hereford refused to be prælector, he was to pay £20 a year to that officer, who was elected either specially or from the prebendaries by the dean and chapter, and received other payments and had chambers in the vicars' college. He had, after the dean and bishop's prebendary, a preference for election to a residentiaryship. He was to lecture on Tuesdays and Thursdays during ten weeks in each quarter. (Stat. 1583, c. 9.)

Maytinantes, or *Matutinales.*—Clerks who sang at the night services and matins.

Meriglerius, Meligerius, Marrelarius.—A custos, or church keeper. He derived his name from the marel, or token of lead which he gave to the canons and chaplains present in choir, as a qualification for the Saturday distribution. Marrancia denoted absence from choir. Marcaclarius, or Mareglier, or Marguillier, are other forms of the word.

Mistral.—A provost or bailiff, a corruption of ministerialis. The mistral of Vienne was a canon, the archbishop's delegate, acting as prefect of the city.

The *Œconomus* of the Greek Church was a dignitary who took charge of the goods of the church and the offerings of the faithful, of repairs and building of the fabric, the sick and poor, of the payment of stipends, and of the lands. The provost of canons in the Western Church corresponded to this officer, at Chartres, Tours, and elsewhere; and Morinus says his duty related to the temporal goods of the canons. (P. iii. exerc. xvi. c. v. § ix.—xvii.) By the

Council of Trent (Sess. xxiv. c. xvi.) an œconomist is appointed by the chapter in the vacancy of the see. The proctor of S. David's was the provost or œconomist. The œconomist of the house is the same as the dispensator, proctor, or cellarer, who presided over the granary, from which the canonical bread or wheat was furnished. (Molanus, i. c. xvii.) A cellarer is mentioned in connection with the fabric at S. Asaph in 1372. (Edwards, ii. 90.)

Organist and Master of the Choristers.—In some of the old cathedrals he is called master of the songschool, at Exeter clerk of the chapel, and usually is a lay vicar. At S. Paul's he was appointed by the præcentor to keep the table and instruct the boys. In the thirteenth century obituary of Hereford a clerk of the organs is mentioned. In the statutes of the New Foundation he is officially mentioned, and has a statutable stipend. At Salisbury he receives £20, and the wage of a lay vicar, besides £60. 14*s*. 4*d*. as instructor. At Lichfield he has £4, and is a lay vicar, receiving by statute of 1699 £4 a year. He was to sit among the vicars during the singing, ranking according to the position his master held. At Chichester, by stat. 1613, he was also to take his part in choir, when not engaged in playing on the organ. The master of choristers was to be paid £10 a year. At Wells the archdeacon is called in the early statutes archiscola. (Ang. Sac. i. 561.) At Hereford the organist and master of choristers received four silver marks from the residentiaries, and £8 from vacant vicarages. (Stat. 1631, c. iii.) At Exeter, being also master of the choristers, £200. At S. Paul's he is a lay vicar, and also master of choristers, £75. At Durham, £209; at Ely, £150; at Carlisle, £100; at Gloucester, £90 and a house; at Manchester, £150; at Worcester, £93, a house, and corn rent equivalent to £10; at Chester, £150 and a house. At Canterbury he receives £115; at Winchester, £170. At Ripon, in 1635, he had £16; and at Rochester, by statute, as master of the choristers, £10; but now has £119 and a house. At Peterborough he is master of the choristers. At S. David's he is a lay vicar; at Bristol his statutable pay is £10. At Rome the organ, as if an innovation, is never played in the presence of the Pope; and also at Liege, where, in order to be peculiar and unlike other churches, two bands of musicians were arranged on either side of the choir. (Molanus, lib. ii. c. x.) At Lyons there has never been an organ, or instrumental music.

Penitentiary.—(See Fleury, i. c. xix. p. 193.) This officer was appointed in order to remedy the disuse of confession, from a repugnance, on the part of many, to going before the ordinary person to receive it. "In cathedralibus ecclesiis ubi sunt sæculares canonici confiteantur ipsi canonici episcopo, vel decano vel cæteris personis ad hoc per episcopum vel decanum et capitulum constitutis." (Lyndwood, b. v. c. xvi. p. 327.) In some cathedrals, as at Carlisle, Kilkenny, Ely, Salisbury, Bangor, and Chester, as formerly at Lincolu and Chichester, there is a parish church; and abroad there is frequently a parochus, the dean's deputy or curate, who has a subordinate cure of souls, (Frances, 223,) the dean having cure of souls in the close. (Coke's Inst. c. lxxi. p. 155.) At Hereford he was the bishop's vicar, and had preference next to the dean for a residentiaryship, and could be prælector, if he chose; he paid no fee on admission, but £20 a year to the prælector. He could not leave the city with chapter-licence in his lifetime, and had no share in the commune after death. The dean of Exeter, or a deputy, received the confessions of all canons and members of the choir, 1225. (Barnes' Report, App. iii.) A penitentiary in foreign cathedrals must be a canonist or theologian of forty years of age, and is collated by the bishop. (Ceccop. ii. 121.) The bishop at S. Paul's appointed the penitentiary. There were four grand penitentiaries at Dunkeld, which was, in 1127, like Glasgow, founded on Salisbury, in place of Culdees. The foundation comprised dean, præcentor, chancellor, treasurer, archdeacon, subdean (the commissary and rural dean of the diocese), succentor, ten canons, four Abernethy vicars, ten vicars, one being the vice-penitentiary, six choristers, c. 1480. (Vitæ Episc. Dunkeld, 24, 29, 30, 68.) After 1236, residentiaries only shared the commune (p. 10.)

Personati, in foreign cathedrals, were pensioned clergy, stipendiaries, holding their benefices for life, and answerable for the discharge of the choral duties.

Petty Canons, Vicars Choral, and other Ministers of the Church.—Canon xlii. The origin of vicars choral is thus given by Ducange (v. 537) "Dimisso domicilii mensæque communis statu, redditus commoda ac preventus atque adeo ipsa prædia Ecclesiæ diviserunt in portiones quas præbendas appellarunt, substitutis ingenti disciplinæ Ecclesiasticæ detrimento mercede conductis honorariis psaltis qui quotidianum psalmodiæ laborem in choro ipsorum vice perferrent, inde vicarii chorales qui in officiis ecclesiasticis in choro vices canonicorum peragebant." The chief of these were, by an easy transition, called minores canonici, as representing the major canons, and parvi prebendarii, as receiving either (1) portionem diurnam cibi et potus quæ præbetur canonicis, or (2) certa stipendia; and as præbenda was often construed as beneficium, on the continent they were known as beneficiati. There is no earlier mention of vicars than in the middle of the twelfth century, and they appear at first to have been merely temporary substitutes for the canons, but about a century later the rule of having a vicar became permanent. Within a hundred years later as the chapter, the bishop's council, had rendered itself as independent as possible of the bishop, and each prebendary had secured his own prebend and patronage and local jurisdiction, so the vicars, assistants of the canons, became as independent as they could of their masters, and were then incorporated as colleges in the

English cathedrals of the old foundation, at S. David's, Armagh, S. Patrick's, Kilkenny, Limerick, Cashel, Tuam, Cork, Cloyne, Lismore, Ross, and Ardfert. Minor canons, after serving five years, have a claim in the disposal of patronage with canons, shared with any lecturer or master of the cathedral school (3 and 4 Vict. s. 44), but not beyond six miles from the cathedral (s. 45); and seven months' residence is required on the benefice. (1 and 2 Vict. c. 106, s. 39.) Canons were bound to sing service on feasts. (Scarf. iii. 148.) In S. Patrick's, according to Dr. Jebb's MS. notes, Archbishop de London founded the vicars choral, who in Archbishop Alan's time (1528—1534) were sixteen, but in 1635 only twelve. The fourteen capitular members had each his vicar, one represented four prebendaries, another two, and four prebendaries contributed to the general fund. Each vicar maintained a chorister or personista, ranked between a residentiary and prebendary, and sometimes held a prebend. All were in priest's orders, the senior was subdean, and the second succentor. The vicars, petty canons, and singing clerks were known under the generic title of vicars choral and ministers. The former were called Perpetui Vicarii at S. Asaph; Parvi Prebendarii at S. Paul's; Vicars Choral at York, Chichester, and Salisbury; Priests Vicars at Lichfield, Hereford, Wells, and Exeter, (vicarii de choro); Chaplains at Christchurch, and at Manchester till the recent act; and in the cathedrals of the new foundation Minor Canons, a name now made improperly general by the Act of Victoria, minor canons denoting in the old foundations peculiar officers, and in the new foundations a new order, stipendiaries of the dean and chapter; at Bangor for a century after the Reformation they were known as Conducts, i.e. stipendiaries without endowments. There was one vicar originally allotted to each prebendary, as his deputy to celebrate mass at the high altar, at S. Paul's, and attend the hours day and night, the masses of the Virgin, the Apostles, and chapter: they were priests, they wore the almuce of grey fur, and were to be elected from the secondaries. (For the customs of S. Paul's, see Rawlinson MS. 145, fo. 28.) At Lichfield, the vicars are still called, 1, the dean's (acting now as succentor); 2, the chancellor's; 3, the prebendary of Offley's; 4, the treasurer's; and 5, the præcentor's; they wore the almuce of Calabrian fur. At S. David's there is a bishop's vicar, the bishop there having been pro-dean; at Exeter the dean's vicar has a house. In the foreign cathedrals there were portionarii or assisii, so called from holding only a portion, or part of the profits, such as food, &c. They were also called Mansionarii, because bound to be perpetually resident and present at Divine Service: besides these there were inferior beneficiaries, in contradistinction to conducts, stipendiaries, having no freehold, called in Spain, chaplains of the cope; and also demies, as at Beauvais, Sens, Auxerre, and Seez, tertians, and quartans, named from the proportions allotted to them. (Frances, p. 231.) In Germany they were called Socii Vicarii. (Mayer, i. 23.) At Paris the Prêtres Perpetuels sat in the high stalls. (Moleon, 68.) At Lyons, Angers, Bourges, and Rouen, they were called Chantres Semiprebendes. At Vienne the Prêtres Chantres sat in the same row as the canons, but did not wear the amess (Moleon, 10) in the second range were clerks and clergeons-choristers. The master of the choir or chief of the chaplains sat at the head of the second range, (Scarfantoni, iii. 138,) and they were never to occupy the seat of an absent canon (148) but might exceptionally sit in the same line with them (143) otherwise their place was in the second row (i. 32, 96.) The subaltern members of the establishment at Rouen included eight petty canons, (four being called "of five marks," and four of "fifteen livres,") four colleges of chaplains-choral, the first called Dernetal, the second Albanes, the third Clementines, and the fourth of the Holy Spirit, or Flavacour. There were seventy chaplains, titulars of the chapels founded in the church. The number of chaplains permitted to wear the habit might be increased to 120. In 1453 there were eleven dignitaries, fifty-two canons, eight petty canons, forty-eight chaplains in four colleges, four enfans d'Aube, and sixty-nine chanting priests. At Pisa there were two classes of chaplains; 1, of the quinterno or register who shared in the daily distribution; 2, of the second order, who had no such share, sat in a lower range, and wore a cowl. The former constituted a college or university who had a steward, a chancellor, and four superintendents. (Ceccop. ii. 326.) At Urgel the vicars were called statores from standing in their masters' places. (Villanueva, ix. 181.)

At Wells the vicars (Statutes in MS. Harl. 6968, 1682) originally fifty-two in number, one for every canon except three (although only forty-nine are mentioned in the chapter) and founded or endowed by Bishop Jocelyn, 1223—1237, (Ang. Sac. i. 564,) were incorporated by Bishop Ralph in 1347; they received, in lieu of common bread of the grange which they had every second day, after 1242, a penny a day, the quotidian or petty commons, provided they were present at matins and the canonical hours, or were absent by permission from the dean or subdean. All others who hitherto had a whole commons of bread daily were to receive a penny a day and a farthing for half commons. (Wilkins, 684.) They also had their stall wages. They followed in choir the order (stationem) of the prebendaries their masters. If a well known candidate (A.D. 1263) presented to a vicariate could sing and play on an instrument (and was accepted by the vicars as a candidate, 1321,) he was admitted and approved by a majority of the vicars as acquainted with music (MS. Harl. 1682, fo. 176,) on probation of his morals and diligence in learning by heart the antiphonar, Psalter, and hymnal, for a year, under the charge of a person (auscultator) deputed by the præcentor, receiving his wages all the time, but forbidden to stand in superiori gradu or sing high mass; but if he was unknown before he was admitted to probation he was to be received without payment during fifteen days for reading and singing alone and with others. Canons were not compelled to entertain their vicars (A.D. 1252 and 1331) because they received wages from their masters and commons from the church; and vicars kept at their master's (dignitaries) table, were to receive nothing more, 1252, (MS. Harl. 6968, fo. 133, 6,) nor the mark (1331) due otherwise for doing the priest's office. (MS. Harl. 1632, fo. 14.) If guilty of indecent gestures during Divine service, or performing miracle plays or shows for sport, or wearing huge masks, 1321, (Comp. Synod. Worm. 1316,) they were deprived of their commons; if they revealed secrets of the chapter were excommunicated, and if absent for six months after recall were deprived. Aged or sickly vicars received their quotidian. Absence was noted by the tabular. No vicar altarista or chorister was to read gospel, epistle, or lection, until he had been heard to read it correctly as regards accent, pronunciation, and "sillaba." Vicars were to attend processions on Sundays doubles "quarta et viferiis pro rege," to use habits of comely length, and never to enter the church for ordinary service except in their habit, to forbear to summon another before a secular judge, to be suspended for a month if they were absent at their turn to read epistle and gospel, to rule the choir or celebrate the high or chapter mass, but for two months if slovenly in their office or talkative in choir, if hawkers, hunters, and anglers, idlers about the streets, or noisy loud singers abroad, if tavern-keepers, secular traders, or public players with dice or at games of hazard; for three months if tardy in choir or leaving it before the service was done. Commons at the end of the week were given to those only who had attended the hours and high mass. By Stat. 1243 and 1259, vicars were to be in the same orders as their masters, and to live two and two in houses, (MS. Harl. 1682, fo. 10); in 1298 all vicars were to attend matins, the Mary mass in choir, high mass, vespers and compline, and other hours, especially when None was said after dinner: six to be present on the dean's and six on the præcentor's side; on pain of losing their daily penny for absence at prime, high mass, vespers, and compline. (Ibid. fo. 7, b.) They were not to leave the choir during service to talk in the nave or about the pillars with lay or suspected persons. In 1263 their position in choir was determined by the order of the stall to which they had been admitted. (MS. Harl. 6968, fo. 130.) They were not to frequent market in their choir habit; but were required to consult the table to see whether their master or themselves were noted to begin the invitatory or rule the choir. The hebdomadary, priest, deacon, and subdeacon, were always to be prepared for the mass to which they were inscribed; the former on Sundays after procession and collect was to go at once, with a light carried before him to the roodloft and there say the appointed prayers which all in priest's orders must attend. Rectors of the choir under pain of losing their day's wages were to know the hymns and psalms which they had to begin; and to intone the psalms in the proper mode. After prime vicars were to attend in chapter to hear the gospel of high mass read and to be corrected, if offenders, by the president of chapter; they were to attend all processions and to lay aside their processional copes until after the collect in choir, at night they were not to wear a silken over the black cope. Those tabled for the chapter mass were to say Placebo and Dirige in the chapter house or library daily. Vicars receiving the distribution for the dead and not attending the whole service forfeited an equivalent on Saturday out of their wages; if they neglected to say annuals they were delated by the sworn spies (exploratores.) The vicars were married at this period although their wives lived in the town and were visited by them under certain restrictions. When reconstituted by Queen Elizabeth, 1582, there were to be not more than twenty nor less than fourteen vicars, but now there are only four (besides five laymen) who are recommended by the chapter to the college of vicars for election, and serve one year of probation. They live on the profits of corporate estates and receive a quarterly payment of £1. 14*s*. 11*d*. from the chapter. Their chief called the principal is assisted by five seniors chosen annually Nov. 8.

Altaristæ, or vicars, 1321, who carried arms or committed robbery in the church or cemetery at Wells were to be deprived: if they neglected their service to the priests at the various altars between sunrise and high mass they lost their wages for the week: their duties were also to take charge of the altars and say a psalter for the canons and departed, and another for the bishop, chapter, and benefactors. The Altaristæ were properly the deputies of chantry priests, officiating clergy. (Scarfantoni, i. p. 11.)

At York there were thirty-five vicars, nine persons, six deacons and subdeacons, two clerks of vestry, twelve thuriblers and choristers. (MS. Harl. 6971, fo. 133, b.) About 1390 they swore on their admission that they would dine in the Bedern hall; they must have come before the end of the Gloria Patri, at matins of the Venite, and at vespers of the Psalms to obtain their quotidian. They appear to have been in a disgraceful condition; they came before the gospel and left after the consecration, and evaded great part of the services on anniversaries, and yet claimed their quotidian; they scarcely sang three months in the year, frequented taverns, and made great noise and singing till midnight, while the service was in church, and had the Bedern gate left open at night for their return. Scarcely eight vicars attended choir at a time, and the books were left uncorrected. In 1291 no vicar was to be admitted except by the dean, or in his absence by four or five prebendaries at least unanimous in their choice. (MS. 6971, fo. 48.) He was required to have a good voice, and to wear in the city a close habit without a hood thrown back or chequered hose. (Ib. 4200, fo. 20.) Every canon was required to maintain a priest vicar and pay him forty shillings a year at Martinmas and Pentecost. In 1294 vicars coming tardy to choir or talking therein lost their daily penny, which went to the custodes chori, who delated the absent and offenders to the chamberlains. They were to ask leave of absence from the dean or a major (one who had kept the Greater Residence) or a canon, or the major de choro, under pain of losing commons for eight days, and still attending the services on penalty of excommunication. Only those present at matins were invited to dinner by canons. In 1252 he received 1*d.* a day, paid weekly. One was deputed by the dean and chapter to pay at Martinmas 10*s.*, and at Pentecost 10*s.*, to each vicar as stipend, the residue passed into communia. The choir services were divided into 1, Major, and 2, Minor Offices. The first included matins, prime, high mass after tierce, vespers, and in Lent comprised compline with Placebo and Dirige. The second tierce, sexts, nones, compline, and, out of Lent, chapter mass. The time of the hours varied according to the season. All the thirty-six vicars were present on major and double feasts, twenty-four at the hours and high mass, and thirty on vigils. Prime was said at 7 a.m., but between 8 and 9 on doubles and Sundays. Then chapter was held, followed by the chapter or Our Lady's mass. High mass, so called because accompanied by music and celebrated at the high altar, succeeded after tierce. The vicar who omitted his duty lost his 1*d.*, but he might miss matins once a week, or one major, or two minors a day. Vicars and clerks of choir were to attend chapter for correction on Saturdays. Vicars and clerks of the sacristy received the linen clothes and carpets of the bier of a dead canon. The chamberlain or custos noted absences, rendered his accounts twice a year before one canon and four vicars, and then divided the residue at the rate of 2*d.* for every major feast and solemn octaves. They were incorporated 1252 and again 1264, and under a custos in 1461. They received corporate estates in 1252, confirmed 1269. There are now five who receive from £150 to £200, and £30 from the chapter: formerly they were paid by their prebendaries. Two are always to be in attendance.

At Exeter there were originally twenty-four vicars, one for each canon (attitulati singuli singulis canonicis;) they in 1205 received the church of Woodbury from Bishop Marshall who required them to pay the chaplain 40*s.* a year. In 1237 Bishop Brewer bound the dean to pay twelve marks to the vicars in consideration of additional services. In 1268 there were twenty-four members. In 1540 there were twelve secondaries or clerks of the second form, who were eligible by the dean to become vicars choral if learned and expert in music. (Rawlinson MS. fo. 40.) In 1613 they were required to pay to the lay vicars, £100 a year, with the moiety of the tithes of Woodbury, after a deduction of £20 and the provision of a house for the curate. They still pay £100 and one half of the net proceeds of Woodbury to the lay vicars: their present income is about £200, derived from £80 out of the rent charge of Woodbury, £66 from head rents and land tax, and £8 or £10 from the rent of a vicarial house, and the remainder from fines on the renewal of leases. They receive at Christmas £4 under the term of "choir feast money." They were incorporated Feb. 26, 1401, being twenty in number under a custos. Their charter was renewed May 5, 1558. In 1547 they were reduced to eight; in 1563 there were six; in 1613, four, the present number. There were twenty-four, besides the twelve secondaries. If a canon did not appoint a vicar within a month after his appointment on the occurrence of a vacancy the preferment lapsed to the dean. Vicars present at high mass and the canonical hours received the portions of the absentees and of vacant offices: they received all burial fees less than one shilling; they were to attend the mass of the Virgin after matins; to dine and sup in their common hall, and to sleep in their houses in the Kalendar Hay, founded in 1388 by Bishop Brentyngham. Vicars attached to chantries attended the canonical hours. The vicars who did not do reverence to the dean were to stand before the cross without the choir, before which a lamp burned perpetually at all the canonical hours, during one whole day and night. They wore the grey almuce lined with black and were required to play on an instrument. They provided a weekly deacon and subdeacon. For non-attendance at high mass and the canonical hours they were deprived of their quotidian for a week; if they continued contumacious they forfeited their stipend to the fabric fund and were removed by the bishop, dean, and chapter. Their annual wage was 20*s*. They kept perpetual residence except when granted absence by their respective masters, or at times of blood-letting when they were allowed to be away during two nights. By Stat. 1540 a canon was to appoint, within a month after a vacancy, a vicar expert in music; or in default the dean appointed after eight days, but the bishop if the canon was beyond seas. The dean or president of chapter punished delinquents. (MS. Rawlinson, fo. 40.) In 1286 as in the other cathedrals of England, the canons were to sit at either end of the choir after the dignitaries, the vicars occupying the middle stalls on each side; the order of canons was in choir and procession, seniors in date of installation before juniors, but priests before deacons and deacons before subdeacons. (Ib. fo. x. b.) They forfeited the week's cotidian for absence on a single day after three warnings. They were examined before admission in singing and the use of an instrument: they remained in their position for one year after their master's death at a stipend of 20s. The licence of the dean was required for the admission of clerks of the upper grade or second form, and vicars if absent were appointed by the dean and chapter. (Barnes, App. iii.) In 1358 there were twenty-four secundarii, the number of the canons, and to the same proportion the annuellars and secondaries were reduced: they were forbidden to keep public banquetings and drinkings in the church, specially in the choir, and to talk during divine service. No vicar or secondary might have leave to be absent beyond eight or fifteen days at one turn or different turns for so long in the year, and then many on the same grade or in the same choir (decani v. cantoris) might not be away together. He was not invited to table by a canon unless he had attended matins. The dean or president of chapter corrected offenders. All were to dine and sup in the common hall except guests of a canon or some respectable host, they were to sleep in their chambers. Those present at prime were to attend the chapter.

At Chichester they were incorporated June 15, 1334, and confirmed in 1464. Their charter for principal and commonalty was granted in 1277. Their number in 1396 was twenty-eight (Reg. Rede,) in 1409 twenty-six, including all ministers; in 1415 thirty vicars, priests, deacons, and subdeacons, (Chichele, Reg. 194, b.;) in 1429 twelve; in 1441 twenty-six, (Praty, Reg. fo. 73, b.;) in 1478 twenty-two, (Storey, Reg. fo. 70;) in the episcopate of Sherborne eighteen; in 1527, twenty, (Reg. Sherborne, ii. 98;) in 1521 fourteen, and two clerks, (Reg. fo. c.;) twelve in the reign of Henry VIII., and from five to eight in that of Elizabeth. In 1342 there were four called minor canons, out of a college of twenty-nine priests, while there were besides five chantry priests, twelve choir boys, and a subtreasurer. Henry de Garland, dean of Chichester, left a tenement and 27*s*., its yearly produce, for distribution; viz., to the four vicars who are called parvi prebendarii each 3*d*.; to twenty-five other vicars each 2*d*.; to the subtreasurer 3*d*.; to the commonalty 3*d*.; to the twelve boys of choir each 1*d*.; to the chantry priests each 1*d*. (Swayne MS. fo. 299.) Before the Civil Wars there were twelve singing men and eight boys. Their president was called principal. They received "stall wages" for singing high mass from their respective prebendaries, and an ample allowance of bread. In 1583 they dined together in a common hall on the first Thursday in every month. Since the Restoration there have been only four who have corporate estates and receive each £6. 13*s*. 4*d*. from the chapter, and £12 partition or common bread-money, in commutation for wheat and flour. They were required to be in the close before curfew rang, and not wear a sword except when going into the country; to keep no dogs within their precinct, and to ask no person to dinner without giving notice to the cook. They were not to delay in the hall after evening bevers 7 p.m., but to keep silence within the precinct from 7 p.m. to 7 a.m. Dinner was served after high mass, and supper after the last anthem, sung before the cross in the nave. The Bible was to be read during dinner, and an anthem sung at its close. In 1197 three communars were appointed, to pay 12*d.* weekly to residents, 3*d.* to vicars, and quotidian if attending mass or vespers. The priest vicars received one mark, deacons half a mark, subdeacons 40*d.* a year. A vicar received every Saturday 3*d.* besides the penny paid by his master. No vicar was to be admitted who was in an inferior order to his master. (1232.) On the four great feasts each vicar received 6*d.* in lieu of the wine hitherto dispensed on those days in choir. As he was maintained at the table of his master when resident, the quotidian pence were given to his master whether the one or the other attended the night office. If absent from any office to which he was tabled he was fined 1*d.* or 2*d.* In case of sickness he had to supply his place in choir by deputy. In 1345 the subdean is mentioned with the vicars as appearing at a visitation; and in 1466 there is a notice of the subdeanery or perpetual vicarage at S. Peter's altar.

At Lincoln they were first established by Bishop Hugh, and were incorporated 1396 and 1441. They have each a house, and £19. 6*s.* paid by the chapter, and a share in their corporate estates, amounting on an average to £43, to each of the four members. In 1534 there were twenty-five vicars. They received 40*s.* a year as wages, and could be dismissed by their masters with a notice of three months; they were presented by their masters to the dean, if they could sing and read, on probation for two years, in the first of which they were required to learn their hymnal and antiphonar, and in the second the psalter by heart. The vicar was then admitted, having sworn obedience to the dean and fealty to the Church and his master. If a canon failed to appoint a vicar he still had to pay the wages, which went to the vicars' commune. Every year they received half a mark over and above their wages. Bishop Oliver procured the erection of the vicars' close. (Schalby, MS. Harl. 6954, fo. 6.)

At Lichfield they were incorporated and received houses in 1240: in 1374 they had a common hall presided over by the præcentor, and it was not disused until the time of the civil wars. In 1340 they had a collegiate seal. In 1348 their wage was 1*d.*; in 1390 3*d.* with commons daily. By Pateshull's statutes they had a house at Stow for the reception of superannuated members. The corporation consisted of five (at the Reformation fourteen) priests and seven secular clerks. One vicar was called the hebdomadary, the celebrant or officiating priest of the week. Absence was granted for three days in each month. The fines for non-attendance were 1*d.*; 2*d.* paid to the fabric fund, and loss of commons. Their income is now 3*d.* a day for commons; stall wages varying from £1. 6*s.* 8*d.* to £2. 6*s.* 8*d.*, and rents of official houses valued at from £3 to £20 a year, averaging about £100. They receive each 40*s*. more than a vicar choral. 6*s*. 8*d*. payable on the renewal of every lease are paid among the members in rotation. Each dignitary and the prebendary of Offley had his vicar among the whole number of five; they rank by statute of 1699 as follows: succentor, dean's vicar, chancellor's vicar, and sacrist or treasurer's vicar. The treasurer is now a canon residentiary, and the prebendal stall of Sawley is not held by him. By recent statute fourteen vicars' stalls have been refilled, four held by priests being the vicars of dignitaries, and ten by laymen, one being organist; and the vicarial stalls of Gaia major and Sandiacre have been also restored. There were once thirty-one vicars. Bishop Hacket fixed the number at twelve, five being priests. The vicars choral of the four persons were to be in priests' orders, and wear the calabre amess, receiving 6*s*. 8*d*. over their yearly wages to supply the place of a canon at high mass at the high altar, and to furnish two rectors of choir to a canon when celebrant. A vicar entering choir without his habit forfeited 1*d*. They could not leave the town for three nights without the dean's licence, nor be blooded without public leave from the chapter. The prebendary of Offley's vicar represented the fifth residentiary. No vicar could be absent for more than two days without leave: for a first offence in the thirteenth century he was corrected "like the religious;" for a second fault punished more severely; and on the third occasion expelled. Aged vicars were allowed to retire to a hospital at Stowe for life. No vicar could be removed except by the dean and chapter. Every canon, whether resident or not, was bound to maintain a vicar; and on his neglect for two months to fill a vacancy, the dean and chapter appointed. Priests were not admitted to a clerk's stall except they knew the canticum organicum, or consented to serve as clerks. Vicars frequently absent from day or night hours were to be removed, or punished as perjurers. No vicar might hold two offices; one noted the absence of his fellows and the "two chaplains." If a vicar tabled to sing or read was absent, he lost the commons of two days; if absent at an obit, he forfeited his portion. No vicar, under pain of excommunication, might remove a book from the choir or vestry without leave. Four vicars, two in each choir, received the "insigne" on certain feasts monthly. If a vicar wished to leave the choir, he asked leave of the dean, senior canon, or succentor. At the least peal of matins and vespers the hebdomadary commenced the service. To prevent the vicars leaving church after receiving their pay, the night wages were paid during the singing of the Benedictus, and the quotidian given at the last hour in choir before dinner. The newly appointed vicar was presented by his master to the dean and chapter, and examined by the præcentor or succentor to serve as a probationer. If finally approved, the succentor presented him for admission to the dean and chapter, when he had first taken the oaths of due service to the Church, obedience to the dean and chapter, and observance of the statutes. He received 20*s*. from his master yearly, but had larger wages if a priest, to be agreed upon between them. There were formerly twenty-seven vicars, but they had been reduced to twenty-one or nineteen in 1504. At the Restoration there were only six; they had previously sixteen houses. The new vicar, in the time of James I., had to give a "service feast" at the end of his year of probation, at a cost of £8 or £10. The four vicars of the dignitaries officiated on doubles in the absence of the residentiaries. By Pateshull's statutes they wore black copes, black almuces, and surplices; and on doubles, in processions, silk copes. The dignitaries' vicars wore a calabre amess, and received 6*s*. 8*d*. over their wages, as they were to supply the place of canons at high mass, as celebrants. The matin, or Lady mass, sung by the chaplain of S. Chad, and attended by workpeople and servants, preceded prime, and was followed by chapter, and in Lent by the requiem mass. High mass was sung before nine a.m. After nones and dinner vespers were said, succeeded usually by compline; but occasionally a collation or spiritual conversation was interposed. In summer (from Trinity Sunday to Nat. B. V. M.) there was an interval, because matins were said after compline. In winter an interval was to be made between vespers and twilight, for the compline hymn began, "Before the daylight dies away." According to a different statute, nocturns were said from Christmas to Easter at midnight, and from Easter to Trinity-tide at dawn; and on feasts of nine lections, after vespers, till Sept. 8. Then followed the Lady mass, prime, chapter, with reading of the Martyrology, the Preciosa (Precious in the sight of the Lord is the death of His saints,) the Tabula (the weekly roll of services and officiating clergy;) on Saturdays and eves of doubles benediction and business, and in Lent commendation. Then mass in chapter, sung without deacon or subdeacon, tierce, sexts, high mass, at nine a.m., on doubles, with two deacons and subdeacons, and two thuriblers and two acolytes in silken copes, with two crosses preceding the Gospeller, before whom went the taper-bearers. Then nones (dinner and peal for the dead;) vespers (an interval in winter occurred between twilight and vespers, but a longer space in summer followed supper and compline before matins;) and compline (in Lent succeeding collation in choir in commemoration of the dead.) From Trinity-tide to Sept. 8, on feasts of nine lections matins were said immediately after compline, until, owing to abuses at supper, the custom was restricted to certain days only.

At Hereford, they were incorporated, Sept. 6, 1396, under a custos. There were twenty-seven in the time of Richard II.; at the Reformation, twenty; in the time of Elizabeth, twelve; and just before the civil wars sixteen, all graduates, and ordained. There are now six, instead of the statutable twelve; they have corporate revenues. The body receives £12. 3*s*. 4*d*. yearly, and each member twenty-six bushels of wheat from the capitular revenues. Besides these, like the foreign habituez, were "frequentantes chorum," who were neither canon's vicars nor recipients of certain stipends, but attended in choir at irregular periods. In the third form were canons and priests, in the second deacons and subdeacons vicars, in the third all clerks of inferior orders. Before admission into choir the introduction and maintenance in board and lodging by a canon or licence of the dean and chapter was requisite. The new vicar had to learn the hymnal, psalter, and antiphonar within a year, and a day. Only a canon priest or the dean's vicar might celebrate at the high altar, except in case of necessity, when the senior vicar was to supply the vacancy. The deacon or subdeacon, hebdomadary canons, might, on all but the greater feasts, be represented by their vicars. If a vicar spoke disrespectfully of a canon, he was suspended, and for the third offence deprived. They were to attend matins in the cathedral at 5 or 5.30, according to the season, daily. Their quotidian was called secta chori. No vicar was to be admitted except by introduction of a canon, who was to maintain him in board and lodging: if he left his master, the dean and chapter might retain him. The perpetual vicars, who received a certain portion in the church, were those of S. Nicholas' or Cawkbridge, S. Agnes', S. Margaret's or Philip Hayes, S. Michael's or Kingston, S. Mary's or Ann Bohun, and those of Diddlebury or Hom Lacy. Two were to bury the dead. (Stat. 1584, c. iv.) No vicar was admitted except after examination in music by the succentor and vicars, (c. vii.) The subdean is only mentioned in the Laudable Customs as serving at the high altar as the dean's vicar on certain occasions, and rendering an account of the rents of the four capitular manors. Absolon, clerk, founded the vicarage of Holy Trinity; Canon P. Rufus, another vicarage; Roger de Cawkbridge another (Obit. p. 11;) W. de Hamme, clerk, another; Canon W. de Haye, the vicarage of S. Francis' altar (ib. 14;) Canon P. de Haye another (ib. 23;) Matthew de Cygonia, Canon, that of S. Nicholas' altar (ib. 19;) and Master Alexander, the secular, another vicarage (ib. 25.) Perpetual vicars were to attend all the hours, they were the actual ministers of the church; the other vicars were maintained by endowed canons. A vicar who refused to sing or read in choir when tabled was delated by the succentor in choir; and if a deacon or subdeacon was flogged on the bare back by the hebdomadary; and if a priest besought pardon on bended knee. Vicars of the second or third form also received discipline for failure in singing, and those of the first form had sharper punishment. By Statute, 1637, there were to be twelve vicars choral and four subcanons, deacons, or subdeacons;

the latter (Stat. 1583) might be laymen, but were required to live in the vicars' college. They constituted "the lower chapter," and consisted originally of eight persons, all in holy orders. According to the Consuetudines, there were four vicars of the abbots of Lyra and Corneilles, and six vicars, two priests, two deacons, and two subdeacons, founded by Bishop de Maidenston, receiving twenty marks from Diddlebury a year; the priests three marks, deacons 20*s*., the subdeacons two marks; four priest vicars, one celebrating at the Cross, another in the Lady Mass, a third for Philip Rufus, and the fourth for Master Alexander; all these were to attend all the hours in choir. In 1637 (Hargrave MS. 246, 357; Harl. 2983, 4343; Benet Coll. MS. cxx. 485) there were to be twelve vicars choral and four subcanons, deacons, and subdeacons. There were two Diddlebury, two Hom Lacy vicars, a De Haye, a Cawkbridge, and an Agnes vicar, so called from their foundation, the four minor canons probably represented the four junior canons. They were required by weeks to say matins at 5 a.m. daily between Annunciation and Sept. 1, and at other times at 6.30 on pain of a fine of 1*d*. a day, and of losing their whole share for a year in sportula sectæ chori, if they did not attend lecture in their college chapel on all Sundays at 3 p.m. (St. 1583.)[1]

At S. Paul's they were incorporated in honour of Queen Anne by King Richard II., on August 1, 1395; but they had lived in a college since 1353. They still retain their offices of (1) subdean, (2) succentor, (3) divinity lecturer, (4) senior and (5) junior cardinals, (6) librarian, (7) gospeller, (8) epistoler, (9) almoner, (10) warden: there are still twelve. They by old usage presented two candidates, of whom the chapter chose one; but by 3 and 4 Vict. c. 113 the election is absolutely in the chapter. They all attended on Sundays and litany days, and two at other services. They have a share in the "cupola fund," and possess corporate estates and hold benefices. Minores prebendati sacerdotes, or minores canonici, were often to confess to the penitentiary, ut celebrantes ad majus altare solempniter cum ministris inferiorum officia ministrorum non presumant. (MS. Camb. c. 5, 21, fo. xxvi. b.) In 1295 the subdean held only an office and ministry in order to supply the place of the dean, and oversee the proper conduct of the services (fo. xlix.) by the inferior ministers, minor canons, and others. He received one white loaf and a bolla of bitter ale. Besides the minor canons, there were thirty vicars, one for each canon, (Ib. fo. xxvi. b.,) who were to be expert in music, to be in

[1] The following rubric occurs in the MS. injunctions of the Bishop of Worcester, commissioner to Cardinal Pole, issued to the cathedral church of Hereford, July 17, 1558, § 5:—"At the naming of Jesus in singing or saying, every man shall give token of reverence with vailing their bonnets and bending their knees, and likewise when the verse *Sit Nomen Domini benedictum* is sung, and the psalm *Laudate pueri Dominum*; also in the creed at the saying of the verse *Et Incarnatus est Spiritu*, and these words, *Et Homo factus est*."

holy orders, and say the Lady matins before mass. They wore plain black almuces of black cloth, and by day, pileum duplicatum (fo. xxvii.,) two priests were to superintend the vicars' houses, and mark them in, (fo. liv., lv. See also Tanner MS. 145, and Rawlinson, 371.) In S. Paul's there were three masses, the Lady, the Apostles', and the high or chapter mass, followed by a mass of requiem for their founder, sung by the minor canons, who were required, being all priests, to represent in turn the canons at the three daily masses at the high altar, and were bound to attend the day and night hours. (Dugd. 252.) They were to be chosen from ministers of the church, if possible. The only other instances of *minor canons* as distinct from vicars are those of S. Patrick's, instituted in 1431, (Const. Abp. Talbot; Mason's Hibern. p. 34,) the eight moindres chanoines of Rouen, and the petty canons of Toledo. There were also four minor canons at Chichester, but at Salisbury the minor canons were greater canons below the order of deacons; the parvi were in all inferior orders. At Hereford there were four minor canons or subcanonici (formerly two deacons and two subdeacons, Stat. 1585, c. vii.) among the vicars. The two vicars of Diddlebury are the deacons, the two vicars of Hom Lacy the subdeacons. (Stat. 1631, c. v.) The major canon at York, 1294, was defined to be one who had completed the great residence. (MS. 4200, fo. 43, Harl.) At Hereford, Dr. Jebb says, the four minor canons, forming a corporation, officiated as priests under the residentiaries; whilst the vicars choral in orders took the lessons and litany. In case of dispute, the decision was in the præcentor, or, in case of his inability, in the chapter.

At Salisbury (Tanner MS. 327) they were incorporated in 1410 under a proctor or advocate. There were in the fourteenth century twenty-one priests, eighteen deacons, and eleven subdeacons vicars, besides seven chantry priests. (Lamb. Reg.) In 1468 there were thirty-one vicars choral and thirteen stipendiary priests. The chapter pays now £42. 13*s.* 4*d.* among the four members, as their share of the communa: they received, by Stat. 1268, each 1*d.* when the canon had 10*d.*, and were appointed as probationers for one year. The rule for attendance at all the hours was peremptory. By Stat. 1214 they received 2*d.* for attendance on doubles, rogations, and S. Martin's day; might accept legacies, and were not removable except for "enormous and manifest offences." By Stat. 1222 and 1319 the vicar was a probationer for one year, in order to learn his duties, the psalter, and antiphonar, by heart. On his admission he took the oath of canonical obedience to the dean, and of fidelity to his master. By Stat. 1268 he was confirmed in his right to a quotidian and bursary from his master, as the stipendiary representative of a prebendary. He forfeited the quotidian if absent from matins. He might supply his place by a convicar, if required as a bailiff, or in domestic business, by his master. He might by licence be absent if unwell, or attending the funeral of a friend; and in 1338 the vicars received licence from the Crown to acquire lands for the increase of their commons. Punishment was inflicted if they ran disorderly, or skipped out of choir, or lifted or let down their seats (stallos) noisily. In 1605 there were six vicars choral, at a stipend of £12 a year. The lay vicars were their substitutes in choir. (For the regulations of choir see Rawlinson MS. 371, fo. 80; and for the statutes, Tanner MS. cccxxvii.) In 1197 the order was: south side—dean, archdeacon of Dorset, subdean, canons (according to rank,) priest and first deacon vicars, archdeacon of Wilts, chancellor; north side—chanter, archdeacon of Berks, succentor, canons, priest and first deacon vicars, archdeacon of Wilts, treasurer. In the second form minor canons, deacons, and clerks; in the first form petty canons and other petties, according to age.

At Bangor there are two who divide the tithes of Bangor, £800, and comportions of Llandinam, £140. In 1504 there were the dean, præcentor, chancellor, treasurer, archdeacon, five canons, two vicars choral, three chaplains, one being chantry priest of S. Catherine's, and the third a conduct. (Reg. Warham, fo. 220.) At S. David's they form the lower chapter, and originally consisted of eight members in holy orders; but at an early date the organist was a layman. The numbers afterwards fluctuated between six and five, the others being laymen, of whom the organist was one. The college now consists of a subchanter, two priest vicars, and three lay vicars. The minor canons have estates and £85 a year. At S. Asaph there are four receiving £50 a year, and acting as vicars of the parish. By Bishop Leoline's ordinance, 1296, confirmed 1558, there were to be a dean and fourteen canons, including the dean, archdeacon, vicedean, præcentor, and treasurer; four minor canons or vicars choral, three chaplains (or vicars of the dean, præcentor, and chancellor), to sing in church and serve their cures; an organist, four choristers, found by two prebendaries, a subsacrist and aquæ-bajulus. (Edwards' S. Asaph, ii. 74, 134.) Ten vicars are mentioned in 1346 (ib. 85) as serving in the Lady chapel. These in 1380 are described as four perpetual vicars, and six minor or petty vicars of choristers. (Ib. 91.)

At Llandaff the senior vicar receives £273, the junior vicar £60, and each has £6. 9*s*. 3*d*. preaching money. Hugh de Bohun founded two chaplain priests 1292. (Cole MS. xxix. 41, b.) At Kilkenny, according to Dr. Jebb's MS. notes, there were four vicars choral, four stipendiaries, and four choristers, founded by Bishop St. Leger in the thirteenth century, who occupied a college and common hall till 1641. In S. Patrick's the original number was six; the college was founded by Archbishop Talbot in 1431. The vicars choral were founded by

Archbishop H. de Londres. In the time of Archbishop Allen there were sixteen vicars; five have always been priests; but in 1615 and 1639 there were only twelve. Provision for sixteen was made in 1664. The fourteen capitular members had each his distinct vicar (1528—34;) four prebendaries had one between them, two had one, four paid a stipend to the body generally, and two contributed nothing. They were called choristæ (as at Dunkeld,) or personistæ, and had rank between the residentiaries and prebendaries; sometimes they were appointed prebendaries by the dean. At S. Patrick's the vicars hitherto celebrated mass at the high altar in absence of the canons; they were to attend at all daily offices (except certain services,) all on holydays, and two on weekdays. All were in priest's orders; the senior was subdean, and the second subchanter, "horum officium est interesse Divinis quolibet die et inservire Ecclesiæ, in matutinis et vespertinis." At Ardfert, by the royal visitation of 1615, there ought to be five vicars. (Supp. to Irish Eccles. Reg. 1822.) In the time of Harris there were five stipendiaries at Tuam. (Harris' Ware, vol. i.) Lismore has five clerical vicars, founded by Bishop St. Christopher in 1230. At Kilkenny there were four clerical vicars, founded by Bishop St. Leger in the thirteenth century, with four stipendiaries and four choristers, founded 1553—65. (Ib. p. 418.) At Cashel there are five vicars, nominated by the five dignitaries; at Limerick, six; at Cork and Cloyne, four. At Leighlin four minor canons were instituted by Bishop Mulgan, 1422—33. (Ib. 459.) Waterford was founded by King John, for twelve canons and twelve vicars. (Smith's Waterford, p. 173.) There were at one time six minor canons (Cotton's Fasti, i. 37;) in 1615 there were four dignitaries, four prebendaries, and four chaplains (ib. p. 17.) Bishop Muirhead, 1452—73, built the vicars' college at Glasgow. The canons lived in Drygate and Rotten Row in houses built before 1445. At Aberdeen twenty vicars choral were added in 1506, with eleven choristers. By statutes both of the old foundation and of the new foundation, all the inferior ministers are removable after three monitions.

By the original constitution of the New Foundations, the number of vicars was equal to that of the canons. They were to be perpetually resident, except by licence of the dean and chapter, under penalty of the forfeiture of their stipend for three months, if absent so long, or a mulct in proportion to their absence. The fine was 1*d.* on ordinary days, or 2*d.* on Sundays and feasts, for absence from matins, litany, or communion; 1*d.* was levied on all who came after the Venite at matins, or at the end of the first psalm at evensong; 2*d.* was the fine for disobedience to the præcentor; and at Canterbury, if less than twelve of the ministers was the number present, absentees were fined 1*s.* These fines were distributed at the end of each quarter among those who had been present, proportionably to their times of attendance. The oath of a minister ran thus:—

"Ego, ——, ecclesiæ cathedralis in ministrum electus, juro me nihil solvisse promisisse vel soluturum esse directe vel indirecte pro acquisitione hujus loci vel muneris, et insuper quòd quamdiu in hâc ecclesiâ morabo, omnes institutiones et statuta quatenùs me concernunt, pro virili meâ inviolabiliter observabo; ad hæc decano et canonicis debitam obedientiam et reverentiam exhibebo, denique commodum et honorem hujus ecclesiæ diligenter procurabo, sicut me Deus adjuvet et hæc sancta evangelia."

In Chester only, of these cathedrals, the minor canons have a common property. By the Caroline statutes of Canterbury, the twelve minor canons appointed by Henry VIII. were converted into six minor canons and six substitutes; the latter were united with the former in 1723. The Caroline statutes of Ely (MS. Benet Coll. cxx. 207, 407; Harl., 6385, 7049) reduced their number from eight to six, and the same principle has been followed in the other cathedrals. [The Act 3 and 4 Vict. c. 113 now fixes the number at not more than six, nor less than two, and the stipend at not less than £150; but there are insuperable difficulties where the minor canons form a corporation, owing to the omission of a definition in the Act whether the stipend is to be paid from the common fund of the Ecclesiastical Commissioners, or from the chapter property. No benefice but the city chapelries was tenable by a minor canon. By Act 3 and 4 Vict. c. 113, s. 46, no future minor canon may hold a benefice beyond six miles from the cathedral. Sometimes they have houses, sometimes a money allowance in lieu.] There are now five, instead of six, minor canons; each receives £22. 10*s*. and a house, or lodging allowance. They are to be always resident, except by leave of the dean and chapter, and hold the four city chaplaincies. For more than forty years before 1840 the service was not intoned. One as deacon or epistoler receives £8, one sacrist £1. 6*s*. 8*d*.; two divide the duties of the prælector theologus, appointed 1666, and receive each £40. The auditor receives £7. 10*s*., the librarian £7; the precentor has an additional stipend. At Canterbury there are six (instead of the statutable twelve,) appointed by the dean and chapter, continually resident, except by leave of the dean, vice-dean, or canon in residence; two must be present on all Litany days. They received £80 (instead of the statutable £5. 12*s*.;) £1. 1*s*. for a sermon, on Wednesdays and Fridays in Lent, preached in turn, and the value of one acre of underwood; they now have £150 a year, with sermon wages. A minor canon might hold a benefice within twenty-four miles of the city, and claimed, after a canon, a share in the capitular patronage. At Winchester there are four (instead of six,) two being present at each service. Soon after the Reformation the twelve divided £140, when each prebendary received £31. 6*s.* 8*d.*, and the subdean £3. 6*s.* 8*d.* additional. (Bacon, p. 917.) At Carlisle there are three (instead of eight;) they received the statutable £3. 10*s.* 8*d.*, a further sum of £4. 9*s.* 4*d.*, and a share of a lease, £60; they now have £150. At Chester there are four (instead of six;) they received £50, now made up to £150. At Gloucester there are three (originally six,) two attend daily; they receive £150, the librarian receives £4. The fine for disobedience to the precentor was 2*d.*; and absence, for even one day or one night, was strictly prohibited. At Bristol there are three (instead of six;) they had formerly £40 for attendance in one week in ten; they have now 30 guineas divided among them for preaching afternoon sermons. Their statutable fee was £5. 2*s.* (B. Willis says £10;) the precentor and sacrist have also each £1. 6*s.* 8*d.* (according to statute, Willis says, £6. 13*s.* 4*d.*) in addition, as at Gloucester still. At Norwich there are four (originally eight, who took one week in two months;) two receive £20 and hold benefices; the precentor receives £244, the sacrist £97. At Peterborough (Benet Coll. MSS. cxx. 523) there are three (originally eight,) who receive £150 and a house; the precentor receiving also £5. 10*s.*, and the sacrist £1. 10*s.* At Worcester (Benet Coll. MS. cxx. 409) there are four (originally ten) who receive £60, the stipend by statute being £5. 2*s.* They were to be chosen by the dean or vice-dean and chapter, and to be perpetually resident, but might hold livings within twenty-four miles of the city. The fine for absence from any hour, or tardiness at mass, was ¼*d.*, and for disobedience to the precentor, 2*d.*: these fines to be distributed among those present. At Rochester there are four (originally six, to be reduced to three,) who received £5. 2*s.* as stipend, £3. 18*s.* for commons, and £1 for livery—in all, £10; they have now houses. The two seniors receive each £40 a year, and £11 for preaching turns, and a benefice; the two juniors are paid £150: the former take one week, the latter two weeks in six. At Durham the minor canons, before the civil wars, resided in small houses, or rather chambers in a common house, unfit for married persons, and maintained a common hall. After the Restoration, five good houses were built for them, as their hall as well as the guest hall had been destroyed. A minor canon might hold a benefice within twelve miles of the city; they were not to be absent a whole day or night without leave. The fine for absence from morning service was 1*d.*, from evensong or for disobedience to the precentor 2*d.*, for tardy attendance ½*d.* There are now six (instead of twelve,) appointed in general chapter; two are always present at the services. Their statutable wage was £5. 2*s.*, but they now divide £1,420 a year. At Christchurch the eight chaplains are appointed and removable by the dean; they have chambers in college and commons in hall; they cannot marry, nor, without special leave, hold other preferment. They receive the same dividend as the senior students, varying according to the price of wheat in Oxford market: one is master of the choristers. At Ripon they receive £300 a year; at Manchester and Bangor, more. At Manchester the two minor canons received, as vicars of the parish church, £7. 10*s*. and fees; but now £250. At Ripon the two minor canons receive each £300, besides fees and rents of lands. In 1605 the precentor was paid £14, and as vicar choral £13. 6*s*. 8*d*. At Westminster there are six: those appointed before the Act of 1840 receive, statutable, 14*s*. 8*d*., and augmentation, £98. 19*s*. 4*d*.; those appointed since that date have £150. All have houses or compensation. By Act 3 and 4 Vict. there were to be not less than four, nor more than six, minor canons in each cathedral; but the corporations of the old foundation were evidently not affected by that provision.

The minor canons in the New Foundations—with the deacon, subdeacon, and master of the choristers—alike are responsible and capable for taking part in the services of the Church, being required to be skilled in singing, and be present in choir. The choice of the deputies of the precentor and sacristan to be nominated by them in their absence is not limited to minor canons. The lessons belong to the exclusive care of the dean and canons, and the gospel and epistle to the deacon and subdeacon. At Lichfield a vicar choral, being in holy orders, may be required to undertake clerical duties assigned by the præcentor or succentor. (Lloyd's Stat. App. Rep. Cath. Comm. p. 45.) In the old foundations the dean and canons read the lessons; at Lichfield the canons, when tabled by the præcentor on doubles (Stat. Nonant. Mon. Angl. vi. 1256;) at S. Paul's by the chancellor, or to sing, if named by the præcentor (Dugd. 249;) the dean read from his stall at York (Monast. vi. 1200) and S. Paul's (Dugd. 258.) The canons in their courses were hebdomadaries; celebrants, and gospellers, and epistolers at the high altar; and on great feasts the non-residentiaries at S. Paul's ruled the choir, beginning hymns, psalms, and antiphons; but in all cases (Dugd. 249, 240; Monast. vi. 1255-6-60) the canons could sing the service, and the minor canons or vicars were only their choral substitutes or representatives and auxiliaries. Their responsibilities are only of a strictly subordinate character, whether of constant attendance in choir, except by leave of absence, or of officiating in turn by direction of the chief authority. The weekly arrangement or course is merely conventional, revokeable and changeable by the latter; and all inferior ministers are required by the statutes both of the old and new foundations to be perpetually present, with a few trifling intermissions and exceptions. The control of the entire conduct of Divine Service, with its hours and times and those who officiate, saving the statutable privileges, rights, and duties of the dignitaries in choir and Divine

Service, resides in the dean and chapter, and with it the assignment or partition of duties to all the subordinate ministers. The preaching turns of the prebendaries no doubt represent their dominical and festal turns of celebration; and the only reason why they no longer sing the services, at least occasionally, is from ignorance of music. The chaplains mansionarii, who correspond with the English minor canons or priest vicars, are not allowed to occupy the vacant seats of canons; but where the immemorial custom has prevailed, may sit in stalls immediately after the canons, and in the same line. (Ceccop. iii. 143, 40.) But ordinarily they occupy the second range of stalls (i. 84,) with their chief, the magister chori, who is chosen by the chapter, at the head of this line of seats (iii. 138,) subsellia inferiora. The upper stalls were reserved to canons from the time of Urban II. (Thomassin, i. l. iii. c. 10,) and if chaplains sit in the same line, their stalls are to be distinguished by the absence of cloth-covered kneeling-mats or hassocks. The rule at Salisbury, by the Constitutions of S. Osmund, was:—"In the second form minor canons are to be regarded as first in order; then deacons, afterwards the other clerks. In the first form petty canons are regarded as first, then the rest of the petties according to age. In the stalls after canons are priest vicars, and the first deacons, according to age and character, are tolerated in the upper rank by dispensation." At Hereford, in the third form sat priest vicars, in the second deacon and subdeacon vicars, and in the third clerks in minor orders. At Exeter the vicars sat in the upper forms, eastward of the canons, next the archdeacons; the annuellars, chaplains, and clerks occupying the second form.

Porter.—There were usually two; one acted as barber, the other kept the gates open, or shut them, as the dean required, and was guardian of the keys. At Canterbury there are two, one receiving £25, the other £15, instead of the statutable £3. 11*s.* 4*d.*, and having each a house. At Peterborough there are also two, one at the west gate having £8. 11*s.* 4*d.*, the other at the east gate receiving £2. 2*s.* At Winchester the porter has £30; at Carlisle £6. 16*s.* 8*d.*, and a house; at Durham £35, and a house.

Portionist.—A beneficed person, who, having private means, received only half or a moiety of his prebend; the demiprebendary of foreign cathedrals, called in Spain rationero.

Precentor.—In cathedrals of the New Foundation he is a minor canon, of maturer years, excelling in morals and learning, and able to be their leader and give the note and direction to the singers. At Norwich the dean or vicedean yearly chooses the precentor and sacrist. At Rochester the office is held in rotation. He is chosen by the dean and chapter, being minor canon and precentor, with authority only in choir, and removeable. In cathedrals of the New Foundation he is to lead the choir, all members of which were to obey him in chanting; to keep the choir books; and, like the punctator of German and Italian churches, to note absences of the dean, canons, and all the ministers of the choir every fortnight in chapter. The dean is rector chori. At Vienne the precentor and chanter were only personats, but were capable of holding a canonry. (Le Lievre, 192.) At Beverley the precentor was also a "person" merely. [In collegiate churches of Cologne the chorepiscopi were præcentors. (Gerb. i. 298.) Eadmer and John Thanet at Canterbury, Symeon of Durham, Thomas Walsingham of S. Alban's, and William Somerset at Malmesbury, are instances adduced by Gerbert that in England the præcentors of cathedrals and minsters were usually selected for learning as well as musical knowledge. He also gives many instances of the promotion of the chanter, who was a dignitary, to foreign bishoprics and abbacies.[1] His duty in France was regir le chant, and in Spain regir los clerigos, as in England regere chorum; so his duties are defined by the Councils of Cologne, 1260, 1536, c. iii. (Maillane, i. 384, 442.) For a complete list of the Constitutions of French collegiate churches see Maillane, i. 463. At Hereford, in 1583, the unseemly practice of murmuring when any one came late into choir was forbidden.] At Durham he noted absentees, whom he delated to the dean and chapter every fortnight, examined choristers, arranged the services, had charge of the choir books. All ministers, and on great festivals the officiating prebendaries, were to obey his directions. By most of the statutes he was required to note the absences of the dean and canons. At Norwich, Peterborough, and Rochester he has a house. At Ripon he is entirely responsible for the good order of the choir and arrangement of the services, and the conduct of the organist, singing men, and lay clerks, subject to the discretionary power of the dean and canon residentiary: he is bound to attend both the daily services. At Norwich he receives £20 in respect of his office, in addition to an income of £224. At Peterborough he receives £175 a year. His statutable allowance at Bristol is £1. 6*s*. 8*d*. as precentor. At Gloucester he receives certain fees. At Ely his duties are defined to assist in leading the choir, in the direction of the minor canons and clerks in choir, in taking care of the choir books, and in noting and delating absentees fortnightly before the dean and chapter in the chapter-house. At Chester he is chosen annually by the dean and chapter, to appoint the order of the music in the Divine Services, to lead the singers in choir, to take charge of the choir-books, to delate in the chapter-house every fortnight all absentees, including the dean and canons. As long as the common hall was kept up, he presided at the first table, and acted as "morum censor" in all cathedrals with Post-Reformation

[1] By the custom of the monastery S. Evratii the præcentor sat on the right, and the succentor on the left. (Gerbert de Cantu, lib. ii. p. i. c. ii.)

statutes. At Durham he is chosen annually to be present on all Sundays and festivals, and generally at all the daily services; to select music for the choir, subject to revision by the chapter; to recommend fit candidates for choristerships; to instruct the boys, to examine them twice in the year, and give them additional instruction if they desire it, with the approbation of the dean and chapter, on a small additional payment. His statutable payment is £2; he also receives 3*s*. 4*d*. at the installation of a canon. At Canterbury he receives the additional statutable payment of £2, and a further addition of £40. At Chester his official stipend is £2; at Durham 40*s*. yearly, and 3*s*. 4*d*. on the installation of a canon, and fees for preaching sermons on Good Friday and Ash-Wednesday: he also received an allowance of £100.

Prior.—This office appears to have held the same relation to the dean which a dean possessed with regard to a provost: the office existed at Cologne (Innoc. III. de Cler. excom.) and in several Spanish churches. Priors were called deans in the middle of the twelfth century. (A. S. i. 796.)

Proctor.—Equivalent to attorney or representative; the president of the minor canons' college at Salisbury, he looked after the vicarial houses, and at S. David's he was a canon, and managed the affairs of the vicars. There was a similar officer in S. Bertin's abbey, his name designating his duty—to represent and defend the privileges of the minor canons.

Procurator.—The churchwarden, or provost in charge of the goods or rents.

The Provost, the name given to the bishop by S. Cyprian and Tertullian, in the early monasteries, (Bened. rule, c. lxviii.) ranked next to the abbot, his nomination being vested at first in the bishop, and subsequently in the abbat. When the provosts gave themselves up to temporal concerns, and became too powerful in consequence, the deans were established to keep up Church discipline; or very probably, when the chapters emancipated themselves from the bishop as the head of the chapter, they exchanged the name of the provost, who had been his immediate deputy, for that of dean, allowing his merely temporal duties to devolve on an officer bearing his name, the dignity thus again becoming, as it were, a mere obedientiary. The title has been revived at S. Ninian's, Perth, as the dean of a Scottish diocese is simply an archdeacon. At Utrecht the archdeacon was called provost. At Vienne the archdeacon was provost (Counc. Valent. 855, c. xxiii.;) the same person was indifferently called archdeacon, primicier, and provost, by Chrodogang, being at once financial treasurer, steward of estates, and, in the absence of the bishop, his vicegerent. (Counc. Aix. 816, c. cxxxviii.) The Council of Mayence (813, c. xi.) substituted deans for provosts, and the second Council of Rheims (c. xxiv.) ranks the provost and vidams as seculars. On the multiplication of officers the archdeacon became the bishop's external officer, and the provost his internal representative; the provost served in the monastery, and the vidam in the cathedral. The vidam was the bishop's mayor-domo or chamberlain, but gradually his authority extended over the laity, as that of the provost over clerks. The provost acted often as the dean's subordinate. (Counc. Aix-la-Chapelle, 817, c. xxxi., xxxii.) In English cathedrals he resembled the French econome and the Spanish primiclerus, being a paymaster of stipends. (8 Counc. Toledo; Migne's Dict. ii. 690, 981.) In Sweden the dean was the dom-prost. When the provost and dean, as in German and other churches, co-existed, the former had charge of the estates with the cellarer and chapter; could convene chapters, but had no voice in them, being not necessarily a canon; could correct the dean, give longer absence than eight days to canons, had cure of souls, celebrated on the greater festivals, and installed canons, but had no vote in their election or in that of a dean. The dean (Mayer, iii. 214) was appointed to control the choir, presided in chapter, and gave leave of absence for eight days to canons. The deanery was a subsequent foundation at Upsala (Benzelius, 38) to the provostry, as at Urgel in 1289. (Villanueva, iv. 133, 408.) There was a provost at Aarhus and Lunden. (Soderström, Alleg. i.) In 673 (Lib. Eliens. l. i. c. 43,) at Ely, it is said, archipresbyterum et præpositum constituebant, and the provost existed at Lichfield, 822. (Ang. Sac. 1, 463.) The word provost, as representing the head, may have died out when the common table was divided into prebends, and then subordinate provosts appointed. When great lords and kings usurped the titles of abbots, provosts, priors, &c., with their revenues, and in the remoter large churches, the word dean was used in lieu of it; but it may have been owing to the dignity and power of the senior dean over the junior deans in monasteries which gradually made the title very honourable. (Kennet, Antiq. ii. 340.) At Lincoln he was chief of the vicars choral, but in the earlier constitution (1212) the provost of canons found the charges for writing new choir-books. (Wilkins, i. 536.) At Solsona the early government was by a provost or prior till 1409. (Villanueva, ix. 59.) The prior or provost of Urgel in 1299, as elsewhere at the close of the thirteenth century, was succeeded by a dean. (Ib. 185.) In 1131 there were twelve provosts, reduced in 1161 to eleven. The provostry which existed in the eleventh century was not an office of jurisdiction, but of economical and financial government, as in other cathedrals; which, when the cost of collection and distribution was greatly increased, was divided between twelve provosts, who took their names from the months in which they served. At Vich, Barcelona, and Gerona, although churches of regulars, the provostry was an obedientiary from the beginning of the eleventh century, and not a presidency, being shared at Vich among twelve persons, for the distribution of the revenues. (Ib. vi. 63, 255.) The provost at S. David's was master of the fabric; at Wells, by Bishop Jocelyn's Statutes, he was not a dignitary, but an œconomus, or financial treasurer, with an "office of burden" next in rank to the succentor; and paid the fifteen prebendaries of Combe, of whom he was the first, and their vicars, £100 sterling yearly, and the vicars of S. Mary's and S. Martin's chapels £20, in quarterly portions. There had been previously two provosts. (Gent. Mag. 1864, ii. 627.) He was rector of Buckland and Wellington. (Ecton, 21.) At Beverley Minster he had charge of the bedern and vicars' hall, presided over the granary, and made payments to the canons through the chamberlain. (Monast. viii. 1310.) At Toulouse the provosts acted as gospeller and epistoler. (Martene, i. 218.) The provost was a dignitary at Milan, Seez, Tuam, Kilmacduagh, Elphin, Killala, and Achonry, and in other cathedrals of Connaught. In the archbishoprics of Aix, Arles, Toulouse, and Rheims the word provost was retained by the head of the chapter; but it seems from Dr. Cotton's Fasti that in Connaught the provost and præcentor were the same dignitary. The provost at Vienne, as head of the chapter, is mitred, and chancellor of the university. (Etat de l'Allem. ii. 73.) At Lavantz he wears a mitre and cross. (Ib. 92.) At Mayence the provost, dean, and chanter since 1244 have been mitred (i. 4.) At Cologne all the dignitaries, including the grand provost, were mitred. (Ib. 283.) This use of the mitre seems in some cases to have arisen from a misapprehension of the meaning of mitra, the part of the almuce which was shaped like a hood, and fell next the arm; it is worn by the celebrant at Cambray. (Molanus, ii. c. ix.) Such provosts were the dignitaries mentioned by the canonists, Isid. (Etymol. l. vii. c. 12,) Rabanus (de Inst. Cler. l. i. c. 9,) Innoc. III. (Epis. l. i. p. 44; l. ii. p. 452,) Durand. (Rat. Div. l. ii.,) &c.; and Frances says in different churches the first dignitary was called dean, archpriest, or provost, but of right the order was, archdeacon, archpriest, dean, provost, primicerius, and treasurer or sacristan (pp. 40, 41.) The provost was president of S. Elizabeth's, Winchester, Eton; Oriel, Worcester, and Queen's Colleges, Oxford; King's College, Cambridge; Wengham, Glaseney, Cotherstoke, Hemingburgh, Rushworth, Rotheram, Wye, and Wingfield; and the prior at Merewell. The provost was head of the minor canons' college at Lincoln and S. David's, where he was master of the works, or œconomist. De Maillane attributes the abolition of the provostry to his unpopularity with the canons (Dict. du Droit Canon. iv. 489,) but the dean and provost were not distinct titles till the twelfth century. (A. S. i. 463.) In either case it must be remembered that the bishop is always required to be obeyed by canons as the abbot by monks. The Council of Aix therefore defines the provostship to be a priorate (c. cxxxix., cxliii.,) and the Council of Mayence calls it a mastership or ministry; but from an office it became a benefice, and from an obedience a dignity. (Molanus, ii. c. iv.) In some churches there was a secular abbot (c. v.,) and in others a prior (c. v., xxxiii.,) probably relics of an elder or concurrent monastic establishment. Many cathedrals, however, in France and the Low Countries, were called minsters, as at Lincoln, York, Salisbury, Beverley, Wimborne, and other secular churches in England and elsewhere, as a term of honour, as early as by the Councils of Tours (c. xxxi.,) and Mayence (c. xix.; Molanus, lib. i. c. xii.) The monastic deanery is said to have been founded on the model given by Moses. (Exod. xviii. Comp. S. Aug. de Mor. Eccl. lib. i. c. xxxi.; Cassian de Inst. Cœn. c. vii.) The archpresbyter of Louvaine, Brussels, Vilvorde, Tene, and Mechlin was the rural dean of the city (Molanus, ii. c. viii.,) like the chorepiscopus of Utrecht (c. xxxii.,) who is the archsubdeacon (Counc. Autun, c. xvi.,) or the dean of deans of Liege, or the city prior of Seville, and in other places "the subdeacon," which probably was the reason that frequently the English subdean is called subdeacon in ancient documents, and markedly in a letter to Lincoln by Innocent III. as the vicegerent of the dean in the close and suburb; and it is an observable fact, ranked next after archdeacons. The subdean of York, the archbishop's penitentiary, is called in the mediæval statutes subdiaconus. There was an archpriest at Aberdeen and Dunbar, and at Ulcombe, Haccombe, Penkivell, Beer Ferrers, Whitchurch, in the early part of the fourteenth century; but they were probably rural deans merely, being not exempt from the jurisdiction of the ordinary and archdeacon (Oliver, Mon. Exon. 287;) and rural deans are called archpriests by Benedict XII. (Const. Spelman's Conc. 505.) And at Chichester the subdeacon, as he is called in the Valor Ecclesiasticus and Cranmer's Register, or subdean, who appears to have been a secondary, and is classed with the chaplains royal, sang the founders' and benefactors' mass at the subdeacon's altar in the Lady chapel, and was a parish priest, vicar of S. Peter's the Great, or subdeaconry, being summoned with the city curates to the bishop's visitation. It was a parish church in the time of Henry III., and in the fifteenth century was appropriated to the commons of the dean and chapter. (Tanner MS. cxlix. 24.) The archdeacon of Llandaff was the bishop's representative in choir when he was absent; being president according to Bishop Henry's ordinance, who appointed twelve or fourteen prebends some time before 1218. (Cole MS. xx. fo. 38, b.) Until about 1119 there had been twenty-four canons. (A. S. ii. 673.) Until recently the bishop was dean, and the archdeacon subdecanus or vicedean. (Cole MS. xxix. fo. 28, b.) Bishops were called provosts by S. Cyprian; and so the text Heb. xiii. 7 was translated "Obey your provosts." In process of time the bishop's deputy in a cathedral and the abbot's vicegerent in a monastery was called the provost, the dean being a subordinate dignitary. (Reg. S. Bened. c. lxv. Counc.

Aix. c. cxxxviii., cxxxix., eos vocari præpositos qui quandam prioratus curam sub aliis prælatis gerunt.) In the Council of Mayence he is called master or minister. The provostship in Belgium had been an office, obedience, magistracy or ministry; but before the sixteenth century had become a benefice, dignity, and titular presidency, with the right of the first place and the best rental, and privileges in collation of benefices reserved, but without necessity of residence. By the Council of Cologne, 1549, the provost was bound to maintain the rights and statutes of his church. The provost of Beverley had civil authority and government within the domain of the church, as well as within the church, but without a vote in chapter or stall in choir. (Leland, Coll. iii. p. 103; Oliver, p. 101.) At Worcester Bishop Oswald removed from S. Peter's Collegiate Church to S. Mary's Minster; at Sherborne and at Winchester, by Athelwold, the clerks were compelled to embrace monachism, or retire. At the Norman invasion these three churches were monastic, but all the other cathedrals except Canterbury, founded by S. Augustine (Malm. Gest. Pont. i. c. 1461, ed. Migne,) and Durham, inheriting the tradition of Lindisfarne (Sim. of Durham, c. xlix.; Bede, Hist. iv. 27,) were secular; but in the former church in 1020 the president was called dean. (Angl. Sax. Chron. s. a. Gervase, 1650.) Giso at Wells, Leofric at Exeter, and Thomas at York established a common refectory and dormitory, which appears to have been the rule for Anglo-Saxon canons. (Thorpe, Anc. Laws, pp. 130, 134; W. Malmesbury, Gesta Pont. ii. c. 1548; Stubbs, in X. Script. 1708-9, Eccles. Doc. pp. 17, 22.) Gundulph introduced monks at Rochester.

The Provost was a bailiff or steward of a manor, who collected the rents. (Kennet's Par. Ant. Gloss. s. v.) Gervas. Dorob. [in Egilnotho] says the provost after Lanfranc's arrival was called prior. At Utrecht and Deventer the archdeacon was called provost.

The Receiver General was a canon, called, like the vicedean, an officer in cathedrals of the New Foundation. His duty was to collect and receive all moneys, rents, and other payments due to the church, and to hand them over to the treasurer. He had general superintendence of all outlying buildings and estates, and was to see all dilapidations thereupon duly repaired. He was also to accompany the dean or act as his substitute in the annual visitation of the estate. He was annually elected. At Carlisle the canons hold the office in rotation; at Gloucester it is obsolete. His statutable fee was £2 at Rochester, 5 marks at Gloucester, £5 at Chester, £6. 13*s*. 4*d*. at Durham, £10 at Ely, where by Stat. of Charles II. the office is merged in that of treasurer. At Bristol he was also treasurer. At Canterbury he is elected annually on Nov. 25; at Durham it is merely nominal. At Chester the treasurer and receiver are still responsible, but the chapter clerk acts as their deputy in the receipt and payment of the capitular funds. At Peterborough the canon who holds the double office receives £20 a year. At Worcester he is elected annually Nov. 25. The receiver in foreign cathedrals attends to the temporal affairs of the chapter; the distributor of the quotidian is called in them sometimes also præsentiarius. (Molanus, l. ii. c. l., li.)

Subreceiver, Deputy Treasurer, Subtreasurer.—The chapter clerk at Carlisle is deputy treasurer and steward. At Durham there are both a subtreasurer and deputy receiver. At Peterborough the subreceiver has a salary of £10. At Ripon the subtreasurer was keeper of the treasury, and receiver of certain rents belonging to the communa, and tithes, except corn, wool, hay, and lambs belonging to the prebendaries; mortuaries, offerings at marriages, churchings, &c., which were paid to the inferior ministers and officers at certain principal feasts, and for serving at Easter. In the cathedrals of the New Foundation the subtreasurer is usually a minor canon. At Canterbury his statutable fee is £2, with Easter offerings and surplice fees; at Ely and Bristol £1. 6*s*. 8*d*.; at Norwich £1; at Peterborough, £1. 10*s*., and as præcentor £5. 10*s*. At Durham his duties under the dean and treasurer were to take care of the ornaments, furniture, and necessaries for Divine Service; to receive oblations, to have charge of the vestry, the bells, books, and clock, the cemetery, and cleanliness of the fabric, and to exercise pastoral supervision in the precinct. He now assists weekly at the Communion Service, collects and distributes alms, officiates at funerals, and discharges other ministerial functions. He was librarian of the chapter and school, but could only lend the books with consent of the dean or vicedean. He receives 40*s*. yearly by statute, and £50 additional to his stipend. At Chester he had charge of the interior of the fabric, records, and furniture; was to provide lights and wine, take charge of oblations, and visit the sick and whole within the precinct. At Ely he had besides the charge of the monuments, and pastoral charge of all members of the church and residents within the precinct. At Gloucester he was chosen by the dean and chapter, received his charge from the treasurer, and with his advice provided all necessaries for Divine Service.

Rectors of the Choir (as Hincmar says, præcentores qui chorum utrinque regunt sunt duces,) at Exeter, noted the absence or irregularity of the vicars, and delated them to the president of chapter and clerks of exchequer. On all the great festivals the præcentor in person ruled the choir. The rectors walked to and fro on either side of the choir, with rector's staves in their hands to mark the time of the chant. At York they wore copes, and delated vicars who did not sing. At Lincoln they sang with the præcentor at the bench in the choir. (Wilkins, i. 537.) At Exeter

(MS. Harl. 1027) they had faldstools covered with leather, and carried staves of ivory and boxwood, as apparently they did at S. Paul's. At Lichfield they wore silk copes in choir always, precious copes on Christmas-day, white at Easter, red on certain feasts, and embroidered or changeable on some other days, at the sacristan's direction. The choir was ruled on Sundays, doubles, and nine lections, and other principal feasts. The rectors were weekly punctatores. (MS. Rawlinson, fo. 4.) On the doubles there were four, the two principals being chaplains, the others secondaries, deacons, or subdeacons. On the greater doubles the præcentor appointed two vicars of the dignitaries as principals; on simple feasts the hebdomadary, who was tabled on the Sunday table, ruled the choir, and on ordinary days the secondaries acted. All clerks and rectors ministering wore surplices, but not rochets under their copes; the rectors observed that the choristers behaved properly. The rectores chori are the Spanish præcentores sceptrigeri. (Villanueva, ii. 25.) In collegiate churches, as Chester-le-Street and Astley, the dean acted as rector chori, there being no præcentor. At Chichester two of the calabre amyces were high rectors in principal feasts, with two of the priests' stalls as second rectors; on lesser feasts two of the priests' stalls were high rectors, and two de secunda forma, second rectors; the rectors' course of the latter to last two weeks alternately. The substitute who "bore the cope" for one in course to the rector received a Venite loaf, which was forfeited by the absentee. At Hereford they began the office and Kyrie in the mass. At Wells, 1298, they forfeited their day's wages if they did not know the hymns and intonation of the Psalms. (MS. Harl. 1682, fo. 7, b.) On greater doubles at Salisbury, 1305, there were present a principal rector, with his collateral, and a secondary rector chori, with his collateral. They wore white copes at Easter time, on the Feast of Annunciation, Michaelmas, S. John Evang., and the dedication of the church; red on all Sundays except at Easter-tide, and on all feasts of Apostles and Evangelists out of that season, and on festivals of confessors gold-coloured (croceis) and of silk. The major canons wore black copes and surplices, but on feasts which had solemn procession—Christmas, Epiphany, Purification, Easter, Ascension, Pentecost, Trinity, All Saints, the dedication of the church, and major doubles occurring on Sundays—all wore silk copes in procession, and until the Agnus Dei at mass. At the Gloria in Excelsis on Easter Eve the clerks put off their black copes, and appeared only in surplices. Black copes were used by all but the rectores chori when the choir was ruled. The rector chori was to learn from the cantor, as at other times, especially on principal Sundays and simple feasts, when the choir was ruled, the "antiphon, intonation, and difference of the Psalms." The choir was set for alternate weeks, it being considered to be successively the dean's and the chanter's choir.

(Rawlinson, MS. A. 371; MS. Harl. 1001, fo. 121, b.) By the Statutes of Bishop Roger, 1305, the persons and canons were to have almicias de minuto vario interius et exterius de griseo (Tanner MS. 327, fo. 24, b.,) while vicars were to have black copes reaching to the heels, and surplices of the same length as the copes. (1278, fo. 99.) At Exeter, 1268, canons, vicars, and clerks were to have only black almuces, and not of green or red sendal; but canons might wear almucias duplicatas, and vicars black almuces, of a grisoforaria material. At Salisbury the choir was ruled every Sunday and double feast, and feast of lections; from the first vespers of Christmas to the octave of Epiphany; on its octave and vigil when not falling on a Sunday; through the weeks of Easter and Pentecost, and on certain feasts falling in Easter time, viz., S. Mark, SS. Philip and James, S. Barnabas, &c.; in the octave of the Ascension, the octave of SS. Peter and Paul, the octave of the dedication of the church, &c. (MS. Harl. 1001, p. 121, b.) The choir by weeks alternately was called the dean's or cantor's choir; but on all double feasts always was the dean's throughout the year, if he were present to do his office, except at Christmas, Easter, and Whitsun weeks, when the choir was united. At certain times the table was made out by weeks or days. On doubles or simple principal feasts the rector of choir was to learn from the præcentor the "intonation and difference," in what grade the singers were to be, who should commence, and who the singers were to be, and then communicated with the principal secondary. Sometimes four rectors of choir acted as leaders.

Rectores chori cum duo tantum habentur sequantur regulam clericorum de secunda forma. Cantor stat in medio chori cum ceteris rectoribus chori scil. in festis majoribus duplicibus tantum; deinde principales rectores chori ex utraque parte sui; exinde duo rectores secundarii, postea chorus more solito. (Martene, i. 240.)

The Registrar was first appointed at Canterbury and Ely in the seventeenth century; in the latter cathedral he is auditor and clerk of accounts, and chapter clerk at Ripon, Lincoln, and Lichfield.

Sacrist.—His office is described in the canon law as keeper of the church ornaments. (Decret. Greg. ix. l. i. tit. xxvi., xxvii.) Where there was no permanent sacrist, a canon, named præfect of sacristy, was appointed, with a clerk as subsacrist. (Scarf. ii. 71.) There were two sacristies, one for the canons and the other for chaplains. He was the treasurer's vice-custos (Frances, c. xx. n. 18,) being the treasurer's vicar or deputy. At S. Paul's he opened at matins and vespers the doors of the sacristy, which contained three rooms for the choir masters, and kept the approaches to it clear of idlers. He admitted at first peal the rectors of choir and sick ministers desirous of saying the hours privately. He had under him subsacrists and valets serving as organ-blowers and bell-ringers. He kept the choir clean and the vessels clean, repaired breakages, saw the books were bound, and preserved order in the vestibule or outer sacristy. In the old cathedrals he represented the treasurer in taking charge of the fabric, altars, vestments, books, and ornaments; providing lights and wine, visiting the sick within the precinct, and in ministration of sacraments. He is now, as at Lichfield, a minor canon, but a canon acts as honorary treasurer, responsible for the early parochial service. (Lloyd's Stat. Cath. Comm. Rep. App. 45.) At Wells, 1298, he was punished if trading occurred in the church, and was removed if he permitted noise. (MS. Harl. 1682, fo. 8.) At Vienne the sacristan, mistral (ministerialis,) and chancellor were only officers. In the Decretals of Gregory IX. (tit. xxvi., xxvii.) the offices of sacristan and custos are distinguished, both being subject to the archdeacon. In 1269 both offices existed at Lyons. (Molanus, lib. ii. c. xiii.) Archbishop Willibrord is called custos of Utrecht, and Roderic, Bishop of Zamora, speaks of the treasurer or custos (Spec. vit. hum. lib. ii. c. vi.;) but at Lyons and by the Decretals the sacrist was superior to the custos, as the præcentor was to the cantor. The sacristan in France was the cheficier, the keeper of the chevet (capitium) or sanctuary, in charge of the furniture and ornaments necessary for Divine Service. His duties are to solemnise marriages, administer Holy Baptism, officiate at burials and churchings, and register them, and to superintend the bells, lights, and furniture, and furnish the sacred elements, receiving the fees for these duties in the cathedrals of the New Foundation. The duty of finding the sacred elements and the food for the common table devolved in foreign cathedrals on the cellarer. (Molanus, ii. c. xvii., xviii.) At Bangor the office, which is endowed with lands, is held by the parish clerk. At Hereford he received one loaf daily for carrying the collectarium. At Exeter the treasurership was founded 1133. At York the subtreasurer (1290) was elected by the dean and chapter to keep the ornaments, charters, relics, books, and vessels, and received 50 marks a year and a house. (MS. Harl. 4200, fo. 19; 6971, fo. 46, b.) By the dean or president's orders the sacrists warned canons of a chapter, opened and shut the door, kept the chapter-house doors shut, rang the bells, and preceded and followed in processions. He had under him five ministers, two clerks of the vestibule or outer sacristy, and three sacrists, the former receiving 20*s.*, the latter 24*s.*, from the treasurer. The sacrist's chamber was near S. John's altar. (MS. 6972, fo. 141, b.) The bells for matins rang through the whole time of the Lady matins, and for prime while a man could walk from Loughtenton to York, in 1291. (MS. 4200, fo. 43.) This inferior use of the word sacrist as applied to the treasurer's servants is noticed by Bishop Storey at Chichester as recent in the fifteenth century. (Reg. 1480, fo. 71, b.) The duties of the dignitary, called variously treasurer, custos, cheficier, and sacrist, seem to have been originally for 1, the treasurer, the charge of the treasures proper, the muniments, the relics, and more costly sacred vessels; 2, the custos (fabricæ,) the superintendence of the bells, altars, and fabric; 3, the cheficier, or chevet-keeper, the care of the sanctuary (at Westminster there is a custos, or scrutator sanctuarii;) and 4, the sacrist, the charge of the sacristy, vestments, and furniture, and provision of lights and necessaries of Divine Service. The subtreasurer is mentioned at Chichester in the fourteenth century, being a vicar. At S. David's there is a deputy treasurer; at Hereford the subtreasurer ranked after the succentor. According to the ancient obituary, he sang the benefactor's mass. At Girgenti there were four sacrists, one being a priest. In cathedrals of the New Foundation he is required to be an active man, and of much credit; and his duties are to take charge of the church, altar vestments, books, chalices, monuments, and ornaments of Divine Service; to find wine and lights, visit the sick members of the church, and receive all offerings for the use of the church.

The office of sacrist still exists at Canterbury, Peterborough, Durham, Ely, Gloucester, Carlisle, Rochester (where it is held in rotation,) Norwich, and Worcester. In the latter he had charge of the church, altars, chapels, vestments, books, plate, and tombs. There was a sacrist vicar at Mayence. (Mayer, i. 24.) At Angers he was the corbelier (cubicularius) or chamberlain, who administered sacraments to canons and clergy of the choir. (Moleon. 83.)

Scriptor Tabulæ.—The officer who made out the weekly table of duties at S. Paul's. (MS. Camb. E. e. 5, 25.)

Secular Canons.—Those who, giving up the common life of the cloister, and becoming possessed of property, lived among laymen and in the world. (Molanus, i. c. xxvi.) Owing to canons at first living in common, Pius V., in Bulla ante Offic. Lateran., called S. Augustine the reformer of the Apostolical order. (Comp. Sozomen, l. vi. c. 31.) But some lived apart from an early date. (See S. Aug. de Com. Vitâ Cleric.; Prosper de Vit. Contempl. l. ii. c. xi.; Pope Gregory, in his Answers to Bishop Augustin of Canterbury; and Pamelius in S. Cyprian. Ep. lxvi.) Those who observed the common life, although not bound by the three monastic vows, were called canons, as living by rule. Eusebius, Bishop of Vercelli before the institution of S. Augustine (Epist. D. Ambrosii, lxxxiii. ad Vercellens.,) made his clergy live in a monastery. The plan was imitated by S. Augustine at Hippo. Fulgentius made his monks act as clergy. (Victor Utic. c. xxix.) Prosper of Aquitaine and Pope Gelasius introduced the order of canons into France and Italy. (Molanus, i. c. x.) The distinction was that monks lived outside the city, and canons in towns, either with the bishop or as parish clergy; but in times of persecution or war monks were received among the canons, who in turn adopted portions of their rule. From the similarity in their mode of life, and their dwelling in community and a distinct building or cloister, the houses of canons were called familiarly monasteries, and their churches minsters. (Counc. Mayence, c. xix.; Tours, c. xxxi.) The earlier canons who lived with the bishop, or by his direction under a provost (per eum præpositum) used a common dormitory and refectory. (Counc. of Mayence, c. ix.; Gratian. Dist. xxxii. ex lib. v°. capitular.; Counc. Tours, c. xxiii.; Aix, c. cxvii.; Decret. Leon. i. ap. Gratian. causa xii. quæst. 1; Alex. ii. ib.; Dist. xxxii.; Jacobus de Vitriaco, Hist. Occid. c. xxx.) Gregory of Tours says that Baudin of Tours established the canons' table in that city. Bishop Wolfgang at Ratisbon instituted the common dormitory and refectory. (Ap. Surium. Oct. xxxi. c. vii.) Canonical bread is mentioned in the life of S. Rigobert. (Ib. ad iv. Januar.) But about the year 975, within the episcopate of Theodoric, the canons of Treves threw off the common life, and were followed by those of Arras, Coblentz, Mayence, Worms, and Spires, (Trithemius in Hirsaug. Chron. ad ann.); at Paderborn, in the middle of the thirteenth century; at Liege, under Bishop Ralph; at Utrecht, where, in the episcopate of Godbald, the dean first received a prebend; at Cologne, under Philip, the forty-fourth bishop (Molanus, i. c. xiv.;) and at Besançon only in 1300. Canons were forbidden to adopt the dress of monks (Counc. Aix, c. cxxv.,) and their rule, instead of vows, was limited to the observation of the canons of councils and provincial synods. (Counc. Rheims, 813, c. viii.) They were to use a simple but not sordid dress; and were to receive equal portions of bread, pulse, and alms. (Counc. Aix, xxii., cxxii.) S. Rigobert, at Rheims, adopted a similar rule to that of Chrodogang at Metz. The word canon sometimes was used to signify a prebend or benefice, or clerical income, as by S. Augustine and canonists. (Molanus, i. c. v.)

Steward.—The Council of Chalcedon, 451, appointed an œconomus, steward, to be chosen by the clergy, in every diocese, to manage the church property, under the bishop's directions. (Can. xxvi.) The vidam or vice-dominus was the bishop's steward (Conc. Chalc. c. xxvi.; 2 Nic. c. xi.) in the administration of the revenues of the Church. (Paul's Hist. of Benef. p. 241; Can. Volumus ii. et Diamonum iii. dist. 89; Decret. p. i. dist. lxxxix.) At Bamberg a canon acts as vidam of the bishop, superintending the fifteen bailliages in Carinthia. (Etat de l'Allemagne, i. 194.) At Vienne the archbishop's mistralis (i.e. ministerialis) was a canon, who acted as præfect of the city. (Le Lievre, 192.) At Patti a secular priest is œconomus. (Græv. Sic. iii. 872.) At Roeskilde and Littomissel there was a procurator fabricæ. The steward or œconomus of Windsor collects the rents and profits, and superintends the chapter estates, while the treasurer had charge of the fabric and buildings, and distributed all the money payments. At Hereford, 1583, œconomus denoted a churchwarden (Stat. c. viii.,) but originally the bailiff, who rendered an account of the rents of the great commune. In 1631 there was a præfectus fabricæ, who looked after the repairs of the cathedral. (C. x.) The master of the fabric, by Cardinal Pole's injunctions, saw that the church was kept clean. At Milan there are two æditui, at Catania two melinglerii, and at Monte Regale four merigmerii, a corruption of margouliers. At Genoa, Milan, and Paris were bedels and singers, called massaconici or mace-conchi; and machicots or ecotiers, from their massa or mace-like verge. They may, however, have derived the name from the massa, the church roll, or capitular fund, as stipendiaries. At S. David's he acted as treasurer. At Exeter, being called œconomus, he provided the choir-books, was paymaster of stipends, and keeper of the fabric and common fund. At Hereford the œconomi or bailiffs rendered, twice a year, the computatio, or account of the rents and perquisites of the greater commune. The high steward, seneschallus libertatis, was an officer appointed by an abbot to hold his courts of the banlieu. The stewards or seneschals of the year or month were minor canons, whose duties became obsolete with the disuse of the common table, as early as 1559, at Canterbury. The common table was established first by the Council of London, 1554, (c. viii.) The œconomus of Westminster is a canon, who had charge of the servants and common table. The two stewards at Exeter, 1485, one a canon, the other a discreet minister of the Church, received the payments of the farmers and others to the commune, and laid them up in the sacristy chest, rendering an account quarterly. (Rawlinson, MS. fo. 45.)

The Steward of the Courts is a layman, found in cathedrals of the New Foundation. At Durham he is called clerk of the court; at Canterbury and Carlisle also clerk of the lands; at Rochester, where he presides in the manorial courts, also counsel, with a fee of £6; at Peterborough also chief clerk, with a fee of £40. At Gloucester and Chester he is the chapter clerk; at Ely the registrar, as at Winchester, having the profits of copyhold business. At S. Paul's, with the receiver-general, he held an annual court in every chapter-manor.

Subsacrists and *Vergers.*—Molanus suggests that the virge carried by the bastinarius represented, like the Roman fasces, their dignity and jurisdiction (lib. ii. c. 54;) but Prebendary Dennis says that the virge contained a virge, or wooden rod, whence its name; which, being unscrewed, was the instrument of flagellation for the choir-boys who were ordered to be punished in the weekly chapter. (Key to the Regalia, p. 40.) At Messana the dean and præcentor, as at Syracuse (Græv. Sic. ii. 649,) Neti, and Catania, used silver staves, as the canons wore silk mitres. (Piccolo, p. 143, ap. Græv. Sic. ii.) At Palermo the senior canon carried a silver rod, and the apparitor or bedel, wearing a gown, carried a silver mace on his shoulder before the other canons. (Pirrus de Eccl.

Panorm. 166; ap. Græv. Ital. Ant. xxix.) At Wurtzburg (Etat de l'Allem. i. 51,) in order to keep out princes and nobles from the chapter, the postulant for a canonry had to pass naked at the girdle through two lines of canons, who beat him with virges on the back. In very many of the Italian and German cathedrals some of the canons were required to be of noble blood, and at Lyons were called counts; and in some churches the lesser grade were called chevaliers. The precular (or Lord Robert's bedesman,) when he was no longer a chantry priest, had charge of the cloisters, at Chichester, "to purge the churchyard of all hogs, dogs, and idle vagabonds, and lewd persons that play or do worse therein; and to scourge out all ungracious boys with their tops, or at least present them to the old man of the vestry." In 1480 Bishop Storey mentions the servants of the treasury as of late time called sacrists. Their duties as subsacrists were, to fold up the vestments, light the candles, apparel the altar, and keep the church clean; and, as vergers, to precede with a virge or mace the bishop, dean, and choir in procession: usually there is a dean's verger and a canon's verger. They kept the sanctuary and choir free from laics who were not to pass the screen, opened the church doors, saw that all was safe before closing them, cleaned the building, and allotted graves in the yard. They were usually acolytes, or ostiarii. The sacrists have now general charge of the church, keep order during Divine Service, and seat strangers; while the vergers attend the dean and canons. At Wells, in 1298, if a sacrist allowed trading in the church, he was punished, and suspended if he suffered a noise. There were three servers at S. Paul's, one of whom, hebdomarius serviens, attended church in his week, being relieved at meal-times by a groom. They had charge of the vestry, doors, lights, vestments, cloths, banners, veils, palms, and the carriage of the furniture from the vestry into the church; to keep the vestry door closed when bishops assembled in it; to cleanse the church on festivals, and the processional path round the cemetery; mark out the places for graves, ring the bells, light the lamps at dusk, close the west doors of the choir when service had well begun, and search the church after the doors were shut at night. (Dugd. 270.) In the New Foundations one of the two subsacrists was to carry the verge before the cross before the bishop, or in his absence the dean, when entering or leaving the church. At Lincoln there are two statutable stall-keepers. At Durham they annually delivered up their verge to the dean in the chapter-house. At Bristol there is one subsacrist, with statutable fee of £2. 18*s.*, and a gratuity of £37. 2*s.*, and one verger (by the statutes also a porter,) with the fee and a gratuity of £17. 2*s*. At Gloucester there are two subsacrists (sextons) at £12 (formerly £6. 13*s.* 4*d.*,) and four vergers at £4 each. At Ely there are two vergers at £6; one being porter receives £6 additional. There are two vergers at Chester. At

Carlisle a bedesman acts as verger, receiving £2. 11*s*. 8*d*., and as butler £4. 10*s*.; and for attending the dean £7. 18*s*. 4*d*. There are two subsacrists; one receives £26, the other £31, acting as singing men, and in charge of the communion plate. At Durham there are two vergers at £160, and eight under-vergers. At Canterbury there are two vergers who formerly received £2. 18*s*., but now have £20, with fees; and two subsacrists or vesturers, formerly receiving £3. 11*s*. 4*d*., but now £6. 13*s*. 4*d*., with fees for showing the church. At York there are three vergers, who receive £11. 9*s*. 8*d*.; the clerks of the vestibule and sacristy in 1430 acted as valets to the canons. At S. Paul's there are four vergers at £100 a year each. At Ripon there is a dean's verger at £23 a year, receiving as subsacristan (sexton) £3, with fees; he has charge of the church and bells, attends to the fires and lights, and shows the cathedral, receiving in all about £69. The deputy-sexton, who sweeps and cleans the church, receives £8 and a coat, and has one-third of the church-showing fees, about £19. The canon's verger receives £25 a year. At Lichfield the senior verger, by Statutes, 1699, is sergeant-porter and gaoler, at £120, and the under-verger is sergeant and common apparitor within the precinct at £60. At Winchester there are two vergers at £20, and two subsacrists at £12 each. At Worcester there are two vergers and two subsacrists. At S. David's the verger receives £6 a year. At Rochester the first subsacrist receives £52, the second, who is also porter, £36. At Westminster one, as master of the choristers, receives £100. At Wells there are three subsacrists or clerks, acting one as dean's verger, the second as canon's verger, the third as door-keeper. At Ripon, Manchester, S. David's, and Bangor, there is a parish clerk. At S. David's and Durham there is a dog-whipper. Frances mentions the Perrero at Lima in 1541. The order of processions was, in going into choir, the minister with his verge to clear the way, attendants, acolyths, the subdeacon, deacon, priest, or executor officii, the choir, boys, clerks of the second grade, clerks of the upper grade, excellentioribus subsequentibus. (Process. Sarisb. fo. viii.) In leaving the order was reversed, excellentioribus præcedentibus (fo. lxviii.;) and for the reception of a great personage duæ excellentiores personæ stood at the west door, (fo. clix.) Bp. Sherborne, when received pontifically, was preceded by a verger carrying a small hand-bell.

The Subchancellor or *Scribe*, the notary of foreign cathedrals (Molanus, ii. c. 53,) or matricularius, the registrar, the senior chaplain (ibid. c. xxxvi.,) is mentioned by Bacon at Lincoln. In 1289 he appears as scriptor librorum at S. Paul's. He was the chancellor's deputy librarian, substitute as lecturer, and assistant secretary. The chancellor there gave the book to the bishop in his throne when he read the lection. At Hereford he was a regent M.A., who tabled the readers, heard the lections read, and attended choir on festivals. At Wells the chancellor was required to find a deputy who should lecture on all saints' days. At Lichfield in the thirteenth century the dean was empowered to appoint a common clerk to write letters for the chapter. At York the subchancellor apprised the dean and other persons of their turns to read, and provided that there was no defect in reading in chapter or choir, and in the offices of thuribler and deacon. His wages were 20*s.* a year paid out of the grammar school. In 1285 the churches of S. Neweline and Stoke Gabriel were annexed by Bishop Quivil to the chancellorship of Exeter, on condition that he read lectures in the city, and instructed the cathedral clergy in theology and the decretals, or found a deputy.

For *Subdean* see *Provost* and *Petty Canon.*

Subtreasurer.—The subtreasurer made the chrism of balsam and oil, and received 1*s.* from each of the archdeacons; and had for every funeral not a canon resident optimam supellectilem quo ornatur feretrum. He received installation fees from the prebendaries. (Swayne's Lib. Epi. Cicestr.)

The Succentor is the Spanish sochantre and French chantre, and answers to the ὑποβολεῦς mentioned by Socrates (H. E. lib. v. c. 22.) It would seem that originally the succentor led the antiphonal chant on the side opposite the præcentor, as S. Augustine includes under cantores the præcentor, qui vocem præmittit in cantu; and succentor, qui subsequenter canendo respondet (in Ps. lxxxvii. 1; so Isid. Etym. l. vii. c. xii., and Gratian. Decret. p. i. dist. xxi. c. 1;) and Amalarius, De Ord. Ant. c. 18, "Præcentor in primo ordine finit responsorium, succentores verò eodem modo respondent, dein præcentor canit versum." He is the vicar and deputy of the præcentor. (Molanus, ii. c. xi.) At Amiens, as chantre, he ranked next the prechantre; installed canons in the lower stalls, governed the choristers, and with the præcentor admitted and dismissed them. His stipend was 260 livres. The subchanter at Rouen in 1530 had a prebend attached to his office, but had no precedence, except that on certain days he occupied a particular stall. He ruled the choir mass, commencing all the offices on doubles, and on Sundays informing the chaplains what was to be sung. He also gave the note for the response and anthems in processions, except the anthem at the entry of the choir, which belonged to the chanter. He had charge also of all processions. At Seville he tabled the ministers for church service, and was the deputy of the chanter in ruling the choir. (Estat. de Sevilla, fo. 10.) At Girgenti the subchanter ranked next to the terminator as a "person," and led the choir opposite the master of the schools in alternate verses. (Græv. Sic. iii. 769.) At Placencia the succentor, in the præcentor's absence, made out the matricula, tabled the chanters and readers; while the præcentor's duties were "disponere chorum et idoneos in chorum introducere." At Paris he was a dignitary appointed by the chapter. (Maillane, i. 442.) The succentor-major of canons was instituted first at Wells, 1130—74. At Hereford the succentor or præcentor presented absent vicars. (Etat. 1583, c. viii.) The subchanter at York directed the major canons, and the succentor, as in other cathedrals, was the præcentor's vicar with regard to vicars choral and songmen, and delated offenders in the Saturday chapter. The office was founded at Wells and York by Robert of Lewes, 1252—69; at S. David's, 1287; at Exeter by Bishop Quivil, where he tabled every Saturday the vicars for their duties in the common week. He received (1358) 53*s.* 4*d.* from the præcentor. (MS. Rawlinson, fo. 43.) The succentor's name nowhere occurs earlier than at Salisbury in 1096. In 1282 he was merely called the præcentor's vicar at Chichester, and sang the Lady mass in S. Mary's chapel (Praty's Reg. 74, b.;) and the secondary sang the mass of requiem. He on Saturdays tabled the vicars for the weekly masses there. (Ibid. fo. 78.) His wages were more than those of other vicars in 1358. At York to the vicar's succentor it belonged to delate offending vicars on Saturdays, mark out the table, and warn those whose names were on it, or in their absence appoint others to supply their turn; to hear them sing their part for the first time, and punish them if necessary; and in the name of the præcentor to rule the choir and order its services, and to give the antiphon to the dean. (Stat. fo. 7, 11.) At Salisbury, as at York, he ranked after the archdeacons. (MS. Harl. 6985, fo. 31, b.) He supplied the præcentor's place when absent, and ruled the song-school by his official. These were his duties at Lichfield, where also he enjoined all chants not noted in the table;—to arrange the method and order of processions; to enjoin lections on greater doubles and in masses; to watch and observe the time for beginning mass and the hours; and on Saturdays, after Benedicite in chapter, to arrange the services publicly for the ensuing week. By Wolsey's Statutes he ordered processions. He is the præcentor's vicar, and is appointed by him. By the Statutes of 1699 he regulates in his absence anthems, services, &c., tables the order of Divine Services, and ministers weekly; sends citations to prebendaries, receiving a fee of 1*s.* 6*d.*; installs them, receiving 8*s.* 6*d.*; and delates offending vicars, and orders punishment for choristers. He was originally the master of the ceremonies on great occasions. At Wells he supplied the præcentor's place, and on Saturdays in chapter regulated the service for the coming week. He was bound to assiduous residence. At S. Paul's he acted in the præcentor's absence, as regards the regulation of the chanting in choir, and in this matter was to be obeyed by major canons, minor canons, and all other ministers. At Chichester, 1232, he gave seven or fourteen stripes to boys misbehaving in choir; with the master of the schools he selected them. He received 40*s.* a year from the præcentor out of the archdeacon of

Chichester's synodals. At Hereford his duty was to bear the "burden" of the psalmody and chant; to table the choir for singing and direct the rectors of choir; to distribute copes on the greater festivals; to order processions. He could chastise with stripes clerks of the first form who were not of the family of a canon, and suspend others offending. He delated offenders in a table, and their names were read out for punishment daily in chapter after the martyrology. He received 12*d.* out of every mark or bequest which was given to clerks of the choir. He took care that the singing was reverently conducted, and appointed five boys of clerks of the first form, removeable at his will, to sing the antiphons, and to carry tapers and thuribles, who were to wear a honest robe, shoes, and stockings. At Hereford and S. Paul's he is a minor canon.

Trefonciers.—Terræ fundarii, lords of the soil, a title assumed by the canons of Liege.

Virger.—The bastinarius of foreign churches; from the virge, "the fasces" of the dean and chapter, and sign of their jurisdiction and power.

Vicedominus.—He was the bishop's steward. (Counc. Chalc. c. xxvi.; Nicæn. ii. c. xi., in the administration of the Church revenues; Paul's Hist. of Benef. p. 24; Can. Volumus ii. et Diamonum iii. dist. 89.) The vidam of Chalons was the same as the provost of other cathedrals, who was a kind of bailiff of Church lands. (Ducange, 815.) The vidam of Cambray was appointed by the chapter to take charge of the property of the see during a vacancy. The vidam was sometimes the general of the Church contingent, or the advocate and protector of the church at Lincoln, Rouen, Chartres, Parma, Sens, Cambray, Laon, Beauvais, Amiens, and other cathedrals. The vidam in some places acted as the bishop's guestmaster.

Warden.—The president of the college of minor canons at S. Paul's; called custos at Hereford and Exeter, principal at Wells and Chichester, proctor at Salisbury (the procurator or quæstor existed at Otranto and Rieti, and also at Littomissel; and in a capacity similar to an œconomus as supervisor fabricæ at Roeskilde,) provost at S. David's (founded 1287 as master of the works,) and Lincoln. At York the subchanter is the president or keeper of the college of the bedern, founded 1256; he receives a seal fee of 6*s.*, paid by the lessee for affixing the corporate seal to each lease, and certain fees at the installation of a prebendary. At Lichfield and S. David's the subchanter is now head of the college. At Wells Ralph de Salopia built the vicars' and choristers' houses. (A. S. i. 569.) At Lichfield Bishop Langton, 1295—1322, first established (feoffesavit) the vicars in their houses. (A. S. i. 442; Vesp. E. xvi. 33;) and by Bishop Burghill's will the chantry priests had a house built, c. 1424. (Ibid. i. 452.) Bishop Oliver Sutton persuaded the dean and chapter to build the vicars' close at Lincoln. (MS. Harl. 6954, fo. 6.) It must be understood that the offices held by minor canons carry no right of precedence. By the Stat. of S. Paul's, "Cum equalibus suis, viz., cum minoribus canonicis in charitate maneat (Dugd. 252,) alius alium fraterniter adjuvet (ibid.,) subdiaconus tametsi hoc ministerium et officium habet, tamen quæ sunt minoris canonici nihil mutabit, sed par erit reliquis suis fratribus." (P. 241.) And the precedence of the precentor in New Foundations being restricted to supervision of morals in the common hall, negatively proves that he has no superior place in choir, there being no mention of it there. Like the office of sacrist minor canon, and those of vicedean, treasurer, and receiver, held by canons, the appointment was merely elective and temporary; and the precentor and sacristan of New Foundations correspond to the succentor and subtreasurer of Old Foundations. In Spain (Counc. Merida, c. ix., x.; 15 Toledo) the primiclerus of the college was head of the vicars' college. The primicerius was anciently the head of the inferior collegiate clergy, and sometimes acted as punctuator, marker of members absent and present, as well as succentor. Primar was the old title of the principal in Scotch colleges. Primicerius was the præcentor's ancient title at Aberdeen, Milan, Venice, Toul, Verdun, Metz (Fleury, xvii. 172, n.,) and Forli; and capiscol, as if caput chori in some places. (Maillane, i. 384.) At Languedoc and Abergwilli, and S. Mary's at S. David's, the præcentor was president; the warden at Winchester college, Astley, S. George's, Windsor, S. Mary's, Ottery, Sudbury, Tonge, Noseley, Maidstone, and Totteshall. At S. Patrick's the vicars lived in a collegiate manner in 1615. The college of Limerick still partly exists. At Hereford the college contains a cloister, chapel, hall, library, and common room, and is still occupied. At Wells its chapel, hall, and separate houses remain; and the college at York, founded 1252, is still in existence. So lately as 1561 the college survived at S. Paul's, and portions of the building may still be seen at Lichfield; and the hall at Chichester, of the fourteenth century, and Exeter, c. 1388.

In all cathedrals of the New Foundation, the model and form of the other cathedrals are prescribed as a rule for Divine Service, but the Statutes of Carlisle and Peterborough enjoin the Use of S. Paul's, London.

In 1833 the first measures of spoliation were proposed by the administration of Lord Grey; and it was stated in the Royal Speech that "attention would also be directed to the state of the Church, more particularly as regarded its temporalities and the maintenance of the clergy." (Hansard, xv. 88.) The subject was again more distinctly introduced into the Speech from the Throne in 1835, by the advice of Sir Robert Peel (ib. lv. 983,) when it was determined to "consider the state of the several cathedral and collegiate churches, with a view to the suggestion of such measures as may render them most conducive to the efficiency of the Established Church." (Ib. xxvi. 66.) The Ecclesiastical Commission was the result of this recommendation. The last fatal measure was proposed by Lord John Russell in 1839, in which the determination was made to make a "distribution of capitular revenues." It had already been provided in 1838 that no clergyman should hold more than one cathedral preferment with a living—a very just enactment; but the commissioners, who were bishops, had resolved that the number of canons was unnecessary, and most cruelly and without judgment agreed that it would be sufficient to have a dean and four prebendaries residentiary attached to each cathedral, while the rest of the revenues were to be applied—or in other words confiscated—to the augmentation of poor livings. (Ib. xxxv. 19; xxxviii. 854.) In the face of an eloquent and argumentative opposition in Parliament, the Bill was passed by the Commons April 9, 1839. (Ib. xlvi. 1303.) The framework of our Church polity was broken up (p. 206,) and one-half of the capitular revenues was taken away from the cathedrals to which, as Sir Robert Inglis truly observed, "the Church of England, and indeed their common Christianity, was indebted, for some of the ablest—he might say the largest and best part—of the theological literature of the country; and their members were at the head of all the diocesan societies of charity and general benevolence." (Ib. liii. 594, 1019.)

Twenty-two chapters memorialized the Commissioners, the Crown, and Parliament; the great body of the parochial clergy protested against the measures of destruction; thirteen visitors of cathedrals and both the Universities opposed the scheme; but, led by the Bishop of London, the Primate unhappily became responsible with him for the provisions of the Bill, and rejected the proposal made of a voluntary contribution from the capitular members towards the augmentation of the income of poor livings. Parliament then deliberately preferred a Bill founded on suppression to that proposal which involved suspension only, and chose confiscation rather than contribution, (Hansard, lv. 199, 200, 206, 988, 991, 1002, 1115,) and with its enactment followed the loss of many rewards for merit and homes of lettered ease. It was calculated that sixty-five dignities and canonries residentiary, and three hundred and sixty prebendal stalls, with an income of £134,000, were suspended by 3 and 4 Vict. c. 113, and the ancient polity of the Church of England was ruthlessly broken up. The crowning mistake was that no endeavour was made to impose new duties, or reinforce, according to oath, those statutable requirements which had fallen into desuetude, and so preserve or revive these ancient and venerable institutions in their integrity. No doubt in many particulars a sound and practical reform was required, to render them more efficient for the purposes for which they were designed. The warning might have been given; and if the performance of duties was again neglected, then the time would have justly come for the abolition of such offices. The mere reduction in numbers obviously could not effect a reform, although it impaired any prospect of greater efficiency.

I append a few expressions of opinion on the subject of cathedrals by Sir Robert Peel, the Bishop of Exeter, the Lower House of Convocation, and the Dean of Westminster.

Sir Robert Peel said that "he regarded cathedral establishments with the greatest respect, and any interference with their efficiency would be a positive evil. Viewed in connection with the monarchy, it is of importance that the wealth, station, and splendour of the Church should bear some proportion to the wealth, station, and splendour so easily acquired by the other branches of the community in this great country." (Hansard, xxxviii. 874.)

Bishop of Exeter.—"The residence of a body of men of superior education, tried experience, and of endowments of a high order, gave to provincial districts a high tone of sentiment, a love of literature and a respect for all the best institutions of the country. It is of inestimable importance to the country that there should be gradations in the clergy, in order that every rank of society should receive spiritual instruction. The connection of the poorer clergy with their brethren who hold offices in cathedrals was calculated to gain for them a respect and a consideration which otherwise they could not, perhaps, receive, and a kind of moral elevation in society. The non-residentiary canons connected the diocese with the cathedral, and that is the centre of ecclesiastical union." (Ib. lv. 1119.)

The Convocation (Lower House,) July 2, 1863, represented that the effect of legislation had been, by the abstraction of their funds, to diminish, without equivalent advantage to the Church, their power of performing their proper function, as institutions designed, and in their original condition most available, for the maintenance in its highest solemnity of the worship of Almighty God, the support of effective diocesan administration, the preservation of sound theology, the advancement of religious education, and the promotion of works of Christian charity.

Dean Stanley.—"Shall every cathedral, with all its various ministrations, be transformed into an ordinary parish church? Great is the need for those many offices of worship, of administration, of reward, of dignity, of learning, of repose, which our cathedrals are intended to furnish; which, if not furnished by them, are assuredly furnished nowhere else, which, if lost in them, can assuredly never be recalled. It is surely something to feel that we are still living members of an institution older than the throne of these realms. It is something to feel that we are servants and ministers, not of some obscure fugitive establishment, for which no one cares or thinks beyond our narrow circle, but of a cathedral whose name commands respect and interest even in the remotest parts of Europe. It is wholesome to be reminded how its grandeur at once redeems our own shortcomings; how, in working under its shadow, our own vain and selfish aims are put to shame; how the errors or the sins even of the humblest amongst us bring discredit on the body which we share. Like the heirs of a noble ancestry, we have a lineage which it is ours to hand on with honour or with disgrace to those that come after us. We have an interest and a cause beyond our own to maintain and to advance; we have a debt of gratitude to discharge to the beauty and nobleness of an edifice, of a history, of a worship, which elevates us even in spite of ourselves, which recurs to us in delightful recollections when we are far away, which soothes and sweetens, even if it does not hallow, the life which is spent within its precincts.

"The duties are not indefinite; they are sharply prescribed by statute, some more some less distinctly. Where there is freedom of choice, the individual member must, as in other grave matters of life, use it aright for himself; and in this particular case as having a joint interest and duty of co-operation in a common purpose, the highest that can engage the work of man—the glory of God, and the well-being of this Church and country."

The practical good sense of the present day has detected the wrong and folly of precipitate and ignorant legislation. May we hope the day of restoration may be at hand, when these great institutions shall be restored more fully to their high and holy purposes, so as to be efficient to the greatest degree possible, as temples for the worship of Almighty God, in Whose honour and for Whose service they were raised; as seats of learning and theology, diffusing the blessings of a religious education; as councils to assist the bishops on various spiritual matters relating to their dioceses, and as connecting links between the higher and lesser ranks of the Church, to keep the whole body in harmony together. Above all, we want a more constant residence of the capitular members. The daily services celebrated in these ancient and glorious churches, we may learn one day in the great hereafter, were more efficacious walls and bulwarks of England than the wise statecraft of her senate, the courage of her unrivalled army, or the power of her magnificent navies.

CPSIA information can be obtained
at www.ICGtesting.com
Printed in the USA
LVHW101933050422
715402LV00003B/42

9 783752 587890